D1123162

FRATERNITY

ANDY MIENTUS

FRATE

RNITY

ANDY MIENTUS

Cataloging-in-Publication Data has been applied for and may be obtained from the Library of Congress.

ISBN 978-1-4197-5470-8

Book design by Deena Fleming

Published in 2022 by Amulet Books, an imprint of ABRAMS.

Printed and bound in U.S.A.
10 9 8 7 6 5 4 3 2 1

Amulet Books are available at special discounts when purchased in quantity for premiums and promotions as well as fundraising or educational use. Special editions can also be created to specification. For details, contact specialsales@abramsbooks.com or the address below.

ABRAMS The Art of Books
195 Broadway, New York, NY 10007
abramsbooks.com

For me, then, and for them, now

AUTHOR'S NOTE

The summer between my sophomore and junior years of high school, I attended a boarding school for the arts in northern Pennsylvania.

My upbringing was unremarkably middle-class—public school, suburbs, malls—and so I found the Gothic look of the school and the traditions held within its ivy-cloaked walls mysterious and intoxicating. As a budding queer kid, I also found the place erotic and alarming, because for the first time, I was living with dozens of other boys. I'd always kept female friends (an early tell), and now, living among these creatures, I truly knew I was different. Their comfort around each other, the language they spoke, the bonds they seemed to form instantly just by possessing a kindred maleness—all of it was foreign and exotic. And locked away from me.

But this was an art school after all, and where there is art, there is queerness. A secret sect of students found each other, and through our late-night conversations (and conquests), we each found ourselves. It forever changed my notion of what being "one of the guys" could mean, redefining boyhood and fraternity in a way that kind of saved my life.

❖

The school was also notoriously haunted, but I don't want to give too much away.

◆

I took a few cracks at telling a story like mine with modern queer kids and fell on my face every time. Besides the obvious horrors of a thirty-something trying to put believable words in the mouths of current teens, I realized that being queer now means something very different from what it did when I was growing up. I thought about setting it in the exact time period I'd had my awakening, but then, I realized that if I pitched the setting back even a decade further, I could still tell the story I wanted to tell while also including some queer history I wish I'd been taught, growing up.

Thus, this story takes place in Nineteen Ninety-One, and I've done my best to make the words my characters use and the situations and relationships they find themselves in feel accurate to that time. I share this with you now, before we start, as a warning. Some of those situations, relationships, and—specifically—words may be upsetting to a modern reader. The characters of color will experience racism openly, sometimes casually. Characters from this time won't have nuanced language for trans identities and will describe such folks with the imperfect words they had available to them. You will read one particular queer slur many, many times in these pages, because I can promise you that, growing up, I heard it many, many times myself: lobbed at me as a weapon, or through my headphones in hit songs, or as a punch line in a big-budget movie. I hope and pray that any discomfort you feel in reading that slur today is due to it being much less familiar to you than it was to me in my young life.

To not include these details would be to whitewash history and deny the characters the reality of their intersectional experiences as they would have lived them. Just like the characters in the story, I believe we must look some of the demons of history right in the eye to overcome them. To that end, I endeavored to look back to Ninety-One as unflinchingly as I could.

—Andy Mientus

PART ONE

CHAPTER ONE

ZOOEY

I want to be frank, right from the jump, about the elephant in the room (on the page? Christ, I'm already messing this up): There's absolutely *nothing* remarkable about the story of a shy kid navigating life at an ornate and mysterious old boarding school.

I wanna get that out of the way, because I'm sorry to tell you, that's the story we've begun.

I will say that the plot is kind of appropriate, though, because there's also nothing remarkable about the shy kid at its center. Or at least there wasn't when his story really began, en route to Blackfriars School for Boys on a *foggy. Autumn. Morning.*

Oh, you'll also learn in due course that our shy protagonist has a terrible secret and an absent parent.

I know what you're thinking: *Groundbreaking. Dare I hope that he'll also have an athletic bully and a stern schoolmaster with a dark, dusty office and an even darker agenda*? Well, my friend, cringe along with me as I inform you that you'll meet both of them before the end of his first semester.

So, let's take stock:

New kid, fish out of water.

Spooky boarding school.

Dark secret.

Bully.

Dead mom.

Yeah, we're walking, shall we say, *well-trod* territory. Cliché, one might say. Hell, *I* would say. If you're still reading, I applaud you. You're damn polite. A saint, really.

If you're still here, let me assure you that as painful as all this probably is for you, for a sixteen-year-old, feeling cliché is actually quite a privilege. Cliché means Normal.

And as the town car carried Zachary Orson Jr. (Zooey for short) ever closer to his new life at Blackfriars School, Normal seemed like a place they'd zoomed past hours ago.

I can tell you this with authority, because maybe my biggest regret in all of this is what I have to tell you next: Zooey Orson is me.

(The redhead over my shoulder is scolding me, so I'll just get on with it.)

❖

"Apologies, Mister Orson," our chauffeur, Max, called back after the car had taken the jolt of a pothole at full speed. "These New England highways sure could use some . . . attention."

"That's one way to put it," Zachary Orson Sr. (never anything for short) replied. It was the first thing my father had said in the three-odd hours we'd been in the car, even though we sat directly next to each other. I was grateful for the solitude of my Walkman.

(The Smiths. It was my moody phase, which I consider ongoing.)

The serpentine route we drove along was a particularly unloved stretch of Massachusetts highway, dotted with crags and cracks, with the dense black woods on either side threatening to engulf the pavement completely.

(OK, yes, I used a thesaurus for "serpentine." And "engulf." And probably every word over four letters long in this damn thing. I'm trying to dress this up for you. If it can't be an original story, it can at least be pretty, right?)

"Between this fog, the rain, and the obstacle course you have to drive through, I truly don't know how you're doing it," my father said.

"Just doin' my job, sir," Max proclaimed. "Anyway, we're almost there."

No, Normal was farther away. Antarctica. On the moon maybe.

The car turned off the highway onto an even more rustic dirt drive, and looking up the hill that we began to climb, I could see through damp greenery glimpses of the monolith (too showy?) I would come to know as the Blackfriars Common Building.

My father cleared his throat.

"Think of it as a fresh start, Zooey. Not everyone gets that."

His barrel-aged voice broke through the atmosphere like unexpected thunder.

"Be grateful," he added, probably trying for sincerity but sounding draconian. (That was definitely too showy. It means severe. My dad had all the charm of a bank statement.)

I nodded.

The car rolled to a gravelly stop in the Common parking lot, and as Max began to unload my trunks, my dad and I stood for a few moments in deeply uncomfortable silence.

Eventually, he managed to say, "It's just a few months until Christmas; here before you know it. Focus on your studies. And . . ." before abandoning words and, instead, extending his hand for a shake.

When I met his handshake, I felt a bit of paper folded into my palm and knew instantly what it was. Money had always been a reliable barrier between us Orson men and our feelings. He usually greased his palm with cash like this before touching me, sorta like how you tuck your hand into your sleeve to grab the handles on the subway.

(I just realized that you might not have a subway where you are. I'm from New York. Not trying to be a snob. I'm just saying, the handles are gross and so you don't wanna touch them and so when my dad gave me the money it was like . . . you know what, you get it.)

I looked down. A hundred.

He must be feeling extra sorry for me, I thought.

"Shall I come and help with—"

"I'll be fine," I interrupted.

Max had already loaded my luggage onto one of the trolleys that were made available at the edge of the drive. He refused my offer of help to take them up to my room.

"You got enough going on ta-day," he began to say in his Queens-inflected mumble before his eyes turned glassy and he scooped me up into a bear hug. Slightly shocked, I couldn't bring my arms up to return the affection (though I think about that moment a lot and wish I had). Instead, I looked at my dad, who looked at the pavement as we both waited it out.

"Take care, Zo," Max said, wiping his round red face with a paw-like hand.

My dad patted my shoulder squeamishly and then I was on my way, solo, to the towering, dark-wood front doors of the Common Building.

Were I actually the average, all-American guy I was posing as when I passed through those doors into the vaulted main lobby, I might have first noticed the incredible light pouring into the space through tall, arched windows overlooking the green of the grounds beyond, or the carved bannister of its impressive wooden staircase that split in two as it ascended to a second floor walkway, or the imposing oil paintings of distinguished alumni, or the ornately carved lions that held up the general information desk. The sights of the Blackfriars Common should be a feast to any young academic, but alas, my eyes drank their fill of the only kind of beauty that seemed to inspire awe in me these days: the beauty of the throngs of identically suited male students.

OK, so, while we're being frank, there is *one* remarkable thing I can tell you about myself, though on that morning, I'd have denied it to the death.

I like boys.

Even if I wouldn't, couldn't, admit it then, of course I *knew*. In a way, I'd always known.

I remember discovering each new tell and thinking that this is how my mom must have felt when she discovered a new lump, a new rash, a new symptom of the cancer that would take her life earlier that summer, before my transfer to Blackfriars.

This is what it's like, I'd think.

There were the early signs: a preference for stories about fairy tales over stories about battlefields, for coloring pictures over tossing footballs, for Mom over Dad. I remember being called "sensitive," "creative," "tidy." "A joy to have in class!" raved my elementary art teacher.

My symptoms were concerning but not terminal.

The disease really took hold when puberty hit, though.

I remember the Christmas I was gifted a tape recorder and gleefully recorded a whole news briefing on what presents each member of the Orson family—Mom, Dad, and Dog—had received. I was about as happy as I'd ever been until I played the recording back and heard my voice for the first time, my sibilant S hissing back at me louder than the reeling of the cassette.

The recorder went under the bed.

I remember spending most of my freshman year back at Hansard baffled at the way other guys in my class began to firm up and fill out like cattle or racehorses, while I elongated in all the wrong places like some graceless colt.

(A colt is a baby horse, right? Or is that a foal? Like I said, I'm from New York. The only livestock I saw growing up were the horses with their carriages lined up by the Plaza Hotel for tourists to visit Central Park without getting mugged. Just trying to say I was awkward. You're shocked, I know.)

Worst of all, I remember becoming exceptionally good at keeping secrets, which is the gravest symptom.

For kids like me, keeping that one big secret is absolutely key to survival, so secret-keeping becomes a well-honed skill.

(Looking back, it's completely amazing that I could keep mum about so much from my time at Blackfriars. You'd think by the time I was spitting my own blood into a ceremonial fire in hopes of invoking a prince of Hell to slay my enemy, I might have called home to say, "Dad, I think I'm in over my head." But I'm getting ahead of myself.)

Some guys have everything, I caught myself thinking.

And while there were plenty of completely average-looking guys scurrying about with their proud parents and sulking siblings, they were as invisible to me as I was to them. It was as if my fancy new contact lenses had a special filter that allowed me to see only those who *did* have everything: the broad shoulders, the smooth skin, the floppy hair, the smiles that were symmetrical to the point of being presidential.

I caught a glimpse of my own reflection in the glass of a trophy case, twig-thin for a sophomore, swimming in a black Lacoste polo and pleated khakis, and remembered that I had exactly *none* of those traits.

This wasn't such a bad thing, though. Back then, my physical flaws were actually a source of safety.

Back at Hansard, when I did allow myself to steal a glance at one of the guys who had everything—the shoulders, the hair, the symmetry—I would tell myself that I was looking not because I *wanted* him but because I wanted to *be* him. Turns out, there's a razor-thin line between envy and attraction, and if I'd been blessed with physical perfection like they were, I'd have known all along which side of that line I was doomed to live on. But I stared at the models on the boxes of underwear my mom delivered to my room only because I longed to be more athletic. *Inspiration*, right?

(I feel you rolling your eyes, but I'm telling you, these mental gymnastics were the only sport I was any good at.)

Besides, what regular guy wouldn't want to look more like them if he looked like me? When I looked at my reflection, the boy I saw looking back was just to the left of good-looking. If I were a film actor, my sloping shoulders, hollow cheeks, and constellations of freckles would make me seem sensitive and mysterious. Tragically, I wasn't—I was only an anonymous sophomore who had to look at the grand total of all of those almost-good-looking features and still face the world with some modicum of confidence.

Festive handmade signage led me down a hall to registration. After waiting in a line of sheepish-looking freshmen enjoying some final coddling from their teary-eyed mothers, I arrived at the front to greet a silvery, smiley middle-aged woman whose brass nameplate read "MRS. WESLEY, HEAD SECRETARY."

Her office, much like the rest of Blackfriars School for Boys, was a leather-bound temple of academia; the walls slick with polished dark wooden wainscoting, the smell of paper and pencil shavings greeting the smells of September where they met on the panes of opened stained glass windows.

“Good morning!” she practically sung. “Checking in?!”

“Yeah. Orson.”

She began flitting through a box of brown envelopes pleasantly, but her smile faded when she reached the O’s and didn’t seem to find what she was looking for.

“First name?” she asked.

“Zooey,” I replied. “Err, Zachary. Zooey’s for short.”

Once again, she came up empty.

“Odd, I don’t see it. Theo?”

She called back to the spectacled boy who looked drowsily up from his filing.

“We have a freshman here without a welcome packet. Maybe there’s been a mistake?”

“I’m a sophomore, actually,” I said. “Transfer.”

“Oh, so you’re the *TRANSFER!*”

It was as if I’d approached her deli counter with a winning lottery ticket.

“Yes, I set your packet aside, special. I’ve been waiting for you! Just—oh—one second!”

She made a giddy little jog to a deeper part of the office and returned to the desk with her prize.

“Orson! Here we are! Class of Nineteen Ninety-FOUR! Goodness, where does the time go, it’ll be Two Thousand within a decade! We practically live in the future!”

She opened the file and arrayed its contents on the desk in one deft movement, like a fisherman gutting his catch. (Before you call bullshit, this I actually have seen firsthand at the South Street Seaport.)

“Here’s the keys to your dormitory, Bass Hall, room number is on the key ring—Oh! A single! Normally, single rooms are reserved for *prefects* only. Prefects, meaning the upperclassmen who chaperone the dorms. But you've got one, too! Someone must love you very much!"

With my father's unceremonious farewell still fresh in my memory (and the ice-cold hundred-dollar bill in my pocket), I wasn't quite sure how to respond to that, so I just tried to match her smile as best I could.

"This is a welcome packet with some history about Blackfriars," she said. "I know most boys usually chuck this right into the trash, but I promise you, it's *fascinating*. I think the distinguished alumni list is incredibly inspiring for new students. I bet you'll know this name: Representative Charles Eldridge!"

I stared back blankly. She deflated.

". . . The congressman from our district? Well I suppose you might not be following . . . Anyway, here's your class schedule, student handbook, code of honor, all the rules, basically. Call over from the phone in the Bass Hall common room if you have any questions at all. We have someone here all night."

She retrieved a roll of printed tickets from her vast cherrywood desk and began tearing a strip away.

"Now usually the Dining Hall is for students and faculty only, but on arrival day, we invite the families to enjoy a meal with their boys before heading home. Eases the transition . . . and gives the fathers a taste of what they're paying for! How many vouchers do you need?"

"Vouchers?"

"Dining vouchers," she said. "Did your mom and dad both come to see you off, or just one? Any siblings?"

"Oh," I said, suddenly humiliated. "I got dropped off."

"You mean—"

"It's just me."

Mrs. Wesley's glow was instantly snuffed out like a candle.

"Well, maybe we can find your roommate and—oh, right, no roommate. Well . . ."

She looked left and right, as if searching for some solution to spring miraculously from the wainscoting.

"Oh! I know! Your prefect will be standing by for move-in issues, and I'm sure this counts as—oh! Theo?!"

The student employee turned once again to Mrs. Wesley as an exhausted little sigh escaped his lips.

"Yes, ma'am?" Theo asked.

"Would you call over to Bass Hall and see if Humphrey Meier can come by and show Mister Orson here around the grounds?"

"Sure thing," Theo said, slipping away into the depths of the office.

"Humphrey is a senior, your prefect at Bass Hall, and a wonderful first friend to make." she said. "You two'll take a nice walk around your new home. Enjoy the fall air!"

◆

To my complete horror, the upperclassman who eventually came by to collect me was maybe the most textbook gorgeous guy I had seen so far that day. Picture a young Kennedy, fresh out of the shower, having spent his morning rowing down the Charles, or whatever guys like that do to achieve their broadness. Now triple the severity of the jawline. He looked like Mount Rushmore's hot grandson. I was devastated.

I leaped up from the bench where I waited and tried to instantaneously metamorphose into a version of myself who could pass as his peer. Alas, when I introduced myself as "Zooey Orson," the S in my last name hissing at him like a venomous snake, I could see from the furrowing of his thick brows that Humphrey's first impression of me was of immediate distaste. I couldn't blame him, of course.

". . . Zoe?" he repeated, telegraphing his bewilderment across his Cro-Magnon forehead. "Isn't that a girl's name?"

Fuck, his voice is deep, I thought. *Fuck, he's tall. Fuck, he's hot. Fuck. Fuck. Fuck.*

"Short for Zachary," I said.

Damn it, I should have led with that.

"Why not Zach?" he asked.

Why not *Zach, actually? Zach sounds like a normal guy. Hey, I'm Zach. Zach Orson. Good old Zach. Zach-attack.*

"Um, it's, like, a family thing?" I explained.

We stared at each other like two strange cats sharing a living room.

"Huh," Humphrey finally said. "Well, let's get this over with."

I nodded and followed him down a very gray hallway, out a heavy wooden door, and away from the Common Building, stepping out from the shadow of its imposing bell tower into the bracing cool air and fiery color of the sweeping Blackfriars quad.

(I'm dressing my words up again, but I do actually love fall. Or I did. Until what happened *that* fall. Shit, one thing at a time.)

Humphrey read a canned history lesson about the campus from his clipboard like he was reciting a grocery list.

"*Nestled in the hills of deep northernmost Massachusetts, Blackfriars has stood isolated in its mountainy perch since colonial times. Named for a monastery that sat on the grounds for only a few years before being disbanded, legend has it that the school was too selective even for several direct descendants of Founding Fathers, and its reputation for an elite student body, demanding curriculum, and strict code of conduct endures today.*

"Strict is right," he warned, looking up from his notes. "I don't know if I'd agree with 'elite student body,' though."

He nodded toward a chubby kid who was sprinting across the quad to greet his pimply friend and gave me a look like he expected me to laugh at them. I'm embarrassed to say I did. (Listen, has anything about this story so far made you think that I'd be brave enough to argue?)

We pressed on.

The quad was lined with ghostly birch trees whose leaves were already changing color due to the early chill brought by the fall of Nineteen Ninety-One. Today it was teeming with students, in uniform and in street clothes, accompanied by parents and running free with friends. The Gothic architecture of the campus was objectively stunning, but Humphrey guided me though the points of interest with all the enthusiasm of an elderly docent at a third-rate museum.

"Library, Dining Hall. Gym is there between the dorms, weight room is open most nights and mornings, but don't make any of the varsity guys wait for a machine or they'll tag you for Hell Week for sure."

"Hell Week?" I asked.

"Homecoming," Humphrey said. "Normally they only tag freshmen, but since you're new, you count, too. And no offense, but you look like an easy target. I'd be careful."

Noted.

He went on to describe the gym's features with the most energy I'd seen from him all afternoon, bragging about its Olympic-size pool, weight rooms, and manicured athletic fields. I nodded along as if I'd ever set foot in a gym in my life. Secretly, I was way more excited by the quiet and solitude of the last two buildings on the grounds, reachable by separate woody paths: the ornate library and the severely steepled chapel.

We made our way around the quad and into one of the four dormitories, which Humphrey introduced as, "Home sweet home: your sophomore dorm, Bass. Or, as everyone calls it, 'Ass,' cuz you'll notice it stinks like shit. Rumor is the pipes got clogged up from too much splooge. So, try to nut into a sock or whatever."

Noted.

The common room of Bass Hall was a cozy little den with hunter green carpets running along warm wooden floors and accents. The deep velvety darkness of the place was interrupted here and there by glinting brass fixtures and stained glass windows. Its ancient couches held impressions shaped by generations of naps and study sessions. Each of its built-in knotty bookcases were packed to the brim with old trophies, photos of sports teams long disbanded, and ephemera (meaning, *junk*) left behind by class clowns, rugby legends, and big-men-on-campuses past.

"Lemme see your room assignment," Humphrey said.

I rummaged through my packet for my keys, which Humphrey examined a moment before exclaiming, with raised eyebrows, "Single, top floor. Damn. Nicer than mine. What'd you say your name was?"

"Orson," I all-but-whispered.

"Well, again, I'm Humphrey, your dorm prefect. I'm in Three F, if you need something, but honestly, dude? Please try to be a grown man and figure it out yourself. I only took prefect to be in a single so I wouldn't have to hear my roommate's mac-and-cheese-sounds in the dead of the night."

He demonstrated by swishing some saliva about through his teeth suggestively, exactly what mac-and-cheese sounds were, tugging the air with his right hand for added effect.

. . . *Noted.*

"Anyway, I'm sure I'll see you around," he said.

He turned to go when I blurted, "I was gonna head to the Dining Hall . . . for some food? If you wanted."

Humphrey looked at me like a child looking at a plate of steamed vegetables.

"Actually, man, I gotta hit the gym."

❖

Luckily, when I exited the elevator on the top floor of Bass Hall, there were no boys in towels chasing one another from dorm room to showers as I'd feared. (I know, I know, but when you like boys and are sent to boarding school, these are the images that haunt you for weeks before you get there.)

Bass was eerily quiet and seemingly deserted.

Right, I remembered. *Dinnertime.*

And though I'd invited Humphrey to join me to the Dining Hall just minutes before, I actually couldn't imagine keeping any food down that night. My stomach had been in anxious knots for hours.

No, what I needed most right then was solitude, and it awaited me just a few steps down the hall in my new room, Four A. I turned the key in the door and practically slammed it behind me after I entered.

It was a simple room: a single bed, a desk with a little green office lamp, a floor-length mirror, and a dark wooden dresser upon which my luggage had been dutifully placed.

Thanks, Max.

Its best feature was its silence. I felt my shoulders release, ever so slightly, and my breath begin to steady. I thought about my girlfriends back at Hansard (as in, friends who are girls. Which was all of my friends. I'd never had a *girlfriend* girlfriend). They'd always joke about the feeling of finally taking their bra off after a long day, and I had to think it must feel kinda like this. *Ahhhh.*

Remembering them made me freshly homesick, though. The feeling would have crushed me if I hadn't dodged out from under it with a flurry of unpacking.

I started with the clothes: an array of colorful Lacoste polos, Brooks Brothers oxfords in white and blue, some Ralph Lauren sweaters, some Dockers khakis, one lone pair of Wrangler jeans for the weekend. When I opened the dresser to put them away, I found my pressed, clean new Blackfriars uniform waiting for me. That navy blazer and striped green-and-navy tie would be my identity now, and that was just fine. The thought of being anonymous in a crowd was the most welcoming thought I'd had in weeks.

Once the clothes were put away, I returned to my suitcases and arranged my toiletries in the handy caddy my dad ('s assistant) had bought me for easy transport to and from the common bathroom. I outfitted the desk with the pens, pencils, and notebooks I'd been instructed to buy.

I reached into my pockets and emptied the contents onto the desk: from my left pocket, the dorm key and a pack of Wrigley's gum. From the right, the now crumpled hundred-dollar bill. I stuffed it inside a sock in my underwear drawer for safekeeping.

And then there was just one last item to unpack: a framed photograph of some younger (alien) Zooey Orson, a warmer and more vivacious Zachary Orson Sr., and a still-living Sonja Orson, her coarse black hair still full, her cheeks not yet hollow, her fate not yet sealed. They were all posing in matching white-and-khaki outfits on a beach I couldn't remember the name of. I wrapped the photo in a sweater and hid it in the bottom dresser drawer where I was least likely to happen upon it. It was a problem for another day, and I was exhausted.

I changed into my flannel pajamas and took refuge under my blanket. I became aware that I'd left my teeth unbrushed and face unwashed.

I then realized that no one would scold me for this anymore.

I was my own keeper now.

That was the first time I let myself cry in months.

(OK, when I say cry, I actually mean Meryl Streep sobs, wet and ugly. If I'd had a roommate, he would have either run away terrified or he would have handed me an Oscar for the performance.)

I don't remember how long it took, but I must have run myself dry and drifted off, because suddenly it was morning and time to face my first real day at Blackfriars School.

If I see this story in the frame of its clichés, you have to understand why I still cling to them. I have to remember it in a frame that seems familiar, because the portrait hanging in that frame—one of occult knowledge, arcane texts, and secret societies, of sex and drinking and revelry and tragedy—is so brutal and bizarre in hindsight that, without a frame, one might not recognize it as a portrait at all.

I also think of my story as cliché because, like everyone, I saw myself as the protagonist when, in reality, I was just a bit part in a much bigger story, one with many protagonists, of which I was joining not at the beginning but somewhere in the middle.

Perhaps the protagonist should have been a different kid from the class of Ninety-Four. Maybe the promising, junior varsity athlete. He fit the picture of a leading man exponentially more than I did.

Or maybe the quiet genius. God knows his is the story I wish I knew better. If only he hadn't been so damn quiet.

Then again, nobody told a great story quite like the playboy; the one with the fire-engine-red hair who made a startling discovery while trying to change a grade.

He understood as much then as I did on my first lonely night at Blackfriars.

Luckily, we'd all soon find each other, as boys like us always do.

CHAPTER TWO

DANIEL

"A.

"Ae.

"Ae.

"Am.

"A.

"Ae.

"Arum.

"Is.

"As.

"Is.

Shit, I thought. *I don't remember this. I don't remember any of this.*

"Good boys! Really good," Professor Reyes said. "Now I know declension endings is freshman year stuff, but it's all about drilling it. And restoring whatever brain cells you undoubtedly killed over the summer."

The guys all laughed. I wished I could join them.

Sure, just too much partying and sun and Sega. I'm not an idiot. It'll come back.

But I knew the truth. I hadn't drank away my first-year Latin. I'd been a damn saint all summer. *So that could only mean—*

"Preston?" Prof. Reyes said. It took me a few blank seconds to realize he was talking to me. My shoulders, already tense from the early morning, seized up so hard that my back felt like it was one solid piece.

"Yes, sir?" I replied, pulling myself back into reality.

"You good? You look like someone just stole your girlfriend."

More laughs. I played along.

"Speaking from experience, Professor?" I replied. That got everyone rolling, Reyes included.

"I'm good," I said. "Just trying to warm this brain back up."

"We'll get you there," Reyes said. "By the end of the semester, you'll all have better Latin than a Roman senator." When he said, "I promise," looking right at me with a smile of genuine encouragement, I knew he meant it.

All the students loved Reyes. He was the youngest professor by at least fifteen years, charismatic as hell, the funniest by a mile. He sometimes wore his tie loose. He seemed like one of us.

I identified with him extra because aside from a few spare others scattered across the campus (mostly groundskeepers and food staff), he was one of the only other melanated faces I saw day-to-day at Blackfriars. I remember the time last year, when he briefly grew a mustache, until Headmaster Westcott stopped by to check in on class and told him he looked more suited to picking fruit than teaching classics. He laughed along with the guys in class but shot me a private look I'll remember forever. The next day, he was clean-shaven.

The best thing about Reyes was that out of all the faculty, he was the least likely to throw the book at you if you fucked up in some way that didn't actually have any serious impact on yourself or any others.

For a teacher, he was a *person*, you know?

Thus, when this skinny kid crashed into the room a full ten minutes late looking like a mouse being chased by a cat, Reyes chose to show mercy.

"Sorry," the kid muttered. "I got lost, sorry."

"No worries, my friend," said Reyes. "But you gotta work on your cover story. Every guy here had Exploratory Language in this very room freshman year. You can just say you overslept."

The first thing I noticed about him was that I didn't know him. At a tiny school like Blackfriars, with just about a hundred students per class, no one was anonymous. I guessed, though, that if any kid was gonna go unnoticed, this one was a good candidate. He looked like he weighed a buck twenty-five soaking wet, and he seemed to shrink further by the second, crushed by the attention of every eye in the room now staring at him.

". . . What?" He looked confused. "Oh—no, I'm a transfer."

"Oh! Well, that explains it," Reyes said.

That explains it, I thought.

"*Relax!* It's all good!" Reyes said. "If you had to be late to any class, you chose right. There's a nasty rumor going around that I still have a bit of human compassion left in me, and it's one hundred percent true. What's your name?"

"Orson," the kid said. "Zooey Orson."

There were a few chuckles and snorts around the room. Was it the weird name alone or the poor kid's lisp? I hated that I knew it was both.

Someone in the back shouted, "Isn't that a girl's name?"

"Hey!" Reyes scolded, but before he could level any punishment, a robotic voice two seats down from me droned out above the noise.

"It is short for Zachary. I believe. Like in Salinger."

Hillman, I thought, rolling my eyes. *Be cool.*

I knew before I had to look. Only Steven Hillman would know something like that.

Everyone turned to look at Zooey's defender. His head hung down in a slouch, like he was apologizing for how tall he was, about six foot three. Thick dark curls and Coke bottle glasses covered his eyes, so his only defining facial features were a pimpled nose and some wiry peach fuzz on his lip and chin.

"J.D. Salinger, author of *Franny and Zooey*," he said in that damn monotone. "Zooey Glass is one of Salinger's famed characters, the Glass children. Short for Zachary."

"Thank you, Mr. Hillman?" Reyes looked a little lost himself. "I'm sure that's right. Is that right, Zooey?"

"Yeah," Zooey said, looking equally surprised.

"Well, there you go, lads," Reyes announced to the room. "Just be glad this is Latin and not English. I won't tell Professor Douglas what a bunch of unread swine you are!"

And thankfully, the room laughed again, and I could tell that the new kid and Hillman were both off the hook for now.

"Mr. Orson, why don't you take that empty seat next to Mr. Hillman," Reyes said, gesturing to the vacant desk. Truth is, there was always an empty seat next to Steven Hillman. He was beyond nerdy, like someone going as a nerd for Halloween. "You two seem well matched to pass notes on all things Salinger. Just don't go all Holden Caulfield on me."

Zooey took his seat as Reyes returned to his position at the front of the classroom.

"Now, here's a little secret: To help memorize the declension endings, I like to sing them to the tune of 'Row, Row, Row Your Boat': *A, Ae, Ae, Am, A. Ae, Arum, Is, As Is*," he sang in a surprisingly smooth baritone. "Give it a shot sometime, won't sound lame in front of any girls, now will you?"

The room roared again, Zooey took his seat next to Hillman, Reyes started back into the declensions, and I tried to unclench my back and shoulders enough so that I could actually hear what he was saying and get this mind back up to speed.

It's not that I was a bad student. My grades were about as good as the average sophomore, and definitely better than most guys in JV rugby. But that word, "average." It was one of my dad's sharpest arrows when he was in one of his rages.

He *himself*, he'd tell me every chance he got, had never been average. He hadn't had the luxury. If he had been average, then we all would be back living in that tenement house in the South Side of Chicago with his sister, my Aunt Deb, barely making rent, like all of the Prestons who had come before us. My white friends could be average. But not me. To be Black and average in America in Nineteen Ninety-One would mean to be left behind.

I knew what he meant. I was running the race with a handicap. But I wish I could have told him that shouting about it from the sidelines wouldn't help me run faster.

Thankfully, with each verse of "Row, Row, Row Your Boat," the cobwebs came off my Latin, and by the time the bell rang, I was feeling more myself.

In the hallway outside the classroom, I took another look at the new kid. Reyes had swooped in on him while everyone else filed out. He was saying something encouraging to him, smiling, patting his shoulder.

He must have known what I knew: Zooey Orson was a sitting duck at Blackfriars. Another one he'd be looking out for. I was feeling something near jealousy when a voice like a bleating goat cracked over the hallway chatter.

"There's the virgin!"

"Godfrey," I sighed as I turned to meet the stubby blond kid with the shit-eating grin who strode up to me. "I won't keep replaying this situation with you."

"I want Theo to hear you explain it for yourself," he said, nudging our lanky, bespectacled teammate who walked alongside him. "How

I served him up the single hottest girl in the Hamptons, *served her up* like a goddamn Roy Rogers buffet, and he still managed to fumble it!"

I defended my honor as we walked toward the Dining Hall.

"For the thousandth time," I said, "she was too drunk that night and I wasn't into it the next morning. You were the one who waited until the last day of the team trip to introduce us."

"For dramatic *effect*!" Ryan squealed. "Girls like Marissa Levine don't put out until the timing is absolutely right. I was working on that all summer for you. I could have killed you."

"Nah, man, I hear him," said Theo, running a hand through his medium brown curls. "I'm not down for morning sex, either. Morning breath, hangover. The only way I'm sucking a titty before noon is if there's coffee coming out of it."

"That's why you never get any, Theo," Ryan said. "Too picky. And you have no excuse, Daniel. If I had that jungle dick, I'd be railing little women morning, noon, and night."

Sometimes a compliment isn't a compliment. Sometimes it's just super fucking racist. Like when Professor Douglas tells me I'm "so articulate." But just like I do with Douglas, I smiled through Godfrey's line, not wanting to make it a whole thing. Trouble is, when I keep shit like that to myself, it doesn't go away, it just builds up in my shoulders like a backpack someone keeps filling with bricks.

I heard my dad on the sidelines again.

"Anyway, stay a virgin for life," Ryan said. "You flew all the way from California to spend the week with us and I thought I'd repay you with a little strange and this is how you accept my kindness and I know that now."

"You're such an asshole," I said as we reached the Dining Hall and joined the back of the line.

After so many meals alone in my parents' vast, vacant house in Beverly Hills, the blast of sound as we passed through the double doors into the Dining Hall fed a hunger I didn't know I had.

My family was what the kids at Blackfriars would call "new money." Never to my face, because "new money" was a dis. The old money families were legit, while the new money families had snuck into the party somehow. And the *Black* new money families?

Anyway, like I said, we grew up in Chicago living with my Aunt Deb, broke as a joke. That all turned around, though, when a few of my dad's old friends wore his designs in their music videos and his brand, Darius, named after the man himself, exploded. Back in the Eighties, the whole world—including the white world—suddenly had its eyes on the Bronx, Atlanta, Oakland, and even our little block in Chicago as they discovered hip-hop for themselves. When they saw the kings and queens of this world for the first time, they saw them all wearing Darius, and they wanted a piece of that crown.

Having lived through disco, my dad knew that fads came and went fast. He knew he had a small window of opportunity to build an empire and get us out of Chicago for good, but he also knew that his talent alone wouldn't be enough. He was already an excellent designer, but he had to learn to be an excellent businessman, an excellent leader, and an excellent public face. His hard work got us out of the neighborhood and into a dream house in sunny Beverly Hills by the time I was twelve. It came at a cost for me, though, as his increasingly busy schedule also meant boarding school, summer vacations with other families, and Pizza Hut dinners all to myself. I'd catch myself missing the crowded house and Aunt Deb's smelly cooking and constant fussing.

All this to say, even dining conversation with Ryan Godfrey was better than none, and as he relayed the plot of the new Freddy Krueger movie to us using his meat loaf and ketchup for bloody effect, I had to laugh.

I did notice that skinny kid again, sitting by himself at a long wooden table across the room, picking at his meat loaf silently. For a second, I saw myself with my Pizza Hut personal pan.

Poor kid.

Cruelly, my gym period this term was scheduled just after lunch. Ryan, Theo, and I trekked across the quad and through the double doors of the gym zombified from bellies full of meat loaf.

The massive main hall looked especially handsome as hazy sunlight poured at an angle through its tall windows onto the wooden floor, still sleek and undisturbed from summer vacation. Doors to either side of the space had signs pointing to the weight room, the pool, and our destination, the locker room.

When we descended the stairs toward the locker room, we were greeted thunderously by a once-solid-now-sloppy-looking man, somewhere around his mid-forties, who wore a dingy white polo, pleated khaki shorts, and a rusty whistle.

"There're my boys!"

"Hey Coach Carpinelli," I said as he clapped a clammy paw down on my shoulder and immediately began to probe my flesh with his fingers.

"Not feeling *too* soft, Preston," he said. "You kept up conditioning! That's good. Spring season'll be here before you know it."

"Did my best, sir," I said as I slipped free.

"And Godfrey, Breckenridge," he said to Ryan and Theo, respectively, "you run your drills this summer?"

"'Course, Coach," Ryan said. "How else are we all gonna get to varsity?"

"Too true, men, too true. Well, I'm gonna make sure we all get back to our fighting weight, starting today! Hope you ate a light lunch!"

I groaned and immediately regretted the little cartons of milk and orange juice that had washed down the meat loaf.

I got to my locker and was unpacking my gym uniform, a white tee with "Blackfriars P. E." printed on the front and matching green athletic shorts, when I noticed that kid again, trying to disappear into the locker across from mine as he changed. He'd definitely chosen the wrong size uniform. He looked like someone's kid sister who got into her brother's dresser; his skinny, hairless legs jutting out from the billowing shorts daintily.

Poor kid.

Once changed, Coach Carpinelli led us to the athletic quad, down the hill from the main campus. There were tennis courts, a baseball diamond, and a track that circled around a grassy, all-purpose field. Beyond those, there was a decent-size stadium with silver bleachers topped with towering chrome lights for night games.

Carpinelli led us to the all-purpose field and blasted his whistle, unnecessarily, to get our attention.

"All right, fellas," he barked. "Our first unit is going to be track while it's still warm enough to use her. Now, according to national standards of youth fitness, you need to be able to clock in a mile under ten minutes . . . But this is *Blackfriars*."

A few groans rang out into the September afternoon. My stomach made a sound like bad plumbing.

"The *competitive* male average is four minutes, thirty seconds. I understand that we're not all gonna be competitive runners, but we do need to hold ourselves to a higher standard than 'average.' "

That word again. My dad on the sidelines, always.

"So we gotta be able to run it in six minutes. Until we all get there together, we gotta run it every day."

Louder groans followed, but I sighed in relief. Tuning out the voice in my head all morning, willing my shoulders to relax, rewiring connections in my brain that had gone slack all summer—it had felt like a sprint. To just sprint, *literally*, actually sounded relaxing.

"But first, we stretch," he said. "Every time! Touch those toes, let's go, boys."

After leading the group through a few stretches without properly explaining how to perform them or why they were important, Coach had us all gather at the starting line. With a sharp blast of his whistle, we were all running.

Ryan, Theo, and I broke ahead of the pack easily, though Ryan seemed to exert himself doubly to catch up and keep pace.

A little too much fun in the Hamptons? I thought, and smiled.

Around the second lap he drifted back, and Theo and I drifted ahead, then I was alone for a bit. Soon I saw a shadow stretch across the track next to mine and I turned my head to greet Theo once again. To my surprise, it wasn't Theo, but that kid, Zooey Orson. He turned his head and his brown eyes met mine for an instant, before he snapped his gaze forward and continued to make his way around the track.

After the fourth lap, we skidded to a stop, me just seconds ahead of him. I nodded to him as I wiped my brow and panted for breath, *well done,* and he nodded back. That was the first time I saw him smile. It spread across his face for just a flash, disappearing a breath later as other guys reached the finish line, but it was a moment that has stuck with me. It said, *I see that you see me.* I've never felt invisible. I generally feel the opposite. But that's feeling *looked at,* not feeling *seen.* So it was something we shared for a second. Then the rest of the class caught up and Carpinelli blew that whistle again and yelled, "That's time!"

"Fucking HELL!" bleated a voice from a distance down the track.

"LANGUAGE, Godfrey!" Carpinelli barked. "And you're gonna have to do a lot better than that to make varsity!"

I looked down the track to where Ryan was panting, yards shy of the finish line. That little shit hadn't made it.

As Ryan walked, panting, toward the finish line, flanked by a couple softer kids, some nerds, a stoner, and a handful of others who'd failed, Theo called out, "Don't feel bad, dude, you have, like, half as much legs as everyone else!"

That got the pack howling. Ryan was rich as hell, reasonably popular, and decently funny when he wasn't being annoying, but when you heard the name Ryan Godfrey, the first trait that came to mind was short. He'd tell people he was five eight, but I'd guess more like five six and a half. He compensated in the weight room, putting on considerable size for his age, but on that little frame, the weight looked silly, like an overfed lap dog. Some of the guys called him "Chode."

I had to ask what that meant. I wish I hadn't.

Godfrey reached the pack and said, "I got a damn stomach cramp! The poison they feed us here."

To which Theo ribbed, "It's probably what stunted your growth. Like a crack baby."

And then everyone was laughing again, even Zooey Orson, which I immediately knew was gonna be trouble for him.

"And who the fuck are you?!" Ryan spat as he turned on Zooey, flushed red and fuming, getting right in his face. Zooey's smile fell, and he looked to the ground.

"Sorry," he muttered. "Never mind."

Ryan gave him a hard shove that sent him to the gravel and whipped the pack into a frenzy of "OOOOOH"s and "Oh shit!"s.

I didn't help him up.

Whether growing up on the South Side of Chicago or in the suburbs of Beverly Hills, you learn about the importance of timing.

For instance, I learned that to walk around after dark in either place could be dangerous, with the South Side dealers who saw me as prey or the country club neighbors who saw me as predator. The times I got caught up by either, I learned to make a split-second calculation about whether it was time to run, or time to argue, or time to just hand over my wallet to the man with the gun, whether he was in a hoodie or a navy blue uniform.

I wanted to help the kid, but now wasn't the time.

We marched back to the gym and stripped down. As I felt the steaming spray of the shower hit my back, my shoulders finally began to relax. The run had brought the day's anxiety to the surface of my skin in rolling beads of sweat, and now the water flushed it down the drain. Clean. I could have stayed there forever. But then I heard Godfrey's voice cut across the shower room in a tone so ugly, it made my shoulders lock up instantly, worse than before.

"Hey, flamer!"

My eyes snapped open, but when I looked to where Ryan stood at the showerhead to my left, I saw that he wasn't calling out to me but rather to the scrawny, dark-haired kid showering a few heads down to the right.

Orson again.

I turned just in time to notice he had been glancing, downward, at me. The sound of Ryan's voice brought the kid's focus to my face, and my brown eyes met his again; this time, the kid looking caught, like a scavenging animal illuminated by a flashlight.

"Yeah, *you*. Do you mind?" Ryan said, covering himself theatrically. "This is a locker room, not a goddamn peep show."

Zooey turned fully toward the wall, his face blank as if nothing had happened, though he was now scrubbing the soap from his body in wild swipes, like it was acid. Ryan didn't let up.

"I mean, I know Dan's dong is impressive, but you trying to memorize it?"

Sometimes a compliment isn't a compliment.

"Shut *up*, Ryan," I heard myself say. The last thing I wanted was to get involved in another of Ryan's juvenile little wars, but my brain didn't have time to decide if it was worth making myself a casualty in this current battle. Ryan gawked.

"Dude, he's literally getting a boner," Ryan shouted. "Oh my god, look, he *is*!"

I looked, and Zooey was.

"Seriously, cover yourself up, no one wants to see that!"

Zooey, not fully rinsed of suds, grabbed for his towel, dropped it, then pulled the soaking wet mess off the shower floor and wrapped it hastily around himself as he dashed out of the showers, nearly slipping as he disappeared behind a cloud of steam.

I performed a pitiful little laugh before rolling my eyes at Ryan and declaring, "You're *such* an asshole."

And suddenly, normalcy was seemingly restored. Ryan and Theo were talking about the Patriots, and I was clean, back in my blazer and tie, and a bit more ready to take on the rest of the day.

The moment nagged at me, though. Ryan had called out *flamer*, and I had flinched. Luckily, it seemed like no one noticed.

Why had I assumed Ryan was talking to me? Ryan lobbed "flamer" and "pansy" and "faggot" at dozens of kids, even teammates, when they wronged him in some insignificant way, sometimes for no reason at all, but never at me. Had I made some other slip he'd noticed?

I decided I was being paranoid. It was a subtle mistake, though I quickly remembered that *excellent* boys don't make any mistakes, subtle or otherwise.

My dad on the sidelines again.

I'm always sprinting.

❖

I saw Orson from afar a few more times that day, slumping, turtle-like, across the quad. It turned out we shared English together. When Zooey was called on to announce what he'd read over the summer, (like everyone else, *Outlander*), my ears perked up at the sound of his voice. It was the most I'd heard him speak all day, and now I was sure that I hadn't misheard that little lisp when he spoke in Latin class. And then there was the way he moved: When the bell rang, he gathered his books with a grace and care that didn't match his awkward, outsize limbs.

That night, just before sleep finally unlocked my back for good, I discussed all of this with my roommate, who, as always, put the pieces of the puzzle together: the voice, the movement, the solitude of Zooey Orson. And he *had* gotten hard in the shower, after all. We were fairly certain that Ryan's dis, *flamer*, wasn't just a dis in this case. Zooey Orson might just be exactly what Ryan said he was.

The next morning, I spotted Zooey a few paces from the entrance to the Dining Hall. I had to sprint toward the terrified-looking kid, who gripped the straps of his backpack as if it were a jet pack he would activate at any moment to fly to safety.

"Hey, you! Hey, *Orson*, wait!"

He turned to see me, eyes wide with assumed danger, and kept pace toward the Dining Hall.

I opened my mouth to call out to him but only emitted a sigh, which escaped visibly into the cold air. Zooey disappeared into the crowd.

I needed to talk to him before he had to face Godfrey again, but that would have to wait until Thursday, because today, gym class was cancelled, along with everyone's after-lunch period, for an all-school assembly in the chapel. There would be some general announcements, but the main event was the welcome speeches from the deans of the school and Alister Westcott, the headmaster himself.

When the time came, the entire student body lumbered into the Blackfriars Chapel, with its massive cathedral ceiling and rose window that cast shafts of colored light through the dusty air like a kaleidoscope. They moved slow because they needed a nap, but I moved slow because churches were complicated for me.

One of the plus sides to boarding school is that you get to be your own man a lot earlier than most guys, who have to wait for college. Little by little, you stop hearing your parents telling you what to pick up for lunch at the Dining Hall, or when to clean your room, or how often to shower (though I wish some of the guys on my team had better clues about that one). You start to live by your own rules. The rule that was hardest for me to break, though, was church. At the beginning of my freshman year, I'd go every Sunday, because that's what my family always did. For my mom and dad, it was obviously spiritual, and while I still wasn't sure if I actually believed in a big man in the sky, for me it was always at least meaningful. Church was where we caught up with neighbors, gathered for big and small moments of joy or sorrow, and felt some peace and communion with folks like us. It was the one part of LA that felt like Chicago. But then, the more time I spent with myself over freshman year, the more I got to know myself, and the more I got to know myself, the less I identified with what I heard every Sunday. I stopped going altogether at some point, and so now, whenever we'd gather there for school assemblies, I'd always feel a weird mix of guilt and shame and nostalgia all at once.

In these moments, it was my mom on the sidelines, praying for my salvation.

Anyway, I sat in the back with Ryan, Theo, and some of the other rugby guys and tried to scan the crowd for Zooey without the others seeing.

Mrs. Wesley rang a small hand bell from her post to the side of the stage, signaling for quiet. The assembly began.

After some whispery orders of business from the mousey dean of students and some slurry nonsense from the obviously alcoholic dean of faculty, Headmaster Westcott himself took the pulpit.

For the status he carried at the school, he actually looked pretty slight: a bald, wiry man somewhere in his seventies with bad posture and arthritic-looking hands. He pulled some folded sheets of paper from his breast pocket, cleared his throat, pulled the pulpit's microphone toward his brittle lips, and spoke in an antique-sounding voice.

"We the youthful sinewy races, all the rest on us depend,
Pioneers! O pioneers!

O you youths, Western youths,
So impatient, full of action, full of manly pride and friendship,
Plain I see you Western youths, see you tramping with the fore-most,
Pioneers! O pioneers!

All the past we leave behind,
We debouch upon a newer mightier world, varied world,
Fresh and strong the world we seize, world of labor and the march,
Pioneers! O pioneers!

"These are the words of the poet Walt Whitman," he continued. "A giant in the American cultural landscape. Some might say a god."

Also, a homo, I thought. *Also, a racist.*

"But before he was a god, he was a man, and before he was a man, he was a boy, like you all, dreaming of a newer, mightier world. He sat, bored and uncomfortable, in chilly pews just as you sit bored and uncomfortable today, listening to some old man grumble about how he ought to behave and who he ought to become. Like him, I don't suspect you'll want to listen to me, but I do hope you'll listen to him, you youthful, sinewy pioneers. What trail you take in your adventures here is up to you alone, but know that if you go boldly and with honor, you too may leave here with something godly to offer to the world."

Wednesday raced toward Thursday and the morning sprinted toward the afternoon when suddenly, it was time for gym.

I prayed for peace. I did still catch myself praying sometimes.

I saw Zooey enter the locker room and cut a path straight for his locker, but he failed to avoid Ryan Godfrey's detection.

"Cover up, boys! Prying eyes have arrived!"

Theo and some of the others laughed. I laughed, too. *Timing.*

◆

Out on the field, Carpinelli hoarsely proclaimed that we'd all get another chance to make time on the mile next week, but until then, we'd need some conditioning.

Blow of the whistle.

Back and forth.

Yard line to yard line.

During a relay, a neighboring foot caught Zooey's, sending him skidding painfully into the gravel.

I knew whose foot it was.

"Watch it, faggot," Ryan spat downward, mid-stride.

Not yet. Timing.

Blow of the whistle.

Sprints.

Kamikazes.

High knees.

Gym shorts.

Not time.

Clock ticking.

Burpees.

My dad on the sidelines.

Clock ticking.

Time running out.

Sprint.

Run.

Push.

"Stop!"

Blow of the whistle again.

Time's up.

❖

As my winded classmates ascended the hill and I noticed Zooey trailing behind, a scrape along his thigh, I knew the time had come.

"Hey, Coach!"

I jogged up to Carpinelli and discreetly told him, "Orson took a fall back there, don't know if you saw."

"That so?"

"He's bleeding."

Carpinelli turned back lackadaisically to confirm the report.

"Well, damn. Orson!"

Zooey lifted his head, and a panicked look swept across his face.

"I see you got a little ding there," Carpinelli said. "Need to see the nurse?"

"I . . . I'll be fine."

"Don't be stupid, man," I interjected. "You wanna bleed out? . . . In the *shower*?"

I tried with all of my might to telepathically transmit the subtext, but fucking Orson, he just stood there, frozen.

"Come on," I said. "I'll take you. That OK, Coach?"

Carpinelli barely nodded before he joined the pack of boys, leaving us alone on the grassy hillside.

We stood there a moment, and when everyone was out of earshot, I offered, "Zooey, right?"

"Um, yeah?"

"We haven't officially . . . I'm Daniel. Daniel Preston."

"Right?"

I extended a hand and Zooey flinched.

"You OK?" I asked.

"Can we just get this over with?" Zooey whispered.

"Get what over with?"

"You're gonna kick my ass, right? Look, I'm sorry for yesterday. I didn't mean to—"

"Zooey."

Were this any other kid, I would have been offended at the way he expected violence from me by default. But this wasn't any other kid, and I knew too well that kids like Zooey expected violence from everyone. For once, this wasn't about my skin.

"You don't have to apologize; you weren't even doing anything."

"Um . . ." Zooey looked stricken.

"Ryan is such an asshole," I said. "He just wanted to call you out 'cuz he was embarrassed about failing. He overcompensates, I think, 'cuz he's totally unremarkable, despite being one of the richest kids here. He's also fuckin' short."

I laughed at my own dig, hoping to give him permission to laugh, too, but Zooey just stared at me. A chilly wind swept through the leaves of the birches lining the quad.

"Anyway," I continued. "You were fine. I didn't care, truly. Don't give it another thought. It's hard enough being new."

Zooey's face twisted, like he was trying to solve a complex equation, but he managed to say, "Thanks?"

"'Course. Anyway, I'm not actually gonna walk you, but you should go to Nurse Gleason and get that taken care of. And get a note to be excused tomorrow. Ryan will forget about it over the weekend. Hopefully. Either way, it couldn't hurt to be off his radar."

"OK. OK, cool."

I turned to head for the shower when a thought occurred to me, all at once, like a clap of thunder. I knew I was right about what we all saw in Zooey. The signs couldn't be clearer.

Plus, the timing was undeniable.

I knew what I had to do.

"You know what, actually," I said, turning back, "there's a party tomorrow night. There are . . . well . . . There's this, like, club I'm in. It's having its first gathering of the year on Friday, and I can bring someone in. You should come."

"Um . . ." Zooey squinted off in the distance for a moment. "You don't have to do that."

"Do what?"

"Trick me. I said I was sorry."

Poor kid.

"Whoa, whoa, whoa," I said, raising my hands in surrender. "Not a trick, I swear. What do I have to do to convince you I'm not a bad guy?"

Zooey's shoulders dropped a bit.

"Sorry," he said.

"That was your last apology," I said. "Anyway, I just think the guys there will be more your people. Not everyone here is an angry little Napoleon like Godfrey. Some of us are actually friendly. Maybe you can make some friends. Find your pack, you know?"

Zooey nodded. Was he even stifling a smile?

"Tomorrow night, ten o'clock, Maxwell, the senior dorm. You know where that is? Go around to the very back of the building and there're stairs leading down to this, like, service entrance. We'll leave a tie on the doorknob. Knock once, then twice."

I demonstrated, knocking my fist against my chest in a syncopated rhythm. Zooey once again opened his mouth to speak, his face showing all the signs of protest, but I interrupted before he could.

"I know, I know, but I promise it's legit. If it ends up being a trap, you can go right to Headmaster Westcott and rat me out and have me expelled, right? So you're safe."

And with that word, "safe," I saw Zooey's own shoulders unlock. He looked down at the lawn and must have finally noticed the severity of his injury as the blood had now run down over his white sneaker.

"I'd better—"

"Yeah, you'd better. But seriously, come tomorrow," I said. "Everyone needs friends."

My dad would never approve of a kid like Zooey Orson.

He seemed to possess every single quality that Darius Preston had raised me to reject. Zooey Orson was not excellent in any way.

But the older I get, the more I wonder if excellence doesn't mean different things to different people. There's the obvious kind of excellence: power, skill, the confidence to show the world exactly how much excellence one possesses. That's my dad's brand of excellence.

There might be another kind, though. A quiet excellence, operating in secret to do what needs to be done.

And something needed to be done about Zooey Orson.

CHAPTER THREE

LEO

"She's *HERE!*"

I practically sang my entrance into the room, loud as Maria Callas in a shower stall, buttoning the beat by slamming the crate of bottles I'd procured thunderously down onto the bar.

By "she" I meant me, of course, and before you even think it, yes, it *was* completely absurd that I needed to announce myself so baldly, singular as I was in the group.

We'll get to that.

Of the early bird crowd, a handful boys of varying years who milled about greeting each other and setting up for the party, some still wore their school uniforms, while some had already retired into their street clothes for the weekend. *I*, however, was the only guest in attendance serving The Works: perfectly coiffed, emanating a pleasing aura of Calvin Klein's Obsession, draped in *vintage* silk paisley pajamas, thank you *very* much.

The first thing you need to know about Yours Truly, Leo Breyer, is that I *live* in pursuit of what my dear mother calls The Works. It's a concept she taught me from my earliest days, taking in half-price matinees of classic movies at the local Cineplex. If she was going to spend some of her hard-earned tip money on entry to the film, you'd better believe that tight as her budget was, she was going to invest a few dollars more to get the popcorn *and* the soda *and* the Junior Mints. We'd arrive in time to get the best seats and see every frame of the coming attractions. After the film, we'd linger until the final credit drifted to the top of the proscenium. It was those few dollars more that made a half-price matinee into an *experience*. The Works, you see. In fact, Mom had baked The Works into my very DNA, blessing me not just with ginger, or rusty, or strawberry blond hair, but with a mop of the reddest shade possible without a box of Vidal Sassoon Colorific.

Despite arriving at the party sporting The Works from fiery tip to flowery tail, I had recently acquired a, shall we say, *talent* for the art of nonchalance, and if I didn't make myself known to the room in the most crass and obvious manner, even Daniel might have passed right by me—and all ego aside, I was the one with the drinks.

"Good haul, Leo," Daniel said cheerily as he sauntered over (and what a saunter it was). He was providing, let's call it, traditional support to the mise-en-scène in a simple white tee and light wash jeans, but then, this was Daniel Preston, so of course he looked devastating all the same. "Whatta we got?"

"We have whiskey, vodka, gin, maraschino, and something peppermint?"

"Where did you get it?" he asked, admiring a tall bottle of Luxardo.

"Never mind where I got it, I *got it*, didn't I?" I said as I snatched the bottle back.

I loved that line. It made me feel like one of those fast girls in a Fifties pulp, smoking cigarettes in the bathroom.

Tonight's drinks program was a slightly meager stock for a fete of this scale, but at least the accoutrements were first-rate, with heavy highball glasses, a silver ice bucket, a matching soda gun, and a bowl of bar-fruit for garnishes, all arranged smartly next to the bottles. Someone's swish uncle was a barman in Boston. Lucky us.

Speaking of luck, I will never get over our good fortune in claiming the old, abandoned student pub for our Batcave. It was a goddamn miracle: an honest-to-God full-size, ornately carved, gorgeously appointed, stodgy old pub, laying buried right beneath the senior dorm like a lost ruin of another civilization. Rumor had it, some senior with a groundskeeping work-study stumbled upon it in the Eighties, went through every key on the ring until he found the one that unlocked it, and then made copies for all of the members and stashed the original. Every class to come after him had added furnishings and bric-a-brac to build it up to what it is today. But given the membership of this particular student club, the shock wasn't how well it had been made over but rather how well it had been kept secret.

Our pub was looking especially dear tonight. The cloudy mirror that stretched behind the vast wooden bar reflected the glow of candles and crimson-shaded cabaret lamps, which lit the space, casting eerie, sensuous shadows here and there. Heavy, bloodred velvet drapes hung over the walls, which were lined with small tables and a few booths. At the far end of the bar, a jukebox glowed green and gold as it emanated crackly, ghostly jazz for a presently empty dance floor.

Oh *bitch*, this was gonna be good.

The first annual gathering of the Vicious Circle was a special enough occasion to demand such attention to detail, but I already knew the surprise of the night: We had a new chick in our flock, and I'd be damned if I didn't give good nest.

We put on the Cole Porter, and I swept about the space, making sure everything was in complete readiness. My kingdom for a white-gloved finger I could drag across a surface and hold aloft in triumph.

Soon, the rest of our guests began to trickle in and start on the drinks and the many reunions that come at a first meeting of the year: "how ya been"s and "look at YOU"s and "did you *hear*"s.

I was already effervescent from the hum of the party, but my cork absolutely popped when I overheard some confusion coming from the pub's entrance.

"No, ORSON," a voice complained. "Zooey Orson. I sit next to you in—"

"I do not see it on the list," droned another. "Who invited you?"

Zooey looked ready to turn on his heels and dash back up the stairs and into the cover of night when Daniel swooped in for the rescue.

"Jesus, Steven, I did! I *told* you I did! He *is* on the damn list!"

Steven Hillman, who was working the door this year now that our former concierge had graduated and shipped off to Yale, shrugged and let Zooey pass.

"Thanks, hey," Zooey said to Daniel as he stepped inside.

I gave him a quick scan. He looked uncomfortable, and I *don't* mean because of the tapered Wrangler jeans and moth-eaten flannel he wore. I mean in his soul. Thankfully, his visible anxiety gave way to awe as he took in the room.

"What is this place?" Zooey asked.

"Oh right, duh," Daniel said, slapping a palm to his forehead. "Not bad, right? Before the drinking age was raised to twenty-one in the Seventies, the seniors had their own pub on campus! It's obviously defunct now, but some guys have been passing the keys down for, like, a decade." He gestured broadly to the crowd, which had grown to ten or so as more students filed in, hugging hello.

"Welcome to the Vicious Circle, one of the secret societies of Blackfriars."

"Secret society?"

"Everybody!" Daniel called out to the room. "If you haven't yet, meet Zooey Orson, the new sophomore!"

The crowd of guests waved and shouted a few various greetings. A few even approached to shake Zooey's hand warmly.

"That's Barton, Reinhardt, Richardson, Osmon—you'll forget all this, of course, say hi again after a drink or two."

"And *we* haven't had the pleasure," I said to Zooey as I emerged from Daniel's shadow to greet him. "Leo Breyer."

"Oh hey," Zooey said. "Sorry, I didn't see you there!"

I smiled like Mona Lisa.

I'll never know exactly what Zooey's first impression of me was, but I'd like to imagine his first taste of my company read something like this:

The boy who stood on tiptoe to give Zooey an air-kiss on each cheek was practically swimming in his paisley pajamas, trim as he was, but despite his diminutive height and slender build, he carried himself with utmost poise and confidence. Gravity was the wrong word for his bearing, though, for he seemed light as a feather; not weak, but gossamer, like a ballet dancer en pointe. His crimson hair, coiffed exactingly into a slick pompadour, gave the impression of the flame that keeps a hot-air balloon aloft.

That's how I'd describe myself anyway.

"Zooey Orson," the boy said, as I descended from my kissing.

"*Zooey*," I repeated. "How utterly *chic*. And Orson, what's that?"

"Just, like, English, I think?"

"No, as in textiles? Real Estate?" I even dared to imagine, "*Hotels*?"

"Stop that right now," Daniel scolded. "He's peacocking. Zooey's already been the victim of one peacock this week."

"I *heard*," I sighed. "Ryan Godfrey, right? Forget that knuckle-dragger, you're among friends now. Well, friends and Steven. You're acquainted? Hold on."

I trotted to the pub entrance and shouted down the corridor, "Steven, *dear*, come be social for a mo'.

"The iceman cometh," I announced, as Steven appeared, hunched, in the doorframe. "There we are. Steven Hillman, meet Zooey Orson." That *name*. I savored each syllable like beluga caviar.

"We actually have Latin together," Zooey replied as he shook Steven's hand.

"Oh, with Reyes?" I asked. "Ugh, a literal Latin lover."

"He's a teacher!" Daniel cried, giving me a playful smack.

"And I have a lot to learn."

"Imagine living with this nightmare," Daniel said to Zooey. "I got a predator for a roommate!"

"*Roommate*?!" I scoffed. "We don't have to call it that, here. And as for my animal nature, it's a jungle out there, so I won't deny it." I raised up on my toes once more to give Daniel a kiss. "And as prey, you really didn't put up much of a fight."

It wasn't a social air-kiss, but the kind of kiss Daniel and I could give each other only in our room at night and here, in the safety of the Vicious Circle. As I pulled away, I saw the look of complete stupefaction on Zooey's face, and it all came together.

Daniel, you idiot, I thought. *You didn't tell him* anything, *did you?*

Steven, who'd been staring at the ground, silently sulked away back to his post by the door.

"Anyway," Daniel said, turning back to Zooey, "You still need a drink! What'll it be?"

All language seemed just beyond Zooey's grasp. He stood there, catatonic.

". . . Do you drink?"

"You OK, kiddo?" I asked.

"I . . . I think I should go," was all Zooey could manage before making an abrupt move for the door. Daniel grabbed both of his shoulders.

"Whoa, whoa, I'm sorry," Daniel said. "Did I . . . misread? I mean, you . . . *are* . . . aren't you? *Family*, I mean. *Are* you?"

But before Zooey could even begin to search for an answer to a question he'd not even managed to find language for, I swept in to rescue him.

"Why don't we just start with the drink? My expert assessment tells me we need a little liquid lubrication for that particular line of questioning. And I am a medical doctor. Stand perfectly still while I fetch us all some medicine. Oh Nurse?!"

Zooey followed orders and waited for his antidote to come.

Something else one must understand about me, to understand how I operate, is that I never ever believed in Santa Claus.

That fact alone would have been a clear indication of my preternaturally analytical mind, but that's not all. From an early age, I actually had the mental maturity to *pretend* I believed in Santa Claus, for my mother's sake! Yes, from infancy, I could plainly understand reality, but also deeply understand the value of *fantasy*.

What good would it do, I reasoned, to deny my mother a game that seemed to bring her such joy at a time when her work shifts doubled as her expenses tripled. She would arrive home from the nail salon every night stinking of cigarette smoke and heavy with exhaustion but would still barter some of her precious sleep to stay up and tell me the most fantastical tales of that jolly old elf. One time, when we were in the grocery store, we'd passed a man in a red sweater who stood by a collection bucket, ringing a bell and asking for donations.

"What is he collecting for?" I had asked.

"For less fortunate kids," my mother replied. "So they can get something for Christmas."

"Doesn't Santa like the poor kids too?" I asked. I'd meant it as a joke but felt immediately terrible when I saw my mother's face. Not only had I blown my own cover as a nonbeliever, but I'd reminded us both of how poor we were ourselves, forsaken by Santa and every other benevolent spirit that year. From then on, I went along with the ruse until my mother revealed the truth herself. When the time came, I acted dutifully devastated. I was a natural actress.

Similarly, I always knew the truth about myself and felt no shame for it. I recognized my affinity for the female characters in the *Wizard of Oz* and my proclivity for talking the neighborhood boys into playing doctor but paid those things as little mind as I did any other fact about myself. They were as natural and elemental as my red hair or freckled face.

Thus, when I came upon cases like Zooey Orson, I had to put myself in their shoes and exercise patience and understanding. Of course, I'd known what Zooey *was* the moment he walked in the door, but it wasn't Daniel's place to *say* as much, out loud, right to the poor boy's face. Unlike dear Daniel, I understood that such fragile, budding specimens must find their way to the conclusion on their own. For this, I learned, alcohol was the chief fertilizer.

"Have you ever tried an Aviation?" I asked as I manned the bar. "I'm told it's the only blue cocktail one should ever be caught dead drinking. We don't have any crème de violette, but I think I can improvise."

"Uh—go for it," Zooey said.

Step one, I thought.

I wondered what would be the biggest obstacle to overcome in helping Zooey reach enlightenment. Religious dogma? Sexual prudishness? A father?

I myself was fortunate to have been born with none of those things. For all her faith in Santa, my mother never had much love for Jesus. Santa only disappointed her once a year, whereas Jesus abandoned her at every turn. As for sexuality, I'd learned all I needed to know and more from the pulpy romance novels she left lying around our trailer. And a father?

Legend had it, my father died of a drug overdose when my mother was pregnant with me. Or he'd killed himself. Or was murdered. The mythology changed slightly depending on how many drinks Mom had enjoyed when she began to reminisce.

Whatever the reason, my mother adored me for who I was, and so I had only ever known acceptance. I remembered how after Daniel and I finally crossed the line from curious flirtation to full physical exploration, we'd discussed the terms of the deal and decided that our romance must stay an absolute secret. The reason? Not for fear of scolding from the dean of students or slander from our classmates. Or, not only. Principally, it was the fear of his father finding out. It occurred to me that even among some of the most economically privileged boys in America, I possessed a privilege they couldn't imagine: the ability to grow up outside of some father's shadow.

The drinks were mixed and drained, and we all found a seat on a rotting leather chesterfield in the corner.

"The Vicious Circle has been convening in some secret space or another here at Blackfriars for—well, for generations, right?" I said as I passed out the second round of drinks.

"Since the Twenties, at least," Daniel said. "Those are the first entries in the guest book. But some of those early entries talk about past members, so we think it went on longer."

"And here we are today, and again on the first Friday of every month," I said.

"And no one has found you out?" Zooey asked.

"It's not exactly the kind of *scene* one brags about to the uninitiated," I replied. "And besides, we're just one of the secret societies at this school, and one of the smallest ones at that. Westcott and the deans absolutely turn a blind eye. It's a bit of fun in the middle of goddam nowhere."

"Leo got spotted by an upperclassman, well, *immediately*," Daniel said, earning another little slap from Yours Truly. "The upperclassman invited him, and then Leo brought me in later, once we, well—"

"Once we got to know one another," I said.

"Wait," Zooey said. "So you're roommates. Leo, you're a sophomore too?"

"C'est moi."

"Why haven't I seen you before?"

I shot Daniel a confidential little glance.

"Oh, well, I'm not sure. I suppose because we don't have any classes together. I'm in remedial everything. A total idiot."

"Don't say that!" Daniel protested.

"What? I'm not ashamed, it's true! I'm charming, not academic."

"Then how are you here?" Zooey asked. "At Blackfriars, I mean. It's . . . selective, isn't it?"

I drained my drink in one.

"Because of the family curse, of course," I said.

"Leo's a Breyer," Daniel explained. "Meaning he's a legacy. Descended from one of the school's founders."

"Which means I got in easy and I'm very, very hard to get rid of. Like crabs. I've *heard*."

In addition to the gift of his absence, my father had left me with a guaranteed space at, and free ride to, Blackfriars School. My lineage also granted me a certain status around campus, as the legacies were understood to be very rich, because usually they were. No one at Blackfriars knew the truth about my—call it *humble*—upbringing and constant economic hardship, and I had absolutely no intention of catching anyone wise. Why let reality spoil a great fantasy?

"I can help you study, if you want," Zooey said. "I mean, I'm no genius, but I do OK."

"You're sweet, but what would be the point? Polishing the brass on the *Titanic*. I just need to survive this place and get myself to New York. I'm going to be an *actress*."

"He played Puck in the school's production of *A Midsummer Night's Dream* last spring." Daniel said proudly. "A lead role as a freshman! He was amazing."

"The competition wasn't *exactly* brutal," I said, taking Daniel's hand. For all the obvious, external appeal of Daniel Preston, his pride in me was completely confounding and very, very lovely.

Just then, the jazz record on the jukebox came scratching to a halt and after a moment of silence, a new song began mournfully. Synthetic strings and low tones created an air of mystery until a woman's voice commanded us to strike a pose.

Then, the song erupted into an ecstatic pop beat and several of the boys emitted excited cheers and took to the dance floor, jerking their bodies around with wild abandon.

"Ah! They got the new one!" Daniel said as he leaped up off the couch.

"Our Lady calls," I informed Zooey. "We must dance for her!"

It was Madonna's "Vogue," of course, her newest single. The Queen of Pop had always hinted at love and acceptance for the gay community, but with this new single, celebrating a dance style emerging from the Black and brown gay scene in New York City, she was absolutely screaming it. It had become our anthem.

I grabbed Zooey by the hand and all-but-dragged him to his feet. Daniel rolled his eyes but joined the throng, bumping and grinding with the others. Zooey stood on the sidelines like a child at a pool party, hesitating at the end of the diving board.

I clocked his reticence immediately and sprung into action, natch.

"Come on, Zooey! You're missing a *moment* here! I absolutely won't stand for it!"

I pulled him into the stew. Our goddess continued her spell as we devotees offered ourselves to her fully.

I turned Zooey under my arm like a ballroom master and struck a pose. Zooey cracked a genuine, toothy smile, the first I'd seen from the lad all night. That's when I knew I'd unlocked something. We danced until reality became fantasy.

Step two.

The song ended and the small crowd cheered and hugged as if we'd just nailed a high stakes public performance. I dared to hug Zooey too, and I felt him ease a bit between my arms. Mission accomplished.

Our trio made another round of drinks and crashed out once again on the couch in the corner of the room. Someone put a slow song on the jukebox, and Chris Isaak began to croon "Wicked Game."

Boys began to slow dance.

I noticed that Barton and Reinhardt had chosen each other as dance partners, something I'd predicted at the end of last year. Barton, thin and blond, took Reinhardt's auburn curls in his hand and pulled him in for a kiss. I smiled, feeling like Dolly Levi herself, but turned to see Zooey watching the scene in astonishment.

Right, I thought. *Gently.*

"This is . . . crazy," Zooey whispered.

"It's *uncommon*," I replied.

We all sipped our drinks and watched, for a bit. Then, alcoholically emboldened, I said, "Zooey, I don't want to darken a beautiful evening, and I promise, we'll get back to our scheduled programming momentarily, but we have to talk some unfortunate business. Your little gym class problem."

"Oh," Zooey muttered, gazing down the barrel of his glass.

"Daniel told me all about it. Godfrey has you in his sights now. He won't let up. Trust me."

Daniel put a hand on my thigh, and I knew he remembered *that* unfortunate era of our lives as vividly as I did.

"Now, I wish Daniel here could stand up to him in front of everyone, but that's just not possible. It's bad enough his roommate is the only clockable faggot in school. Zooey, you need to learn to protect yourself."

Daniel nodded sadly.

"But . . . he'd beat the shit out of me," Zooey protested.

"Then you'll have to be very clever," I replied. "Weakness is unacceptable. Show any sign of it and the Ryan Godfreys of the world will devour you for sport. I said it before, this place—it's a jungle. Now, we can't be kings of the jungle, you and I, but we can be poisonous snakes. We can be black widow spiders. We can take down even the greatest beasts, we just have to be very, very—"

"Clever," Zooey said, then finished his drink.

Step three.

Before I could elaborate further, a tall, broad-shouldered boy whose chiseled physique bulged invitingly through his unbuttoned shirt staggered over to us.

Oh no, I thought. *It's Meier time.*

"Preston, you good with locking up again tonight? Some of us are ready to head to the after-party."

". . . Humphrey?" Zooey asked, sounding profoundly shocked.

"Oh damn," Humphrey said, noticing Zooey. "Orson. Fancy seeing you here. I—who brought you?"

"I did," Daniel said.

"Ah, yeah, makes sense," Humphrey said. He scratched the back of his neck, clearly spinning. I leaned in to enjoy the scandal. "Sorry, I shoulda made the invite, I mean I had a feeling about you, but. You know."

"So . . . you're . . ." Zooey began to ask a question he didn't seem to be able to finish.

"Is *she*?!" I roared. "She's the club *president*!" Humphrey narrowed his eyes at me.

There was a time, I'm told, three years back, upon his arrival at Blackfriars School as a new freshman, that Humphrey Meier was fat. I don't mean gay fat, I mean *fat* fat. I've seen the photos. Apparently during Hell Week, the seniors all chased Humphrey through the quad, shouting with glee about his "bitch tits." Anyway, I learned from another Circle member who used to suck him dry and then act as his therapist in the afterglow that, at the time, he didn't blame *himself* for being fat. His fatness was but one symptom of a greater cause. You see, he'd been raised entirely by women; a single mother and two older sisters who, in his estimation, fed him garbage, babied him far too late, and gave him no proper example to look up to. It took time, but a single-minded focus and a changing adolescent body conspired to rebuild Humphrey Meier over the course of his freshman year. When he arrived on campus the first day of sophomore year, he noticed guys notice him. Humphrey Meier had gotten buff, and henceforth, he *had* to be envied. He *had* to stay thin and fit. And he could certainly never be feminine again. It was troubling how much he associated femininity with weakness, but I've read that the psychological associations one makes during one's adolescence can be all but impossible to break, and moreover, he was a student at an elite, all-boys school as the Nineteen Eighties became the Nineteen Nineties. His misogyny was troubling but certainly not surprising.

I hated gays like Humphrey Meier, which was just as well, because they despised me.

"And of course we'll lock up, darling," I assured him. "Just don't forget all this dues-paying when you're endorsing your successor."

Humphrey rolled his eyes.

"Remember, bottles in the woods," he said. "Don't get sloppy."

"Same to you, *dear*," I replied, with deep subtext.

Humphrey turned to go but then lingered a moment before turning back.

"Hey, Orson. The after-party is at mine tonight. Usually upperclassmen only, but since you're in the building, swing by if you're feeling it."

"Oh," Zooey said. ". . . OK, thanks! That's really nice of you!"

"Maybe I'll see you there, then."

I half-stifled a laugh as conspicuously as possible. Humphrey shot daggers.

"Night, Preston," he said. "*Breyer*."

When he was a safe distance away, Daniel and I fell into absolute hysterics.

"What?!" Zooey asked.

"Dear, sweet Zooey," I said through tears. "He wasn't being nice, he was being a dog. The Vicious Circle after-parties are . . . carnal affairs. NOT that I've been, mind you."

"Carnal?"

"Don't go unless you want to get off with them," Daniel said. "All of them."

"WHAT?!"

"We won't judge if you do!" Daniel assured him.

"*I'd* judge," I snorted. "Meier has a gym yard body but a jail yard face, in my opinion, though I know it's an unpopular one. If it weren't for his fake ID and the beer can between his legs, I think it would be an after-party of exactly *one*."

"That . . . happens every time?" Zooey asked.

"Boys will be boys," I said, laughing, but then I saw Zooey's face. He looked like a rowboat that had just been cut free of its mooring and was drifting out to sea.

"I think I need the bathroom," Zooey said getting up.

"Oh, you poor thing, you look absolutely haunted!" I said. "I'll take you. And get you a refill, which you need desperately."

I led him, practically limping, to the restroom at the end of the bar and waited for some time outside. When I heard no water, no flushing, no vomiting, or any other activity occurring therein, I knocked on the door.

"Zooey? You all right?"

Getting no response, I opened the door to find him staring at himself in the mirror.

". . . Zooey?"

"This is what it's like," he said.

"What?"

He turned back, seeming to notice me for the first time. I could tell the alcohol had hit him upon standing up and now was abstracting his thoughts and blurring his vision.

"This is what *what's* like, Zooey?"

"Oh . . ." He considered for a second. "Well, I was thinking that this is what it's like to be drunk. I've never been drunk."

Rats. I really am a bad influence.

"Oh! I'd thought, being from New York, you might have—"

"But then when you asked, I thought . . . this is what it's like to hang out with . . . I mean I've never had any friends who were—"

"Boys?" I offered, half-joking. He got the punch line and laughed.

"YES, that too! I always sat at the girls' table in grade school. But you know what I mean."

"I do."

"It's like a little club."

"A little fraternity," I said. That made him laugh. At what, I wasn't totally sure, but I laughed, too. And we stood there and laughed at each other until an argument blooming a few yards away grew so loud, it couldn't be ignored any longer.

"Yes! Yes *of course* we deserve to drink and flirt and listen to Madonna, but not without *any action*!"

It was Matthew Dell, a balletic-looking blond junior who was perpetually furious about the state of the world. He had Frank Costa, Italian stallion of the VC, in his clutches and was not letting up. I knew that Costa only truly cared about round backsides and his mother, so I was surprised to see that he was standing there, taking the onslaught, rather than simply walking off, but I suppose Dell did fill his khakis well enough.

"Dude, I'm seventeen, what action are you suggesting?" Costa said, sipping a watery whiskey soda.

"That's no excuse!" Dell said. "If we can be organized enough to keep a goddamn secret BAR going, stocked with contraband, frequented by—what—fifteen closeted fags? I think we could manage to take a bus down to Boston to march for AZT."

"I don't even know what that means," Costa said, listless.

"EXACTLY!" Dell shouted. "Everyone is here for the party, but when we get out of here and join the real world, you're all in for the wake-up call of your lives."

"What's he talking about?" Zooey asked me. I turned to him, unsure if I should answer.

"I believe there's meant to be a demonstration in the city this weekend for access to a new drug."

"A drug for what?"

"For . . . well, for AIDS."

Immediately I knew I should have talked around it. Zooey Orson hadn't even said the word "gay" yet. That word was enough of a specter; "AIDS" was an absolute monster.

"Does . . . does that kid have it?" he asked.

I almost laughed, but then I realized he was deadly serious.

". . . No," I said, incredulous. "Zooey, no! He's a teenager, probably a *virgin*. Matthew Dell doesn't have AIDS."

"But then why does he want to go to Boston for medicine?"

"He doesn't need the medicine, he wants to march for *access* to the medicine . . . for the cause, you know? People are dying, after all."

Another mistake. I'd drunk too much. Death? *Good one, Leo.*

"Anyway, let these two bark it out," I said. "Let's us find out where—"

"Actually, I better get going."

I could see his wheels spinning and I didn't know how to stop them.

"But it's so early," I said. "We haven't even played any party games."

"I'm tired," he said. "It's been a long week and I . . . I think I just need to sleep."

"Oh. Well maybe we can walk you—"

"I got it," he said. All I could do was nod. "See you around. Tell Daniel I said thanks."

I went in for a hug, but Zooey peeled away, heading straight for the door.

"Drink some water before bed, Zooey!" I called after him. "Two glasses!"

But he'd slipped through the velvet curtain at the entrance and was gone.

I sighed. It was not the way I wanted this night to end for him, but I knew that progress had been made and that such a project needed to be gradual. Anyway, we did have work ahead of us that night and it was time for me to get focused.

"Good night, sweet prince!" I called after the final guest as he staggered from the pub into the crisp September air. "Choirs of angels and all that!"

Luckily it's a short walk, I thought, chuckling.

After Humphrey had taken the most beautiful upperclassmen back to his room for the after-party, the festivities had grown more quietly social until they died down to the crackling of a record that had reached its end and the flicker of a candle that was all but burned out. Now, all of the boys had gone home save for three stragglers who prepared the space for an event of a different kind.

Daniel was picking up plastic cups and putting them into a trash bag while Steven worked quietly, scrawling Hebrew characters in chalk on the floor. It was part of an elaborate circle he was copying from a thick tome bound in black leather.

"Do you need anything, Steven?" I asked as I circumambulated the room, swinging a thurible of burning incense.

"No," Steven said, curtly.

I could tell that bubbling beneath that stiff upper lip was deep resentment that we were actually going through with this. That was none of my concern. He was doing what was needed of him.

"Did you get the thing?" I asked Daniel.

"Oh . . . yeah," Daniel said as he put down the trash bag and walked behind the bar to get his backpack. Of course, his trepidation was obvious. Ryan Godfrey was his friend, on some level. But I didn't offer him any comfort, because mine would have been cold comfort indeed. Even though Godfrey was his friend, he was also undeniably dangerous. And he was about to get a taste of what he deserved.

Daniel fished around in his backpack until he found what he was looking for, zipped in an inner compartment.

"Will this work?"

"I think it's perfect."

It was a grubby jockstrap with "RYAN" written on the waistband in black marker.

Steven had finished the circle and now was working on drawing a separate glyph on the floor: a triangular pattern this time, a few feet away from the circle.

I put down the incense and opened my own backpack, unpacking the supplies I'd picked up from the shop in downtown Adders Lair last night: some candles, a vial of an oil with a planetary symbol on the bottle, a few plastic bags loaded with clumps of pungent herbs and roots, and a small figure of a man carved from wax.

"Now we have about an hour until sunrise," I said.

I tore the waistband from the jockstrap and began to wrap it around the wax figure.

"We'd better get to work."

CHAPTER FOUR

ZOOEY

This is what it's like.

That was the phrase that turned over and over in my mind while I turned over and over in my bed, trying to mold my pillow into a shape that would shield my eyes from the sun, muffle my ears from the weekend chaos raging in the halls, and support my aching head all at once.

I was hungover.

I thought of scenes from movies where business executives would suavely roll up to the office with sunglasses and a cigarette, take a swig of Pepto Bismol, and get to work. This was not like the movies.

This is what it's like.

As I mentally scanned down my body, I took stock of the symptoms I'd seen in those movies: the headache, the light and sound sensitivity, the nausea.

Check, check, check, check.

What the movies didn't accurately capture was the strange, existential sense of doom I was experiencing.

I remembered the night before like it was an R-rated movie I'd watched through my dad's fingers as he shielded my eyes from the grown-up parts: Underage drinking. Boys kissing. An invitation to an "after-party."

The details were somewhere at the bottom of a cocktail glass beneath the senior dorm. The room undulated around me as I drifted between fitful sleep and nameless dread.

I felt dirty. Not just because of the things I'd seen.

See, the only thing more insistent than the pounding in my head was the throbbing in my pajama bottoms.

Turns out, hangovers make you horny.

The position in which I found sanctuary from light and sound (flat on the stomach, pillow wrapped around the head) crushed my boner so uncomfortably that I felt like my upper and lower portions were two nations at war.

Finally, I knew my hand, like an ambassador between the two opposing camps, needed to intervene and mediate.

(*Why is he telling me this,* you're right to ask. I promise, I'm not some exhibitionistic freak who gets his jollies telling strangers about his stiffies. There's a point. So read on, you naughty little minx. I'm kidding. Or am I?)

I reached under my elastic waistband, and for a moment, Head, Eyes, Stomach, and Boner all let down their guard.

But then, pesky Mind roared onto the battlefield deploying images that I'd kept locked away since last spring like napalm:

Breath on the ear.

Broad shoulders.

A hairy chest.

A man's tie on the floor.

A wedding ring on the nightstand.

My inner war shifted from a conflict between my senses to one between arousal and shame.

I felt dirtier.

My hand surrendered its hostage, and I turned on my side, defeated, begging for sleep like a lonely solider waving a white flag.

(All this to say, that's how the memory would come back to me. Never when I wanted, and never in a way that felt good. It was an attack. He was an attack.)

It was past five o'clock and already turning to twilight when I emerged from the dorm, showered and dressed and hopefully not still reeking of gin, to get dinner in the Dining Hall.

A whole day wasted, I thought.

There was that dread again.

As I picked over a gray burger alone at one of the tables, I thought about how quickly I'd been *identified*.

(No jokes, I really thought I was stealth for a minute there. The hard truth was that my secret was as obvious here at Blackfriars as it had been back at Hansard. Less than a week in, and I'd been spotted, pursued, and seduced. *Real* stealth, Z.)

I thought about last spring.

I thought about Mr. B.

I felt the dirtiest and sickest I'd felt all day.

At least I was exhausted, and sleep came easily.

❖

Sunday was as good a day for penance as any, even though I opted not to attend chapel like some of the other, more religious kids. (After last year, I didn't have much faith that someone was watching over me who deserved to be praised and sung to, let alone beseeched for some favor.)

I knew I had to make amends for the sins of Friday night on my own, and so after an early morning jog around the track, a steaming hot shower, and a breakfast of granola and fruit, I hit the library and attacked my homework with more puritanical fury than any Sunday sermon could hope to inspire.

I wolfed down a quick, solitary dinner at the Dining Hall, then headed straight back to Bass to do my laundry, sweep out my room, and make my bed. It was already so much colder than any September I'd ever known in New York (where summer tends to rise again like a stinking zombie every couple of weeks until Christmas), but still, I threw the windows open and let fresh air rush bracingly in.

I brushed my teeth, washed my face, donned my flannel pajamas, set my alarm, and, finally, treated myself to a restorative wank. (Again, I swear this is narratively important, and sharing it is harder for me than it is for you. Bad choice of words. Anyway—)

This time, when my mind threatened to ruin the day with inconveniently arousing memories, I focused on newer, more potent images instead.

Daniel, shaking his hips as he danced.

Daniel flashing a devilish grin.

Daniel in a towel.

Daniel not in a towel.

My head snapped back against my pillow.

Release.

Relief.

Then, Regret.

Clarity came flooding back to me (the way it sometimes does in the moments after shooting a good wad, you know, fellas?).

I'd been at Blackfriars only a week and already I'd broken every rule in the Code of Conduct with the exact kinds of kids I should be avoiding, given what had happened back at Hansard. I'd been handed a fresh start, and this is how I was treating it, like a drug addict who walks out of rehab with a certificate of success and marches right down to the corner to find his fix.

This is what it's like.

I reminded myself that tomorrow was a new day, a new chance to be better. I hoped that this weekend was one last purging of my addiction, and, now expelled, I could toss it out in the morning along with the wadded-up Kleenex I dropped onto my nightstand.

I strode into Reyes's Latin class with a steaming thermos of coffee many minutes before the bell.

I was a new man. Focused. Better.

I slid my backpack under my desk chair and began to situate my textbook, notebook, and pencil case when I felt a tap on my shoulder.

I was startled to find Steven Hillman towering above me.

"Morning, Hillman," I said. "Good weekend?"

(Because of *course* I hadn't seen him at any unauthorized student party. *God* no.)

"This is for you," Steven droned, handing me a folded note.

"Oh?"

"It is not from me. It is from Leo."

Shit, I thought. They had my scent now, the sexual deviants of Blackfriars.

Steven turned without another word, returned to his seat, and waited, blankly, for class to begin. I sighed and shifted my attention to the note.

I unfolded it to reveal a funny little doodle of a coiled snake, ready to pounce on a stick figure in a Blackfriars tie. The caption read, "*Hiss hiss, bitch.*"

I crumpled and hid it, as if it were my own signed confession of a terrible crime. The note was, of course, about Ryan Godfrey, and I was suddenly aware that our reckoning was just a few periods away.

❖

I sat down to lunch and began nauseously picking at my chicken breast when the sound of a tray slapping down across from me made me jump and nearly bathe myself in Marsala sauce.

"Come here often?" Leo said in a filmic whisper.

"Oh, uh—hey," I mumbled, already on the defensive.

I looked around, paranoid, to see if anyone had clocked the pair of us. I was already certain that I stood out enough on my own. After all, Daniel had thought to invite me to the Vicious Circle after just one conversation. The last thing I needed was an exclamation mark like Leo Breyer to scream out in such a public forum.

"I know what you're thinking," Leo said. "Lucky for you, I'm exceedingly inconspicuous. Look around. Anyone whispering?"

I took a scan of the Dining Hall and was relieved to see that everyone seemed to be completely oblivious to us.

"Sorry, hi," I said.

"Can I join you?"

"Um . . ."

"Fair enough, then I'll be quick," he said. "I wanted to apologize for this weekend. I hope we didn't overwhelm or, dare I say it, offend you. Daniel just wanted you to know that you had a place here at Blackfriars, and so he invited you to the party. I should have known that it was maybe a bit . . . extreme. For a new student, I mean."

"Thanks," I said. (I'm not sure why I couldn't just leave it at that, but even in such a private conversation with someone who seemed genuinely respectful of where I was at, I just *had* to continue with—)

". . . Because I don't know if I . . . *am.* Like you guys. I mean. I don't think I'm one of you."

If my statement disappointed Leo, he didn't show it.

"Of course. Our mistake," he said, smiling. "But I *do* have to beg a favor, then . . . You won't tattle on us, will you? Daniel would never forgive himself if he accidentally invited a narc to the VC and it ended in the disbandment of such a storied little club."

"You don't have to worry," I assured him.

"You're a doll," he said.

My eyebrows must have shot up because he quickly countered with, "I mean, thanks . . . *dude.*" He lowered his voice theatrically. "You're a real pal, buddy!"

"Shut up," I chuckled.

"But seriously," he said, light tone and pronounced S returning, "if you ever want to hang again and just play cards or whatever, Daniel and I are in Two C. Knock anytime. And of course, if you ever do want dining company, I usually eat alone, too. We could be alone together."

"Why don't you eat with Daniel?" I asked. "I mean, if you're . . . roommates."

"I'm adventurous, dear, not suicidal," Leo said as he poked at a limp mushroom on his plate like a janitor inspecting something left in a toilet. "He's happy as a clam over there with the rah-rah set, natch."

I turned to see Daniel with his usual crew, laughing as Ryan Godfrey seemed to demonstrate some oral sex act upon an unfortunate peach from the salad bar.

"Doesn't it bother you?" I asked.

"What, dear?"

"That he's your . . . well whatever he is, behind closed doors, but out here, he gets to be a BMOC and you have to be—"

"Myself?"

Leo smiled, somewhat pitifully.

"You know what I mean," I said.

"Of course I do," Leo said. "And to answer your question, of *course* it doesn't bother me."

"Why?"

"Look, maybe I watched too much *Dynasty* as a kid, but I quite like having a secret," Leo said, leaning back on his chair regally. "I mean, it's kind of glamorous, isn't it? The coded messages, the hidden rendezvous. You said it yourself, actually: It's like being in a members' club. And those are only as good as who you *don't* let in. Besides, what's the alternative, being like everyone else? No *thank* you!"

With that, he plunged his fork into his chicken and tossed it, devil-may-care, over his shoulder.

I gasped, but even as the chicken slapped wetly on the floor like a mishandled organ transplant, no one even turned his head. Leo threw his fists up in victory.

As much as his presence made me nervous, that was the first good laugh I'd had since . . . well, the last good laugh I'd had, which was *also* courtesy of Leo Breyer, at the party.

Then, the bell rang and my smile evaporated.

Gym class was next up.

Leo uttered some kind of farewell as he picked up his tray and departed, but his voice was drowned out by the ticking clock in my head, a time bomb counting down relentlessly toward the explosion I knew was coming.

❖

That first gym class, after I'd finished the run ahead of the pack and shared that victorious nod with Daniel, I felt for a brief moment what the Ryan Godfreys and Theo Breckenridges and even the Daniel

Prestons of Blackfriars must feel all the time: that unteachable, automatic camaraderie shared between guys who see each other as kindred.

This is what it's like, I'd thought. (Stupid.)

In the endorphin-fueled high of the finish line, I actually believed that in this place I might be "one of the guys." But then, like a bath of ice water, Ryan Godfrey caught me ogling Daniel as he showered and reminded me that I was not, nor could I ever be, "one of the guys."

I couldn't even imagine it.

What is a school day like when gym class is a chance to be exceptional around people who look like you and talk like you? What is a school day like when "gym" doesn't stand out on your schedule like a tumor glaring on an X-ray, threatening to metastasize and overtake your whole day? What is a school day like when you are like everyone else and not like me?

Pondering that alternate universe was tempting but futile, since it was a universe I could only dream of and never escape to. Today, in my reality, the bell had just rung, signaling the end of lunch and the beginning of my personal hell.

◆

Before I'd even entered the locker room, I was met with a familiar, athletic smell of dampness, bleach, and boys. Back at Hansard, the locker room had always been a confusing space for me, a cauldron where my deepest fantasies and darkest nightmares bubbled together.

Ryan, Theo, and Daniel hadn't arrived yet, thank God. I changed with all the speed of a Broadway dancer trying to make an entrance (and probably with all the femininity, too). I was first out onto the athletic quad, stretching and pacing in preparation for this week's mile run test.

"Good fight there, Orson," Carpinelli called out to me when he saw me there. "I like that hustle!"

The rest of the class tottered down the hill and assembled.

I stole a quick glance at Daniel. It was amazing the way the same cotton tee and polyester gym shorts could make me look like a noodle and him look like an Olympian, but here we were. I didn't look long though, because I could already feel Godfrey's eyes find me. He'd locked onto his target. I'd just need to be faster.

Blast of the whistle.

I was so full of adrenaline and so empty of the lunch I was too nervous to eat that I felt as if my feet never touched the ground. This time around, I didn't even allow myself to keep an eye out for Daniel on the track. My focus was singular: finish the run, get to the shower, get dressed, get out. I was so in my head that I didn't notice I was on my fourth and final lap until I saw Carpinelli walk out to the edge of the track with his stopwatch. I crossed the finish line and skidded into the lawn, winded but relieved.

"Good God, Orson! You're on fire!" Carpinelli shouted.

I looked around as I caught my breath. Every other student, Daniel included, was still running. I'd beaten them all.

Any other kid would drink in such a victory, but I just turned to Carpinelli and pleaded, breathlessly, "Can I shower and get dressed?"

"Sure, kid," he said, with a wave.

My legs were Jell-O, but they carried me up the hill and back into the locker room, where my shower looked more like a NASCAR pit stop. (That's a butch-er image than a Broadway quick-change, isn't it? But of course, Broadway came to mind first. You can see why I was a hopeless case.)

I was already getting dressed again at my locker when I heard a voice behind me say, "Orson! I oughta call you the Flash!"

I turned because I recognized the voice to be Daniel's. His T-shirt was now drenched in sweat, and he was still breathing heavy, but somehow, he looked even better than before.

"Carpinelli's gonna ask you about track in the spring for sure," he said. "Or maybe even rugby with us. I've never seen a kid run like that, even the guys on Varsity."

I smiled.

There was that feeling again, just like when he'd nodded to me at the finish line that first time.

One of the guys.

This is what it's like.

But then Daniel stripped off his tee, revealing his heaving chest and flat stomach, all glistening like polished silver, and I remembered the truth, once again.

And then, the nail in the coffin of my fleeting victory, came Ryan Godfrey.

"Daniel, he bothering you?" he barked in that shrill, pubescent whinny of his as he approached us.

Daniel turned away. I was on my own.

"I think you're in the wrong class, buddy. This is gym, not anatomy."

My heart sank. I couldn't even turn to face him. I just stood there, taking the hit.

"You know, when I saw you rushing up here to be the first in the shower, I thought, 'This faggot isn't gonna miss a *second* of the action,' but seems like he's just got his heart set on Preston!"

Theo and other guys laughed wickedly.

"Preston's too polite to do anything about it—you're lucky. If *I* caught you looking at *me*? Forget it."

I knew that if I didn't nip this Godfrey problem in the bud, it would grow out of control for the rest of the year, hell, even the rest of my tenure at Blackfriars. They'd warned me plainly, back at the party: Once Godfrey had selected a target, it would take a miracle to get him onto some other prey.

Then, I thought of Leo, the predator.

Hiss hiss, bitch.

"If you *caught* me doing anything, it would be a goddamn miracle," I heard myself say. "Seems like you can't catch shit, the way you run."

Ryan's mouth fell open as the other guys took notice.

"What the *fuck* did you say?!"

Ryan stepped toward me. I could see Daniel out of the corner of my eye. He looked impressed but poised for violence to break out at any moment.

"Come on, man," Daniel said. "You threw a jab, and he threw one back. You don't want shit, don't start shit."

"No, no, I wanna hear him say it again," Ryan said.

I looked to Daniel, whose eyes said that he couldn't help me further.

Still, I knew there was only one way forward here.

"You heard me," I said. "Or did you? Sound might not travel all the way *down there.*"

I sent my venom right to his jugular: his height.

Hiss hiss, bitch.

"Keep talking, faggot," he said, seething.

"And what, you'll get on someone's shoulders to punch me in the face?"

Now the whole room was laughing again, but this time, they weren't laughing *at* me, they were laughing *because* of me.

I tasted blood.

This is what it's like.

"And you're calling *me* the faggot," I said, winding up for the killing blow, "but you're the one always talking about Preston's cock. Though I guess it's hard not to fixate on it when it's always at eye level."

Howls from the other boys echoed off the tiled floor and walls, multiplying and merging into a wave of torment that seemed to hit Ryan Godfrey straight in the heart. Was he about to cry?

No, he was about to strike.

He raised a fist, red and angry.

"YOU'RE DEAD, ORSON!"

Though I raised my chin defiantly, I'll never know if I was actually prepared to take the shot or not, because just as he started to charge toward me, Godfrey hit a slick, wet patch of the tiled floor, sending his feet flying out from beneath him.

It happened as if in slow motion, underwater:

His face changing from intense fury to curious surprise, like a cartoon who just realized he'd run off a cliff.

His chin sailing down toward the wooden bench between the rows of lockers.

The dull crack when they connected.

His jaw flying to the left as the rest of his face stretched to the right.

A blast of spit, blood, and bits of something gritty spraying out over the white tiled floor in front of me.

The realization that they were his teeth.

Reality resumed as the other guys sprang into action.

"WHOA!"

"Dude, fuck!"

"You OK?"

Ryan staggered to his feet and covered his mouth as bright red blood flooded between his stubby fingers and began to drip.

". . . Cn't . . . ah cn't move muh . . ."

He struggled to speak, but his jaw was frozen in that grotesque bent angle and the blood wouldn't stop coming. He looked up at me, equal parts scared and enraged.

"Come on," Theo said, throwing an arm over him. "I'll get you to the nurse."

Some of the other guys followed them out, others gawked at the bloody mess on the floor.

Daniel looked up at me, shaken, and whispered, "He deserved that," before exiting himself.

I looked down at the blood on the hem of my khakis.

I smiled.

"No, *you're* the faggot! BAM! CRACK! Teeth OUT! I love it!" Leo roared.

He was now standing on his bed in excitement after Daniel and I had relayed the events of Ryan Godfrey's (literal) fall from grace.

"It was so gnarly, for real," Daniel said. "They had to take him to the hospital in Adders. Nurse Gleason said his jaw was definitely broken. He'll need dental work, too."

"That's what you get for messing with our Zooey!" Leo said as he mussed my hair.

The rest of my classes that day had flown by as I replayed the locker room incident over and over in my head. By time the final bell rang, I knew I needed to debrief with somebody—anybody—so I took Leo up on his offer and came knocking on their dorm room door.

If I hadn't known the nature of Leo and Daniel's relationship, looking at the setup of their room, I would have thought that they were siblings who hated each other. There was an invisible but undeniable line down the middle of the room that separated it in two. Daniel's side was tidy, with a couple of posters of the LA Lakers and A Tribe

Called Quest. Leo's side was completely chaotic, with clothes flung here and there, Broadway musical posters and brochures covering an entire wall, and handkerchiefs over the lamps like it was some kind of bordello. Given the two occupants, this seemed completely appropriate.

"I didn't even do anything," I said, fixing my hair. "It just kinda happened."

"No way, Z," Daniel said. "Your digs were GOOD. You got him right where it hurts. It took him off his balance, *literally.*"

"I just hope he's not too hurt," I said. (Lied.)

"Fuck that," Leo said. "He drew first blood, didn't he? Now he'll think twice before opening his mouth. If he even can after this!"

He fell over laughing into Daniel's lap. Daniel cradled him and looked at me, laughing himself, shaking his head.

(I'm embarrassed to say that I bristled a bit, seeing them together like that.

Of course, I knew the truth about them. They'd told me, straight-up. Still, when I thought of them together, I admit, I'd only thought of two extremes: one where they were roommates like any other pair, annoying each other with keeping the place clean or coordinating study time; and one where late at night, they gave into their hormones and got what they needed from each other. This easy tenderness surprised me. As Leo howled in Daniel's arms, Daniel stroking his hair gently; they didn't look like roommates who occasionally got off together for convenience's sake. They looked like a couple. I realized I'd never, ever seen two boys together like that before.

I'm embarrassed to say that I was uncomfortable.

And that I was jealous.)

Just then, there was a knock on the door and the two instinctively shot apart.

"Come in!" Leo called.

The door cracked open to reveal Steven Hillman, towering and glowering per usual.

"Hillman!" Leo said as he trotted to the door and blew two air-kisses. "To what do we owe the pleasure?"

"Oh . . ." Steven said, as he noticed me sitting there. "I did not know you had a guest."

"It's not a guest, Steven, it's Zooey," Daniel said. "He's our friend. He's *your* friend."

"Hey, Hillman," I offered. He didn't seem impressed.

"I was hoping to speak to you," Steven said to Leo. "Alone."

Leo looked back to Daniel, who nodded.

"Sure thing," Leo said. "Smoke break out on the quad?"

"You don't smoke," Daniel said.

"I ought to smoke, it would be so good for my character."

"Oh, are you cast in another play?" I asked.

"No, dear, *this* character," Leo said, gesturing to himself. "The one I'm cultivating daily. Anyway, Hillman, let us take a stroll around the grounds before curfew. Back soon, kids."

They left, and I turned to Daniel and asked, "What was that all about? Is Steven OK?"

"Ah . . . he will be," Daniel said. "I think he might be a little jealous of you. The new baby."

"Oh, I mean, I don't wanna mess anything up."

"You're fine. Hillman is complicated. I'll make sure we all do something together soon, break the ice."

"I'd like that," I said.

(Yeah, I had it bad. I'll say it before you have the chance.)

"So does that mean we're keeping you around?" he asked. "Leo said you were maybe regretting coming to the party. That maybe I'd . . . misread. I'm sorry about that."

"No, no," I said. "Well . . . I don't know. The party was a lot."

"Dude, I fully get it. The first time Leo brought me, I felt like I'd been a part of some backdoor drug deal. Still do, sometimes. I forget, then remember all at once. I just thought you being from New York, it wouldn't be so shocking."

"There are as many different New Yorks as there are New Yorkers," I said.

(God, I sounded like Leo. Probably on purpose.)

"I hear that," he said. "Well, I'm really glad you came by tonight. I was hoping I'd get to check in on you after all that. I'm sorry I couldn't stand up for you better, but with the team it's . . . tough."

"It's OK," I said.

"No, it isn't," he said. "It's fucking horrible. I have to act like my friends, my . . . Leo even, are strangers when I see you in the hall or at meals. When you're getting shit from guys like Godfrey. But if I speak, I'm suspect, you know? If you think what you hear them say is bad, you should hear them when it's just us. It fucking sucks and I hate it and I wish I had the guts to do more about it."

I hadn't really considered all that Daniel had on the line when he came to a Vicious Circle party and let others see his true self, unafraid. Any one of the guys there could blow his cover and ruin his life. He'd risked everything by reaching out to me and inviting me in, just because he could see that I needed to know I wasn't alone. If he could be that brave, I knew that I could be brave myself.

"Be who you need to be outside the VC," I said. "I get it, I really do. I know who you really are. And I'm excited to get to know him here . . . and at the next party."

(REAL stealth, Z.)

His face lit up.

"So you're coming to the next one?" he asked.

"Maybe . . . Pencil me in," I said.

"I'll take it," he said.

I learned the next day that Ryan Godfrey had indeed broken his jaw and would need to have it wired shut for six to eight weeks.

As much as I tried to muster my inner New Yorker and say, "not my life, not my problem," I couldn't help but feel bad.

So, on his first day back at school a week later, when I spied him sipping his breakfast through a straw at the Dining Hall, I decided to offer an olive branch. As I approached him and Theo at their table, I could see that they were in the middle of a hushed argument of some kind.

I heard the tail end of Theo saying, ". . . I could get in trouble! Expelled, even. Wesley watches that office like a hawk," when Ryan caught sight of me and interrupted.

"—Ut do oo ant?"

He was asking what I wanted through his clenched teeth.

"Hey, man," I said.

(*Man. Dude. Bro.* Those terms of endearment sound so natural when other guys use them, but out of my mouth, they sound like a line being regurgitated stiffly by an actor on a soap opera.)

"I just wanted to say that I'm really sorry about what happened and that I'm glad to see you back. I wanted to call a truce."

He looked at Theo and then at me and, smiling as much as his bound and broken face could create a smile, he extended his hand.

". . . Druse . . ." he said.

I shook.

"Truce," I repeated.

To anyone watching the scene, it might have seemed like a heart-warming little moment of mutual respect. Maybe even the beginning of an unlikely friendship. I trotted away from the table with a self-satisfied grin, feeling like the Godfrey problem was in the rearview mirror.

(Unfortunately, I'd learn the truth all too soon.)

As October arrived with a blast of cold and color, Blackfriars was suddenly wonderfully boring.

With Godfrey out of gym class and thus my life for the foreseeable future, my mind was free to focus on studying. I asked Steven for help with my Latin, half because I needed it, and half because I wanted to get in his good graces and let him know I wasn't trying to steal Leo and Daniel away. As for them, I took to going over to theirs or hosting them at mine most days after class. I was still squeamish about talking openly about the boys I liked (mostly because the boy I liked best was Daniel himself), but I got more comfortable speaking with their lingo, recognizing their pop culture references, and witnessing their affection for each other.

On Friday the fourth, I even joined them as they dressed for the month's Vicious Circle party and offered to walk them there. I wasn't even sure myself if I would then escort them inside and actually stay for the party until the moment we greeted Steven at the door. I did manage to get all the way through the door and this time, without the shock of that first visit clouding my senses, I was actually able to meet the others.

There were fifteen of us in total: five seniors, five juniors, us four sophomores, and one precocious freshman named Mikey Moore. I learned that usually, no one located any eligible freshmen until near the end of the year, but Frank Costa, prefect of the freshman dorm, noticed Mikey lingering in the showers and that was that. Everyone called him "The Kid" and suddenly, I wasn't the new baby anymore. "That's gay life," Leo said with a sigh.

I met Matthew Dell, the perpetually angry leftist.

I met Brett Richardson, the British one.

I met Stephen Schaefer, whose father was an ambassador.

I didn't meet The Kid, because Costa was hoarding him like a precious resource.

That was fine by me. The sophomores stuck together. I knew they were my real friends.

After a round of doing the "Locomotion" around the dance floor, we four sunk into the old chesterfield couch for a breather.

"So Zooey, now that we're official, I'm deadly curious," Leo said. "Tell us, what *did* bring you to Blackfriars, so happily into our arms? You're an Upper East Sider. Why aren't you at Hansard or something?"

And suddenly, the warmth in my heart turned to ice. I was so focused on where things were heading for me and my friendships at Blackfriars, I had almost forgotten all that I was coming from. I considered, for just a moment, telling them the whole truth. But just as quickly, I realized that these guys were all that I had here. I knew that if they learned the truth, they'd never want to be my friend. Even here, in this secret space full of friends who all shared the same secret, I knew that I could never reveal everything.

"Actually, I was expelled," I lied.

"You're kidding," Daniel said.

"Academic failure or disciplinary action?" Steven asked.

"I'm *fascinated*," Leo said, leaning in the way he did when the gossip was good. "She's a bad girl on the run! What did you *do*? I mean, what happened?"

I opened my mouth, preparing to ad-lib some story about cheating on a test or something when Daniel interrupted.

"Never mind," he said. "That's who you were then. You can start over with us. Be who you are now."

(Yes, the guy so perfect on the outside was actually *also* that perfect on the inside. Come on, I didn't stand a chance.)

"Because we love who you are now," Daniel said. "I can't believe there was a time before you were part of the Circle!"

He put a hand warmly down on my thigh and I about shot through the ceiling. I was embarrassed that a moment so casual for him could be so charged for me.

Or did he know what he was doing?

"I'll drink to that!" Leo said. "And one for Mahler!"

Daniel, Steven, and I looked at him, stumped, and Leo gasped, offended to his core.

"Oh come *on*, boys, Stephen Sondheim's musical breakthrough, *Company*! Elaine Stritch's legendary performance of 'The Ladies Who Lunch'! What kind of degenerate sissies are you?!"

"You've totally lost me," Daniel laughed.

"No, you've lost *me*, dear! I can't be with a man who doesn't know his musical theater."

After more drinks and dances and another thinly veiled proposition from Humphrey Meier, I was presented with the Vicious Circle guest book, a pen, and a choice: to sign or not to sign. "The Kid" went before me and happily scrawled his full name to toasts and cheers of, "One of us! One of us!"

And that's what I'd always wanted, wasn't it? To be a "One of us?" One of the guys.

This is what it's like.

I took up the pen and signed. Daniel and Leo embraced me tightly.

That night, when I returned home from the revelry, I slipped into the best sleep I'd had since my arrival the month before.

It was the kind of sleep you can only achieve in a place that feels like home.

"My darling, where are you hiding?"

Though I'd told myself when I squeezed into the tiny space between my bed and bookcase that I would stay there until I was a very old man, the sound of my mother's voice was still as hypnotizing as ever, and so I stood.

"There he is," she cooed, smiling. She walked across the room, passing through a shaft of golden afternoon light that poured from the bedroom window, and took me into her arms.

"What's got you all worked up?" she asked, tucking an errant strand of my slick black hair behind my ear.

"You threw up," I heard myself say, softly. I shook my head, bringing the strand back down over my eyes, cover for the tears I felt coming.

She sighed.

"I did, yes," she said. "But we talked about this, didn't we, darling?"

She paused to make sure my roving eyes found hers again before continuing.

"Mummy is going to get sick after she gets her treatments, but that's just because the medicine is so strong. It's sometimes too much for my body to take, but that's a good thing, because that means it's stronger than the cancer. I have to get a bit sicker so that I can get a lot better. Do you understand?"

My eyes filled with tears. I nodded and mirrored her smile as best I could.

"Anyway," she said, "I'm feeling much better now. So good, I think I might just make myself some bungeo-ppang. With chocolate filling, I think. That wouldn't bother you, would it? If I made myself a sweet and chocolatey treat? I know you *hate* chocolate."

I twisted up my face, confused.

"I wouldn't want you to throw up, too," she said. "I know how much you can't stand sweets."

"But Mom!"

"On second thought, maybe bungeo-ppang isn't a good idea. Maybe anchovy pie instead."

"No!"

"Or liver on toast."

"Mom!"

"Brussels sprouts smoothies!"

"MOM!"

"Zooey. Zooey, you OK?"

"Mom?"

"Not your mother, dear, your sister. It's *me*, Leo!"

❖

It took me several hazy moments to remember where and when I was. Though the room was very dark, the details of it began to form around me until I was aware that I was in my room in Bass Hall and that Leo stood above me, hands on my shoulders, jostling me back into consciousness.

"Leo . . . what in the—"

"Get dressed," he whispered sharply. "All black. And meet us downstairs."

I sat up and looked at the clock on my desk: ten thirty. I'd only turned in for the night about an hour earlier. My mother's haunts were coming so quickly now.

It was a Friday night, and until this rude awakening, October had been happily unremarkable. Halloween was the week after next, though, so I shouldn't have been surprised at a midnight scare.

When I was awake enough to be certain that I wasn't still dreaming, I rose from the comfort of my flannel sheets, as our leader commanded.

"Leo, what in the world—"

"Now, Zooey!" he whispered, ominously. "We don't have much time."

CHAPTER FIVE

LEO

When, after a few minutes, Zooey tiptoed drowsily down the stairs into the Bass common room wearing all black as instructed, I couldn't help but feel a little disappointed in everyone's choices for our macabre little fashion show.

I mean, it's not every day one gets an after-hours demand to dress for danger and mystery. You'd think the chance to wear a *disguise* would inspire any self-respecting homosexual to try on a bold new identity, but Zooey's black cardigan, polo, chinos, and Converse were as blank and nondescript as I knew the boy himself longed to be, Daniel looked reliably sporty/tactical with athletic pants and a hoodie, and Steven was odd and academic as ever in a strangely formal corduroy blazer (the only black thing he owned, apparently).

I, on the other hand, was *completely* transformed by a leather jacket one of my mom's boyfriends had left behind, a little big on me, but weathered and dangerous looking, some Bruce Springsteen black jeans, and pugilistic little watch cap to match. *The Works.* I even considered adding an eyepatch but then thought better of it due to night visibility. Altogether, the clothes really did make a new man. If I kept my mouth shut, you might have thought I was *straight*. NOT that I'm paying myself a compliment with that assessment, but I figured my image could use the shot of testosterone for the mission ahead.

"Is everything OK?" Zooey whispered. "Where are we going?"

"No questions," I warned. "Do exactly what I say when I say it and you'll be safe."

Zooey swallowed hard, and with a militaristic little cock of his head, Daniel motioned for us to fall out. We all slipped clandestinely through the doors of Bass Hall into the dank night air.

Lit only by the full harvest moon hanging above, we prowled through trees, avoiding the lantern-lit paths of the campus to stay cloaked in shadow.

Blackfriars had lost a lot of its initial charm for me as the mundanity of class and homework and bland meals rendered even its most impressively Gothic structures banal. By night, however, the whole campus took on a pagan sort of ancientness as the insects, winds, and earthen smells of rural Massachusetts took up the space left when we throngs of students retired for the evening. Blackfriars belonged to the woods again at night, and its sylvan mystery filled even my jaded little heart with a dark awe.

Soon, we'd met our first checkpoint: a lonely shed positioned near the southern border of the property.

"You're on," Daniel said to me as we approached the shed door, sealed as it was with a heavy-looking padlock. Undaunted, I retrieved a pair of bent paper clips from my pants pocket and started to work on the lock.

The feeling of picking a lock is not unlike how it felt getting to the bottom of Zooey Orson over the last few weeks. Each bit of shame and trauma I'd uncovered in him through our conversations at meals and in the dorm felt like a new chamber coming loose as I needled my way deeper and deeper toward the core of the enigmatic boy. I still hadn't tripped the pin that would unlock him completely. I knew there was more he was hiding. But I was as skilled in psychology as I was in thievery, and I knew I would get there eventually. The lock in my hands popped open. If only Zooey Orson were so easily cracked.

"Nice!" Daniel said as I pulled it free from its latch and unsealed the door.

"Agreed, impressive," Steven muttered.

"How do you know how to do that?" Zooey asked, clearly shocked.

"When you grow up like I did, you learn all sorts of useful skills," I replied, pocketing my tools.

Whoops, I thought. *Don't give too much away.*

My mother swore that when she and my father were together, they had a respectable house in a nice little village. She'd sold it after his death and lived comfortably on the nest egg for some time during my infancy. Perhaps too comfortably, as we moved, over the course of my childhood, from a nice duplex to a small apartment, and finally to one of the finer trailer parks in Worcester County. My upbringing there left me prepared for very little in life, but I did learn the ins and outs (mostly ins, as it were) of lockpicking from a nice girl two trailers over. Together we'd slip into shops and groceries under the cover of night, taking what we needed; the Bonnie and Clyde of North Mass.

Of course, I didn't elucidate that bit of history. I preferred to maintain a mystique of privilege and glamour.

I swung the shed door open to reveal our prize: a fleet of stored black bicycles.

"Let's do this," I said.

Daniel, Steven, and I each straddled a bike, but Zooey hesitated.

"What's wrong, Z?" Daniel asked.

"I . . . I don't know how to ride a bike. I never learned."

"Damn, Orson," I said. "You're richer than I thought!"

"Shut up," he moaned.

"No, I mean it, how devastatingly civilized! She doesn't ride, she's *driven. CHAUFFERED!*"

"You're an idiot," Daniel laughed.

"What do we do?" asked Steven, ever ready to get to the meat of the matter.

"He can ride with me," Daniel said. "I'm the strongest, he can ride on my seat while I stand and pedal."

"You sure?" Zooey asked. "I can just hang back."

"Don't be silly," Daniel said. "We ride together."

We walked the bikes to a path at the back of the property that led into the woods. Eventually those woods fed out onto a country route that would take you, if you knew the way, to Adders Lair, the little fishing town a few miles away and the nearest civilization to Blackfriars.

When we emerged from the woods to meet the black paved road, Zooey once again asked, "Where are we going," to which I again replied, "No questions!"

We straddled the bikes and started down the hill. I thought of *E. T. the Extra-Terrestrial*, lit as we were by the spotlight of the full moon, Zooey acting as our precious alien cargo.

I'd made this delinquent little journey about a dozen times since it was first revealed to me by a VC member in my freshman year, but getting to take a new passenger along, I suddenly felt like a tribal elder, passing wisdom to the next generation.

We sailed down the hill, a navy blanket adorned with filigree of silver and gold stars hanging above. I felt the song of rebellion rise up in my lungs and, totally out of character, I let a whoop of sheer youth and freedom escape my throat. I turned to Daniel, who smiled back as he pedaled, and then noticed something curious.

As discussed, Daniel stood, working the pedals and steering the handlebars as Zooey sat perched on the seat, holding his waist for security. The strange thing was that Zooey didn't look ahead at the road, but rather, had his face pressed to the side of Daniel's back. He wasn't just holding on to him to stay on the bike. He was embracing him.

The moment probably didn't even register with Daniel as significant, but I saw everything when I saw that embrace. I thought of our early days as strange roommates, learning to make him laugh, daring to let my hand linger on my shoulder as he gasped for breath. That lingering touch was how I first recognized my own feelings for Daniel, so I recognized it immediately when I saw it again, reflected on Zooey Orson.

A creature less evolved than myself might be filled with jealous rage at the sight, but I'm a true romantic, through and through, always have been. I saw nothing but beauty. I wanted simultaneously to be Daniel, wrapped in an adoring embrace; to be Zooey, seizing the opportunity to turn a simple bike ride into something more; and to remain myself, getting to watch it all from my vantage point like a poetic film, moonlight and all.

I was so entranced by the moment, I was almost disappointed when our bikes whizzed past the carved, painted sign declaring our arrival in "Historic Adders Lair." Then I remembered our mission.

Adders Lair was, I shall say, *rustic*, as far as the towns of northeast Massachusetts go. There used to be some kind of mill here where a tributary of the Merrimack met the ocean, which might have provided jobs and denizens to energize the compact little town. That mill had long since closed, and now, unless you were a fisherman or an employee of one of the small shops and restaurants that existed for the summer crowds, the weekenders, and those passing through on their way north, Adders Lair didn't seem to offer much. There was a bit of life along Main Street, though most of its customers had headed back to Boston or New York as the summer wound down.

We skidded to a stop in a small, derelict little park in the center of town where we dismounted and stashed the bikes in some bushes.

"Are you sure these are safe here?" Zooey asked.

"Darling, this journey is old hat for me," I said. "And also, *no questions*! Now, lemme just prepare myself for my next act."

I retrieved a small brown vial from my jacket, unscrewed the cap, and turned it over my finger before dabbing the drops behind my ears.

"NO," Steven gasped, looking at the bottle with alarm. "You did not tell us you'd be using that."

Drat, thought I. I'd hoped Steven would just be cool, but I should have known better.

"OK, what on earth do you have planned, Leo?" Daniel asked.

"Oh my goodness, can everyone *relax*?!" I pleaded, eyes rolling.

"Leo . . ." sighed Daniel.

"Wait, *you* guys don't even know what we're doing here?" Zooey asked the others.

"QUESTIONS!" I reminded him.

"What was that?" he asked, despite my instruction.

"It's . . . cologne," I said. "To make me seem more mature. You brought your fake ID, right?"

I tipped my head toward the bar across the street: a squalid-looking little dive whose flickering neon sign read "The Forecastle." Bikers and tattooed townies swarmed the entrance, smoking. One of them fell drunkenly, crashing into the gutter. Another was bleeding from the face but didn't seem to notice or mind.

Zooey caught my drift and instantly looked scandalized.

"No!"

"Zooey, I'm fucking with you," I said. "I'm *convivial*, not downright alcoholic. We do hang out without getting blind drunk, you know.

Besides, look at that dump, do you think I'd be caught *dead*?! No, tonight, we're having a cultural outing. A special midnight screening."

I gestured down the block to The Community Theater, a decaying two-screen movie theater.

"Ohhhh," Daniel said, laughing. "I should have known. He's been talking about this for weeks."

"Not to me," Steven said, squinting at the theater.

I put that little comment in my back pocket and said "Let's go," and we made our way toward the theater.

There were a few men of various ages loitering around outside, stealing glances at each other as if they were wondering who had the next line. I figured they were interested in seeing the same movie as us, but without our youthful boldness. In comparison, I waltzed up to the ticket booth without fear and announced, "Four for *My Own Private Idaho*, please."

"*Really?!*" Zooey gasped.

I gave him a nudge in the ribs just hard enough to send the message.

The woman working the booth, a picture of dour North Mass conservatism, let's call her "Susanne," because she looked like one, scanned me up and down.

"Do you *kids* know what this movie is about?"

Do I know what it's about?!

The whispers about *My Own Private Idaho* among us VC boys had been damn near screams since word first got out about the film after its premiere at a festival in September. That's because it stars River Phoenix and Keanu Reeves as gay hustlers, and apparently, it features graphic gay sex and male nudity. Now, in case you are reading this in the far future, this was a *big gay deal.* River and Keanu were both *straight* movie star heartthrobs, the James Deans of their generation, rising to A-list fame, and they'd chosen to take on these roles and ostensibly do all manner of gay things to each other. Also, I'd heard you see River's dick. Listen, I'm a man of taste and refinement and I was sure the film had its cultural value, but I'm also a man with red blood running through his veins, and the idea of River and Keanu in the throes of gay passion got that blood pumping enough to orchestrate this late-night outing to catch the one showing of the film scheduled within a fifty-mile radius.

"It's *about* two hours, if I'm not mistaken," I said to Susanne.

Susanne didn't love my cheek.

"IDs," she commanded. "It's rated R. No one under seventeen permitted."

"Oh, *Susanne*," I chuckled, looking to Daniel, amused, for dramatic effect.

"That's not my—"

"We never bring those around anymore! I haven't been carded for a simple *movie* in ages! It's not like I'm trying to buy a bottle of whiskey or a gun or something. We didn't even think to bring them."

Her eyes narrowed. It occurred to me that I hadn't planned for the glass case that separated Susanne from myself and my undeniably persuasive aura. Luckily, I'm a goddamn secret agent. I fumbled in my jacket pocket with the little bottle, clandestinely unscrewing the cap with one hand as I fished for my wallet with the other.

"I do have a student ID from the university, which ought to be good enough, wouldn't you say? I mean, unless you know some child genius that attends university. Now there's a movie I'd like to see!"

I got a bit of the stuff on the tips of my fingers and screwed the cap back on.

"And may I say, I'm just absolutely *chuffed* as they say across the pond, *chuffed*, that this humble little theater in Adders of all places is daring to show a film of such cultural import. Even if we do need to turn up in the dead of the night just to see it, like we were slinking into some coin-operated porno house."

I opened my wallet and pulled out my library card, slicking it with the secret formula before tossing it into the metal slot at the base of Susanne's window.

"But truly, it's better than nothing. I hope you take pride in your position at a movie house with such a passion for progressive, artful programming, Susanne, I really do. *I* would."

She looked at the card.

"What the hell is this supposed to—"

And then I saw it happen in real time.

It was in her eyes. They seemed to glass over slightly as her focus drifted away from my face to an indistinct middle-distance.

"Something, wrong, Susanne?"

". . . Susanne," she whispered. Her face looked puzzled, as if recalling her own name were as complex as reciting all fifty state capitals. "No, nothing wrong, honey. Go on in, enjoy the movie."

"Susanne, you're too kind, but we do need to *pay* for these tickets, don't we?"

"Oh? Oh, sure, right . . . twenty-four dollars, even."

"You heard her, Steven," I said. "Well, come on now, don't be stingy. We know you're good for it."

Steven was, in fact, good for it. In retrospect, I feel guilty about all the times I asked Steven to pay without a second thought, but truly, twenty-four dollars was about as relevant to the Hillmans as I was to River Phoenix. Once a family hits a certain level of wealth, money just becomes numbers that go up and down, a game of Monopoly with no stakes at all.

Anyway, he shelled out and we stepped into the theater.

“You’re ridiculous,” Daniel chuckled. “I can’t believe that worked.”

“You knew it would work,” Steven said, gloomy. “It always works.”

“We don’t *know* that,” Daniel began to say, but as I saw Zooey’s bewildered expression, I knew that we were about to pull a thread that needn’t be pulled, and so I steered us toward the snack bar.

“The popcorn was probably made in the early Eighties, but still, I’d like a large with all the fake-butter product they can sully it with! The Works!”

We stocked up on snacks and found seats near the back. The men from outside the theater began to filter in, one at a time, looking guilty as puppies who’d chewed up the cushions.

“Now boys, before we take the plunge, let’s take the *official* tally,” said I. “Keanu or River?”

“Keanu,” Daniel said without hesitation.

“Really?” I said. “I would have taken you for a River. He’s *almost* ginger, after all. Strawberry blond, I’d say.”

“I just know what I like when I see it,” he chuckled.

“Well, that’s lucky for us, because I’m a River man. I mean, get me a paddle and I’d navigate that River like Huckleberry Finn. If we ever meet them, we’ll divide and conquer!”

“I’m not enough for you?” Daniel scolded.

“Oh, come on, it’s a *hypothetical,* darling. What about you, Zooey?”

In truth, it was his answer I was interested in all along, not because I actually wanted to know but because I’d been on a mission to keep needling through to the real Zooey with little questions like this. If I could normalize talking about boys and gay life for him, I reckoned he’d have an easier time bringing up such subjects himself someday.

Like I said, I’m a secret agent.

“Um . . . why choose?”

“Ding ding ding! We have a winner,” I said, mussing his hair affectionately from my neighboring seat. "You know, you look a bit like Keanu, all that gorgeous dark hair and those soulful eyes. No! Don't argue, dear, take your compliment like medicine and sip your Coca-Cola. Steven? Which of our leading men take the lead for you?"

"I need to use the bathroom," he said, standing abruptly and sidling out of the row.

I looked to Daniel, who shrugged.

"I'll get it," I said. I knew this mood was my fault anyway.

❖

Let's take a mo' to discuss poor Steven Hillman. You're probably wondering why a goddamn delight like myself would keep such a notorious wet noodle in my social circle. I very often wondered that myself.

We met in Reyes's Exploratory Language course in freshman year. At Blackfriars, before you decide on which language you'll major in from sophomore year onward, they make you take a little platter party class where you have to sample each of them. I knew, going in, that my heart was set on French so that I could become just exactly like Catherine Deneuve in *The Umbrellas of Cherbourg*, but the first on our tasting menu was Latin.

My mother and I were practically allergic to all things religious, but we did pop into the Catholic church down the street every Christmas Eve for the caroling (and, I'd later learned, for the charity she was able to get for last-minute presents), and I found all that "mea culpa deus maximus dominus" noise so damn *depressing*. My ears actually went deaf to it, I swear!

So, a few lines into Reyes's chanting, I'm already lost, but this kid in the seat next to me, he's raising his hand every time Reyes has a question. Up, down, up, down: It was actually very Catholic. And every time Reyes does call on him, he aces it! So, after the bell I turn to the kid and ask:

"Sorry to bother you, friend . . . what's your name?"

"Steven Hillman."

"Hillman, Leo Breyer, a pleasure. *Say*, I noticed you're kind of a wiz with Latin!"

"I am fluent in Latin," he said flatly.

I chuckled, but he just stared back, deadpan.

". . . Seriously?"

"Yes. I am fluent in four languages. Proficient in several more."

I waited for a punch line that wasn't coming.

"Then . . . why are you taking this class?"

"Because I will get an A."

Hot damn, I thought.

"Have lunch plans?"

What followed was a strange little courtship where I would sit with him at lunch and regale him with fascinating conversation, and he would essentially do my Latin homework for me, *quid pro quo*. Besides, I'd been sitting all by my lonesome anyway, so I actually didn't mind having a stone such as Steven upon which to sharpen my tongue.

Imagine my surprise, then, when one day, right in the middle of learning about feminine endings, our study session took quite a masculine one when Hillman leaned over and planted one on me, right on the *osculum*. When my shock abated, I informed him I wasn't interested, but I knew just the little gathering for him to find someone and asked if he would join me at the next Vicious Circle.

We became something like friends, though anytime I tried to get into anything too personal, he'd retreat. Last Christmas break, I'd phoned his house in Connecticut to ask about an essay project for Reyes's class. The butler who picked up needed to shout over the party that was in full swing at the Hillman home, and when he could finally make out that it was Steven I was asking for, he was bewildered. I guessed that it was rare, if not unprecedented, that anyone called for dear Steven. I held for a full twenty minutes before he could be located, not because he was in the swing of the festivities but because he'd locked himself in the attic.

When Steven went off on his own, you knew there was something he wasn't telling you.

❖

I sped through the neon and mirrored lobby, past a Ms. Pac-Man machine, and into the men's room.

It was as glamorous and sparkling clean as I expected, which is to say, not at all. Among the innumerable scribbles memorializing romances (TS + MW 4EVR), political positions (DIE FAGGOTS), and local lore (SOMETHING DARK SLEEPS IN THIS TOWN) on the walls around the urinals, I found Hillman staring into a cloudy mirror, seething.

". . . You OK, Hillman? The movie's gonna start soon."

"You said you had gotten rid of the bottle," he said.

I knew that was it.

"Did I?"

"You *know* that you did."

It was rare bit of spice from him. I was really in trouble.

". . . So I forgot! And I found it again when I was unpacking this semester, and I thought we may as well use it. I mean, it worked, didn't it?"

"*Furthermore*," he said, "I thought you said we would be done with *all* of that stuff when we returned the book for the last time. But now, this is the second time you've used it in a matter of weeks. All to show off for someone we barely know."

"Why, Hillman," I said. "Are you jealous?"

"How can you say that?" he sneered. "I did the work to get Godfrey off of his back. You could not have done it without me, and I helped, even though you know I did not want to."

"Yes, you did, and we are very grateful," I said. "So that was the *one* more time, to help a struggling boy who needed the help. And this?"

I pulled the bottle out of my pocket. He winced at the sight of it.

"This we already made ages ago! I didn't even think of using the *product* as engaging with the . . . *process.* I didn't think it counted! Honestly, Steven, I didn't. I was just excited about the movie, which we're about to miss, and I wasn't thinking. I promise. We're really done with it. Actually, here, you take it."

I handed him the bottle.

"I do not want—"

"So throw it away, or whatever you want. But this way you're in control."

He pocketed it.

"How are your dreams?" he then asked, abruptly.

"What's that?"

"Since that first party, back when we . . ." he searched for the words. "How have you been sleeping?"

"Like Judy wrapped in valium, dear, why do you ask?"

There was something in his eyes I'd never seen before. He looked vulnerable. He looked *human.*

"Never mind," he said.

"Steven, if it's happening again, you have to tell me—"

"I am fine. Let's get back to our seats. I know you will never forgive me if you miss seeing that boy's penis."

I didn't push it. I'd known Hillman long enough now to know when the vault had closed.

Also, he was right about the penis.

"Now that we can agree on," I said.

❖

We shuffled back to our seats to find River already three stories high before us, looking absolutely devastating alone on a desert highway.

"There you are!" Daniel whispered.

"How's the bird-watching? Did I miss any peckers?"

"No, no, it's just starting."

The movie told the story of two hustlers (that's gay for prostitutes) as they survived a gritty underworld and navigated their lives. River was on a quest to find his mother, while Keanu was trying to get away from his father, who was a mayor or something, very wealthy. River's character seemed to be in love with Keanu, while Keanu said that he only slept with guys for money. In one scene, River tries to kiss Keanu, who turns him down. They go to Italy in search of the mom and Keanu meets a girl who he falls for, having sex with her noisily while River lies awake in the room downstairs in agony. By the end, Keanu takes his money, marries the girl, and ends up in high society. River never finds his mom and ends up unconscious on the side of the road.

The kind of gay romance I'd come to expect, actually.

And I was lied to about the nudity. There were breasts but no dick. Of *course.*

When we lumbered out of the theater, it was past two in the morning. We walked toward the park where we'd stashed the bikes.

". . . So, reviews?" I asked.

"It was sad," Daniel said. "I mean, beautiful, but obviously really sad. And I wish there'd been, like, a *single* Black person in it."

"The acting *was* very good," I said. "I didn't know dear Keanu had it in him. Now, I wouldn't expect you boys to know, so I promise I'm not being a *snob*—"

"Here we go," Daniel laughed.

"Well, forgive me for *educating*, but Keanu's plot was based on Shakespeare."

"So that's why they were talking like that," Daniel said. "It was *almost* enough to kill my boner. Almost. I can't believe they showed that blow job scene!"

"Barely," Steven said. "It was an abdomen and the back of a head."

"But what an abdomen," Daniel said. "You know, maybe I *am* a River man, after all."

"What about you, Zooey, did you like it?"

"No," he said, cold.

I was taken aback.

". . . Care to elaborate?" I asked.

"Well . . ." he looked deeply uncomfortable. "Those young guys with those older men. Taking advantage. You really found that hot, Dan?"

"Well, no, of course not, I mean that guy was a troll," he said. "But River!"

"I guess so," Zooey said. "Anyway, I didn't blame Keanu for wanting to get away from all that in the end. I mean if that's where it ends, otherwise."

Suddenly I realized that the whole night had been a miscalculation.

It seemed that every time I tried to expose Zooey to some facet of the gay world, I managed to show him the dark side. I'd need to be more careful, lest I scare him off forever.

There wasn't time to mull it over, though. Daniel interrupted my racing mind with a grave, "*SHIT*."

We'd reached the bushes where we'd ditched the bikes to find that the bikes had ditched us.

They were gone. We were stranded.

"Goddammit," Daniel sighed as he looked around helplessly.

"Yeah, I kinda thought . . ." Zooey began.

"Let's not relitigate this, please," I interrupted, trying to keep cool. "Like I said, this spot has always been safe."

"How are we going to get home?" Steven asked. "It is the middle of the night."

"We'll just have to call a cab," I said.

"Where?" Daniel asked. "Even the bar is closed now. And where would we wait for it? It's looking sketchy as hell out here . . ."

He was right. The few film enthusiasts had scattered, and now it was just us, the night, and a few ominous-looking zombies who still wandered the dark streets. I didn't want to find out what would happen if one of them caught our scent.

I allowed myself to despair for exactly four seconds before a plan B manifested in my cunning little noggin.

"What about Poison Ivy?" I asked. "She lives down the block."

"Who?" Zooey asked.

"A friend," I said. "Err, an acquaintance."

"She'll be asleep," Daniel said.

"You really think Morticia Addams is asleep before the witching hour? She's probably up breaking chicken's necks or something diabolical."

"I do not want to go there," Steven said.

"Well, darling, if you've got a better idea, I'd love to hear it," I snapped.

He looked at the ground.

"Fine," Daniel said. "I'm really sorry about this, Z . . ."

"Zooey's fine, aren't you, Zooey?" I said, desperate to keep the ball in the air. "Just a little wrinkle to add to the adventure. This will work and we'll be home in no time."

"It'd better," Daniel said, shooting me a look.

I could tell he was pissed. I was just unsure whether it was more to do with the bikes or the fact that we were about to expose fragile Zooey to one of Adders' most venomous spiders.

We hurried the short distance to a weather-worn little bungalow tucked between two vacant storefronts. I knocked on its crumbling door. A flake of ancient red paint gave way beneath my fist and fluttered to the ground.

Silence.

I knocked again.

I allowed myself a few more seconds of panic.

Then the door creaked open, the light from within slicing a golden blade across the slick black pavement before us. A dark pair of eyes glowered at us through the crack.

"You've gotta be *kidding* me," croaked a young female voice dripping with annoyance. "*What* on earth do you want?"

"Oona, my angel of darkness," I cooed. "So sorry for the late hour. We're in just a bit of a bind and we need to call a taxi to get home, lest the ghouls of Adders Lair take us directly to Hell instead. Can we use your phone?"

"Do you know what time it is?!"

"Were you sleeping?"

"Well . . . no," she said. "But it's the principle of the thing! I brought you here during *business* hours. That wasn't an open invitation!"

Daniel and Steven looked to me to fix this.

"Really, we just need to use the phone and wait for the taxi," I said, stepping in close to the door, hoping I was still as *persuasive* as I was when I'd talked our way past Susanne.

"Be a pal?" I pleaded.

She huffed, exasperated, but then softened suddenly. I noticed her eyes change the same way Susanne's did; subtle, but undeniable.

"Fine," she said, undoing the chain on the door and swinging it fully open. "Just don't touch anything."

Secret. Agent. I'm telling you.

"Darling, you're a legend. Fellas?"

I ushered us all into the safety of her place.

"Thanks, Oona," Daniel said. "We'll be quick."

Oona's house was a small little fisherman's shack left over from the boom years of Adders Lair, though while it was begging to be decorated with nautical touches like rope and seashells and copies of *Moby Dick* lying here and there, she had opted for a more *dramatic* look, all black velvet, flickering candles in glass pillars, and wafting incense. It was like being in Stevie Nicks's beach house.

You see, Oona worked down the block at a little shop called Ouroboros that specialized in candles, crystals, incenses, herbs, and other trappings of the occult. She worked there because she herself was a self-described witch, and she dressed the part, too.

"*Loving* the look, by the way," I said. "I read about grunge in Vogue. SO '*right now*'!"

She looked like she was drawn from chalk and charcoal the way her pale skin played against her dark makeup and macabre sense of fashion: black flannel tied over a black tank, gray-and-black plaid skirt, black stockings, black Doc Martens. Her red lipstick was the only accent of color in the whole portrait, a way to draw your attention to her words, which I knew to be generally deadly.

"One, *uck*, those are posers," she said. "Two, last time I saw you, you said I looked *drab*."

"Drab is chic! Rococo went out with the Eighties, the Nineties are minimal—"

"THREE, what the hell are a bunch of—what?—*sixteen*-year-old prepsters doing out so far past their bedt— Wait! Let me guess, that gay movie at the Community?"

"You really *are* a witch," I said.

"Phone is just in the kitchen there," she said, pointing down the hallway. "There's a card for the cab company taped to the wall."

"I will get it," Steven said. He'd never been comfortable in Oona's house, and I could tell that he was eager to leave. I think for someone so totally oriented toward numbers, physics, and logic, the idea of the metaphysical realms and the people who earnestly dabbled in them were as unsuited to Steven as the Charles River would be to Oona's black cat. I suppose I couldn't blame him. Our previous brushes with the dark arts had been . . . unnerving for all of us.

"How was the movie, by the way?" she asked. "I thought about going, but I'm no longer consuming art made by white men."

Daniel let a laugh escape. I was grateful for the levity.

"Well, naturally, I have a LOT to say."

I dove into my shot-by-shot commentary. Invested as I was in giving my full critique of the film, I failed to keep my eye on Zooey, who'd begun to wander around her spooky little abode, poring curiously over the scarves and curios and tarot decks and taxidermy.

"What is all this?" he asked.

We turned to see him stretching a finger toward a white pinwheeled blossom of one of the plants growing beneath a bluish grow light in Oona's indoor garden.

"DON'T TOUCH ANYTHING, I SAID!"

Zooey pulled his hand away like he'd submerged it in boiling water as Oona rushed over to the plant.

"I . . . I didn't actually touch it," he said.

"Good," she sighed. "Sorry, I didn't mean to yell. That's just . . . very poisonous."

"Are you . . . I mean, do you *poison* people?"

I felt Daniel's eyes find me. I shot him a look as if to say, *don't panic.*

"Not without their consent, of course," she said. "Mostly, I just grow the baneful herbs to learn from their spirits. It's part of my practice as a devotee of Hecate."

". . . What?"

"Say, could I get a glass of water?" I cried, practically sprinting over to them. "All that salty popcorn."

Luckily at that moment, Steven returned and announced, "The car will be here in a few minutes."

"Oh fantastic, Steven, thank you."

"Who is this one, by the way?" Oona asked, focused on Zooey. "I haven't seen you before."

"Uh, hey," he said. "I'm . . . new in town."

"Well duh," she said. "I think I'd have noticed the *single* other Asian person in this town."

"What?" I asked. "Zooey isn't Asian."

"Of course he is," Oona said. "Or some, at least. I'd know better than you, wouldn't I?"

"You're seeing things," I informed her.

"Yeah, preeeetty sure he's white," Daniel laughed.

"Well yeah, I *am* white," Zooey said. "But . . ."

"But?" Oona asked, incredulous.

"Well, my mom is," Zooey said. ". . . Was. Korean."

I about hit the floor.

"She *is*?!" I asked.

"*Was*," he said.

"I knew it!" Oona said. "Me too! Sup, Dongsaeng?! Wow, we got *two* in Adders Lair! One more and I'll have to quit the shop to start selling bubble tea."

"*Korean*! I'll be damned," I said to Zooey, who looked strangely distant. "You're just full of surprises, Orson."

"Sorry, yeah," he said. "Sorry."

"Wait till you find out about Keanu," Oona said.

"What?" I asked.

"I think I see headlights," Daniel said, looking out a porthole window.

"Anyway, that's our cue," I said, rushing up to Oona to give her two air-kisses. "Thanks again, Dark Lady. We owe you one, and I mean it. Give my best to the infernal spirits!"

"Don't let it happen again," she said, though I could tell she was suppressing a little grin.

Once safely in the taxi, zooming our way home at last, Zooey asked, "So who was she? How do you know her?"

I hoped I didn't hesitate too suspiciously long before I blurted out, "My dealer!"

"Your dealer?" Zooey repeated.

"You saw all her plants, she's the only place in town to get a decent smoke."

"You mean like . . . weed?"

"Don't tell anyone, please," I lied. "I don't want to get the reputation of a burnout. It's just so much better for the waistline than drinking. No calories, you know."

Daniel took my hand, privately, and squeezed. I hoped it meant that I'd earned his forgiveness.

We had the taxi drop us at the edge of the grounds so as not to draw the attention of any night security or groundskeepers, and we walked the last stretch through the woods, back to the campus proper.

We bid a hushed adieu to Steven and Zooey. I hoped that Zooey's lethargic response was due to the early hour and not some mounting homosexual dread.

By the time Daniel and I finally slipped back into our room, the sun was beginning to rise.

It had been more of an adventure than I'd bargained for, but all's well that ends well.

We were too exhausted to be intimate, so we just collapsed into our own beds on our own sides of the room.

Before we drifted off, I drowsily asked, "Do you think he had fun?"

". . . Zooey?" Daniel asked, his eyes already shut.

"No. Steven. Of course Zooey."

". . . I think you're pushing him," Daniel said. "But I also think that's what he needs."

"I agree."

"I like him," he said.

"I like *you*," I replied. Daniel opened his eyes and turned to face me.

"I like you, too," he said.

We smiled at each other until each of our eyes began to close.

"*Korean!*" I yawned, still processing the revelation. Daniel laughed at me and turned over, shutting his eyes.

And as my lids became insurmountably heavy, my view of Daniel began to fade.

His face, then darkness.

His face, then darkness.

Darkness, then a face.

But it wasn't Daniel's face anymore.

It was a face I still cannot describe. Something monstrous, foul—

And *watching me.*

I sat up with a sharp gasp. Every hair on my body stood on end. I felt a sense of dread wallop me like nothing I'd known before.

But Daniel just lay there sleeping.

I blinked the moment away.

Hillman putting ideas in my head, I thought, and lay back down to sleep.

❖

I should have asked him what he'd meant about his dreams, back at the movie theater.

There is a lot I should have done when it came to Steven Hillman.

It's hard to pinpoint at exactly which crossroads we'd taken the wrong path, but this is the one that still keeps me up at night, even today.

I should have listened.

CHAPTER SIX

DANIEL

It's amazing what you can get used to, I thought.

I was thinking back to this exact time, the weekend before Hell Week, one year ago. I'd spent the whole weekend training in the gym. I wanted to make sure the senior jocks saw me lifting heavy and knew I was not one to play with. That, and I wanted to show Carpinelli that I was serious about making JV rugby when the tryouts came up in the spring.

I wasn't actually super-psyched about rugby. I mean, who besides, like, a Kennedy or a Trump or something grows up watching or giving a shit about *rugby*? I don't even know where you watch that. Growing up, I wanted to be like Magic and Jordan. But rugby is what Blackfriars had, and so that's what I was gonna play. After my first month and a half at the school and learning how most of the guys here reacted to me, I figured making the team might be my best chance at making some friends.

I had to laugh, because *this* Hell Week, as I stood crammed in the bathroom of the secret pub, trying to get Leo's wig on straight, I realized I had the best friends I could have asked for, but not at all in the way I'd expected. These guys didn't give a shit about rugby, either, but they also didn't give a shit about Jordan. Tonight, Leo wanted to be Anjelica Huston in *The Witches*. Just as badass as Jordan, but a much trickier costume.

"I just really think the hairline needs to come down," Leo said, flustered, as he tugged the slick black wig here and there. "I cut the bangs too short, god*dammit*!"

He'd made another unauthorized trip into Adders Lair last weekend to get the wig, dress, gloves, and jewelry from some thrift shops in town (and he was more careful about where to stash his bike this time). He even brought out that damn incense burner we'd gotten at Ouroboros, loaded it with something pungent, and carried it by its chain so that a cloud of wispy smoke would envelop him all night. Knowing how much work he'd put in, I wished he'd just relax and enjoy himself, but there were prizes for the best looks, and even though he was just a sophomore, Leo was determined to take the gold.

Someone pounded on the door, impatient.

"I *SAID*, take a goddam Xanax!" Leo shouted back. "We'll be out in a second, *CHRIST*!"

Halloween fell next Thursday, so that meant everyone was celebrating the weekend before and that the annual Vicious Circle Halloween party (the Crystal Ball, someone had named it) was tonight, Friday. Of course, the guys couldn't parade around campus in their costumes. For one, they'd give away our location, but worse, most of them would probably get the shit kicked out of them, since the costumes at this party tended to be pretty out there. So everybody had to get ready, one by one, in the club's bathroom, and then make a grand entrance.

As for me, I'd opted for Indiana Jones. It was an easy enough look to put together with clothes I already owned, and with my jump-rope whip, I thought I looked pretty damn good. Leo's only adjustment once we got into the bathroom was undoing two more buttons on my shirt.

"I still feel like we should have done a couples' costume," I said, looking him over. "I mean, you look great, but pairs are better for scoring."

"So we *are* a couple?" he asked, eyebrows raised.

"... Of course we are," I said.

"Just checking. It's nice to be reminded."

He shot me that smile of his, then turned back to the mirror and continued primping.

❖

I was repulsed by Leo Breyer when I first met him, if we're being honest.

I'd checked into my room on move-in day hoping to be paired with a BMOC type to take me under his wing and introduce me around. That, or at least someone quiet. I walked into our dorm to find Leo draping red handkerchiefs over all the lamps in the room and I knew instantly that he was neither of those things. Socially, he was the opposite of an ally; he was a liability. The bullying he suffered was immediate and relentless. As for quiet, the kid only stopped talking when he was selecting just the right insult, like a rich lady picking out jewelry to go to a luncheon. In fact, he seemed to have a sixth sense for knowing when I really needed to study, because it was on those nights that he absolutely *had* to get my opinion on the arrangement of our four pieces of furniture, or something ridiculous.

He was pretty funny, though, when he wasn't infuriating.

There was one late Friday night, right at the top of October, when he crashed into our room stinking drunk and began to hurl into the trash can. I was furious, but I was also afraid of him overflowing the can and ruining our carpet, so I ushered him down to the hall bathroom to yak into the toilet like a civilized person. Between heaves, Leo wept through all the famous death speeches of the stage, from "Alas, Poor Yorick" to "Goodbye, Grover's Corners" (I had to be educated about those later). Like I said, he was funny, so I was howling when I wasn't rinsing splashback out of my pajamas. By morning, I actually felt pretty attached to the little lush.

Then came Hell Week.

Hell Week used to be Homecoming Week when Blackfriars had a football team, but that had been disbanded due to a lack of schools to play against in the area and so now it was Hell Week, because it was also the week of Halloween. Every Hell Week, the seniors got into all sorts of pranks, and you could bet that if you were a freshmen, particularly a short, poor, or faggy freshman, those pranks would involve beating your ass.

By this time, Leo and I had grown closer and closer, spending late nights talking about deep stuff, like how the way we were born might get in the way of who we wanted to become. I wore my burden on my skin, but Leo's was equally obvious and not something he ever needed to confirm. So we were anomalies at school, outcasts together. At the same time, the cool kids began to warm up to me. I'd like to think it was because I had natural charisma and was easy to talk to, but I knew it was more likely because I was a kid from LA who had actually met the rappers playing in all of their Walkmans. Whatever the reason, I became cool, and with that social status came more and more questions about my sissy roommate. I wanted to defend him but knew that I couldn't be *too* accepting, at least not publicly. I was a good guy, but I wasn't an idiot.

So one day, during Hell Week, a senior informed me that he'd really let Breyer have it behind the library—an offering to me, the rising star of the freshman class. I actually *thanked* the kid with a laugh, then raced back to the dorm to find Leo with a black eye, a swollen lip, and what seemed to be a bruised rib. That was the first time I saw him cry. All I could do was hold him.

I practically carried him to his bed, and when I laid him down on his pinstriped sheets, I found that I was still holding him. I reached over to turn the bedside lamp off and surprised myself by hugging him tighter. I didn't know what I was doing. I only knew that I wanted to take this day away from him however I could.

I knew in that moment that I loved him.

The nights went on like that, and soon Leo was returning the love I gave him. Physically, I mean.

I nearly sprinted out of the room the first time he told me about the Vicious Circle and asked me to join him at a party, but because I loved him, I went. And now?

It's amazing what you can get used to.

❖

"Breyer!" Humphrey Meier himself shouted through the door. "We're docking points if you're not out in three, two . . ."

"FINE!" Leo barked, taking one last look in the mirror before popping a cassette into the boom box at his feet and clicking Play.

It was a disco version of "I Put a Spell on You" by some Dutch singer I'd never heard of. Leo had found the imported tape in the bargain bin of the record shop in Adders and built the whole costume around it.

He emerged at last to gasps and squeals; lip-synching the song, swinging his incense around, and bewitching the guys with swirling hands. I noticed as I watched him holding the room how beautiful he was like this. When I tried on the wig, I'd looked like my Aunt Deb, but the same wig turned Leo into a goddess. Not just pretty, but the kind of beauty that supermodels have: half attractive, half intimidating. It was a spell, all right.

When he was done, buttoning the song by pulling a fake mouse from his cleavage (I hadn't seen the movie but got that this was probably a reference), the guys all leaped to their feet, cheering and catcalling.

Barton approached dressed as Marty McFly with a Polaroid camera, saying, "Pose, boys!"

"I can't go anywhere without being hounded by the press!" Leo cried as he threw a black, velvety sleeve around me and held up the incense burner in his other hand.

"Say Halloweeeeeeen," Barton said, raising the camera.

Just then, Richardson, already three sheets to the wind, stumbled into Leo's back, sending his wig forward off his head, a black cloud of fake hair where his face ought to be, just as the photo flashed.

"Dammit, Richardson!" I said.

"Oh, I think it's actually going to be very artful," Leo said, examining the grey outline of us, mid-shove, as we began to take form on the picture.

"Anyway, speaking of getting *punched*, why don't we?" he said, gesturing to the bar, where someone had mixed a vat of some god-awful-smelling drink, black as tar, in a plastic witch's cauldron. We made our way over and I ladled out two cups for us.

"To the devil himself," Leo proclaimed as we took a drink. My sip nearly came right back up.

"That's TERRIBLE," I said, wincing. "My god, who made this shit?"

"I don't think it's so bad," Leo said, swirling the murky dregs of his cup. "There's something licorice flavored?"

"That's a bad sign," I warned.

"Well then, I'll have a double."

"Should we bring one to Steven?" I asked. "Maybe go keep him company by the door?"

"No way," Leo said. "He didn't dress up! And brought a *book*. I think he's sending a very clear message, and I don't want to waste his time or mine."

"Fair enough," I said, though I didn't agree. Steven had been distant ever since we went to that damn movie. I knew he was leaving something unsaid, but I also knew that Steven had to let you know how he felt on his own time.

We took a lap around the party.

The pub was always kind of spooky, but the seniors really outdid themselves with the decorations for tonight. Cotton spiderwebs covered every inch, and they'd swapped a few of the lightbulbs for black light, giving the whole room a strange, otherworldly glow. There was a little corner set up with a game where you could reach into covered shoeboxes to blindly feel "severed eyeballs," "zombie guts," and "Linda Blair's regurgitated lunch," which were all actually cold leftovers from the Dining Hall. In another corner, Reinhardt was dressed as a fortune-teller, reading tarot cards.

He turned over a card depicting a queen holding a sword.

"I'm afraid you're a real bitch that no one likes."

"The cards say that?!"

"Oh, I can't read tarot cards, dear, I'm just letting you know."

That's when I caught sight of Zooey for the first time, sitting alone on a sofa, dressed as a sailor. It was just a costume, but he had a whole new energy in the uniform. He looked older, or more confident, or something. Leo looked beautiful, but Zooey looked damn handsome.

He also looked a bit sad in this private moment, staring into the bottom of an empty punch cup.

"Zooey, hey!" I shouted to him. He looked up groggily, but came a bit more alive when he recognized us approaching.

"Wow, wow, wow!" he shouted as he stood to embrace Leo, then me, clumsily. "You look incredible! Who did your makeup?!"

"Oh, I just popped down to Vidal Sassoon and got a full face," Leo said, sarcastically. "*I* did, natch! Just my Ben Nye stage makeup kit I got for *Midsummer*, accentuated with a lipstick and false lashes I swiped from the drugstore in Adders."

"Thanks again for raiding the drama club storage for me," Zooey said, tugging on his crisp white uniform.

"It's my utter pleasure, Orson," Leo said. "You look so smashing as a sailor, I wish I'd come as Cher. If only I could turn back time."

"What?"

"Never mind. Having fun?"

"Oh yeah, a *blast*, yeah!" Zooey said, maybe too eagerly. I could tell he was pretty gone already, his skin flushed and his eyes glassy.

Just then, "Thriller" came on the jukebox and the place erupted.

"Come on!" Leo cried, "I demand we 'Monster Mash'!"

We hit the dance floor and bopped along to the song, surrounded by a Phantom of the Opera, a dorm toilet paper mummy, a full set of Village People, and what I was told was supposed to be Julia Roberts in *Pretty Woman* but looked more like Little Orphan Annie.

We stormed through "Like a Prayer" by Madonna, "Groove Is in the Heart" by Deee-Lite, and "Emotions" by Mariah Carey.

We took a break for drinks: Us, vodka sodas; Zooey, another huge pour of the punch, which I knew was a bad idea.

"I Wanna Sex You Up" by Color Me Badd.

"Hold On" by Wilson Phillips.

"Rhythm Nation" by Janet Jackson.

I dipped Leo low like Gene Kelly, his wig and long velvet sleeves practically dragging on the floor, and planted a big kiss on him. I rose back up to find Zooey looking lost at sea.

"U Can't Touch This" by MC Hammer.

"O.P.P." by Naughty by Nature.

Then "Nothing Compares 2 U" by Sinéad O'Connor came on, a slow song. Ghosts and vampires and pirates and presidents all began to embrace each other and sway.

Zooey looked left and right for a dance partner, but everyone had found his.

Leo and I just kind of stood there for a second, unsure of what to do.

Eventually Zooey said, "I'll leave you guys to it," and started to walk off.

But Leo grabbed his sleeve, saying, "No, no, I'm hotter than Anita Bryant burning in hell in this wig. I need to freshen up. Zooey, you'll look after Daniel, won't you?"

And then he was off.

Leo was always one step ahead of every social situation, always playing chess when we were playing checkers.

I reached out my hands for Zooey, my face asking, *"May I have this dance?"*

He looked . . . complicated? I couldn't imagine why. We'd been having a great time just moments ago.

"Come on," I said. "Didn't anyone teach you how to slow dance in New York? I thought ya'll were SO cool . . ."

"Shut up," he muttered, smiling, but looking down.

And even as he put his hands on my shoulders and I put mine on his hips, even as we started to sway, he wouldn't look me in the eye. I was pretty sure he wasn't breathing. I decided I needed to break the ice.

"Did you see Schaefer's costume?" I asked.

His eyes met mine at last.

"Oh . . . yeah!" he said. "The ninja turtle, right? Where did he get all that green paint?"

"I dunno, man. Whoever shares his hall bathroom is gonna freak after he tries to wash that all off. Like, it's bound to leave a ring."

"Ha, yeah . . ."

"You know I don't think we've ever gotten the chance to talk, just the two of us," I said. "Or, not since that first time when you scraped your leg."

"Well, it's not exactly easy."

"Right, right. I hate that. I get so jealous seeing you and Leo eating together at meals."

"Jealous?"

"Well yeah, I'd so much rather talk with you guys than watch Godfrey slurp down liquified meat with the other blockheads at our table."

"Oh yeah . . . right," Zooey said.

Man, something is really up with him, I thought.

"I get it, though," he said, sincerely. "You have to protect yourself. You have enough to worry about."

I knew exactly what he meant by that.

And I hated that I knew he was right.

The song faded into another: "Rush Rush" by Paula Abdul. We kept slow-dancing.

"Hey, I've been meaning to ask," I said. "A couple weeks back, the night we saw the movie in town, when you met Oona . . . you said you were white."

"I did?" he asked.

"Yeah, like, Leo said you weren't Asian, you were white, and you said something like, 'Yeah, I *am* white, but my mom was Korean.' And I just thought that was funny."

"Oh, well, yeah, I dunno. It's complicated," he said. "I really look most like my dad. Like, no one has ever noticed before. And all my friends at Hansard were white and we always did, like, *white stuff*."

"White stuff?" I laughed.

"You know what I mean," Zooey said.

"Money laundering?"

"Come on." Zooey chuckled.

"Colonizing?"

"Daniel—"

"Square dancing?"

"OK, that was the wrong choice of words," he laughed. "But . . . Like, my mom changed her name from Soo-Yeon to *Sonja,* and we never saw that side of the family, and so, I dunno. I guess it just never felt like something that was . . . mine. That part of me. You know what I mean?"

I thought about that part of myself I could ignore because it wasn't immediately obvious to everyone else. I knew what he meant.

"I think there's no right or wrong way to be who you are," I told him. "That part of you *is* part of you, so it's yours. It's as much yours as it is anyone else's, and—"

"To be honest . . ." he interrupted. It seemed like the punch was doing the talking now, but I could tell he needed to let this out. "The *other* part of me was always kind of relieved. Relieved that no one could tell that I was Asian, I mean. I have enough trouble feeling handsome. I don't know if you've noticed, but there are no Asian guys on *Baywatch,* or in *People* magazine's sexiest men alive, or in Calvin Klein ads."

Oof, I thought. At least I have Denzel to look to. Imagine having no one, no blueprint for the kind of handsome you might grow up to be.

"I . . . I hadn't thought about it," I said. "But you're right. And it sucks. And I get it. But Zooey, come on. You have to know you're super handsome. Hell, you got the Humphrey Meier seal of approval from the jump!"

He nodded but still seemed far away.

"Is there something else going on?" I asked.

"No, no, no . . ." he said. "Well . . . It's just. I haven't . . . I mean, I've never . . ."

"What?"

"Slow danced with a boy before."

It hadn't even occurred to me that this might mean something different to Zooey than it meant to me.

It's amazing what you can get used to.

And then, Christ, he was leaning in.

He was going to try to kiss me.

I figured he'd just had too many. I didn't want to embarrass him, so instead of firmly reminding him that I was with Leo, I just acted like it wasn't happening.

"Yeah, that turtle paint is gonna be a bitch tomorrow," I said.

Zooey opened his eyes and looked to where Schaefer was trying to dance with Richardson without smearing green all over his toga.

"Yeah . . . yeah, what a mess," he said. "What a total mess."

I averted my eyes and felt his drift off to the side as well. We swayed like that, quiet, until the song finally ended.

"Whew! I'm a new woman!" Leo said as he slid through the crowd toward us. "Thanks for that, Z. Did you boys have fun?"

"Yeah, yeah, thanks," Zooey said with a half smile. "Well, anyway, I need a refill. I'll catch up with you guys in a bit." He started off.

"You sure, Z?" I asked. "Want us to come with?"

"No, I'm good. Just need a . . ." and he trailed off as he walked away.

We watched him go, and Leo sighed.

"Poor boy," he said. "He's got the blues tonight and I wish I could figure out why."

"He tried to kiss me," I said.

"WHAT?"

"Just now, while we were dancing."

"No way! Well *that* explains it," Leo said, looking scandalized but delighted at the same time. "Oh, he must have a crush. Not that I can blame him, you gorgeous thing. And did you?"

"Did I what?" I asked.

"Kiss him."

I was shocked by how matter-of-factly he asked, like neither answer would change his pulse one tick.

"What? No, of course not. I'd never cheat on you."

"Oh, Daniel, come *on*," he said. "The chemistry between you two is undeniable."

"Chemistry has to come from him *and* me."

"Am I wrong?" he asked as we sunk into the sofa.

I looked at him.

"What are you accusing me of?" I asked.

"Oh my gosh, I'm not *accusing* you of a *thing*, I promise! It's not a bad thing, it's no one's fault, and it doesn't bother me in the slightest! Daniel, it's the Nineties, we're young, we're sexual deviants—"

"What are you saying?"

"I'm saying we don't have to play by the old rules," he said. "That if there *was* something there and you wanted to explore it, I wouldn't be threatened—"

"Leo!"

"And I wouldn't get in the way."

I thought he might be testing me, but I could tell he was serious. That was almost worse.

"I . . . I don't know how to feel about that," I said. "You know most guys would be jealous if they thought their boyfriend had feelings for someone else."

"But then, we never really say 'boyfriend,' do we?" he asked.

There it is, I thought. Leo, playing chess again.

I opened my mouth to protest, but damn it, he was right.

"Do you want to?" Leo asked. "Should I wear your pin around the halls?"

"Now I get it," I said. "You're punishing me."

"*Oh* my god, forget it," Leo said, standing. "I'm devastatingly jealous, Daniel, even though you aren't officially my boyfriend, because that would be too inconvenient for *you*."

"That's—"

I realized I had nowhere to go.

He was right. I couldn't have it both ways.

Luckily, I didn't have time to attempt a sensible response, because a voice broke over the crowd yelling, "WHAT THE FUCK?!"

We turned to see Humphrey Meier standing by the bar in a tuxedo, perfect for his James Bond costume, except for the fresh stain of purply black vomit that dripped down his white shirt and bow tie. Standing just in front of him, looking seasick as hell, was our first mate, Zooey.

"SOS," Leo said, as he dashed toward them both.

"I'm sorry . . . I'm so . . . sor—"

And then he was heaving again.

"There you go," I said, as I patted Zooey's back. "Quicker it's out, the better you'll feel."

We were all three sitting on the tiled floor of the top floor bathroom of Bass Hall. We had a hell of a time sneaking across campus with Zooey in this state and Leo in half-drag, but we'd managed it. I couldn't even let myself imagine what would have happened had we been spotted like that. Luckily, we were back safe in Bass, and with Humphrey as the prefect, we wouldn't be found out up here.

"And you've got to stop apologizing!" Leo said. "I heard a rumor they put a *bottle* of Dimetapp cough syrup in that punch! It's actually criminal."

I thought of Leo, that night I'd spent helping him be sick. In the wave of nostalgia that came with the memory, I felt instantly terrible that we'd fought.

Between bouts of puking, Zooey put his head on the cool tile. Soon his heavy breathing slowed and we realized he was asleep.

"Think we need to call the nurse?" I asked.

"He'll be OK," Leo said. "I had the exact same reaction to this exact same punch last year before you joined the club. Wicked hangover, but nothing urgent. Still, we shouldn't leave him alone."

We managed to get him up to his feet and to the elevator. We got out on our floor, the second, and, quietly as we could, took him back to our room.

I took the mattresses off the beds and pushed them together on the floor—a trick Leo and I had learned early on—and Zooey belly flopped right into the center of the bed and was snoring almost instantly.

"He's adorable," Leo said, shaking his head. "You want the left or the right side?"

"I really don't care," I said.

"Well, you get comfy and I'll be right back. I have to get this face off or I'll break out."

"Be careful," I said.

"Or else someone will spot me? Pretty certain I'm safe if I'm on my own."

"Yeah, OK. Yeah."

Though our earlier conversation still hung heavy over both of us, we were too tired to hash it out now.

But as I lay down beside Zooey, my mind was suddenly racing again, and sleep seemed far off. Here I was, sharing a bed with one boy I was pretty sure had a crush on me, and another boy who I was actually dating. A boy who'd straight up offered me to the first boy without batting a false eyelash.

I realized that earlier, when I told Leo about Zooey's pass at me, I hadn't wanted him to feel threatened for some ego trip. I wanted him to be threatened because that's what a normal relationship looks like.

As if this relationship could ever be normal.

I knew it couldn't be as long as it was only something that existed behind closed doors and at secret parties every few weeks.

It's amazing what you can get used to.

"God, I could just get ready for bed until dawn, you know?" Leo said when he reentered, toweling off.

"You do take forever," I said, hoping sleep would come and let me off the hook.

"Hey," he said, in a rare, serious tone. I rolled over and opened my eyes. "I'm sorry we had words. I was honestly just excited that Zooey was even feeling comfortable enough to make a move. I mean, what a step, right? I wasn't suggesting that what we have isn't real just because we can't stroll around the quad holding hands. I'm not an idiot, you know."

"I know you're not. I'm sorry I overreacted. I wasn't angry, I was just . . . sad."

"Sad about what?"

"I dunno . . . all of it?" I said. "I mean, for one, if Zooey really does have a thing for me, it makes me sad that he can't tell the difference between friendly male affection and, like, romance. Like, it makes me wonder if any man in his whole life has ever been good to him."

"That's fair."

"Two . . . I don't want to keep doing this to you."

"Darling, I—"

"And I *know* you aren't trying to make me feel guilty or pressure me about it. I know that. I'm saying for me, it's getting harder. And I can feel you getting frustrated. I'm frustrated, too. But I don't know how to fix it and I just worry—*fear*—that this is what this life will be. Like, maybe this is just what being gay is. Having to make a choice between being yourself and being safe. Being invisible. And that makes me sad."

Leo walked over and lay down on the other side of Zooey. He reached over him, to where I was laying, and stretched his arm over to embrace us both.

"You might be right, I don't know," he said. "I mean, I think you're definitely right about Zooey, about no men being good to him. I think you're just afraid of the men who haven't been good to you, either. So let's just all be good to each other. We have to be better to each other than all of the others are to us. That's what matters most, I think."

With so much on my mind leading up to that first Monday of Hell Week, it's natural that so many important clues about what was to come had slipped through the cracks.

Godfrey finally got his jaw opened back up, but I should have noticed that instead of going back to running his mouth like before, he was weirdly quiet. Every time I joined him and Theo for lunch, I seemed to be interrupting some secret, whispered conversation. If I'd noticed his scheming, maybe I could have asked him about it. I bet he would have told me. I could have talked him out of it.

I should have noticed the day he came crashing over to our table with the energy of a guy who'd just won the lottery because he figured out that he had a cousin who was a current student at Hansard. If I'd made the connection that Zooey had transferred in from Hansard, I might have put together who Ryan was targeting.

I should have noticed the news reports playing on the TV in the Bass common room of a hurricane brewing off the coast of Bermuda, creeping its way north and gathering strength. It would have been a stretch, but maybe I would have reconsidered the timing of our retaliation, knowing the true power of the forces swirling above us.

It will probably haunt me forever that if I'd just noticed any one of those things, I could have stopped the terrible events that were barreling toward us on Monday, October twenty-eighth. That everything that followed could have been avoided.

That if I'd just been more aware, maybe they'd still be alive.

CHAPTER SEVEN

ZOOEY

From the first steps I took on the quad that morning, I just couldn't shake *the feeling.*

(In case you're lucky enough not to know, there's this calculus that boys like us can perform instantaneously to assess our current safety and how it's being threatened at any given moment. Like a sixth sense, we can actually *feel* the violence coming before it comes. We have to. Those who don't hone the skill don't make it.)

On the morning of October twenty-eighth, I had *the feeling* stronger than I ever had in my life.

Any normal guy might have walked into the Dining Hall on that final Monday morning of October simply enjoying the fresh weather, laughing at the seniors who wore their pajamas to class to announce the beginning of Hell Week, and longing for the end of the semester, which inched ever closer.

I, on the other hand, met eyes with a random kid across the hall and recognized his look immediately: the look of someone who has been talking about you.

He pressed his tongue against the inside of his cheek suggestively.

I looked away.

Leo clanged his tray down, its syrupy cargo glistening under the hall's halogen lighting, which they'd turned on early this morning because the day was so ominously overcast.

"Did you *hear* about whose apples got bobbed at the Crystal Ball?!"

He started into his usual torrent of morning gossip, and I tried my best to tune out the sirens going off in my head to really hear him.

That feeling.

By the time I reached Reyes's first period Latin, I was getting truly nervous. I could have sworn that the halls were fully vibrating with whispers and scores of looks just like the one I'd seen in the Dining Hall.

I even recognized that very same look on Daniel's face when I sat down for lunch and caught sight of him across the room.

He seemed to be having it out in a major way with Ryan Godfrey. I squinted to try to figure out what they were saying but couldn't.

"What's up with them?" I asked Leo, gesturing toward the rugby boys.

"I dunno, trouble in paradise?" Leo said. "Probably something to do with a *fantasy league* or whatever the hell."

"It looks serious," I said.

Ryan had now gotten up and Daniel was chasing after him.

"Zooey, the machinations of the Blackfriars sports clubs are as mysterious to me as the Dead Sea Scrolls. Who *knows* what pissing contest is occurring with the rah-rahs. Who cares?!"

I tried to laugh it off, but. That *feeling.*

"Hey, have you heard about this storm they're expecting this week?" Leo said. "We might get a damn hurricane! What if they cancel class?"

A storm is coming. That was the feeling, all right.

Cold anxiety crept up my neck as I entered the gymnasium and made my way down the stairs to the locker room.

And then suddenly, Daniel was there, intercepting me before I could enter.

"Zooey, listen to me," he whispered. His face was deadly serious. "Don't go into that room," he said.

A storm is coming.

"What? Why?"

"I . . ." He looked over his shoulder, paranoid. "Just don't. Cut class today. I'll catch up with you later."

But then the unmistakable voice of Ryan Godfrey rose up from over Daniel's shoulder.

"Orson!" he called. "How you been?! I've missed seeing you around class. But I'm back now."

A storm is coming.

Daniel turned furiously to where Ryan emerged in the doorway.

"I've been anxious to talk with you, because I recently had the most *fascinating* phone call with my cousin, Oscar," Ryan hissed. "You actually used to go to school with him. At Hansard."

The storm is here.

"Yeah, Theo did me a favor and looked through your file in Mrs. Wesley's office, but weirdly, there was no information about your transfer, other than that you came from Hansard. Oh, and it said the matter was *sensitive*."

This is what it's like.

"But lucky me, dear old Oscar was just a call away. *What* a story!"

I was paralyzed, save for my widening eyes, which could only scan the locker room to see what I hadn't seen before: The whole class gathered around my locker, looking at freshly scrawled graffiti: *HOT FOR TEACHER.*

And suddenly there was no color in the room.

No air.

No time.

No sound.

I saw everything that happened next like I was viewing it through a telescope:

"Goddamn you!" Daniel shouted to Ryan as he tried to lead me out of the room.

"What the fuck, Preston?!" he shouted. "This isn't about you!"

Ryan reached out for my shirt at the exact moment that Daniel turned to wave him away.

Daniel's elbow connected with Ryan's freshly healed jaw with a sickening crack.

Ryan made a little yelp of pain.

Everything went very quiet.

As Ryan staggered backward, hands over his mouth, something slick and red slipped out from between his fingers and slapped wetly onto the tile.

We all looked.

It was a sizable piece of his severed tongue.

Ryan let out a primal, dripping scream, spraying bright blood down the front of his gym shirt and barreled into Daniel, low, breaking his balance and sending both of them to the floor. He tried to throw punches, but Daniel wrestled him into a pin and held him down as he spat and raved.

Soon, a booming "HEY! BOYS!" echoed across the tile.

It was Coach Carpinelli, who wrenched Daniel off of Ryan. Once freed, Ryan lunged again for Daniel, but Carpinelli pulled him up by his shoulders and marched him into the shower, tossing him to the tiled floor and turning the water on cold.

"Ooou're 'ead, 'eston!" he screamed as the water poured down his flushed face to where it pooled red around the drain. "You 'oo, Orthon! Fuckin' FAGGOTHS!"

"More water, dear?" Mrs. Wesley asked me.

It took me several seconds to process the sounds she made into words.

I was waiting by her desk in the main office of the common building. Daniel had been led in to see Headmaster Westcott some time ago, and my head was packed to capacity with worry about what was taking place in there.

"No, thank you," I murmured.

Obviously, when called in myself, I would have to explain that this was all my fault. That Daniel was only protecting me and that I deserved to be expelled, not him.

It would certainly mean the end of my academic career; no school would take me now. (That was probably earned. After all, this was just more consequence of what happened at Hansard, the worst thing I've ever done. No one deserves a *third* chance.)

Suddenly, Wesley's desk phone rang. She picked it up, listened for a moment, and said, "Yes, sir."

The storm is here.

"Mister Orson," she said. "The headmaster will see you now."

I passed Daniel on my way in and tried to read his face for news of our fate, but no luck. I was on my own.

❖

Headmaster Westcott's office was a leathery library cast in an otherworldly green light from the colored glass that shaded its brass lamps.

I was met by his stern silhouette, as the window that lit him from behind glowed with amber afternoon light, obscuring the details of his face.

"Have a seat, Mister Orson," he said, gesturing with a bony hand to a straight-backed chair before him. I nodded and settled creakily down.

"You can relax, Mister Orson, you're not in trouble," he said.

I exhaled, perhaps too audibly.

"In fact, Mister Orson, I owe you an apology."

What had already been a surreal day was spinning into pure comedy.

"Sir?"

"When your father inquired about a spot for you here at Blackfriars, I assured him that I'd keep my eye on you personally, make sure that your time at Blackfriars was enriching to your positive development. I fear I may have become derelict in this duty. I regret that I'm only meeting you now, and under such circumstances."

"It's . . . it's nice to meet you too, sir."

"I understand that the . . . details of your transfer have become public and that your gym locker was vandalized?"

"Yes, sir."

"And Mister Preston tells me that Mister Godfrey was responsible? And that he called you a . . . distasteful name?"

I looked at the floor.

"Zooey, I admire your urge to stay neutral, but a Blackfriars man knows when to keep quiet and when to take a stand."

"Yes, sir. It was Godfrey."

"He'll be summarily dealt with, I promise you. Take the rest of the day off and enjoy tomorrow's excursion to Adders Lair, weather permitting, head high. Gossips are of no consequence to your academic progress, pay them no mind."

"Thank you, sir," I said, as I rose to leave.

"One more thing, Mister Orson," he said.

I paused.

He paused.

He seemed to select his next words with surgical precision.

"You're at a crucial age, Zooey. The path you take now will affect the rest of your life. You must be very careful about the choices you make . . . and the company you keep. Blackfriars is, of course, incredibly careful to admit only the finest young men, but naturally, certain circumstances permit some less pristine candidates to slip through the cracks."

Somehow, I knew he meant Leo. How much did he know?

"And Mister Orson, I'll be frank with you, while I truly believe that you are an upstanding young man and an excellent student, given what you endured at your last school, it's obvious you are also easily manipulated. You are vulnerable. Suggestible. Any negative influence on you might have dire consequences. Do you understand what I'm telling you?"

It seemed like he was trying to give advice, but it came off more like a warning.

". . . Yes, sir," I said.

"It's lucky for you that a man like Mister Preston was there to put himself on the line. You'd do well to keep the company of students like him. I hope you'll become friends."

(You can imagine the look on my face.)

"I hope so, too."

When I reached my dorm, there was a folded note slipped under the door.

It said, "Our room," in Leo's handwriting.

I arrived at their door on the second floor, and when Daniel answered, he immediately scooped me up in a tight, long hug. I melted into his strong arms.

(Why did this moment I'd wanted for weeks have to come at such a terrible cost? My famous Zooey Orson luck, the gift that kept on giving.)

"I tried to stop him," Daniel said. "As soon as I knew what he knew, I tried to stop him from spreading it."

I couldn't speak in that moment, but I knew I didn't need to. My first tears of the day came, finally, and once they'd started, they wouldn't stop.

He brought me into the room, where Leo and Steven waited. I sat down on the bed and Leo held my hand while hot, heavy tears poured down my cheeks.

Steven brought me some water when I'd gotten most of it out.

"We don't judge, Z," Daniel said. "We would never judge. We just want to understand."

"But you don't have to tell us anything you don't want to," Leo added.

How could I tell them—these guys who liked me, who trusted me? What would be more ruinous to our friendship, the truth or a lie? By this moment, though, I was exhausted from lying. I knew the point of no return was miles behind me. I knew there was nothing left but to tell them everything.

I found my breath.

". . . He was young. Like, right out of college. He didn't seem that different from any other boy, just—he was a teacher."

I knew by now they already knew this terrible detail, but still, saying the word out loud brought all the shame I'd forced down to the core of myself back up to the surface. I felt it pool behind my eyes and in my throat, threatening to choke me up, but I pushed through.

"He was the first one I told about . . . the feelings I was having. For other boys. And he was *nice* to me. The only one, really, and things just. Escalated. And I know it was wrong, *he* was wrong, but . . ."

The storm is here.

"But what happened was my fault," I said. "Because I wanted it. I wanted it, but when we got found out, I lied and said I didn't, and now his life is over and—"

"*Zooey*," Leo whispered.

Fuck, I thought.

Some truths are too horrible for even your best friends.

He turned my face to look him in the eye. His expression was one I didn't even know a guy like Leo was capable of, gravely serious but also with deepest compassion.

"No," he said. "No, no, *no*. He *was* wrong, no matter what you thought. No matter what you thought you wanted. You were, what, fifteen?!"

"Minors cannot consent," Steven said quietly.

Daniel put his face in his hands. I think he was crying.

"Zooey, he abused you," Leo said. "I need you to understand that. None of it was your fault. Not one moment of it."

I'd heard this before, of course. Somehow, hearing it from Leo felt different.

I remember my parents coming into the office at Hansard to hear the awful revelations directly from the headmaster. My mother was nearing the end then, gaunt and frail from brutal rounds of chemotherapy. She'd been so subdued from the treatments that when she wasn't asleep or being sick, her face was simply frozen. But on that day, as the headmaster slowly unpacked each detail of what he'd learned from my confession, her face regained enough life to contort to an expression of utter horror, shock, and shame. It's one of my last memories of her.

When the headmaster had finished, my father used that word, "abused," first. I remember there was a strange bit of arguing from the headmaster as he suggested I may have coerced Mr. Barrett, or Mr. B, as everyone called him, into what had happened.

That sent my father into a fury I had never seen from him, buttoned up as he usually was.

"Zooey isn't *like that*, are you, Zooey?" he asked.

All three sets of adult eyes on me.

Terrible quiet.

"He forced you," my father continued.

"Yes," I'd said.

And that was that.

When the press ran the story about the disgraced teacher and the abhorrent scandal, they didn't use my name, but everyone knew. There were a few months left in the term, but my parents pulled me out early because the bullying got so bad. My mother went into the hospital and lost consciousness before I could tell her everything I needed to say about it. And then she was gone.

I realized as I relayed all of the details that this was the most I'd said about Mr. B since that day in the office. After my mother died, my father didn't talk to me about much of anything, let alone what had transpired. He merely made the calls and wrote the checks to get me into Blackfriars for the fall term.

And then it was now.

We all sat in silence for a while, the truth taking up all of the air in the room.

Finally, Leo took a deep inhale.

"So. Your dad suspected you might be gay," he said. "So . . . he sent you to an all-*boys* school?"

I looked at him.

I burst out laughing.

Daniel, too. Even Steven cracked a smile.

There was nothing else to do. We were still crying, but now we were howling. We laughed until we were gasping at the absurdity of this life we'd been born into and the joy of sharing it with others like us.

"People see what they want to see," I said, wiping my eyes.

"Amen," Daniel said.

We sat with that for a bit.

There was some distant screaming and laughter coming from the quad. *Hell Week*, I remembered. Probably some poor freshmen being tortured. (It's terrible to admit, but after everything that went down that day, all I could think was, *better him than me.*)

Eventually, I said, "God, I'm gonna miss you guys."

"What do you mean?" Daniel asked.

"I had to leave Hansard over this," I said. "Once kids knew, they wouldn't let up. Even if Ryan gets expelled—hell, especially if he gets expelled—it'll be the same here. I'm sure I'll have to leave."

"You can't leave," Leo said. "You've been initiated! Screw those guys. It'll blow over."

"Will it?" I asked. Despite his words, Leo's face said I was right. "Obviously I wish I didn't have to, but I've been through this before. It's going to be unbearable, unless I can find a way to become *invisible*."

Leo looked to Daniel, who held his gaze for a moment while Steven stared evasively out the window, something complicated overtaking all of their energy.

"Wouldn't that be something," Leo said.

I awoke the next morning to a knock at my door.

I groaned and pulled the quilt over my head.

I thought about being a kid, hiding this way to block out the sound of my mom being sick, thinking that if I could get back to sleep, I'd wake up and realize the whole thing was a bad dream.

That never worked then, and it didn't work now.

"Mister Orson?" Leo said from the other side of the door. "Reception for a Mister Orson? Would you like any towels, sir? The paper?"

I stumbled toward the door and caught a look at myself in the mirror. I looked fucking thirty, my eyes all puffy from crying and lack of sleep.

I knew Leo thought so too when I opened the door. He smiled, but I could see him recoil ever-so-slightly at the sight of me. He handed me a thermos of coffee.

"Hey, gorgeous," he said. "Didn't want you to miss the bus."

He was wearing some god-awful sweater from the Eighties he'd pulled out of a bargain bin, depicting kittens dressed as witches.

"I'm not going," I told him.

"I knew you'd think so, and that's why I came here to personally inform you of your error."

At least there was no class today. One of the perks of Hell Week was a school-wide field trip into Adders Lair for its Harvest Festival. It had been scheduled for Halloween itself on Thursday but moved up because of the approaching hurricane. Newscasters were already calling it the "Perfect Storm," due to some expected collision with a nor'easter coming down from Canada.

As for me, the perfect storm had already hit and decimated what little life I had built up at Blackfriars, and so today, I just wanted to mourn my loss in peace.

"I'm not going," I repeated.

Leo sighed.

"Zooey, our pleasures here at this prison are few, and so when they come along, we cannot let tearer-downers like Godfrey ruin them for us. I simply won't let you. Besides, I have it on good authority that he has been *barred* from attending, and so why would you accept his same punishment for the crime he committed upon *you*? I can't allow it."

He tapped the bottom of the thermos.

"Now caffeinate yourself, pull up them panties, and put on something festive, Mary!"

❖

Once dressed in a pair of gray corduroys and a tartan plaid flannel, I made my way with Leo toward the main driveway, where the whole student body was lined up by class to board buses.

I nearly turned and ran back to my bed and blanket, because I felt every eye on me. Juicy news like my past would spread quickly, no matter what, at a school like Blackfriars.

After the scene in the locker room, the contagion had reached pandemic-level.

"Like Orpheus in the underworld, dear, just keep your eyes straight ahead," Leo told me as we walked past throngs of snickering, leering kids and took our place in line.

"There's Steven," Leo said as he spotted Hillman towering above everyone but somehow still looking lost. "We ought to call him over, right? I mean at *this* point, what's the risk, socially? Rock bottom ain't so bad. STEVEN!"

He waved him over to where we stood and after a moment of flummoxed staring, he gave in and lumbered over.

"Good morning, Zooey," he said. "I hope that you are feeling better today than you were yesterday."

He managed a smile. I returned it. I knew how much effort such a show of emotion was for him.

"All right, sophomores!" Professor Reyes called out as he approached our line. "Who's ready for a little local lore about today's field trip?!"

His enthusiasm was met with an exactly equal level of apathy from us sleepy sophomores.

"Cool, me too," he laughed. He glanced down at a printout he carried and read aloud in a creepy Vincent Price voice like he was narrating an old horror movie.

"'Named for a seventeenth-century infestation of snakes thought to be brought over by early European settlers, Adders Lair has a long history of *spoooooky* occurrences! Some claim that the spells which brought Salem to its knees in Sixteen Ninety-Two actually came from a secret society of English sorcerers who settled in Adders Lair. What sorcery might befall *you* on your journey there today?!'"

He shot imaginary magic rays at a kid near the front who was wholly un-spellbound. He cleared his throat and moved the printout to the bottom of his clipboard.

"OK, some business, boys. Back on the buses at five P.M. sharp and remember, all school rules still apply in town . . . so whatever you do, don't get caught. OK, enjoy Adders Lair Harvest Fest!"

We boarded the bus, and I took a seat near the front next to Steven, with Leo across the aisle. A few of the guys who squeezed past us toward their own seats bumped us a little more aggressively than seemed natural. Then one guy flicked my ear as he passed. I kept my eyes forward as instructed.

Daniel climbed onboard and made his way toward the jocks at the back. I shot him the smallest nod of acknowledgment so he wouldn't worry. He passed by.

Then, a few seconds later, I was surprised to feel his shadow return to where we sat and linger.

I looked up, stunned.

"This seat taken?" he asked, pointing to the open spot next to Leo.

"Um." I didn't know what to say.

"Cool," he said, sitting down. "And hey, Breyer." He threw his arm around Leo affectionately.

Such physical affection between boys is weirdly common and nonsexual at boys' schools like Blackfriars, but for a guy with Daniel's social standing to be so chummy with the school's best-known fag was completely audacious.

I felt all of the eyes that had lingered on me shift away to Daniel and Leo.

". . . Hey, Preston," Leo replied wearily.

"So Orson, ever been to Adders Lair before?" Daniel asked, casually. "It's not much, but there's some cool shops and stuff. I'd love to show you around."

I could hear gasps and whispers coming from behind us as the most popular kid in the sophomore class chatted up the three most unwelcome. If anything could have pulled focus from my scandal today, it was this new one.

"Daniel, *what* are you doing?!" Leo whispered.

"Something I should have done a long time ago," he said.

❖

We rode the few miles into town, chatting when we weren't gawking out the window at the explosion of autumnal color across the hills of Massachusetts. Soon we were let off in the heart of town, just a block or so from the little park we'd stashed our bikes in just a couple of weeks before.

Adders Lair was actually pretty charming by day. Faded but colorful colonial storefronts gave way to beachy little cottages and then weathered wooden docks as Main Street stretched toward the sea. The street was closed to traffic, filled instead with stands selling apple cider donuts, bales of hay covered in jack-o'-lanterns, and smiling parents led around by eager costumed children.

Daniel stuck with the three of us, undaunted, and we prowled one end of the street to the other, trying our hand at a few midway games, wolfing down some funnel cakes, and enjoying some warm apple cider beneath a crimson-hued maple tree in the park. I saw kids looking, but the warmth I felt inside on that gray afternoon was stronger than their icy stares.

Leo wanted to venture down a side street to check out his favorite vintage store. He was hunting for an outfit for the VC holiday party ("Slay, Belles"), which was still months out but "closer every day," he'd insisted.

We turned off Main and were heading down Church when I saw someone I recognized.

Seated on the stoop of a narrow corner storefront, smoking a cigarette, was a girl dressed in a black velvet minidress, black stockings, black boots, and a tiny witch's hat pinned to the side of her sleek black bob.

"Oona!" I called out to her.

She looked up and said, "Oh hey, prepsters," smoke streaming from her red lips. "I thought I'd see you here today."

"Cheers, darling," Leo said, curtly, as he picked up his pace.

"Didn't you wanna come in?" she asked. "I'm technically on a fifteen, but I'll open back up for my best customers."

"What do you mean?" I asked, stopping.

"We're heading to Threads, down the road," Leo said. "Bye now."

"Is this your shop?" I asked, looking at the shop sign above her. It had a picture of a snake forming a perfect circle as it ate its own tail. It read OUROBOROS. Peering through the windows, it looked a lot like her apartment; jars of herbs, bookshelves full of tomes with black and red spines, tables displaying crystals and bones. "You sell, like, witch stuff?"

"Why don't you come in and see?" she said slyly as she grabbed a ring of keys at her hip and unlatched the door.

"I don't think we have time, Z," Daniel said to me.

"It's, like, three o'clock," I said. "We have till five."

I walked toward the shop door and turned back to see that they weren't following. Something was off. Leo and Daniel looked caught—stumped. Steven was blank as ever.

"I just . . ." Leo said, swallowing hard before he continued, "I just don't want to get stuck in the rain, if it starts soon. It's looking dark, isn't it?"

It looked overcast but not urgent. Daniel and Steven mumbled their agreement, all the same.

"I wouldn't want to find the perfect thing at Threads and have it get ruined. Thanks anyway, Oona." Leo began to continue on walking and the others followed.

She shrugged and took a long drag of her cigarette.

"Come on, Zooey," Leo called back. "My wardrobe will wait for no one!"

I took one last look at the curious shop and caught up to the others.

"What did she mean by 'her best customers'?" I asked. "Do you guys actually shop there?"

"Oh, I went through a phase last year," Leo said. "I'd seen *The Witches of Eastwick* and wanted to be just like Cher, naturally."

(That seemed reasonable enough, so I brushed it off. Leo really was a secret agent.)

Shopping took up most of our remaining time as Leo tried on tacky sweaters, alpine fur coats, and literally anything he could find in red or green. As for me, I found a creepy old mask of Michael Myers from the movie *Halloween* that Daniel insisted I buy, even though our Halloween party was over.

At five o'clock we boarded the bus, tired, and rode back to campus as the clouds above grew darker and more sinister. It was already getting dark so much earlier as October ticked by, but with the approaching storm, night had fully fallen before we even reached campus.

The wind threatened to carry us away as we sprinted across the campus back toward the Dining Hall to beat the rain, which seemed imminent. By the time we'd finished our dinner, it was coming down in sheets, and so we all tried to share the one umbrella Steven had been wise to bring as we made our way back to Bass. Safely in the common room, soaking but laughing, we bid each other good night.

When I reached my door, I was surprised to find a note slipped underneath.

I can't put it all in writing—need to tell you how I feel in person. Meet me tonight behind the chapel, 9.

—Daniel

I stared at the scrawl for many minutes.

Daniel.

Daniel needs to tell me how he feels.

I remembered that he hadn't been with Leo in the morning; we hadn't seen him until he boarded the bus. He must have left the note after Leo and I had left the room.

My heart began to pound out of my chest. I sat on the edge of my bed, still dripping rainwater, thumbing the crinkled note with trembling hands.

I thought about him choosing the showerhead next to mine in gym.

I thought about his hand on my thigh at the pub.

I thought about our bike ride into Adders Lair.

I thought about our slow dance.

I thought about the way he hugged me so tightly.

True, he'd put his arm around Leo on the bus, but maybe he'd only done it so that kids would stop staring at me.

It all made sense. He felt the way I felt.

But, oh, *Leo.*

Leo was the best friend I'd ever had. If Daniel really had feelings for me, what would that mean for our relationship?

He's waiting, I thought, as I looked at the time. No time to worry about all of that now.

God, it was pouring. I had to go to him. I didn't know how I would react, but I figured I'd better let him say what he had to say and figure it out later.

I threw on my black raincoat, grabbed an umbrella, and slipped away under the cover of the storm.

I pushed through the pounding rain and wrestled to keep my umbrella from collapsing in the fierce gusts of wind. I realized that whatever happened behind the chapel, there was no going back. My head finally heard what my heart had been screaming for weeks.

I loved him. I wanted him.

(But, Christ, why did such a pure feeling have to be sullied by the complicated reality of things? Why did my heart only ever really want what it shouldn't have?)

I finally reached the chapel, nearly slipping in the mud that was pooling by its front steps, my legs were shaking so hard. I tried to steady my breath as I made my way around the back of the slick stone building.

Just listen. Just listen and then speak. You can do this. You'll figure it out.

I turned the corner and, squinting through the sheets of the downpour, could just barely make out Daniel's silhouette where he waited. He was wearing his raincoat as well, hood up, leaning against the back wall of the chapel.

He saw me there and stood to greet me.

But something was wrong.

He looked as if the pounding rain had shrunken him by a head.

Whoever this was, he was too short to be Daniel.

Then, a handful of other boys in hooded raincoats emerged from the woods around him.

"Orthon," Ryan Godfrey said, taking down his hood. A wad of gauze covered the tip of his tongue. "I knew I wath right about you."

He and the others closed in.

(The last thing I remember before their fists connected with the side of my head is thinking that I deserved this.

For trying to steal my best friend's boyfriend away from him.

For thinking he'd want me at all.

For having to transfer here because of my terrible actions at Hansard.

For being the way I am.

I deserve this, I thought.)

And then they tore me apart.

CHAPTER EIGHT

LEO

How to make a Perfect Storm:

1. Take one cold front from coastal Canada and form into a nor'easter. Send south.

2. Meanwhile, take one tropical storm and upgrade it to a hurricane as it rises north. Name it Grace.

3. Introduce both to the coast of Massachusetts. Combine.

◆

By nine thirty, Bass Hall was in utter pandemonium as every radio blasted warnings about the storm and Humphrey barked out orders in a rare tone of authority as he was forced to actually do his job as dorm prefect.

"Do not hang out in front of the windows. Do not *open* the windows. If the power fails, do not panic, there is a flashlight in your closet for this purpose. No one is to go outside for any reason."

The radio was calling for evacuations, but we had nowhere else to go.

Daniel and I were busy moving our beds away from the window as high winds moaned through its aging frame, threatening to rip the glass free and suck us out into the black torrent of rainfall. Daniel pulled a sheet off his bed and was tacking it up over the window with pins from the corkboard over his desk.

"I haven't been blown like this since freshman year," I joked, but Daniel wasn't laughing.

A knock at the door pierced the moment.

I crossed the room to open the door and chuckled to find Michael Myers himself standing in the doorway.

"It looks smashing, Darling," I told Zooey. "No storm is gonna ruin your Halloween fun, is it?"

Zooey didn't laugh though, and he didn't remove the mask, either.

"Really committing to the character, are we?"

Then, I noticed his collar: soaked, torn, dirty with rusty smears. My smile fell.

". . . Zooey?"

He stepped inside and I closed the door. Daniel looked up from his work. I grasped the top of the mask and pulled it off, revealing what, for a moment, I mistook for a second mask.

The true horror was that it was no mask at all.

Zooey's face was swollen, slashed, and blackened into a face that was nearly unrecognizable, his hair matted with dried blood, leaves, and twigs.

"Zooey!" Daniel cried, racing over.

"My god," I said. "Sit. We'll get help."

"No," Zooey whispered vacantly. "That'll make it worse."

"Worse with who? Seniors?" I asked.

"Godfrey," he said.

Of course, I thought. I knew that chapter couldn't yet have closed. I just never expected the plot to shift so violently so quickly.

"He found out I told on him to Westcott and now he's on academic probation. He said if I tell again, I'll get it double next time."

"Then I'll go to Westcott myself," Daniel said. "This is way more serious than some gossip. We'll get him expelled and there won't be a next time."

"Daniel," I said. "We take math and science every day in a building named after his father. He's not getting expelled."

Daniel knew I was right, of course. He pounded a fist on the desk, hard, seeming to churn with a hundred times the fury of the storm outside.

"We'll handle it, Zooey," he said, pacing. "Don't worry."

"How?" I asked. "He's untouchable."

"We'll make Zooey invisible, like you," Daniel said. "That'll protect him, at least. Then take it from there."

"You'll *what*?" Zooey asked.

Daniel stopped pacing.

He'd slipped, caught up in the moment.

I looked at him.

He looked back, contrite.

"What do you mean, make me invisible?" Zooey asked, forcing the words through his swollen mouth.

I sighed and hung my head. Sometimes an unconscious slip like Daniel's does the hard work for you, pushing you, flailing, off of the cliff that your conscious mind had been begging you to turn back from. We'd leaped. How we'd land all depended on what happened next.

"It's time," I said. "It's time we tell him."

"*Leo*," Daniel warned.

"If not now, when?" I asked. "Besides, I've been saying since the first time, if we're going to do stuff like this for him, he ought to know about it. We didn't know him well enough before, but now? Come on, it's Zooey. He's one of us!"

"Know about *what*?" Zooey asked.

The room was silent save for the banging and wailing of the wind and rain against the window.

"I just . . ." Daniel said, fretting. "I mean, we don't even know what we're doing."

"We know it works," I said. "We know it can fix this."

"You guys are freaking me out," Zooey said. "Whatever it is, just tell me."

Daniel shook his head, then raised his hands in surrender.

I nodded, then sat down on the bed and took Zooey's hand.

"Zooey, there's something we need to tell you—to *show* you—and I just need you to keep an open mind and listen and . . . just trust us. You trust us, right?"

Zooey's face could barely show any emotion, swollen as it was, but I could see the conflict in his eyes. Still, he nodded and squeezed my hand.

I knew there was no turning back.

"Daniel, go get Steven and all of you head to the pub. I'll meet you there when I'm done."

Daniel nodded dutifully.

I got up and took my raincoat from its hook on the back of the door.

"Done with what?" Zooey asked.

"I've got to run an errand."

As I made my way across the campus to the common building, I took a beating of my own, my body pummeled by the gusts and my face slapped by rain, and I thought, *remember this?*

After all, it was the beatings I'd taken throughout my freshman year that had led me to take this illicit journey for the first time.

❖

The name-calling and insults were so immediate upon my arrival at the school, I thought they might have been part of the welcome packet.

Words I could handle, but soon those verbal jabs turned into physical ones, and by the time we hit Hell Week, I took my first actual beating from a rugby senior who accused me of staring. I told him I'd always been fascinated by primates and then I was on the ground.

I learned to dart from class to Dining Hall to bed quickly so as to minimize my exposure to upperclassmen; a snake slithering through the underbrush of the jungle that was Blackfriars. That worked fairly well until the boys of my own class noticed the way I performed in gym and pounced upon me like a pack of lions. The king of the pride was Ryan Godfrey, who quickly discovered that every time he beat me down, he seemed to grow inches taller in the eyes of the other kids. So I was dead meat.

Turns out, if you stop going to a class, you fail it, and as a broke peasant who only got in because of his legacy status, failing was precisely the one thing I could do to fuck it all up. And I was failing gym. I tried diplomacy, pleading my case to Carpinelli, but he had a dictator's capacity for charity.

"Wish I could help you, Breyer, but the grades are already with Westcott. He'll be transferring them into the master grade book by now. You shoulda come to me sooner."

I was left with one option: espionage.

With the spring term coming to a close, my last hope of getting a passing grade in gym was giving one to myself by changing my marks in the master grade book before report cards were printed. The book was, naturally, kept under lock and key in the headmaster's office.

Luckily for me, lock and key were little challenge at all.

After rehearsal for *Midsummer* let out, just like the play's four young lovers fled into the forest, I tiptoed through the darkened halls of the common building, fiddled through the office lock with my trusty pair of pins, and unsealed Westcott's door.

Once inside, I searched the desk, each drawer revealing various files, memos, and manuals. Still, no grade book. But then, as I rifled through some notes in the very bottom left drawer, I felt a hefty volume with a leather cover: jackpot.

I pulled the book out and laid it on the desk, where it caught the moonlight streaming in through the window.

The mysterious tome was the size of an encyclopedia, bound in black leather with some kind of pinwheel symbol embossed into its cover. It closed with a weathered metal clasp, which I released to reveal a well-worn parchment title page.

LIBER FRATRUM

I turned the pages carefully, as they seemed so old and fragile, stunned to find not names and grades but something . . . else. My eyes were pointed in the right direction, but it took several moments to make any sense of what I was seeing.

The pages were handwritten. Some contained paragraphs, couplets, and lists of text in languages I couldn't understand. Others lacked discernible language at all, instead showcasing alien sequences of glyphs, symbols, and signs. Occasionally there were full-page illustrations depicting sinister scenes like men in dark robes standing in elaborate circles, or monstrous entities manifesting from rising incense.

I stared slack-jawed, turning each page until a flash of light in my periphery brought my attention away from the book. It was the beam of a flashlight, scanning the hallway just beyond the main office lobby.

Shit, I thought. *The night watchman.*

I ducked behind the desk as something fell from the pages. The flashlight's beam passed overhead, and I stayed low and still until it bobbed slowly away.

When I was sure the guard had passed, I groped around on the ground for the thing that had fallen. I raised it to the moonlight and saw it was a photograph: men in dark robes and strange square hats standing in front of the Blackfriars campus. I turned the photo over to find a label scribbled on the back.

"The Oldfellows, Invocation, 1968."

I looked again at the men. They were old, mostly, looking sternly into the camera. I gasped when I recognized, unmistakably, a younger Westcott in the crowd. He and the others were situated around a central figure who wore a sash decorated with more of the odd scribbles, his hand on the shoulder of the only young person among them.

I nearly dropped the photo when I saw his face.

It was *my* face, staring back at me.

I knew immediately that it was my father.

Nineteen Sixty-Eight; he must have been a senior at Blackfriars when it was taken.

And though I hadn't completed the mission I'd come for, with this mystery in my hands and my heart pounding in anticipation of the night watchman's return, I slipped the book under my arm and crept out of the common building, across the campus, and to the dorm room of the only kid I knew who could help me decipher the thing.

"What time is it?" Steven asked, groggily, through the crack of the door.

"Steven, I need your help," I whispered.

"I will help you over breakfast," he said, beginning to shut the door. I threw a hand into the frame.

"Breakfast will be too late; I need to return the book before then."

"What book?"

I brought him to my room, where Daniel had been waiting up for me.

"There you are!" he said, darting up from the bed. "Where have you been? Your rehearsal let out hours ago. And what's Hillman doing here?"

"I . . . did something rash."

"*No,*" he said, his eyes widening with disbelief. "You didn't actually go through with it. You broke into Westcott's office?!"

"Daniel, I told you, I can't fail. I'll be out."

"Oh my god," he said, shaking his head. "Well, did you succeed, at least?"

"I couldn't find the grades," I said. "But I did find *this.*"

I slapped the tome down on the desk, swung the lamp over it, and opened its clasp as they peered over my shoulder.

I turned page after page.

We all stared in silence.

"This is . . ." Daniel looked flabbergasted. "What *is* this?"

"Latin, mostly," Steven said, poring over its pages. "Plus some Hebrew, Greek. Something else I cannot place."

"But . . . what . . . *is* it?" Daniel asked again, looking at an illustration of a man in a black robe and hat severing the hand of a hanged corpse at a gallows.

"Whatever it is, Westcott is involved in it . . . and my goddamn father," I said. "Look at this."

I showed them the photo, pointing to the father I never knew standing at its center.

"Are you sure?" Daniel asked.

"Sure I'm sure. My mom still keeps a picture by her bedside. Plus, I'd say the family resemblance is pretty damn convincing."

"The Oldfellows," Daniel read from the back of the photo. "Well, we don't know that this group has anything to do with the book. Maybe Westcott was just using the photo as a bookmark."

"Look at the robes, Daniel," I said. "The guys in the drawings are dressed just like the guys in the photo."

While we searched the photo for clues, Steven was quietly leafing through the book and scribbling notes on a pad on the desk.

Suddenly he dropped the pencil and said, "This is a grimoire."

"A what?" I said.

"A medieval book of magic," he said. "I read about these in my own classical studies. These are spells."

I guffawed.

"Like Dungeons & Dragons?"

"Some of it I cannot make out, like the Greek sections. I do not know much Greek. But of the Latin, I am certain. Each page has a heading for what the spell does, then the formula. Look: 'For Luck in Gambling,' 'To Stop Bleeding,' 'To Become Invisible.' "

"Bullshit," Daniel said.

"Some are quite complicated," Steven said as he scanned the text. "Specific astrological alignments to be observed and fumigations of various herbs to be prepared and talismans to be worn. Others are simple. This one, for instance."

He turned the book to me.

" 'For Good Fortune. Bear this sign about you on clean paper.' "

There was a mathematical sequence of numbers arranged in interlocking squares. These squares were surrounded by those alien-looking characters, all contained in a perfect circle.

"Anything about changing a gym grade?" I whispered as I gazed at the symbol.

"I would need more time to do a full translation," Steven said.

"No, you have to return this thing tonight, before Westcott notices it's gone," Daniel said. "Besides, this kind of stuff couldn't actually work, right?"

With a million questions, zero answers, and my failing gym grade unresolved, I made my way back to Westcott's office. But then, as I set about returning the book to its hiding place, I remembered Steven's translation of the Good Fortune spell. Just write the symbol on paper and keep it handy. It couldn't hurt to try, right? Desperate times, desperate measures, et cetera, et cetera.

I flipped through the book and found the page again. Taking some of Westcott's letterhead from a neat stack at the corner of the desk and his brass pen from its holder, I laid the fresh paper over the symbol and traced a copy for myself. I folded it into my pocket, replaced the book, and, watching out for the guard, made my escape.

The next day I went about my routine, dodging slurs and nudges, struggling to stay awake in class, exhausted as I was from my busy night.

When I arrived in the locker room for gym, though, I experienced something that shocked me awake.

"Mister Breyer, can I have a word?" Carpinelli said when I entered.

A few boys tittered by their lockers as I stepped into his office.

"Yes, *Coach*?"

I hated calling him that.

He looked me up and down pitifully, then sighed, exasperated.

"Listen, Breyer, if you breathe a word of this to anyone, you'll be sorry, but . . . I've had a change of heart."

"Sir?"

My hand went reflexively to my front pocket where I'd slipped the folded bit of paper.

"I know some of my guys here have a- ah- . . . sense of humor . . . that isn't for everybody. And I know you're . . . well, you're obviously not going to be a pro athlete, are you?"

"No, sir."

I hated calling him that, too.

"This office hasn't been organized in years. It's a wreck. I could use the help of a . . . an *organized* student like you. Let's say you help me clean it out for the rest of the semester, during the class period. You do that, and I'll speak to Westcott personally about your grade."

I practically teleported back to the dorm that night to report what had happened to Daniel and Steven.

"It's a pretty crazy coincidence," Daniel said. "But definitely a coincidence."

"Not enough data to prove causation," Steven agreed.

"Then we have to try again," I said. "Something more dramatic this time. Wasn't there a spell for becoming invisible? That one ought to be crystal clear, no pun intended."

Daniel rolled his eyes but was curious from a scientific perspective. Steven was unreadable. As for me, I had to know. So, that night, I made my covert little journey once again and presented the book to Steven.

"We do not have the things we need for this," he told me as he scribbled his translation of the invisibility spell. "We need a specific incense, some tools, some candles."

"I know a shop," I told him. "There's this spooky-ooky shop in Adders Lair. One of the guys in the VC took me there when he went to pick up some candles for the Halloween party. We can go this weekend."

That was the first time the guys met Oona, icy proprietress of Ouroboros, the premier witch shop of North Mass, which just so happened to be in downtown Adders.

"Welcome to Ouroboros, your intuition brought you here," she mumbled, deadpan, without looking up from her copy of *Rolling Stone*.

The store was a trip. It was a tight space, but she hadn't wasted an inch, packing the place full of rows of candles in glass jars, incenses, herbs, and books that apparently told you about stuff like *Divination for Queer Womyn* in earnest. I was feeling just like Samantha Stevens on *Bewitched* as I waltzed up to her counter and slapped down Steven's handwritten translation.

"Could you help me find these items, please?"

She looked at me quizzically, picked up the paper, and began to read.

She looked back up.

"Who are you prepsters?"

"Just some customers with legal tender, ready and waiting," I said. "Is there a problem?"

"No problem," she said. "I just thought from the looks of you, you either came in here to gawk or maybe buy a quartz for science class or something. Your shopping list here is real shit. Do you know what you're doing?"

"I appreciate the concern, ma'am, but I believe the only question you need ask is, 'Paper or plastic.' "

With a roll of her eyes, she set about gathering the things we needed: a specific incense, a thurible to burn it in, black candles, and some chalk made of eggshells for drawing signs of protection on the floor.

That night, Steven and I set up the whole production ourselves. Daniel didn't want any part of it, and he certainly didn't want us scribbling the strange circles on the floor of our room. Besides, burning incense in the dorms was against the rules.

Luckily, the VC's secret pub was available with ample space for our experiment. Its lock was as easy to pick as any other on the campus.

Steven drew the sigils in chalk on the floor while I lit the candles and wafted the incense about the room as the book instructed. When the stage was fully set, it was time for the ritual itself: words to be chanted while some signs were traced on my body.

I made Steven turn around as I disrobed and readied the pen. The spell called for an eagle feather and consecrated ink, but Oona didn't have those, so I made do with a Sharpie. I hoped it would be enough.

He started chanting all that "Hekas, hekas," mumbo jumbo while I scribbled on my body, following the illustration in the book. I finished my work and closed my eyes, imagining myself going cellophane as Steven's chanting reached a crescendo.

"Well? Did it work?" I asked.

Steven turned around and looked me up and down.

"You should get dressed," he said, as he turned his eyes away, respectfully.

We cleaned up and I returned home, dejected.

Daniel was still away at some rugby game when I got in, so I decided to wait up for him reading the bodice-ripper romance novel my mom had mailed in her care package. All that talk of heaving chests and chiseled arms got me going, so I was extra excited to greet him when he slipped through the door. My excitement deflated though when he didn't look at me, didn't even say *hello*, but rather began to unpack his things.

"Hello?!"

He nearly jumped out of his skin.

"Oh my *god*, you scared me!" Daniel said, grasping his heart. "Why did you hide like that?"

My eyebrow raised.

"I wasn't hiding at all; I was sitting on my bed looking right at you."

"Oh, well, I didn't see you there, sorry."

"Daniel, we tried the spell . . ."

I pulled up my shirt so he could see my new temporary Sharpie tattoos.

He looked at me like I was insane and said, "But I can see you, you're not invisible."

"But you didn't at first."

"I'm exhausted, Leo," he said. "I probably wouldn't see my own mother if I was looking right at her. Now wash that shit off before bed. You'll ruin your sheets."

And as I drifted off to sleep, I actually laughed at myself for taking this as far as I had. It was a ridiculous idea. I pictured myself as Mia Farrow in *Rosemary's Baby*, shoving a book about witches in Daniel's face like a raving lunatic.

He must really like me, I thought.

But the next day, I saw Daniel's jump-scare repeated again and again in teachers, other students, lunch ladies; any person whom I interacted with.

"Oh! I didn't see you there!"

"Don't *scare* me like that, Breyer!"

"That's not funny, faggot."

I wasn't invisible like the man in bandages from the movies, but goddamn if I wasn't completely unnoticeable.

At roll call of each class, if I merely raised my hand and didn't also shout, "Present," I would be passed over totally. I could walk right up to a teacher, basically under their nose, but if I didn't make myself obvious, they would just look right past me. Best of all, my usually relentless bullying ceased completely. You can't punch what you can't find. Now, I was convinced.

"It is a compelling development," Steven admitted, though he was looking haunted rather than interested.

"Come on, the spell said invisible. And invisible means *invisible.* Maybe the seniors just got bored of you," Daniel said.

"Then I'll have to steal the book again tonight," I said, "so that you can pick out our third experiment, Daniel. After all, three-for-three would be a pretty unbelievable *coincidence*, wouldn't you say?"

"I do not like this," Steven said.

"No, now I'm invested," Daniel said. "You're on."

That night, we paged through the book with Steven spot translating.

As the final VC meeting of the year approached, Daniel decided that the ultimate test of power would be to make our reigning club president, Dickie Cullman, pass his title on not to Stephen Shaefer, his underclassman boyfriend, as everyone anticipated, but to Humphrey Meier, whom he publicly loathed with an acid vengeance. If we could do that, Daniel reckoned, then we were truly magic.

We selected a spell to craft an Oil of Persuasion: simply apply to the body and all will obey you. We took our shopping list to Oona at Ouroboros.

She looked over the list and then up to us, her deadpan expression deadened further by her mournful makeup.

"What the hell have you boys gotten into?"

"Is there something you don't have in stock?" I asked, butter-wouldn't-melt.

"Well, not *exactly*," she said. "But these herbs. I mean . . . hemlock? Wormwood? *Datura*? Pretty hard core for high schoolers."

"Do you have them, or don't you?"

"Not in-store," she said. "But . . . I have my own garden at home. I grow poisons like these as part of my devotional practice to the goddess Hecate."

"Sounds lovely," I said. "How much?"

"Hard to put a price," she said coolly.

"Would you accept cash?" I said, sliding a hundred-dollar bill across the counter.

Steven received at least one such bill in the weekly letters he got from his parents, so it was a small price to pay in the name of scientific research.

"It's *fine* if you can't make change," I said with a wink.

Oona sighed and pocketed the bill. She grabbed a slip of receipt paper and a pen and wrote down an address.

"I get off at five," she said. "Meet me there at five fifteen."

"It's a date," I said.

We grabbed some coffee at the Sea Salt Diner down the block. Steven seemed despondent, but Daniel was energized.

"I gotta say, this is exciting," he said. "I mean, a backdoor drug deal for *poison?* Didn't see that coming."

"It does not bode well for the work we are attempting," Steven said. "Maybe best to try a different spell. Or just give it up altogether. You got what you wanted, didn't you?"

That was the general attitude about the Book of Brothers among our group. Daniel regarded it with curious skepticism, Steven with genuine aversion. But the vote was two against one, so we pressed on, doing what we were doing.

At five fifteen sharp, we arrived at the little cottage Oona had directed us to and knocked on the crumbling door.

After a moment, she emerged with a few pungent baggies packed with dried herbs.

"That's everything. If anyone asks, you didn't get these here. Is that clear?"

"As a crystal ball," I said as I shoved the bundle into my backpack.

"I hope you're not planning to take those internally," she said. "I mean, I'm sure if you're asking for them you know this, but . . . they can kill you."

Steven shot me a mortified look, but I was undaunted. A little danger wouldn't stop me. By that point I was a man possessed. I told myself that I just needed to know whether or not the book worked to satisfy the kind of curiosity anyone would harbor about such a thing.

Deep down, though, I knew that solving the mystery of the book was just the first piece in a greater mystery: the mystery of the photo in its cover, of who my father was and what ultimately became of him.

Once again, we waited until the campus was sleeping, snuck silently to the secret pub, prepared the space with the signs on the floor and the incense in the thurible, and set about brewing the oil. This time Daniel joined us, and though I could sense his snickering skepticism as he eyed our witchy preparations from across the room, he didn't leave. He did start to laugh when we chanted the prescribed incantations to ward and cleanse the space, but I couldn't blame him. It was all so totally ridiculous.

Steven, on the other hand, was stone silent as he handed me the herbs, which we boiled in oil before straining the batch into a little brown glass bottle. He didn't utter a word through to completion, when we wiped up the chalk sigils we'd drawn on the floor and packed everything up. I could tell he didn't like the game anymore, but me being me, I let my own desire to see things through cloud my awareness of his feelings.

I regret that.

That night, as we were getting ready for bed, Daniel asked, "What is that *smell*? It reeks in here."

"Gotta be the oil," I said. "Maybe we burned the herbs."

"The oil is sealed in a bottle in your bag," he said, sniffing around the room. "Oh my god, Leo, it's *you*! You stink like garbage."

"What a romantic thing to say."

"No, I mean it, you gotta get in the shower. Maybe it was the incense or something, but LORD!"

I showered off, but he complained about the smell for days.

"Maybe it's your upper lip," I joked, but later, I noticed it too, on Steven. We decided that maybe the fumes from the incense had clung to our hair or something.

Luckily, the smell faded by the weekend, and I put it out of mind.

At the final VC gathering, I dabbed our magical oil onto my neck like it was Chanel No. 5 and marched into the pub on our mission.

"Dickie!" I shouted across the room when I'd spotted him, "Congratulations on a legendary run as president! Say, can we have a word in the corner?"

His expression seemed to soften into peaceful complacency, like an enlightened yogi, and he said, "Of course, Breyer. Whatever you want."

Over in the back booth, Daniel, Steven, and I made our case to him as he nodded evenly.

"Humphrey is certainly impressive," he said. "And no one in the school would suspect him."

About an hour later, a knife clanging against a champagne flute signaled it was time to reveal the new president. There were gasps when Dickie handed the bubbling glass to a shocked Humphrey and not his crestfallen, soon-to-be-ex-boyfriend, Shaefer.

We all knew that the magic of the book couldn't be denied.

That was also the first time I saw *the face.*

After the party let out, back in the dorm, I was washing up before bed. As I splashed the water over my face and rose up from the basin, I saw for only a moment that monstrous visage looking back at me in the mirror. I leaped back and wiped the water from my eyes. My unremarkable reflection looked back at me once more.

A trick of the light, I thought.

I believed it, too, until both Steven and Daniel reported their own visions of the terrifying beast in dreams or at the edges of their periphery.

"I think we can agree on two things," I said to them on the last day of classes, as we met in our room. "One, that the book absolutely works. Two, that we're all sufficiently creeped out and never need to lay eyes on it again."

We did agree, and held to that promise.

However, while I never used the book again per se, I did use the oil once more before I went home for the summer, convincing Coach Carpinelli to let me take a study hall instead of gym when the fall semester began. I didn't see the harm in using it, since it was already crafted.

I regret that, too.

I also didn't tell the others that when I returned the book once and for all, I chose to keep the photograph of my dad and the Oldfellows.

One day, after I'd been home for a couple of weeks, I got up the courage to ask my mom about it.

"Where did you get this?" she whispered breathlessly when I showed it to her.

"I found it tucked in an old book at school," I said. Well, it was the truth.

"My god, look at him, so young."

My dad had always been a ghost to me, so to see my mom so immediately emotional at the sight of him was a good reminder that before he was a ghost, he'd been a man with real relationships and a real life.

"And is that your headmaster? Makes sense that they were in the same club. Westcott had so many questions about your dad when I first enrolled you. I think they thought they'd seen the last of the Breyers after your dad. A few guys like this came around asking me questions once he was gone, but they didn't know I was cooking up another Breyer to take Blackfriars by storm."

"Do you know anything about the . . . club?" I asked. "Looks pretty creepy."

"There are a lot of these old men's clubs around the East Coast," she said. "The Masons, the Shriners, that sort of thing. It's all an excuse to drink and get away from their wives, if you ask me. I remember your dad telling me about it once, how his dad had brought him in but he wasn't so keen on the whole thing. It all looks a little queer to me, the costumes and all. No offense, honey."

"None taken," I said.

❖

To be honest, the book had nearly exited my consciousness completely by the time we met Zooey Orson in the fall of the new term. I had no use for it, after all. My invisibility seemed to stick long after the Sharpie signs had worn off, so I was pleased as punch.

But then Godfrey set his sights on Zooey and I knew we needed to take action one more time.

"You said that we would never touch it again," Steven had said, the night of that first VC party back. "You *promised*, actually. Why break that promise for someone we hardly know."

"Because we protect our own, *Steven*," I said. "We'd do it for you, so you need to do it for him."

He didn't argue further.

We discussed making Zooey invisible, too, but even I couldn't figure out a graceful way to talk him into permitting himself to be ritualistically painted in the nude. He just wasn't *that* kind of girl.

Steven did uncover a little spell toward the front of the book, "To Stop a Gossiping Tongue," that seemed promising. Maybe we could shut Godfrey up, at least. We'd need a personal item of the target.

Target. Steven had a particularly hard time with that word.

"This is a curse," he said as we wrapped the jockstrap band Daniel had stolen from Godfrey around a wax figure. "Are we actually going to *curse* somebody?"

"How bad can it be?" I said. "At best, he stops his trash talk. At worst, he can't talk at all, which sounds like a win to me."

That's when I learned that everything we said during a working might find its way into the work, whether we meant it or not. Daniel reported back about Godfrey's jaw and the scene from the locker room, and satisfied as we were with the results, we agreed again that our days as secret wizards were over.

"Until now, Zooey," I said. "Because we'd do anything for you."

I'd explained the whole saga to him in the dark pub, the stolen book in my lap, the ceiling above us creaking as the tempest pulled the entire senior dorm from side to side. Hearing it all play back, I suddenly felt ridiculous. I always prided myself on being unabashedly outrageous, but medieval black magic was a *toe* over the line, even for me. I fully expected Zooey to stand abruptly, inform us that were totally insane, and leave. Remarkably, he instead sat placidly receiving the whole story, still as an oil painting.

"So we can do the invisibility thing," I stammered. "Or try the gossip thing again. That . . . that didn't seem to stop *others* from spreading gossip, did it? Maybe we could use the last of the persuasion oil to talk him into leaving you alone. God, we should have thought of that sooner, huh, boys?"

I looked to Daniel, seated beside Zooey, who looked stumped. Then I looked to Steven, who looked to the ground, ashamed.

"Or . . . we can just forget this ever happened. We can say we were kidding. To cheer you up. That's probably what we should do."

Zooey spat a bloody gob onto the floor and looked up at me with eyes blacker than the leather on that wretched book itself.

"I wanna break his fucking neck."

How to make a Perfect Storm:

1. Take one budding homosexual. Add shame, self-loathing, and trauma. Let fester for sixteen years.

2. Beat until vengeful.

3. Combine with book of black magic.

❖

Zooey selected the spell himself, flipping through the pages until he found an illustration of a man being held over a fire by some winged black demon and translated the title as "For Revenge."

"That is correct," Steven said. He scribbled the rest of the translation.

It would be, far and away, our most elaborate working yet.

First, we needed to prepare the space, drawing out a circle of protection, fortified by the writing of various names of God and archangels in Hebrew, Greek, and Latin around its circumference. This was meant to shield us from a power that we would seek to invoke outside of the circle.

I wish Steven had read a bit further on to know exactly what that power was, but we were in a race against the raging storm and the approaching dawn.

As we completed the circle, we burned frankincense as we walked around clockwise chanting from the book.

"Hekas, hekas, este bebeloi. Nothing unholy here, far be removed the profane!"

Next, we would draw out a triangle, apart from our circle, bound on its three sides by the name of the power: FRATEROTH, as knowing the name of this power allowed you to control it.

We'd place something belonging to the target (that nasty jockstrap coming in handy again) in the center of the triangle with a pot of burning "baneful herbs." The spell didn't specify which herbs exactly, but Steven still had bits of the herbs we'd used in the oil, which seemed "baneful" enough, based on Oona's warnings. We knew not to eat them, but I really wish she'd warned us not to burn them, either. We were to add a bit of "vengeful blood," which Zooey was happy to provide from his still-bleeding mouth.

When all was in readiness, we stepped into the circle, faced the triangle where the herbs sat smoldering, and lit the candle.

Everything was silent except for the crackling of the incense and the groan of the wind and rain, punctuated by occasional distant thunder. The circle of undulating light cast by the candle reached just far enough to make out the swirls of poisonous smoke rising from the triangle a few feet away.

I looked to Daniel and marveled that he was still here. I wondered if it was his love for me or his concern for Zooey that let him take this so far.

"Well," I said. "Take it away, Steven."

Steven opened the book to the page bookmarked by his own handwritten translation and began to read aloud in Latin.

After a few phrases, Zooey reached over and took the translation in his hands, reading along in English, in time with Steven's chanting.

"Brother to all of your Initiated,
The Pain of your Brother is your own Pain,
The Wrath of your Brother is your own Wrath,
The Hatred of your Brother is your own Hatred,
I summon thee forth in fumigation by your own name,
FRATEROTH!"

No one taught or told him to do this. He just . . . did. I stared at him, slack-jawed. I'd never really given much thought to the hocus-pocus

Steven read out in Latin when we tried anything, but hearing it in English, I began to regret ever letting him utter any of it aloud.

"First of us Brothers,
Who dwells in darkness,
Prince of Pain,
Prince of Wrath,
Prince of Hatred,
Awake and arise!
The Enemy of your Brother is your own Enemy,
Make haste unto my revenge,
Awake and arise!"

I noticed that the herbs were burning hotter now, white smoke billowing from the dish, beginning to fill the pub. I started to feel dizzy and flushed, my head pounding and my palms sweating as my heart raced. I noticed I was getting hard, but I didn't feel aroused. I felt terrified.

"Arise Frateroth and find the target of my revenge upon your seal,
Take up mine Enemy who has wronged me as your own,
In the name of your Brother, span the abyss, cross the gate and go forth,
Deliver thy justice, Frateroth,
It is so!
It is so!
It is so!"

I reached out for Daniel's shoulder so that I might steady myself, but my hand found only air. I looked down and saw that he was already on the floor, unconscious.

My knees buckled as the pub seemed to press in around me like a shrinking room in a fun house, the very fabric of our dimension pulsing and constricting as my vision blurred and un-blurred in nauseous waves. As I fell, I saw *the face* again, unmistakably, rising from the smoke, and just before I lost consciousness, I could have sworn I saw Zooey and Steven begin to levitate off the ground.

There was a deafening crash of thunder and a gust of wind that felt like the end of the world.

Then there was blackness.

How to make a Perfect Storm:

1. Allow terrible, unholy powers to find their way into the hands of children. See that those children only half-translate their conjurations, missing key protective details.

2. Have them perform those conjurations at the very height of autumn, the dying of the year, when the veil between worlds is at its thinnest. Make sure they are coming to the work not soberly but at an emotional breaking point, dripping blood, hungry for violence. Aim their violence at another child.

3. Pray for those children.

Terrible consequences await them.

PART TWO

CHAPTER NINE

DANIEL

I awoke to the sound of someone puking, and for a minute, I thought I'd dreamed everything in the drunken stupor of a VC hangover.

I definitely had the headache.

That's Leo in the bathroom again, I thought. *Any minute now he'll come in and take me to breakfast.*

But soon I was aware enough to feel concrete beneath my body instead of that worn-out mattress.

Must have really been a bender.

"Daniel, get up."

Five more minutes.

"Is he hurt?"

"No, he's just—Christ, can you get a trash can or something for Steven?"

Actually, ten. A half hour. I'll meet you at breakfast.

But I couldn't snooze any longer, because Leo was shaking me awake. I blinked my eyes open to see his face, close to mine, a little trickle of blood coming down from his forehead.

"Daniel, get up, we have to go," he said.

Why is he so serious?

"It's dawn."

And then I was together enough to see the room around him: the pub. It all came back to me in a sickening instant.

As I bolted upright and ran to the corner where my blazer still lay folded, I saw out of the corner of my eye Zooey scrubbing that chalk shit off the floor and Steven throwing up into a garbage can. I felt sick myself and still uneasy on my feet as I hastily straightened myself up.

"What happened?" I asked. "I can't remember."

"We passed out," Leo said. "And now it's dawn."

"Class isn't until eight," I said. "We're fine, we just need to eat."

"Daniel, we still have the *book.*"

The book.

We'd never failed to return it before dawn before.

For a second, I wished I could go unconscious again. Maybe wake up in a different life. But I knew the book was a problem that couldn't be ignored.

"Westcott will be in his office by now," Leo said darkly.

"We'll . . . return it tonight, then," I said. "What are the odds he needs that thing today?"

"HOW THE HELL SHOULD I KNOW?" Leo shouted. Zooey shushed him urgently. I'd never seen Leo lose his cool like this. It made me even more anxious.

"We should go," Steven said, wiping his mouth.

"He's right," I said, placing my hands on Leo's shoulders. "All we can do is get to class and figure it out later. 'Cuz we have to get to class. One thing at a time."

"Right," he said. "Right, OK. Let's go."

We finished cleaning up fast, cramming the supplies and the book into Leo's backpack, and made our way to the door.

When I saw the carnage outside, I thought I was still hallucinating.

The rain was coming down lighter than the night before, but steadily, and while day was breaking, turning the sky a weird purple-gray, flashes of silent lightning still lit up the grounds every few seconds.

Red-and-blue lightning.

I realized it was the lights of police cars and fire trucks.

The next thing I noticed was that every single one of the old birch trees that lined the quad were uprooted, lying on their sides like corpses on a battlefield. We traded stunned looks and made our way toward Bass. As we crunched across the quad, I realized we were walking on the broken glass of the academic building windows, all totally destroyed.

Then Leo stopped dead and whispered, "My God."

I looked up to where he stared.

I blinked and blinked again, but the hallucination wouldn't fade.

It could only mean that what I was seeing was real.

It was the steeple, ripped right off of the chapel, sticking out of the side of our dorm at a cartoonish angle, like a rocket that had crash-landed. Teams of firefighters and police swarmed the entrance, all shouting instructions through the pouring rain.

"HEADS UP!" one shouted as a portion of the steeple broke off from its base and fell to the ground below, crashing thunderously into jagged pieces.

Suddenly, I heard a voice behind us.

"BOYS!"

I turned. Mrs. Wesley ran across the quad, soaking wet, looking furious.

"What are you doing out on the quad?! All sophomores are to shelter in the Common Building until further notice and—oh . . ."

Her eyes fell upon Zooey's battered face.

"You're hurt! Was your room near the point of impact? Do you need the nurse?"

". . . Yes!" Leo chimed in, stepping forward. "We were trying to get him some help."

"Poor thing. Come with me."

I took in the chaos as long as I could, because I knew it would take a long time for my eyes and brain to agree about what they really saw that day. Then I turned and followed the others into the common building.

❖

Nurse Gleason, tiny and efficient, patched Zooey up as best she could.

"These injuries were all due to the chapel collapse? That's very concerning," she said.

We all sat silently sipping paper cones of water she'd given us to chase our aspirins.

"I thought the damage was only to one room. I wonder if others are hurt."

"It all happened so fast," Leo said. "I don't even know what *did* happen."

"Someone called it a . . . microburst?" she said. "Some kind of shaft of air? That can happen during big storms? Apparently, they can be very destructive . . . as you may have seen. Anyway, the steeple blew off and must have flown through the air about a hundred yards. It came right in through the window of a dorm room. Just *terrifying*. I pray to God that . . ." She drifted off, shaking her head. "You'll need a stitch here, I think. We'll put this gauze on for now and get you to the hospital in Adders when things settle down a bit."

Just then, there was a knock on the door. Ms. Gleason answered—it was Mrs. Wesley. She was crying.

"Excuse me," Gleason said before joining Wesley in the hallway, shutting the door behind her.

When the coast was clear, Leo turned to us.

"Holy shit!" he whispered. "Our dorm is destroyed! They gotta send us home, right?!"

"You don't think . . ." I hesitated. The rest of the sentence was almost too awful to say. But someone had to. "You don't think *we* did that, do you?"

Leo's face fell and was still a moment. Then he balked.

". . . No! No way! There was already a storm. We knew it was gonna be bad," he said.

"But would it have been *this* bad?" I asked.

"Daniel," Leo said, "are you actually suggesting we controlled the weather?"

"Why not?! We know the book works. We *don't* know the limits."

"Or the methods," Steven said, staring at the ground.

"Speaking *of*, Steven," Leo said, turning on him. "When were you gonna tell me that the stuff you've been chanting when we use it is so damn . . ."

"Demonic," Zooey said, fingering the gauze on his cheek, dazed.

"The other incantations were not like that," Steven said.

"Well, that's just terrific," Leo said. "You could have maybe said something before we got into all that 'awake and arise' noise."

"Since when are you interested in my feedback?" Steven asked.

"We can do all that later," I said. "For now, how are we gonna get that book back?"

"There's no way we can do it before tonight," Leo said. "And even then, all those cops and firemen . . ."

"Why so many?" Zooey asked.

Ms. Gleason stepped back into the office, white as a sheet.

"Boys, buses are on their way to evacuate the campus to a hotel in Adders Lair. I'm afraid that the sophomores won't be able to collect any belongings from Bass before departing. You can get anything you need when you return."

"Return?" Leo asked. "How long will we be gone?"

"I don't know," she said. "There's a lot of damage and . . ."

". . . Ma'am?" I said.

"Oh, it's just terrible," she said, her blue eyes starting to glisten. "I shouldn't say anything—they're going to tell you all at the hotel but . . ."

She looked up as fresh tears rolled down her face.

"Someone has died."

❖

The next forty minutes come back to me in flashes, like remembering a movie I mostly slept through.

"THERE you are!" Humphrey shouted as we staggered up to the others waiting to board the buses. "Where the hell have you been? We were about to call your parents to tell them you were fucking *missing*."

"The nurse," Zooey said, pointing at his bandages.

"For five hours?!" Humphrey said. "Ugh, never mind. Sophomores are in this one. I'll call off the search party."

I remember being taken to the big hotel in town where we were ushered by poker-faced teachers into a big conference room. I remember everybody soaking wet in their street clothes; teachers, too. The sophomores looked especially rough, some still in pajamas, all looking exhausted. They must have been evacuated as soon as it happened. I hoped no one noticed that we four were the only ones in uniform. To seem less conspicuous, I joined some of the rugby guys.

"Preston! You're alive!" one said. "Now we just gotta find Godfrey and Breckenridge. You seen 'em?"

I shook my head weakly.

Of course, I jumped to the darkest possible conclusions about them immediately.

Still, for those forty minutes, my mind was able to do some serious gymnastics to keep in denial about it.

Maybe Godfrey just got his dad to book him a private car home. He'd never sleep in a Holiday Inn. I bet he's home right now being a spoiled little shit.

My mind turned like that until Westcott, flanked by the other deans, strode into the middle of the room and everything went still and silent.

"Gentlemen," he said, gravely. "It is days like today that test the courage and fortitude of a Blackfriars man, and I want to thank each of you for your courage and fortitude in evacuating the campus in an orderly fashion. I was so moved to see students from across classes helping each other like the family we are. I trust you'll extend that same support to your brothers around you tonight and in the days to come. I'm afraid I have some terrible news."

There were screams when he said the name "Ryan Godfrey," and then I didn't hear much else. A few words and phrases leaped out from the static between my ears:

". . . died instantly and painlessly, I'm assured . . .

". . . his roommate, Mister Breckenridge, injured but not seriously, and being taken care of at a nearby . . .

". . . a week or more to make the campus habitable again . . .

". . . your families are being notified and travel arrangements are already being made . . .

". . . pray for the family of Ryan Godfrey."

After he'd finished, we were all told to wait for further instructions. As soon as he and the faculty had left the room, the place exploded into whispered discussions, but I just stared at Leo, Zooey, and Steven, who sat across the room, stunned and speechless.

I needed some air.

"Where's the bathroom?" I asked Mrs. Wesley, who waited by the door.

"Oh . . . well we're supposed to keep everyone in this room. Is it an emergency?"

"It is."

She sucked in through her teeth and looked side to side.

"OK, just be fast, dear. Down this hall on the left."

When I was alone in the men's room, I rushed over to the toilet and heaved, but nothing came up. I put my hand on either side of the stall, gripping on to the world as it spun around me. I couldn't breathe. I couldn't think.

Dead.

Ryan is dead.

The victory dances.

The away games in hotels.

The team trip to the beach.

He told me once about a life-size Larry Bird poster that hung in his childhood bedroom. Every birthday, his mom would mark his height on it in pencil. He stopped letting her when it was the same two years in a row.

No more birthdays now.

Ryan is dead and I'm a murderer.

No, worse. Murderers use guns and knives. I was a monster.

I shut my eyes and pounded on either side of my face, wanting to scream, wanting to cry, unable to do either.

Then, behind my eyelids, I saw a face.

I can't describe the details of that face. I don't think anyone could. All I can say is that it was staring right at me, right *through* me, and that got me screaming. I don't know how long I was screaming on the floor like that before I felt hands lift my shoulders off the ground and pull me up into a hug.

"It's OK," Prof. Reyes said. "Daniel, it's going to be OK. I know. I know."

He took me outside.

The rain had finally stopped and it was already getting dark; the whole day vanished in what felt like an hour. We sat there as I struggled to get my breath. Eventually, someone brought me a ginger ale from the vending machine. It tasted like ashes.

The next thing I remember is a green junker of a car pulling up onto the curb and a bleach blond rushing out, not even closing the door behind her, and barking at Reyes, "Where's my son?!"

"I'm sorry, ma'am, what's your name?"

"*Miss* Scalfani, but my son's last name is Breyer. Leo Breyer."

I sat up.

She didn't look old enough to be his mom, maybe thirty-five at most, though that may have been her crimped hair, mall rat outfit, and bright blue eye shadow, which made her look more like a pop star from MTV than someone's mother.

"He's fine," I said. "I'm his roommate."

She looked at me motionless a minute and then swept down and hugged me so hard I thought I was gonna pass out again.

"You poor kids," she said, wiping blue makeup from beneath her wet eyes with a fingerless, lace-gloved hand. "It's just so awful. Thank God we live so close. I came right from work. Nails."

She extended her manicure, bizarrely, for us to see. I didn't know what to say.

"He inside?"

"Yes, Miss," Reyes said.

She gave me another squeeze before breezing past us into the lobby, her earrings jingling with each high-heeled step.

When she emerged with Leo, I didn't know whether to lunge and attack him or hold him and weep. We locked eyes as he passed. He looked like an animal being taken to a back room at a vet's office. Then my eyes fell to his backpack. The backpack that I knew contained the stolen book. I watched it bob away, still strapped to Leo, not to be returned to its owner for God-knows-how-long.

The backpack was flung into the trunk of the car.

And then it and Leo were gone.

A short time later, the dean of students came out to find us. He explained that he'd spoken to my parents. Flights were a mess due to the storm, so I wouldn't be able to get back to California until tomorrow at least. They'd put me up in the hotel for the night, maybe longer.

But first, someone wanted to see me.

❖

We got off the elevator and I was taken to a room to find Theo, sitting on the edge of the bed, staring at the muted television.

"I'll give you two a minute," said the dean as he shut the door behind him.

I stepped in closer. The TV was set to the news, showing images of the damage brought by the storm. Theo looked totally vacant but physically unharmed, at least.

I swallowed.

". . . Theo?"

He looked up at me slowly, like he was underwater.

"Oh, hey, Daniel."

"They said you wanted to see me?"

"They did? I didn't ask for you."

"Oh," I said. "Well . . . maybe they just thought that since we were both his . . . I mean . . ."

The room was a sad, beige cell, like a seedy hideout in a mob movie. I guessed they'd just dumped him here after he was discharged.

"You OK?" I asked, before quickly correcting myself. "I mean, of course you're not, but I mean . . . I heard they took you to the hospital."

"Not a scratch on me," Theo said. "I think they were just worried about my, like, brain? Because of what I saw. They gave me a pill."

"That's probably good."

"Yeah . . ."

His eyes found their way back to the TV. I didn't know what to do.

"Well, I'm spending the night here," I said. "I think a lot of us are, until we can get home. If you want me to hang out, I'm down to stay with you as long as—"

"It took his head off," he said.

I almost laughed, for some reason. I had to ask, "What?"

"We were sitting in our room, doing homework, listening to the storm. I turned to ask him something and then a giant cross came in through the window . . . and it took his head clean off. I saw everything."

I just stared at him as he stared at the TV. The air conditioner hummed on.

I remembered what Zooey had said.

"I wanna break his fucking neck."

I opened my mouth to speak but nothing came out.

"They gave me a whole bottle of the pills," Theo said. "If you need one."

◆

I remember calling my parents that night and my mom in hysterics.

I remember two days in the hotel watching the news, watching reruns of *The Jeffersons*, watching the walls.

I remember the stewardess demanding to see my ticket again when she found me sitting in first class, assuring me I had the wrong seat.

I remember my mom holding me a long time when she and my dad came to pick me up from the airport.

I remember our dog barking wildly at me despite my dad repeatedly reminding him, "That's Daniel, Valentine! You know Daniel, you love Daniel!" Valentine hid from me under tables and in closets the whole first week I was home, growling suspiciously.

If that wasn't enough to tell me something was off, the smell was undeniable. My dad called it out first, after we'd been sitting together a while my first night back.

"Damn, Big Man, why don't you hit the shower? You must've sat next to someone ripe on that plane."

I showered and even spritzed myself with some Cool Water, but my mom commented on it again after dinner. I told her I didn't smell anything.

"Boys . . ." she said as she shook her head.

I stopped coming out of my room after that, but the solitude wasn't much better.

I tried to sleep as much as I could, but when I closed my eyes, I saw the steeple hanging off the side of the dorm.

Or Ryan's severed head.

Or the monstrous face looking back at me.

"My roommate" called asking for a me a few times. I always said I was sleeping or sick and would call back later. I never did, though. I wasn't ready.

My Aunt Deb sent a care package of her homemade cookies, the ones I always loved growing up. They crumbled tastelessly in my mouth.

That Sunday, my family all piled in the car to go to church together, but when I reached the doors of the chapel, I was hit with a wave of nausea so intense, it bent me over at the waist.

"You OK, Big Man?" my dad asked.

"Yeah, just a little—"

I stood again but then caught sight of the cross on the altar through the open doors. It burned my eyes like I was looking into the sun. I turned into the lawn and threw up.

"Just stress. A stress migraine," my mom said as she walked me back to the car, but I knew it was something different.

That holy place had expelled me like I was a virus. And didn't I deserve it, having traded my place there for a place in the Vicious Circle with all its sinful pleasures?

I couldn't be one of God's chosen anymore.

I had chosen something else.

❖

The bizarre death at the elite school in Massachusetts made national headlines almost immediately, and Godfrey's face haunted me everywhere I went: on TV screens at the RadioShack, on newspapers at the bookstore. His parents even made a weepy appearance on Larry King one night.

"He loved that school so much," his mother said. "That is why our family is increasing our endowment to Blackfriars, to rebuild as fast as possible and get those kids back to their home away from home."

I was watching it up in my room when my dad knocked on the door.

"Have you seen Valentine?"

"No."

"Ugh, that fool dog chewed clear through his line out in the yard. He's probably chasing squirrels and having a hell of a time. I'm sure he'll be back when he gets hungry."

After two days, we put up signs around the neighborhood.

We never saw Valentine again.

Sometime during my second weekend home, my mom knocked on my door with news of another phone call for me.

"Tell 'em I'll call back," I said, as ever.

By then, the side effects of whatever we'd done had passed, but I still didn't leave my room much. A few of my friends from home had heard I was back and called from time to time to invite me to join them on a walk around Venice or to go surfing or drive out to Palm Springs for the weekend, but I just didn't have it in me.

"Well OK, honey, but it's your roommate from school again. He sounds . . . pretty upset. I thought maybe he might have news."

I sighed. I knew this moment was coming, but that didn't make it harder to face. I sulked downstairs and picked up the receiver.

"Hello?"

"Hey, you," Leo said.

Even the sound of his voice brought that night roaring back. I almost hung up, but I didn't, and we held there in silence for a while. Eventually, he continued.

"How are you holding up?"

"Not great."

"Yeah, I'm sure," he said. "I've tried you a couple of times now."

"So is this a guilt trip?"

"No! No, Daniel, honestly. I just didn't know where we stood . . . I know you two were friendly, despite everything, and I've just been worried about you. And . . . and I hope you aren't mad at me."

Mad wasn't the right word. In the time I'd had to myself, my shock over Ryan's death had given way to the deepest regret I think I'd ever felt.

"I never wanted anything to do with that book," I said.

"Now wait a *minute*," he said. "Steven may have expressed some hesitation, but you were downright curious! No one forced you to be a part of any of it. No one forced you to stand in a damn chalk circle in the dead of the night, burning black candles, chanting some—"

"ENOUGH!"

I looked around the living room, checking who heard me. It suddenly occurred to me that either of my parents could be snooping on the other line.

"Look," I whispered, "What's done is done. You're right, I chose to be a part of it, that was my mistake—"

"*Our* mistake, all of us made a mista—"

"And now I just want to forget about all of it. Move on with my life."

"OK . . ."

More silence. Then I had to ask.

"Do you still have it?"

"It's in my backpack still, yeah," Leo said. "Daniel, I can, like . . ." He hesitated. It wasn't like Leo to not have his words under him. "I can *feel* it . . . in there. It's like someone else is in the room with me. All the time. It's giving me the creeps."

"Burn it then," I said.

"But we have to return it."

"Not we, *you*. I didn't take it; I don't have to do anything."

"Right, of course, right. I'll figure it out."

"Anyway," I said. "I should get going."

Leo sighed but didn't protest.

"OK," he said. "Well, it was nice to hear your voice. I really miss you."

Furious and confused as I was, that hit me.

I hadn't thought about Blackfriars much since I'd been home, probably as a defense mechanism. For a moment, though, I let myself imagine it as it was the day before everything had changed: gloomy skies, golden leaves, my navy peacoat, chilly days on the quad among the birch trees. Those trees were all dead now, their torn twigs littering the ruined campus like the bones of my old life, a life that had died along with Ryan Godfrey. I could only move forward into this new life, but I had no idea what that life would look like. Would I fall back into my old rhythm, going to class, training for rugby, eating the damn meatloaf? Would there be secret parties in the pub where we'd done the unspeakable thing that caused all this? Would I feel better by Christmas, opening presents and singing carols? And what about that first rugby practice of the spring season? Would there be speeches and tears, or will we all have just moved on?

And then there was the question at the very front of my mind, in this moment: Could Leo and I ever go back to . . . whatever it was we were doing? Could I even look him in the eye?

"I miss you too," I said. "Sorry, I just . . . need a minute. Good night."

"Wait," Leo said.

"What is it?"

"This is weird," Leo said, ". . . but did you have the smell? And the . . . face?"

My stomach dropped.

"Yeah," I said. "You?"

"Yeah. It's . . . disconcerting. Steven, too. I tried calling Zooey over and over, but he won't get back to me. Have you heard from him at all?"

Right. Zooey.

As stunned and sad and scared as I'd been the last two weeks, it hadn't even crossed my mind how bad things might be for Zooey. I at least had some experience with the book. I got to process the fact that it existed, the fact that it *worked*, slowly, over many months. Zooey got thrown right into the deep end over the course of one night, trial by fire, and that fire was from the bowels of Hell. He'd barely said a word the next morning. When he'd learned of Ryan's fate, he just stared. And then we were all scattered across the country.

There was no telling how he would react to something like this. He might snap and wind up in a loony bin or change schools again and run from this his whole life, or get paranoid and tell everyone what we'd done.

I called a few times over the next week but always got a phony excuse from his dad or a housekeeper. Leo had the same luck, so we started to get really worried.

One night, Leo called me in tears, asking if I'd heard the news, and I feared the worst. But that night, Leo wasn't crying for Zooey but for Freddie Mercury, rock-god front man of Queen and childhood hero to so many of us. He was dead. He'd just revealed his AIDS diagnosis the day before. And now he was gone.

I tried Zooey again that night, not expecting to actually hear his voice on the other end of the line.

"Daniel!" he said when he picked up. "How's your little vacation treating you, man? I bet LA weather beats the hell out of New York right now."

I don't know what was more surprising, how upbeat he sounded or how different the actual tone of his voice was, deeper and more confident. He sounded like one of the guys on my team.

"It's . . . uh, it's OK," I said. "*Really* been anxious to talk you, Z. It's been almost a month."

"Ugh, yeah dude, I know, I'm the worst. Just really hit the ground running here, catching up with people and stuff. You know how New York is. Or do you? Have you been, I can't remember."

"No, I get it, I guess. I've been seeing people too, but I just thought . . . I mean, I was worried about . . . Zooey, are you OK? After . . . what happened?"

There was a moment of strange silence on Zooey's end, then:

"Ohhh, you mean about Freddie?" he said. "Yeah, it's just terrible."

It's worse that I thought. Zooey had completely detached from the whole thing, like it didn't happen. I knew I needed to be gentle with him.

"Oh, well, yeah, it's awful news," I said. "But actually, I meant . . . are you OK after what happened at *Blackfriars*. We never got a chance to talk about it. I wanted you to know that what we did that night was, like, way further than anything we'd tried before. We didn't know how it would turn out. We're all pretty freaked out. And I just wanted to make sure you were OK."

"Oh," he chuckled.

Chuckled. The sound of his voice was like ice water down my back.

"I mean, look, I didn't want to *kill* the kid either, but . . . Oh, Dan, I know he was your teammate or whatever, but, I mean, he might have killed me first, for all we know. I'd say he got what he deserved."

I clutched the phone, shaking. I didn't know what to say.

"But I really am sorry I didn't call sooner," he said. "To *thank* you! I've just had a lot going on here. Actually, I should probably get going. I have plans tonight. A date!"

It occurred to me that since we'd only met a few months ago and only got the chance to hang out in stolen nights at secret parties, I didn't really know Zooey Orson all that well.

"A . . . what?"

"Yeah, I know, we have *so* much to catch up on," he said. "But I promise, this won't change anything when it comes to our friendship."

I looked out the window to where Valentine's leash still dangled, chewed through, in the moonlight. This was all wrong. Something was really, really wrong.

"I can't wait for you to meet her," Zooey said.

CHAPTER TEN

ZOOEY

"What makes a man?"

I remember hearing the question when I was just a kid, suffering through a commercial break, waiting for my Saturday morning cartoons to come back. The ads for toothpaste and cereal and home stereos didn't pull my attention from the Legos in front of me, but that one question hit my ear as it opened a spot for aftershave, and I looked up from my building.

"Integrity," the man in the TV said. "Honor. Drive. Sacrifice."

I didn't know what any of the words meant, but I remember thinking that the TV had it wrong. A man had a deep voice, big muscles, and a hairy chest. Like my dad. Everyone knew that. And the day I had those things myself, I would be a man, too.

(Of course, that day wasn't coming.)

By ninth grade, I had given up on any of the markers of manhood I'd expected to possess and naively thought that maybe the aftershave commercial had been telling the truth after all. Maybe if I led with Integrity, Honor, Drive, and Sacrifice, I'd become a man in the ways recognizable to the men around me.

(That got me abused, humiliated, and beaten to a bloody pulp.)

❖

Then I met the monster.

After the events of October thirtieth, after Ryan Godfrey lost his head, I started seeing the monster whenever I closed my eyes. It was the same monster who appeared to me in the smoke on the night of the storm.

At first, I was terrified.

His face was an abomination, horned and snarling. He reached for me with tentacled fingers. I woke up screaming every night. My dad actually gave me some scotch one night to help me sleep, but still, as soon as I let my eyelids fall, there he was.

After a few days of this, something occurred to me, finally. This being, monstrous as he looked, had appeared to me when summoned. He'd appeared in order to carry out my will. And when he got his order, he'd *done* it, exactly as I asked. So what was I afraid of? What if this thing wasn't an enemy but, rather, an ally?

So that night, I shut the door to my room, turned off the lights, sat on the edge of the bed, and shut my eyes. I waited for him to appear. And soon, rising from the inky darkness, he was with me, and this time I didn't scream.

He stared and I stared back.

"Hello," I said in my mind.

He didn't speak, not exactly, but somehow, I understood his greeting.

I understood that he was asking me what I wanted from him.

I knew that what I really wanted more than anything in the world was to be a man. A real man.

"Power," is what I said back, though.

And in that instant, I knew that the commercial hadn't been right, either.

Power made a man.

Like an alpha leading his pack, or a general commanding his army, or a king atop his kingdom, power was the currency of real men and was the thing I'd lacked all these years.

I looked the monster in the eye and asked for power.

I slept like a baby.

❖

Over the next week, I took stock of my power at Blackfriars. November had brought a seemingly endless stretch of soaking gray days to New York, so I had plenty of time to sit inside and think about what was adding to my power and what was taking it away.

The first thing that came to mind was money. We definitely had that. So did everyone else at Blackfriars, though, so money wouldn't be useful while I was still a student.

I'd heard that knowledge was power, and I considered myself decently smart. But then I thought about the smartest kid I knew—Steven. Any power he possessed was not the kind I wanted, so I gave up on the idea of becoming head of the class.

I knew that I had friends. Maybe my connections could be power? What good were friends whom you had to keep secret, though? Friends who kept you in the know about Madonna singles, River Phoenix's hair, and what our fellow students looked like in the shower, rather than the stuff normal guys talk about? Was their friendship really power?

Leo called to check in on me. I didn't call him back.

Then I remembered those early days in gym, when I'd kept pace with even Daniel. "Coach is gonna be asking you about track, I know it," he'd said. I knew I didn't have the coordination or, frankly, the guts to try a contact sport like rugby, but track would be starting up again in the winter term. I could actually be one of the jocks, if I tried out. I made a mental note to ask Carpinelli about it when I got back to school.

Then there was the matter of the way I presented myself. I always thought of myself as gawky and average, but then, Humphrey Meier had made more than one pass at me at the pub. One night, I took off my clothes and stood in front of the mirror. My face was healing, and I thought the little cut across my eyebrow, the scratch on my cheek, and the hint of color around my eye actually combined to make me look sorta tough. I was too thin, but what I lacked in muscle mass I also lacked in body fat, and I noticed that some lines of definition had appeared in my abdomen. I pictured how my flat stomach would look in contrast to bigger shoulders and a defined chest. I dropped and did twenty push-ups right there.

Better, I thought, as I looked in the mirror.

I vowed to start a fitness routine.

But then I remembered that even if I got a body like that actor from *Thelma and Louise*, I'd still sound like steam escaping anytime I said my own name. Absolutely no one powerful had a voice like mine. I remembered the tape recorder hidden under my bed. I exhumed its box, replaced its batteries, and pressed Record.

"My name is Zooey Orson, I'm sixteen years old, and I live in New York City."

I played it back.

Faggot, I thought.

I rewound the tape, pressed record, tried to force my voice down. I affected a clipped, nonchalant, throwaway attitude and spoke.

"Hey, I'm Zooey. I'm sixteen. I'm from New York."

I played it back.

My "S"es still needed work. I tried morphing them into "Z"s.

"I'm Zach Orzon. Zixteen. Upper Eazt Zide."

I played it back.

Better.

I practiced through the night.

❖

With so much to work on in pursuit of a new, more powerful me, days fell quietly away like the fall colors in Central Park until one night, the week before Thanksgiving, when my dad knocked on my bedroom door to tell me there was a call for me.

"Tell Leo I'm not home."

"It's not from a Leo," my dad said. "It's a girl. From Hansard. Someone called Mallory?"

Hansard.

My whole other life flashed before my eyes. Among the images of New York cool kids, field trips to the Met, society parties, and the leering eyes of Mr. B, I recalled sweet, raven-haired Mallory Gellar. She'd been my friend all through elementary, and we'd been excited to attend Hansard together. I hadn't spoken with her since the scandal.

I trembled as I picked up the phone.

"Mallory?"

"Zooey! As I live and breathe, Zooey Orson, back in New York."

"The prodigal son," I said.

"Wow, wow, wow," she said in her singsong way of speaking. She'd always sounded like a film actress from another time, many years older than she was. She had some strange kind of accent that sounded faux-British but that she'd describe as "mid-Atlantic" when asked.

"Terrible about what happened at your school," she said. "And that boy! Just terrible."

"Yeah," I said (though "terrible" wasn't how I'd describe it).

"Anyway, I heard that the school was out of commish until further notice and then it occurred to me, 'Oh! Zooey is in town!' How are you holding up?"

"I'm just fine, Mal. How you been? How's Hansard?"

"Oh you know, a whole lot of little Ronnie Reagans terrorizing the Upper East Side like a plague of locusts. It's revolting, and I'm through with it. I'm moving to Paris after graduation to become a mime, I really am."

"Maybe I'll join you," I laughed. "I could use the quiet."

"I wish you would. Oh, I've missed you. It's good to hear your voice. You sound more . . . grown up."

"Thank you."

"It's *not* a compliment," she laughed. "I thought we said we'd never grow up."

There was a pause.

"So . . . was there something?" I strained for conversation.

"Oh! Yes," she cooed. "Mummy and Putt-Putt are having a little political fundraiser for some congressman. Oh! Of course, you'll be familiar, he's a Blackfriars man! Charles Eldridge?"

"Right, right."

"Anyway, the election isn't until next fall, of course, but they're being aggressive about cash flow early, for some reason. Honestly, I think they're just looking for a new way to spend their money. They said I could invite a . . . someone to keep me company, and then I remembered you. And the Blackfriars connection is just *too* perfect! So, if you wanna dust off your tux and laugh at the whole thing with me, I'd love to . . . catch up."

❖

I hadn't worn my tux since last Christmas, and I was excited to feel the neck, chest, and shoulders of the shirt and jacket pull a bit as I put them on; signs that my nightly push-ups were already having an effect. A bit of Brylcreem turned my shaggy mane of black hair into a sleek Wall Street pushback, and I borrowed a spritz of my dad's Polo.

Combined, I barely recognized the darkly handsome young man I saw in the mirror.

Better.

I arrived at the Gellar town house, an impressive pale stone palace steps from the Guggenheim, at six thirty sharp, exactly one half-hour fashionably late. The help answered the buzzer and invited me to wait in the lofty foyer, where I checked my overcoat and admired the blown-glass chandelier hanging above me until that singular voice called to me from the top of the stairs.

"Is that James Bond *himself*?!"

I smiled up to Mallory, where she posed at the top of the grand staircase like Eliza Doolittle (There was my Broadway knowledge again. I still needed more work). She wore a deep blue ballgown that sat low on her slender pale shoulders; a perfect frame for the diamond necklace that sparkled over her collarbone. Her smile sparkled brighter, though.

"All that's missing is the martini," I replied.

"We'll fix that," she said.

I ascended the stairs to greet her at the landing with a kiss on each cheek.

(That was something *she* initiated. I actually thought of Leo in that moment and worried I'd blown my cover.)

"It really is so good to see you," she said. "Oh, your face . . ."

Most of the damage had faded away by then, but my eye still stubbornly held its dark purple bruising. I was beginning to worry that it would keep it forever, like the biblical mark of Cain, permanent evidence of what we'd done and who I'd been.

"You should see the other guy," I said.

"Poor thing. It's dignified, though. Like Rocky. Let's put some ice on it. Ice, covered with gin, vermouth, and an olive."

Their living room was packed wall-to-wall with the silvery social set, all clinking glasses and slurping oysters and showing off their plastic surgery.

"Couldn't you just *die*?" Mallory whispered to me, laughing. "Thank God you're here, I was about to drown myself in the fondue, I really was."

"Is that Zooey Orson?!"

A particularly pulled-looking lady swept over, appearing scandalized.

"You've *grown* . . ." she said, scanning me up and down.

"Better late than never, Missus Gellar," I said. "Thank you for having me over. Great party."

"Never in my life did I think I'd be hosting a political fundraiser in my very own home, but desperate times call for desperate measures. Congressman Eldridge has quite an exciting announcement."

"Well, did you know, Mother," Mallory said, "where Eldridge cut his teeth and calls alma mater? Blackfriars School, over in Mass. Same as Zooey!"

"Of course! I forgot that's where you'd . . . wound up. Awful news about the storm—that boy."

"A real tragedy," I said, deadpan.

"You know we've got a house on the Cape that apparently took a real beating too, according to the caretaker. I told John years ago that it was one squall from being swept out to sea. And now . . . Well, I'm glad to see you're all right, dear," she said. "In so many ways . . ."

Luckily, she didn't get the chance to elaborate further as glasses began to clink to announce a speech.

"Oh!" Mrs. Gellar gasped. "It's time!"

"Putt-Putt has been preparing for his big moment all week," Mallory whispered to me.

The guests cleared a space as Putt-Putt himself, the very round, very bald Mr. Gellar, stepped into the center.

"Distinguished guests," he said. "Welcome to my home, and thank you for being here. It is my honor to introduce to you the congressman representing Massachusetts' twelfth congressional district, a rising star in politics, and a dear friend: Representative Charles Eldridge!"

A tall, handsome, relatively young man in his mid-forties emerged from the crowd to shake Gellar's hand. He wore a navy suit, a red power tie, and a gleaming white smile. His generous head of salt-and-pepper hair was slicked back, not unlike my own.

"Thanks, John," he said in a magnanimous voice. "You may have heard that I have an announcement to make tonight, and I hope you can keep an open mind, hear me out, and we can end the evening drinking champagne rather than each other's blood."

Laughter from the socialites. Mallory squeezed my hand confidentially.

"But that's what next year's election is about: coming together. And I'm not talking about Congress, though I do take my role as the sole Republican in deep blue Massachusetts as an extreme point of pride. No, I look at the state of conservatism in this country and I know I need to aim higher. We have to get the markets back on track, fulfill the vision of economic freedom put forward by President Ronald Reagan, and affirm to the world what the soul of America really means. That is why I say to President Bush, 'Read *my* lips. I will be challenging you in the primary to seek the Republican nomination for president of the United States."

There were gasps, then titters, and then, slowly at first before building to a furor, applause.

"We'd better hurry up and get stoned," Mallory said, surreptitiously. "This is about to get very, very boring."

She took my hand and we slipped away from the crowd as Eldridge began grandstanding.

❖

We tiptoed up a spiral staircase to the fourth floor and her bedroom, all floral pink tufts and gold-leaf swirls.

"DON'T say a word, I didn't decorate it," she warned as she entered. I lingered at the door.

"Um . . . are your folks gonna be OK with us being alone up here?"

She stared at me for a moment before bursting out laughing.

"Zooey, if you think Mummy or Putt-Putt will notice a thing tonight besides who finishes the caviar and how much they've donated, you might be stoned already. Now shut that door."

I obeyed as she opened her window, letting fresh November air rush into the room. She had an incredible, unobstructed view of Central Park, the lanterns glowing dimly, the skyline of the West Side glittering in the distance. A cab honked loudly below. I suddenly wanted to forget everything about Blackfriars and stay in New York forever.

"Here," she said, having produced a little rolled cigarette and lighter, seemingly from nowhere. Of course, it wasn't a cigarette; it was a joint. I must have looked nervous.

"First time?" she asked.

"Don't tell the lads back at Blacks," I said.

"Mum's the word," she said. "They kick a little harder than a cig. You'll cough the first time. Unless . . . no."

"What?"

"Well . . . ever heard of a shotgun?"

"Like . . ." I mimed a hunting rifle. She laughed.

"No! No, it's a way to smoke. But it's a bit intimate."

"We're old friends," I said.

"Ancient history," she said. "Come here."

We sat on the edge of her bed, close.

"I'll take a hit and then blow the smoke into your mouth. Just breathe in deep when I blow, OK?"

"Roger."

She smiled, raised the joint to her lips, lit it, and pulled as the tip glowed orange and smoke rose. She lingered a moment, eyes closed. Then, opening them, she leaned in toward me, as if for a kiss. I leaned in to meet her.

Our mouths touched. Then we were breathing.

"Now hold it! Don't breathe out!" she instructed. I felt the smoke burning my throat, but I let her drive. "OK!"

I exhaled a cloud.

"No! Out the window! Shit!" She began to fan the room with a nearby *Cosmopolitan*.

"Sorry, sorry," I sputtered.

She laughed.

"Trying to get me in trouble, Orson?"

"Trouble follows me everywhere I go," I said.

She seemed to like that.

We sat for a moment. Then she jumped up suddenly and trotted over to her dresser.

"Have you heard this yet?" she asked, holding up a CD.

The album art was of a naked baby submerged in water, swimming toward a dollar bill on a fishing line.

"No."

"Oh, it's the *most*," she said, gliding over to her stereo and popping in the disk. "Some dirty-looking boys out of Seattle. Nirvana, they're called. Sound like it, too."

She pressed Play. A dry guitar played a pulsing lick, solo. Then, with a kick of drums, the room exploded with angry, sad, young, sexual rock.

I didn't know if the joint had hit yet. I'd never been high before. But I knew I'd never felt like this.

We lay back on the bed, listening to the music.

Eventually she said, "Zooey, I'm certain you are sick to death of talking about this, so I'm going to bring it up just one time and you don't need to say a word but . . ."

She sat up and looked me in the eye.

"I am so, so sorry about what happened to you. At Hansard, I mean. I was absolutely sick over it. And I want you to know that I never thought of you as anything but a victim in that situation, and I'd never judge you for an instant for it. I know a lot of the creeps in our class declared open season on you, but I just wanted to make sure you were OK. And then you were gone."

She held my gaze. I didn't know what to say. She flopped back down onto her back.

"But now you're back and I wish you could stay. There, I've said it."

". . . Thank you."

I meant it.

"Well, I'm feeling sufficiently elevated," she said, hopping up and smoothing out her dress. "We should probably get back."

❖

As we descended the stairs, I had to hold the railing tight and deliberately place one foot in front of the other just to stay upright. My skin seemed to pulse to meet the air around it as if the borders between it and everything else were growing indistinct. My mouth was dry, and I was slightly paranoid that I still smelled like the smoke, but at the same time, I marveled at the colors of the room's decor, the sounds of tinkling ice, the smells of the hors d'oeuvres.

This is what it's like.

Then, to my horror, Mrs. Gellar approached looking like it was

Christmas morning, with Eldridge himself on her arm, just as my high was really beginning to peak.

"Mister Orson," she cooed. "The next president of the United States would very much like to meet you!"

I slapped a clammy palm into his and shook firmly, trying my damnedest to muster all the sobriety left inside of me. Mallory watched from the cheese table in hysterics as she loaded a cracker.

"Hello, zir," I said, remembering to mind my S. "Zachary Orzon."

"Orson," he repeated. "Say, I've heard of another Zachary Orson. Hotel man."

"My father, zir."

"Of course! I see the resemblance! And I hear you're a Blackfriars man too?"

"I am, zir. New thiz year."

"I hope you and your classmates are holding up all right after the tragedy. Trust that my office is doing everything we can to get the school fixed up and you boys back into class. And to take care of the Godfrey family, of course. Were you two close?"

I swallowed hard. It was as if all moisture had left my body.

"We had gym together," I croaked.

"Gosh, I'm so sorry," he said.

"Congratulations on the announcement," I said. It was a pivot one would have to be stoned to attempt, but I needed to change the subject.

"Oh . . . why, thank you! Yes, it's no small thing to try to unseat a president of your own party, but the sad fact is, President Bush betrayed us. He betrayed us with his tax hike, putting the burden of his deficit on us, the earning class. He betrayed us on immigration, doubling the number of visas granted while our American brothers can't find a job. He betrayed us on spending. Do you know about the CARE Act? The United States Government is now actually *subsidizing* junkies and sexual deviants who wind up with AIDS. While hardworking family men struggle to get food on the table! Someone had to stand up. That's the story of America: each man claiming his own greatness, his own *power*, so that he may join with his brothers to combine their power and seek greatness together."

I didn't know much about taxes or immigration or government subsidies, but I heard that word, "power," loud and clear.

By eight o'clock, most of the guests had left for dinner or the theater. I helped gather up dishes, among the help, as Mrs. Gellar repeatedly told me "you really don't have to do that," even as she shot impressed smiles back at Mr. Gellar.

Mallory walked me to the front door, where Max was waiting in the car.

"You're a saint for enduring that," she said. "I mean, *really*. Thank you."

"You kidding? It was fun," I said. "And so good to catch up."

"I agree. When do you head back?"

"We actually got word this morning. We report back December first to start class the next day."

"So that gives us another whole week," she said, lighting up.

"Yeah, and then it's just a few weeks more until Christmas break," I said.

"Well, suddenly I'm in the holiday spirit," she said. My god, she was flirting. "Here, some homework."

She put something into my hand. A CD. A naked baby underwater.

"Call me when you've got it memorized."

"I will."

We lingered for a moment.

"Well," she said. "Good night."

She ascended onto her tiptoes to give me a kiss on the cheek. Not an air-kiss, but a tender little brush of her pink lips. Then, smiling, she turned with a wink and strode back into her house.

I turned to see Max beaming like a proud father from the driver's seat.

I saw Mallory four more times in the week before I headed back to Blackfriars. Dinner at Tavern on the Green, a performance of *Les Miserables,* a chilly walk through the park with ciders and her arm in mine, and last, another evening listening to music in her room with a joint.

It was the last Saturday of the month, my final night in town. This time, her parents were out at the opera and with no one to bother us, we kissed while Sonic Youth sang about a "Teenage Riot."

"So . . . what is *this*?" she asked when she pulled away.

"Let's figure that out when I'm back for Christmas break," I said. "That's just a few weeks away now. But whatever it is, I like it."

"I like it very much," she said.

What makes a man?

Maybe it's a woman, I thought.

When I stepped out of the car, back onto the Blackfriars campus, I was struck by the blankness of everything.

The trees that had survived the storm were all leafless, and without the steeple looming over the campus, the overcast white void of the sky was more visible than ever.

It was a new month, and I was a new me.

A blank slate, I thought.

I remembered what my dad had said on the day I'd arrived: "Think of it as a fresh start, Zooey. Not everyone gets that." Now, here I was getting *another* fresh start. This time, I intended to use it.

As I made my way into the mandatory, school-wide assembly in the common building and Daniel caught sight of me across the auditorium, waving, and gesturing to sit with him and the others, I pretended not to notice, taking a seat on my own toward the back.

When everyone was seated, Westcott stepped soberly to the podium.

"Good afternoon, students, and welcome back," he said. Westcott was always frail-looking, but today he looked like his own corpse reanimated; his skin gray and sagging, his eyes red and tired, his suit rumpled.

Not so tough, are you? I thought. *Not without your book.*

"I know we normally meet as a family in our beautiful chapel, but repairs will take some time. When it is safe to do so, we will begin meeting there again, and the first of those meetings will be a proper memorial mass for our departed brother Ryan Godfrey."

He eulogized a bit about Godfrey, saying kind things about his character and academic record that everyone must have known was complete bullshit. He led a moment of silence, and I thought we were wrapping things up, but then he rose his head and said, "Before we go, students, I'm afraid there is another matter we need to discuss. A very serious matter indeed. A theft."

I didn't dare to look up for Leo, Daniel, and Steven, but I was sure we were all thinking the same thing.

"It seems that in the chaos of the storm, my office was broken into and a valuable antique was taken. I need not explain how grave a betrayal this would be in normal times, but to take advantage of our tragedy to commit such an offense is as morally bankrupt an act as I can imagine. If anyone has any information about the culprit and the whereabouts of the missing item, I demand they come directly to me without delay."

My mind raced. Had we been sloppy? Had we stashed it someplace, or had Leo taken it with him? I couldn't remember. I wondered if Leo had run his mouth to anyone else about it. Gossip ran through him like a sieve.

If one of them fucks this up for me . . .

"In the meantime, trust that all school rules, particularly our nightly curfew, shall be enforced with zero tolerance. I will find the guilty party and make certain that they receive the precise punishment due for such a heinous act. Good day, gentlemen."

❖

Classes wouldn't start back until tomorrow, so the rest of the day was free for panic. I arrived back at my room to find a note waiting under my door:

Our room.

❖

"Hey," I said, when I arrived at Daniel and Leo's room to find them and Steven waiting.

Leo stood to hug me, and I let it happen.

"I missed you," he said.

I'm sure he could feel my hesitance, though.

"How . . . have you been?" he asked as he pulled away. "I tried calling."

"I've been fine. Busy, actually." I joined Daniel and Steven where they sat on each bed.

"Daniel told me," Leo said. "I . . . had to ask if he heard you correctly."

"You mean about Mallory?"

"Yes, about *Mallory*."

"You sound different," Steven interjected.

"*Thank you,*" I replied coolly. "And is there a problem with her?"

"Well, *Zooey,*" Leo said, looking around to an unseen studio audience, like he was Sally Jessy Raphael or something. "I mean . . . are you bisexual?"

"I'm . . . look, I'm sixteen. I shouldn't need to explain myself or who I date to you or anyone. She's an old pal from Hansard, and I like her. Besides, aren't there more important things to talk about right now?"

"He's right," Daniel said. "We're here to talk about the book."

Leo sighed.

"Well," he said, "getting the book back to Westcott is obviously priority *uno*. And I doubt breaking into the office will be the cakewalk it once was. Maybe we just mail it back anonymously?"

"I expect he'll want to learn who was responsible," Steven said. "And there are a number of appropriate spells in the book for doing so once he has it back: To Identify a Guilty Thief, To Learn Secrets, For Revenge. As soon as it is his, he can find us out."

"We hide it, then," Leo said. "Bury it, or throw it down a well, or into the Charles or something!"

"Or destroy it," Daniel said.

NO, the monster roared, behind my eyes.

"NO!" I repeated, louder than I'd intended.

Everyone looked at me. I realized I'd stood up. I sat once more.

"I mean . . . why don't we just use it?"

"What?" Daniel asked.

"We're talking about giving it back or hiding it or destroying it. It obviously works, so I have to ask, why don't we just *use* it?"

"Because," Leo said, "we . . . I mean, someone is *dead*, Zooey."

"Oh my *Christ*, where is all that 'hiss hiss, bitch' talk now?" I said. "I thought we were supposed to be venomous snakes. It did what we asked it to do, point blank. And it was good riddance. Or did we all forget the part where Ryan Godfrey spread my darkest secret to the entire school and then beat the ever-loving *shit* out of me?"

I pointed to my face, still scarred.

"We've been handed real power, here. We should use it. We could coast through Blackfriars, get everything we want, *be* anyone we want, and send a storm for anyone who tries to get in our way."

No one said a word.

"Fine, you don't want it? I'll take it. You all got free reign with it last year and then you show it to me, rope me in to all this, and then want to play gatekeepers? Fuck that. It's as much mine as it is yours, now."

"Zooey, are you OK?" Daniel asked.

"*What* do you mean?"

"Well, we don't hear from you for weeks after . . . something serious happened. Then you come back here and you're like a different person. You sound different, you look different, you suddenly . . . want different things."

"Why shouldn't I want *different things*?!" I said, my heart beginning to race. I stood. "I don't know if you've realized, Daniel, but guys like us don't tend to get what they want in life anyway. They tend to lead sad, broke, frivolous lives, estranged from any family, lacking any upward mobility, before they get beaten to death, or overdose on some dance floor, or die of fucking AIDS! But maybe that's just not something you worry about. Because you've always been able to hide it, to live in both worlds."

"Like you don't know *anything* about being able to live in two worlds," Daniel said, standing to meet me, furious.

"I wish I could trade with you," I said. "I'd rather pass in the way that you can than pass in the way that I can."

Daniel and I glared at each other. Horrible, tense silence hung in the air.

"Take that back," Daniel whispered. "You're gonna regret saying that."

"May I suggest," Steven interrupted, "that we find a suitable hiding place for now while we figure out what the best course of action might be."

We broke our stare down.

"If you look carefully at your effects here," Steven continued, "I think you will find that your room has been searched. I noticed immediately that some of my things were out of place. And I am very particular about my things."

"No—" Leo said.

He began to pore over his desk.

"You're paranoid," I said.

"No, he's right," Daniel said, examining his dresser. "Everything's just slightly out of place. This drawer is still open, and all my clothes are messed up. Jesus, look at this . . ."

It was true, his dresser drawers were a mess, clothes rumpled and replaced carelessly.

"We are very lucky that Leo had the book on his person and not hidden in the room," Steven said.

"So, they're searching everyone's rooms?" Daniel asked.

"Or he already suspects *us*," Leo said.

"Why us?" I asked.

"I would think the target would point to likely suspects," Steven said. "Who else would have a motive but the targets of his bullying? And Zooey, given the way that Ryan spread your secret, the altercation you had, and the timing of his death, I would guess that you are suspect number one."

That would have been the logical assumption.

How strange, then, that a few days later, when the first disciplinary summons came in, it wasn't for me.

❖

By that time, we'd hidden the book in a rusty cabinet beneath some old tarps in the forgotten shed at the edge of the property. There had been some arguing about whether to replace the lock on the shed door; Daniel and Leo argued that the lock would keep it safe, I argued that the lock made Leo its de facto keeper, Steven weighed all outcomes but decided that if Westcott figured out the hiding place, the lock wouldn't help whatsoever, as he could easily get the key. I won, and the shed remained unlocked.

Anyway, it was lucky we'd done it when we did, because none of us had the book in our possession when Mrs. Wesley came.

A few of us were crowded in the Bass common room watching a VHS of Chevy Chase in *National Lampoon's Christmas Vacation.* We turned down the volume and our laughter went quiet when Mrs. Wesley strode sternly in through the front door. It was after dinner on a Sunday, so it could only mean one thing: Someone was in deep trouble.

"Daniel Preston," she announced. There were a few gasps. We all looked back to where Daniel was sitting with Leo. They both looked stunned.

"Yes, ma'am?"

"Please come with me at once. Headmaster Westcott needs to speak with you urgently."

CHAPTER ELEVEN

DANIEL

I always said my time at Blackfriars was like a sprint, and for the year and a half that lead me to the events of Nineteen Ninety-One, I'd kept my pace up as best I could. I'd been sprinting for myself, running toward a life that I knew was at the finish line but would take every ounce of stamina I had to reach. I sprinted for my dad, hollering from the sidelines.

But maybe more than anything, I sprinted because I was being chased.

I was being chased by the lie I was living. That whole year and a half, I felt it catching up to me, a steady footfall just behind mine, reaching out to grab me by the back of my shirt and yank me down.

When I sat down in Westcott's office and he slid the photo across the desk, a Polaroid of myself dressed as Indiana Jones, arm around a drag queen, I knew the race was over.

He just let me stare at it in silence for a while, not saying anything.

Then, finally, he spoke.

"As you know, Mister Preston, I am investigating a theft," Westcott said. "Last week, just before students were welcomed back on campus, I conducted a few dorm room searches, looking for the missing article. Your room was one of the first I thought to explore. Not because of *you*, Mister Preston. It was your roommate I was interested in. I'll be frank, you are one of the last students I'd suspect of impropriety. But then I found this photograph."

He tapped it with his bony finger. God, I'd forgotten all about it. Barton had given it to me as a souvenir and I'd kept it in my sock drawer.

"Before I tell you what I know about this photograph, Mister Preston, I'd like to give you the opportunity to tell me about it in your own words."

It's amazing what you can get used to.

I'd gotten too comfortable, *too* used to it, the parties, the drinking, the boys. By the night that photo was taken, I'd become so damn comfortable with all of it, I'd actually smiled for the camera. A smarter guy would have knocked it out of Barton's hand. A smarter guy doesn't take photos of things he doesn't want people to know he's doing. That guy wouldn't be sitting where I was sitting.

". . . It was a Halloween party, sir. We're in costumes."

"Well, I should hope *so*," Westcott said with a cruel little laugh. "Last I checked, this is an all-*boys* school, and the person you've got your arm around here is in a dress and wig, so if these aren't costumes, I would be very alarmed indeed. Tell me, who is the other student?"

While my stupid face was clear as day, Leo was an inky black blur, his face hidden by his falling wig. I remembered how Richardson had staggered into us right before the photo was taken.

Lucky Leo, still invisible, even in a photograph.

"I don't know," I lied. "I think he liked my costume."

Westcott's eyes narrowed.

"Well. How about we examine a few more details in this photograph. Perhaps they might jog your memory."

He swung his desk light around low over the photo.

"Where was this photo taken?"

Stick a fork in me, I'm fucked.

I tried to keep my cool, act casual.

"Um . . . had to have been a dorm room. One of the seniors, maybe?"

"Halloween was just a few weeks ago, Mister Preston. You can't remember where a party took place just a few weeks ago?"

"I . . ."

"May I draw your attention to the ceiling in the photograph? Beams. Tell me, do you know of any dorm rooms, even a senior dorm, with such spacious dimensions and exposed beams in the ceiling?"

"No, sir."

"No, I don't, either. Because there are none, Mister Preston. It took me some time to recognize the space in the photo to be the old student pub. I thought it had been converted for storage and had forgotten it completely. Imagine my surprise when I opened it up again to find the *lavish* operation that had been taking place there. A fully functioning bar, right under my nose! The jukebox was an especially nice touch. That, and the *guest book.*"

He laid our tattered guest book down next to the photo on the desk, and I wanted to cry. It was all over. Not just for me, for all of us.

"The Vicious Circle," he said. "It sounds like quite a . . . storied . . . little group. There are even some notable alumni! Alumni whom I suspect would be very troubled to have their history with such a group come to light. Do you know why I suspect that, Mister Preston?"

"Because . . . because secret societies are prohibited at Blackfriars?"

"Because the Vicious Circle is, apparently, a club for homosexuals."

He opened the guest book to a pornographic sketch some kid had done decades ago that spoke for itself. I looked away.

"Now, I know that you were assigned to room with Mister Leonard Breyer."

"Sir?"

Shit.

"I'm sure you're aware that Mister Breyer has a reputation for being a young man of the most frivolous, low, unmanly nature. I regret that you've had to endure such a presence as you've gone about your academic and athletic life. I can't imagine the disruption such a person might pose to a well-meaning student unlucky enough to share his room. And still, I recognize that such a character could have a way of imposing his predilections on vulnerable young men, particularly young men who are unlike their peers . . . for one reason or another. That is to say, I do believe one could be . . . *bewitched* . . . by such a person."

Like I've said, I'd learned a long time ago when it was time to speak and when it was time to shut up and listen. And he seemed to be leading me somewhere, so I shut up and let him lead.

"Naturally, I'll be bringing in Mister Breyer next, before making my way down the entire list of students in this guest book. But I wanted to speak with you first, Mister Preston, because in truth, to be completely plain, I do not believe you to be a homosexual. Not *really*."

He tapped the Polaroid again.

"And while your attendance at such an unauthorized gathering is a serious offense, I also might exercise leniency if your attendance was the result of such . . . bewitchment. *And*, of course, if you could provide me any useful information toward the recovery of the item I seek. A book. A very old, very rare book. Does it ring a bell?"

There it is. Goddamn, he was actually threatening me.

"You are, in every way, the very picture of an ideal Blackfriars man. Except, of course, for your appearance in *this* picture. But I am willing to forget about that if you'll cooperate. Maybe you saw a strange book in your roommate's possession?"

"I . . ."

"Think of your future, Mister Preston. Think of your *team*."

Westcott was smart; he knew just where to hit me. From the

basketball courts in Chicago and LA to the rugby pitch at Blackfriars, I'd always been a team player, loyal to a fault.

But I wasn't just a meathead. I was also a real strategist on any field, and I saw his play coming a mile away.

He'd given me a choice: admit I was a homo and had been at the party willingly or admit that I knew something about the book and help him find it. Now, if I confessed to being at the party, I would probably be expelled, and that would be bad, *bad* news for me. Like, find-another-place-to-live kind of bad news. Expulsion for any reason would be a fatal blow to my excellence in my dad's eyes. But for *this* reason?

On the other hand, if I confessed to knowing about the book, I'd be admitting that I knew a secret about Westcott that no one was ever supposed to know. That I knew what really happened to Ryan Godfrey. That I knew about the Oldfellows. I'd seen enough movies to know what happens to the guy who knows too much.

Plus, Westcott had gotten one other thing wrong about me. He'd misjudged which team I was most loyal to.

Sorry, Dad, I thought.

LEO

"Which one of you ratted him out to save your own ass?!"

Screaming accusations was all I could do to avoid breaking down into anxious hysterics, and so Zooey and Steven were getting the full force of it.

Daniel had been gone an hour, and Bass Hall had exploded into speculation about what he'd done and what would become of him. Most kids linked his summons to the reported theft right away, and some truly insidious commentary followed, right on cue.

"He *is* from Chicago."

"There was always something *about* him . . ."

"They just can't help themselves, can they?"

Having heard enough, I'd grabbed Zooey and Steven and dragged them to my room for an interrogation of my own.

"Leo, it would not make logical sense for us to do so," Steven said. "If we gave him up, he could give us up."

"Well, maybe one of you cut a deal," I said, looking directly at Zooey.

"How dare you?" Zooey spat. "You really think we would do that?"

"I don't know what to think about you, Zooey."

"And what is that supposed to mean?"

"Well, you are full of surprises lately. You fall off the face of the earth after what happened, you emerge with a *girlfriend*, then won't so much as look at us all week. I mean, this is the most we've spoken since the day we all got back, and it's only because we're in deep shit."

"Yeah, deep shit that YOU roped me in to! But sure, I must be the bad guy because I've chosen to separate myself from that, from *you*. It couldn't possibly be because you're ruining my fucking life."

There was a knock at the door.

We stood still, poised like a pack of animals on the hunt.

"Into the closet," I whispered. "I'll laugh about the symbolism later."

Zooey shot me a dirty look but complied, filing into my closet with Steven.

I opened the door. It was Theo Breckenridge, the one-student secret police of the Blackfriars main office. I knew then that I was in for it, but I managed a smile.

"Good evening, Breckenridge, you're looking well. Can I help you with something?"

"You'll need to come with me, Breyer. To see Headmaster Westcott."

I swallowed.

"To see the HEADMASTER?" I repeated, loud enough for Zooey and Steven to hear from their hiding place. "My pleasure."

When we arrived at the common building and made our way back toward Westcott's office, I passed Daniel, who was sitting next to Mrs. Wesley at her desk, on the phone, looking fraught. I only heard him say, "But, Dad—" before Westcott's door closed and I couldn't make out any more. It was all I needed to hear, though. We were finished.

I sat at the desk across from the headmaster, a Polaroid I barely remembered having taken laid out before me.

God, I looked good that night, I thought.

"Mister Breyer," Westcott said. "I've just been speaking with your . . . roommate."

Something about the way he'd said that told me what he and Daniel had been talking about.

"And while he can't seem to conjure up any recollection of this photograph or the identity of the person he's posing with, even in the face of expulsion . . ."

Expulsion. Christ, I'm so sorry, Daniel.

"I have a sinking feeling that you, Mister Breyer, can't have been far from the lens. Given your *relationship.* I already know for certain you were a member of this illicit club. I have the guest book with your own signature. Alongside the signatures of all of your friends."

"Friends is a strong word, sir. Those queens are mostly intolera—"

"ENOUGH," he barked. "I am not in the mood for any cheek, Mister Breyer, I'm really not."

"Fair enough, sir," I said, sweet as could be. "So, tell me, if you already know I was part of the society, why does it matter who it is in the photo? Why not just get on with whatever fate awaits me?"

He sat back in his chair, seeming to calculate his next move.

"I'm not so much interested in the person in the photo. I'm more concerned with what he's holding."

I peered at the Polaroid.

Oh shit.

I was holding that damned incense burner from Ouroboros. I'd pulled it out of our stash of occult stuff to use as a prop for my look. Of course he'd recognize it.

"Do you know what that object is?" he asked, pointing to the picture.

". . . An ashtray?"

"A *thurible,*" he said. "A kind of incense burner, for rituals religious and otherwise."

"You don't say."

"Curious, right?"

We were both dancing around the truth, though I wasn't sure who was leading.

"Curious because I had to wonder where a student might procure such a . . . specific prop for one's Halloween costume in our lonely neck of Massachusetts. So I did a bit of digging. Were you aware that there is an occult store right in downtown Adders Lair? A store called Ouroboros?"

Yes.

"No! How odd."

"Indeed. It just so happens they sell the exact model. Along with all manner of curios, herbs, and supplies used for occult workings."

Bold move, Westcott, I thought.

"The girl there confirmed for me that such an item . . . as well as *other* suspicious materials, were purchased from her by Blackfriars students. However, when I pressed her for details about those students, her memory was suddenly less reliable."

"You don't say."

Thanks, Oona, I thought.

However, I knew that he didn't need Oona to confirm to him that I was one of those students. He wouldn't be taking the interrogation all the way to black magic if he wasn't certain. Still, he didn't have anything concrete to pin on me directly. I knew that my next few moves were critical.

"Well, it seems to me, sir, that whoever this is wanted to add a touch of *realness* to their costume and thought enough to check that store. Good drag is all about the details, you know."

"I'm sure I *don't* know what makes good 'drag,' Mister Breyer, but you want to know what I *do* know?"

"Desperately," I said.

"I know that your *father* would have known where to get such an item. And how to use it."

I blinked my eyes wide.

I thought I was prepared for any twist in our conversation, but I never saw a mention of my father coming.

"And so, I can't help but suspect that it's *you* in the wig and dress, holding the item in question."

My face was still as Lake Placid, even as my heart and stomach were churning like Niagara Falls.

"I never met my father," I said. "He's been dead since I was a baby."

Westcott's brow furrowed curiously, but he didn't respond.

"So frankly, sir, I don't know what any of this . . . occult business has to do with me and a drag party. Unless you're worried about ghosts or witches or both."

He seemed to look deep into my soul as he clenched his jaw and gathered his thoughts.

"I'll be plain," he said. "I think you know where my book is. I think you've used it for terrible purposes and now you're in over your head. And you can either tell me where it is this instant, or you and all of your friends will be expelled."

Checkmate, I thought. He'd given up too early. Now I knew everything I needed to know.

"Sir . . ." I said, performing the utmost confusion and alarm. Like I've said, I was always a natural actress. "I have absolutely no idea what *book* you're talking about with such furor. But it seems to me that whatever it is you've lost, you're willing to go to extremes to get it back. Like, breaching the subject of the *occult* to a student at a simple disciplinary meeting. I mean, to be honest, sir, that's just. Fucking. Crazy."

What did I have to lose? I knew I wasn't getting out of this without being expelled. I may as well enjoy it.

"It tells me a couple of things. One, even if you do have some kind of *magical power*, you're obviously neutered and feckless without said *book* if you need to sit here and beg me for it like a child."

"MISTER BREY—"

"SECOND," I shouted over him, "and this is the really important bit: Your desperation makes me think that as much trouble as I'm in for having my name on the official faggot registry of Blackfriars, you seem to be in a world more trouble should you fail to produce your lost item to whatever society has *your* name in its guest book."

I saw in his wounded expression that I was bang on. Whoever the Oldfellows were, they didn't yet know his book was missing, and he was very, very scared of them.

"So if we're quite finished with all of that esoteric hooey, do you want to call my mother to break the news, or shall I?"

ZOOEY

They're still not back.

It was ten o'clock and neither Leo nor Daniel had come to knock on my door to tell me what had gone down with Westcott. Left unchecked, my anxiety festered into paranoia.

I walked down to their room to check for signs of life. I knocked to no answer. I paced back to Steven's room, where he groggily answered the door.

"I have heard no sign of them. I suspect they would contact you before me anyway."

I needed to move, to work off this sickly, dizzying adrenaline that was pumping through my veins, but now the grounds were being watched by night. I returned to my room, lay down on the bed, and screamed into my pillow.

Why hadn't I run out of the room when they told me about the book?

Hell, why hadn't I run out of the room at the first Vicious Circle party?

Westcott was right, I'm vulnerable. Easily manipulated.

This is all Leo's fault, that fucking faggot.

I should kill him.

The monster was behind my eyes again. I wrenched them open.

Then I cried.

It was all stacking, all a mess, all connected. If my mom hadn't gotten sick, I wouldn't have sought comfort with Mr. B back at Hansard, wouldn't have been expelled, wouldn't have come here, met these people, joined their shameful club, participated in murderous rituals. Maybe Mal and I would have started dating sooner. Maybe I never would have even explored my deviancy. I could have been back in New York, the right girl on my arm, no beast behind my eyes. I could have been normal.

If praying had ever worked for me, I would have prayed. The monster listened, though. So I spoke to him instead.

"Let me survive this. Get me away from this life, these guys. I want to have this girlfriend, do my work, make normal friends. Maybe join track. Just let me survive this. Let me . . ."

❖

The next thing I knew, my alarm was going off.

Six thirty A.M. Time to get up and get to class.

I'd passed out in my clothes on top of the covers and slept through the night.

They must have come by late, I thought. *I must have missed them.*

Surely I'd find Leo and Daniel at breakfast, where they would catch me up.

I grabbed my dopp kit and towel and opened my door to head for the showers. There was a note pinned to my door. For a moment, I thought it must be news from one of the guys. Then, I noticed the official-looking penmanship on the envelope addressed to "MR. ZACHARY ORSON."

I opened it.

12/09/91

Mr. Orson,

You are requested to report to the main office for a disciplinary inquiry with Headmaster Westcott this evening at 5:00 p.m. Please be prompt.

Sincerely,
The Blackfriars School Administration.

I held the note in my hands, frozen to the spot.

Even the damn monster had abandoned me.

I heard some boys coming down the hall, heading for their own morning routine, and I stashed the letter in my pocket like I had been caught with a dirty magazine. I wondered how many had already seen it.

I ran down the stairs to Leo and Daniel's floor, to their door, and stopped cold.

The door was propped open by a doorstop, so I could see before I even stepped inside that all trace of either of them had been wiped clean.

I stepped in and walked around the bare little room, dazed. All of Leo's scarves and posters, Daniel's cork board above the desk, all of their books, all of their bedding, gone. I opened the closet in which I'd hidden just last night to find it empty of any coats or blazers.

"It's fucked, right?" came a voice from behind me.

I turned to see Humphrey standing, ashen, in the doorway.

"You didn't even get to say goodbye. I only saw them off because as prefect, I had to help with the move out. All very hasty. They put Daniel on the first flight out, and Leo's mom came to pick him up, I think around two A.M.? We didn't really get to have any words about it because Westcott, Wesley, and the dean of students were there. I haven't known too many kids to get expelled, but they usually give them a day or two to move out. This way, under the cover of night? It seems cruel. Pointed."

He came in and sat down on Daniel's bare mattress with a sigh.

"I assume you got one of these," he said, producing his note.

"Yeah," I whispered. "What time—"

"I'm one of the first up. Eight A.M. sharp."

"Oh . . . well, maybe it won't be—"

"I was supposed to go to Harvard, get married, run for office. I wonder what I'll do now?"

"You can still do those things."

"Oh, *Orson*," he said, looking up at me with pity in his eyes. "Just being a *member* of a club like this is enough to ruin anyone. I'm the goddamn president."

"Well . . ." I knew he was right.

He laughed, in spite of the moment. "Hey, at least I held office that one time! Well, I'd better go get some breakfast. Wouldn't want to watch my life fall apart on an empty stomach."

He got up and headed back to the door.

"It was nice knowing you, Orson," he said. "I wish you'd have come to that after-party some time. You know, you're cuter than you realize."

Then he was gone, and I finally had the space to panic properly. I began to hyperventilate as reality set in.

Leo and Daniel were expelled and already gone; God knows where to.

Humphrey had a meeting early in the morning, and mine was scheduled for the end of the day. That must mean that Westcott had made time to interview every single VC member. We were all toast.

I would be expelled, too. It had been hard enough to get into Blackfriars after the scandal at Hansard, and I'd only lasted a semester. There wasn't a prep in America that would take me now. I'd be at public. God, what would I tell Mallory? What would I tell my *father*?

But then, as I shut my eyes tight to catch my breath, I saw my monster there, in whatever part of my mind he'd come to occupy, at the ready.

I knew that defeat wasn't the only option.

We still had the book.

◆

I practically pounded on Steven's door.

"Hi," he greeted me, vacant. His voice was flat as ever but his eyes looked bleary, like he'd been crying. I'd never seen him emotional in any way, let alone reduced to tears, but I didn't have time for that.

"I'm sure you heard about Daniel and Leo," I said.

"I went to find them when I got my note. Very . . . unusual. The way they were sent away. I suspect Westcott didn't want them warning anyone else."

"What time is your appointment?"

"Four P.M.," he said.

"Just before mine," I said. "Humphrey's is happening now."

"They must be interviewing everyone in the VC, going by the list in the guest book," he said. "Seniors first, then down the classes. Yours was the last name added."

He might be right.

"So that means we have some time," I said.

"We have class."

"Oh, fuck CLASS!" I realized I was shouting. I composed myself and continued in a whisper. "Is your roommate in?"

"Gone to breakfast."

"Can I come in, please?"

"Um. Sure."

I stepped inside. Steven's roommate's side looked like that of a normal student: clothes strewn about haphazardly, posters on the walls, stacks of papers and half-drunk cans of Coke on the desk, bed left unmade. Steven's side, on the other hand, was so pristinely tidy, you'd think he'd been expelled overnight, too.

I sat on the bed.

"Steven, we can stop this, we just have to act *now.*"

"What do you mean?"

"We have to use the book," I said.

His face darkened.

"Use it for what?"

"Well, you would know better than me," I said. "I mean, who knows, maybe there's a spell to reverse time or change someone's mind or something."

"I do not think there are such spells—"

"But we *do* know one spell that will work," I said.

He looked at me, stone-faced.

". . . Which is?"

"The same we used on Godfrey," I said.

He drew in breath, but I didn't let him argue.

"I mean, we obviously don't have the storm," I said, "but I think we could take him out. Like, if we're specific about it, while we're doing it. Send a . . . like, a heart attack or a stroke or something. Something that seems perfectly natural. He's old. He looked like shit at the big meeting; everyone saw that. Hell, he was probably gonna stroke out on his own anyway, with the stress and everything. I mean, for all we know, he's actually like a thousand years old and the book was keeping him alive. Anyway . . ."

I was spinning. My heart was pounding out of my chest and my thoughts were moving too fast to keep up with. Still, I knew what needed to happen. (I just wasn't clever enough in this moment to put it to Steven gracefully.)

"Anyway, we just give him a little shove to make it happen *today*. As soon as possible. Preferably before more guys are expelled but definitely before our meetings."

"So . . ." Steven's eyes narrowed, as if he was doing advanced calculus in the back of his mind as he spoke to me. "You want to kill Headmaster Westcott to avoid expulsion?"

"Well, not only *that*," I said. "The book is his! I mean, he's part of this Oldfellows thing, whatever it is. He's probably pure evil. We have to stop him from . . . whatever he's doing with that thing. We're the good guys!"

"It seems to me that the good guys in stories do not have to *kill* people," he said. "Typically, the bad guys are the ones killing people."

"Oh CHRIST, Hillman," I hissed. "Did you not hear what I—we'd be cutting off the snake at its head. For the good of the world. If that *also* means we get to avoid total ruin ourselves, then I don't think that's so bad, either. But the main thing is, Westcott is a dark, shadowy goddamn wizard, and we have to take him out."

"I don't want to kill anyone else," he said, plainly. "If you want to use the book, be my guest. You know where it is hidden."

I felt churning black rage bubbling up inside of me, threatening to spill forth at any moment. I bit my lip and drew in a long breath.

"You know very well that I can't read that thing without you. And . . . and, god, what is this sudden fucking moral high horse you're on?"

I stood and paced.

"I mean, you're a goddamn ROBOT every other day of your life, devoid of any spine, until the exact moment I need you. Then, THEN, he's Mother Teresa. Well, you know what, Hillman, you *owe me this*. You know that? You translated every word we uttered from that book. You could have stopped this at any time. But you didn't, and you know why I think you didn't? Because this was the only way you'd ever have any fucking friends."

His face didn't change, but it didn't need to. Some venom is so strong, you know it will be lethal, even if the beast doesn't go down right away.

Hiss, hiss.

"You know I'm right. You wanted to hang out with Leo and Daniel and so you kept on with it. And I *know* you never liked me. I know I got in the way of whatever little trio you thought you were a part of, and I'm sorry about that, but it really isn't my problem. Or it shouldn't be, but your problem became *my* problem when you had me read from that book, read words YOU translated, so now it's time to finish what you fuckin' started. You got me into this and now you're gonna help me get out. If you want friends, Steven, you have to actually be a friend."

And though his face hadn't moved a centimeter in the whole time I berated him, a single tear now streaked down his face to where it dropped off his chin. It was enough of a shock to stop my tirade. He bowed his head to wipe it away.

We sat in silence.

Then he raised his eyes to look at me and said, "Go to class. We don't want to arouse further suspicion, especially if another party tries to investigate us later. Meet me at the shed in the woods, right after last bell. Three o'clock. I'll bring the other materials. We won't be bothered there, and the book is already waiting. We'll be done before our appointments. Then, we can decide what to do next."

I sighed, relieved. Safe. I put my hand on his shoulder.

"Thank you, Steven," I said. "I know it's . . . unpleasant. But it's for the best. And it will be over soon and then we can figure out how to move forward."

I stood and walked to the door.

"Sorry," I said. "If I got a little heated. This is all just so big. Too big. But we're almost out of it. I'll see you at three."

"See you soon," he said.

❖

I wish I could tell you more about the lead up to three o'clock on December ninth, Nineteen Ninety-One, and the twenty-four hours that followed. I wish I knew more. I wish Steven could have told me then or could tell me now.

Here's what I do know.

I walked through the day like a zombie, without a word from any professor or a look from any gossiping student penetrating the roaring static between my ears. I did notice a few things, though: Daniel's empty seat in Latin. How quiet lunch was on my own without Leo rambling on with gossip. I saw Richardson walking back toward Bass in hysterics. I saw Barton and Reinhardt whispering conspiratorially in the quad. I saw Matthew Dell being escorted off the premises with a fist raised. I saw Humphrey carrying suitcases toward the main drive.

I knew my Vicious Circle brothers were dropping like flies, but I knew we couldn't help them. We didn't have time for justice, only for revenge. But soon, at least Steven and I would be safe.

After the final bell rang at two forty-five, I made for the woods as fast as I could without drawing attention to myself. I arrived at the shed, looking left and right for Steven. No sign of him yet. I waited.

The afternoon sunlight streamed down through the leafless trees around me, intensely amber. The days were getting so short.

I checked my watch.

Three o'clock arrived and passed.

I waited.

By three fifteen, I'd begun to get nervous. I looked around, frantically.

That's when I noticed that the door of the shed was hanging slightly ajar. I opened it.

There was no sign of Steven.

A terrible thought occurred to me.

I opened the cabinet at the back of the shed and rifled through the tarps, but instead of the Book of Brothers, I found a manilla envelope with my name scrawled across the front.

No, I thought, tearing open the envelope.

There was a little brown bottle. It was the exact one that Leo had dabbed himself with the night he talked our way into the movie. It was now empty.

There was also a brief, scratchy note paper clipped to a tattered piece of parchment.

It read:

Dear Zooey,

You said some things earlier that made me certain of what I must do.

Chiefly, you said that it is my responsibility to get you out of this, and I believe you are right about that. However, I think you and I will have different ideas about what that means. And what I need to get you out of.

You see, you said some harsh things in a tone of voice that I do not recognize to be yours. I do not believe you are a harsh person. I believe you are a very gentle person who has been overtaken by something harsh. Something I had a hand in unleashing upon you.

I do not believe that your proposed solution to the problem at hand will solve the larger problem in which you have found yourself. I believe that problem can only be solved by the page of the book I have torn out and attached here. Please contact me at my home as soon as you feel safe to do so, and we will make a plan about how and when to perform this one last work.

As for your interview, say nothing about the book. You did not know a thing about it. You do not know me at all. I will make certain Westcott believes those things. All you have to do is go along with it.

You also said that I needed to be a friend. I cannot think of a better way to show my loyalty than the step I am about to take.

I do hope we can be real friends when all of this is over.

Until then,
Steven Hillman

I examined the parchment attached to the note. It was a single page from the Book of Brothers, simpler than the others I'd seen, with just a few spare paragraphs of handwritten Latin text.

My eyes widened and my breath quickened.

I realized what he was going to do, but I had no idea how to stop him.

❖

I know, based on the accounts of VC boys waiting in Mrs. Wesley's office for their own audience with Westcott, that Steven had strode in, pushing past the queue, holding some black leather book aloft in his hands defiantly.

I know he was in that office for over an hour.

I know that the dean of students and school security were called. They arrived at the office, and a few minutes later, Steven was taken out in their custody.

I know that whatever he said in there was enough to convince Westcott that he was the sole culprit. The empty bottle in the envelope suggests that he used the last of the Oil of Persuasion. It was definitely effective. I know this, because when I finally had my interrogation with Westcott that evening, about ninety minutes later than my scheduled time, he didn't ask about it at all.

He sat across the desk from me, looking exhausted but somehow at peace.

"Mister Orson, I'll be brief, as it's been a very long day. Yours is the last name on this list I've recovered from the secret club that's been operating under my nose; a club that seemed to harbor unauthorized gatherings, misuse of campus spaces, drinking, smoking, and . . . immoral conduct. You have also been named by students previously interviewed as present at its gatherings. What do you have to say for yourself?"

I took a deep breath. I knew my entire future hung in the balance.

"I'd just like to say that you were right, sir."

It wasn't the response he was expecting.

"What's that?" he asked.

"When we last spoke, after Ryan Godfrey spread the story about my scandal at Hansard, you said that I was a vulnerable case. Easily manipulated. And you were right. I was brought to that club by Daniel Preston, who I assumed to be a good role model. After all, it was you yourself who encouraged me to befriend him, was it not?"

Westcott leaned forward in his chair.

"I wasn't aware of what kind of . . . gathering it was. I only wanted to make friends, sir. To belong to something. I should have disengaged as soon as I learned the truth about the club, but . . . You were *right*. I was manipulated. And now it could mean the end of my academic career here, my future ambitions, my relationship—"

"Relationship?"

"My girlfriend, sir. Her name is Mallory Gellar. Of the New York Gellars. Her father is working on the Eldridge presidential campaign?"

Westcott raised his eyebrows.

"I know the Gellars well," he said. "And I wouldn't think a sophomore would be up on the presidential primaries this far out. Especially on such a fringe candidate. You know it is very rare to primary an incumbent in one's own party."

"I had the pleasure of hearing him speak, sir. At a fundraising event the Gellars threw for him during our leave. Fascinating stuff."

"So, your political views are in alignment with his?"

Was that a smile on his face? I saw my opening and ran toward it.

"I loved what he had to say about individualism," I said. "We have to each be our personal best before we can come together to make the world better. So many people just grift off the success of other hardworking people. They take advantage. I guess . . . like I was taken advantage of. So, I need to learn to be better. Work on myself before I can try to come together with others. I think if I'd had stronger personal character, I'd have seen through the sordid affair at the pub much faster. But you nailed it on the head, sir. I came to Blackfriars in a sorry state. I only hope I don't have to leave it before I have the opportunity to complete the work I need to do to be the best man I can be."

Westcott relaxed back in his chair and looked me up and down. He looked impressed.

"It's late," he said, looking at the wooden clock on the desk. "I'll bet you're in need of dinner and rest."

"It has been stressful today, sir, knowing I had this appointment."

"Well, I must say, Mister Orson, I expected it to go differently. I have actually very much enjoyed talking to you."

It sounded like he was wrapping this up. And still no talk of punishment. Was I in the clear?

"I enjoyed it as well, sir."

"Have a good evening, Mister Orson. We'll speak again about Representative Eldridge soon, I hope."

"So . . ." *Dare I ask?* "Am I being expelled, sir?"

He sighed and rubbed his eyes with two pinched fingers.

"I think it's far too late in the day to consider all the factors at play here and level punishment with a clear mind. But my gut tells me that you are speaking from the heart. You already seem so different from that first time we spoke, just a few weeks ago. More . . . mature. Sure of yourself. I believe Blackfriars is taking hold of you, Zooey, in just the way the founders intended."

"Thank you, sir," I said. "And actually? I'm going by Zach now."

Fourteen boys were quietly expelled from Blackfriars School that day. Somehow, this massive scandal stayed out of the papers, local or national.

I would have been the fifteenth, if not for whatever I'd said to save myself.

Or, whatever work my monster had done in the place such work happens.

Or, most likely, if it hadn't been for the sacrifice of Steven Hillman, taking the fall for us all and returning the book.

I wish, will forever wish, that I could thank him. That I could repay him for that.

I wish we could have had a real friendship, like he'd asked for.

Sadly, that could never come to pass, as three days later, while eating my breakfast alone at a drafty table in the Dining Hall, frost covering the arched window beside me, I first heard the news trickling through the tables of whispering students.

Steven Hillman was dead.

PART THREE

CHAPTER TWELVE

LEO

Here's what I know about being invisible.

For me, the natural belle of every ball, a legendary raconteur with a rapier wit and dagger-sharp tongue, becoming invisible was a vacation from the demands of being my fabulous self. It's what I wanted.

That's what I told myself anyway.

In actuality, it was the only thing I could do to avoid being beaten and harassed by any number of straight boys who had what I *really* wanted. Everyone thinks they want to stand out from the crowd, but then you learn that there are good ways to stand out and bad ways to stand out. Dangerous ways. I might not want to be like everyone else, but sue me if I want to be myself and be safe at the same time.

Being invisible, while safe, was also existentially lonely. I'd taken for granted simple things like being greeted when entering a room, being waved over to a table at lunch, even being called on in class without making myself known first. All of these things seemed inconsequential before I became invisible, but it turns out they add up to something much more. They remind you that you exist.

If I was in a bad mood and didn't feel like actively inserting myself into conversations, or approaching Zooey at lunch, or raising my hand in class, I could go an entire day without speaking to a single soul. Without even being looked at. I can't imagine the state of my mental health, my sense of existence, if that had been every day, and if it hadn't been my choice.

That is to say, I can't imagine what it must have been like to be Steven Hillman.

The news came a few days after my expulsion, when my mom came into my room just as I was getting ready to get to bed.

"Leo, there's a call for you. From Blackfriars."

It was Friday the thirteenth, so the timing was right enough for some more bad luck.

At first, I thought Westcott had called back with some new, scandalous detail about me he'd learned in his questioning, just to upset my mother. I think he'd been disappointed when she'd come to pick me up and was far more furious that they were making her come collect me in the dead of the night than she was that I'd been expelled. He thought he'd revealed my deep dark secret to her and that he could revel in watching our relationship implode. On the contrary, when she'd arrived at the main office late that night, she wrapped her arms around me, jingling her bracelets, before pouncing on Westcott and Wesley, calling them bigots and cops.

"Tell Westcott that whatever he has to say, I'm not—"

"No, honey, it's a student."

The hairs on the back of my neck stood on end.

Daniel? I hoped.

❖

I'd called his house the day after he would have landed back in California. His father picked up.

"Preston residence."

"Hello, sir, I'm wondering if I can speak to Daniel?"

There was a long pause.

"Hello? I said I'd like to speak with Daniel? This is his . . . a friend. I wanted to check on—"

"Daniel can't talk," he said curtly.

"Oh," I said. "Well, can you please let him know that Leo called and—"

"No, I can*not*," he said.

"Sorry, sir?" I thought I'd misheard him.

"I said, son, that I cannot let him know you called."

". . . Why not, sir?"

"Because Daniel doesn't live here anymore."

I shut my eyes. It was even worse than I'd expected. I thought about those early nights in our dorm, holding each other, talking about what would happen if his dad found out about us, about *him*.

I tried to play it cool.

"Oh . . . well, might I ask where I can reach him?"

His father let out an incredulous little snort.

"Look, kid, if you are who I think you are, you're the last person Daniel ought to be talking to. Leave him be. And don't call here anymore."

He hung up abruptly.

I waited for Daniel to call back and explain the whole thing. It wasn't like him to not be in touch, especially after what we'd been through. I waited three days.

❖

So I thought, *maybe this is him*, as I took the phone from my mom. Maybe he hadn't been expelled after all, had only had a falling out with his dad and was calling from the school to tell me everything that had happened.

"Daniel?!" I said into the receiver.

". . . No," Zooey said on the other end of the line. "It's me."

I closed my eyes and sighed bitterly.

Son of a bitch, I thought. *Still there. He got out of it.*

"And . . . you're calling from Blackfriars?" I was boiling but trying to keep the lid on the pot until I knew more. "So, you're not expelled?"

"Oh . . . no. I mean, not yet, anyway."

"Who else survived the chop?"

"Leo, I don't have much time."

"WHO?" I shouted.

"Only me, OK? Only me."

If I could have leaped through the receiver to strangle him, I would have.

"Now listen—"

"Did you name names?" I interrupted. "Betray us about the book? Or did you *use* it? Some dark pact with whatever that thing is to keep you—"

"Leo, LISTEN to me," he whispered, urgently. "Have you heard about Steven?"

Something about the way he said that told me before I had to ask. Still, I asked, cautiously, "What about Steven?"

He didn't answer. I thought for a moment that he'd hung up, but I could hear him breathing, sniffling.

"Zooey?"

"He's dead."

My mom must have sensed something deeply wrong passing between our telephone and Blackfriars, because she poked her head out from her room on the other side of the trailer and began to mouth to me, asking if I was OK. I waved her off and turned away from her prying eyes.

"I . . . *what*?"

"I don't know much, just what I've been hearing around Bass. They say he dropped dead as soon as he got home and—"

His voice clipped off suddenly, like he was holding back tears.

I was too stunned to do anything except to think, *No. No, that's not right. Something isn't right.*

I kept repeating that thought over and over as Zooey regained composure.

"Leo," he said, "there's more. He turned himself in, with the book. Handed it right over to Westcott himself, but first . . . he left me a note."

He *left* a note.

Steven *left* something.

Left it behind.

Reality was dawning on me with each passing second. Steven was gone. There was a note left behind, but Steven was gone.

"What . . . does it say?" I asked.

"Wait," Zooey said.

I heard the distant, muffled sounds of some kids talking and Zooey rattling off some excuse like, "Only a minute . . . girlfriend . . . New York . . ."

After a few beats of quiet, he sighed.

"OK, sorry. Well for one, the note said not to say anything to Westcott about the book when I went for my interview. He also left the empty bottle of . . . whatever you smeared on yourself to talk your way into that movie. I think he must have used what was left to convince Westcott that it was all him. So you see?"

"Westcott took him out."

"I mean, it's horrible to imagine, but what are the odds otherwise? If he'd successfully convinced Westcott that he was acting alone with the book, then Westcott would assume that his secret would die with Steven. And once he got the book back . . ."

I caught a glimpse of myself in the mirror above the couch and it was like I was looking at a still from a movie. This person, hunched over a phone, face drained of blood, whispering about a dark conspiracy—it couldn't possibly be me, could it? My life had been surreal for a while now, but the fact that it had led me here was still almost inconceivable.

"So . . . what do we do?" I asked.

"I don't know," Zooey said. "I don't think there's much we can do."

"Well, we have to do something!" I was shouting now. "And with Steven gone, Daniel missing, and me stuck in the goddamn trailer park, seems like you're the only one who can!"

"I tried calling Daniel, too," he said. "Do you have any idea where he . . . ?"

"No," I said. "He'll call. I know he will."

"Yeah," Zooey said. "I just . . ."

He hesitated.

"Leo, if I'm right about what I think happened to Steven . . . I just think we have to lay low for a while. Westcott has the book, he thinks he . . . he thinks it's over. And I dunno, this just all seems too big. Too big to fight. I wish you hadn't gotten expelled, I really do, but at least you're alive. I think we'd be smart to just let it go."

I couldn't believe what I was hearing. I took a deep breath, slowly as I could, to keep from screaming.

"You know, that's *really* easy for YOU to say, Zooey," I said. "Some of us are ruined, others are missing, others are *dead*. But you, you're just fine. So forgive me if I don't share your desire to just let sleeping dogs lie."

There was just the sound of his breathing. Then, a knocking.

"I have to go," he said. "People are waiting. I just . . . wanted you to hear it from me. And Leo, I'm sorry. He didn't deserve . . . I'm sorry."

There was a click.

"Zooey?" I asked. "ZOOEY?!"

But he was gone.

I slammed the receiver down hard and put my face in my hands.

◆

I got details about Steven slowly in the days that followed from the guys who began calling each other in the wake of our expulsions. Matthew Dell knew Steven's sister from a camp they both worked summers at, and she'd called him for comfort—and answers—in the wake of the death. Dell shared what he knew with Frank Costa, who told Humphrey Meier, who told me.

Apparently, Steven was found dead in his room the morning after his arrival home. The autopsy pointed to a freak brain aneurysm; lights out, in his sleep. Such things are rare but do happen, even to young people.

Despite the tragedy of such a death, unlike Ryan Godfrey's much-mourned passing, Steven got no headlines, no evening news segments, not even any classes cancelled.

I wondered if the straight kids at school would even care to spread the gossip. If they even knew who he was.

I thought about being invisible.

I asked the others about Daniel. No one had heard a thing.

I grew more and more worried. Soon I was desperate.

❖

I took a bus to Adders Lair to see Oona. If I couldn't find Daniel by phone, maybe I could find him by magic.

"Prepster!" she said, when she saw me. "Long time no see! Some old dude came here asking after you, but don't worry, I covered for you. What the hell is going on? You look stressed."

"I need to find someone who's missing," I said to her.

"Have you tried calling the cops?"

"No, it's not like that . . . can you help me? With a . . . spell or something?"

She raised her darkly penciled eyebrows.

"I'd have thought, given the kind of work you guys were doing before, that you had spells of your own."

"My situation has changed," I said. "Can you help or not?"

"Look," she said, "I don't know what system you were involved with before, but I'm just a Hecatean Wiccan. I can dress a candle for you, for his safe return?"

". . . A candle?"

"Or if you're not turned off by Catholic folk magic, you could try petitioning Saint Anthony? I think? Is he the 'lost things' guy?"

"Wait, so you don't have, like, a book with a spell that can bring a lost person home? You have hundreds of books in here."

"Dude, this isn't the movies. Real magic is like praying. Magic isn't *magic.*"

That's when I learned that what the Book of Brothers was capable of was profoundly different from what we could expect of even a professional "witch."

I bought the candle anyway, though. I lit it every night until it burned down to nothing.

Daniel remained a mystery.

As for Zooey, we wouldn't speak again until just after Christmas, when, much to my chagrin, I needed him.

Santa had come and gone, leaving a haul of Ralph Lauren polos and slacks for me (gently used) and a bottle of Chanel No. 5 for Mom (gently stolen, by yours truly).

Now, in the slushy afterglow of all that merriment, my mom was busy working double shifts at the nail salon to take advantage of all of the ladies preparing for New Year's parties, while I was spending my last days of freedom oscillating between worry for Daniel, anger at

Zooey, and grief for Steven. I was to start at the public school down the road on Monday the sixth of January, which gave me exactly one week to prepare myself spiritually for whatever horrors awaited me there.

The morning of December thirtieth was bright and frigid. I sipped coffee, practically hugging the space heater that hummed noisily at the center of the living-room-themed section of our trailer. Meanwhile, my mom was already in a full face of makeup and chandelier earrings, even though it was nine in the morning.

"OK hon, straight after work, I'm going on my big date," she said, spritzing her hair with ever more Aqua Net. "So don't wait up!" She turned from the mirror to shoot me a sly little wink and I feigned a gag.

"Ew, Mom!"

"What?! One of us has to marry a rich man," she said. "And this guy's a business owner. Pools and hot tubs! Your college tuition is riding on this little black dress." She did a little pose, and I had to laugh.

"Spare me the details," I said. "But good luck."

She gave me a jingly kiss on each cheek, donned her smoky old fur, and stepped out of the trailer into the white severity of Massachusetts winter.

I breathed in the peace of a house to myself.

I had a whole agenda planned of crying, picking at a lunch of Kraft Mac and Cheese, and staring at the wall. However, my plans were dashed when our phone rang and rang again insistently until I finally picked up.

"Hello?" I answered, already gathering my defenses for a row with another bill collector.

To my surprise, the woman on the other end said, "Hello sir, I'm with Saint Vincent's Hospital. I'm looking for a Miss . . . Rona Scalfani?"

Hospital? I thought. My first instinct was that Mom was hiding some illness from me. However, the name of the hospital was unfamiliar.

"Sorry," I said. "Saint Vincent's?"

"Yes, in New York? Is this Miss Scalfani's number? It was listed on an old emergency contact for the patient. Well, *she* was listed. The old number didn't work, so I called Information. We don't usually go to such trouble but . . . he's all alone, so I thought I'd try. Is this Rona Scalfani's residence?"

"It is," I said. "But Rona's not home. Can I take a message?"

"Well . . . hmm." She seemed conflicted. "We're not supposed to leave messages like this, but the situation is time sensitive, and we're slammed. I suppose it couldn't do any harm. I'm calling because the patient's condition has changed and we think any kin ought to get here as soon as possible."

"Kin? Doesn't that mean family?"

"I thought it might be a mistake on the form, given the patient's condition, but these days? Nothing shocks me anymore . . . Anyway, yes, it's her husband. Mister Lucas Breyer."

A cloud of vaporous breath escaped my lips, visible in the chilled air of the trailer.

I nearly cracked the receiver, I clutched it so hard.

This year had been so full of death, I should have expected the arrival of ghosts.

". . . That's a mistake," I managed to say. "Lucas Breyer is dead."

"Sorry?"

"He's been dead for fifteen years."

"Oh . . . um . . . one moment . . ."

I heard the sound of papers rustling and a muffled, whispered conversation before she returned.

"Sir . . . there's no mistake. Lucas Breyer, husband of Rona Scalfani, is in poor condition at Saint Vincent's Hospital. If she'd like to see him, we'd recommend she visit, urgently."

I couldn't understand what she couldn't understand.

And then, all at once, *I* understood.

Of course, I'd been lied to. For my entire life.

I thought about the photo of my father with the other Oldfellows. I thought about my mother's dodgy, evolving answers about his fate.

Of course.

The revelation might have completely overwhelmed me with shock if my anger wasn't stronger. I had no idea why my mother would have held such a titanic secret for so long, but the why didn't matter. She kept it.

She kept *him.*

From *me.*

I never believed her about Santa Claus, but I'd believed her about this.

"Sir?"

I realized I was still holding a phone, still on my feet in a trailer in the middle of rural Massachusetts.

". . . Thank you," I said, hanging up.

Then my mind went blank, but my body was moving.

As if piloted by some alien force, I managed to shove a change of clothes and my toothbrush into a backpack, steal the "emergency money" from under my mom's mattress, and scribble a short note, which I left atop his framed photo on her bedside.

I know about dad. I'm going to see him.
And you'll never see me again.

And then I was out of the door, wincing against the late December wind, which cut straight through my flimsy denim jacket. A blizzard couldn't stop me, though, and so I was soon at the county road, thumb out.

Luckily, it wasn't too long before a truck slowed down along the side of the road.

"Where you headed?"

"New York, or as close as I can get."

The driver looked me up and down lasciviously.

"I can get you as far as Boston," he said. "Then you can grab the bus from there."

"Aces," I said, getting in.

◆

We drove a bit though the white blankness, cheesy seventies pop playing on the radio.

"You're awful young to be on the road alone," he said.

I felt his gaze drift over to me, but I kept my eyes fixed on the highway in front of us. I'd barely looked at him at all when I'd gotten in; I had only a vague sense of his gray-bearded shabbiness. "How old are you, anyway?"

"Sixteen," I said, flat.

"Oh, not *too* young then," he said with a treacly giggle. "When I was sixteen, I knew some things."

I didn't respond. Anne Murray sang about love on the radio.

"What's in New York? Some trouble?"

He slid a hand over onto my thigh.

I drew in a sharp breath. Luckily my mind was still functional enough to know what was happening.

"Actually, the trouble is back in that trailer park," I said. "I killed a john who wouldn't follow the rules. Or maybe just 'cuz I felt like it, I don't remember. Anyway, I bashed his skull in with the hammer I've got in my bag. Left him bleeding out onto the linoleum. I haven't seen that much blood since I was a kid. I gotta get out of the state before they start looking for me. And before I kill again."

He took his hand off my thigh.

Anne Murray said everything was gonna be all right.

We rumbled into Boston and said our unceremonious goodbye.

I found my way to the bus station, slapped down my fare, and before I knew it, I was barreling toward New York City.

My mind began to catch up with me on that bus ride south. What I'd done. What I was planning to do. I began to panic. Even though I'd grown up on Broadway LPs and reruns of *Fame*, I'd never been to the city that never sleeps. I wished I was going to see *Miss Saigon* like I'd been dreaming of since I got the cast recording. But this wasn't vacation. Hell, I didn't even know how to find Broadway. I had no idea where I would stay that night, and it was far too cold to stay on the street. I would be dumped into the biggest city in the world with nowhere to go, no one to turn to.

And then I remembered. Not *no one*.

And so, when we pulled into the Port Authority Bus Terminal, I stepped past junkies, prostitutes, businessmen, and tourists to the payphone bank, fished out my address book, plunked in my quarter, and dialed the number for the one person I could turn to in the city of strangers.

"Hello?" Zooey answered.

About a half hour later, a black town car pulled up where I waited on the corner for Forty-Second Street and Eighth Avenue, the back door opened, and out stepped Zooey, hair slick, bundled in a black peacoat with a fur collar, leather messenger bag, and leather gloves.

"*Keanu . . .*" I whispered as he emerged.

He really did look just like Keanu in the last scenes of *My Own Private Idaho*, wrapped in luxury, living the straight life. I guessed that made me River Phoenix, dirty and sad, destined for the gutter. Then I remembered that I couldn't be River because both he and Keanu were actually straight movie stars who could take this costume off when the director called cut, sit back, and wait for the accolades to roll in. This wasn't the movies. I was gay and broke and homeless for real.

"Hey," he said, his breath rising into the air in white wisps.

"Hi."

He was like a stranger now, but he was also the first of the VC boys I'd seen in person since the expulsions. Since Steven. I ran to him and hugged him tightly, silently.

"Oh . . . um—" he protested, surprised, but he didn't force me away, either. We just held there, in the slushy, filthy, pungent scrum of Manhattan, just outside a porn store and beneath a sign for Cartier watches, stuck in a half embrace, a half reunion, a half reconciliation.

Some cabbie yelled "Faggots!" through an open car window as he passed.

Zooey pulled away sharply and said, "Come on. Max will take us."

❖

It wasn't until I got into the back seat of the car, its heater on full blast, that I realized how bitterly cold I'd been.

We snaked through blaring traffic down Eighth Avenue, heading south out of grimy Midtown.

"Thanks again for this," I said. "I know we haven't exactly been in *touch*."

"Come on, what was I gonna do, say no?" he said. "I'm not a bad guy, Leo, I just . . ."

He trailed off. The sounds of traffic took over for a while.

"Are you gonna tell your mom?" he asked. "I mean, she'll be worried about you, but also . . . maybe he wants to see her?"

"I don't know," I said. "Seems to me that I deserve to keep him from her, the way she's kept him from me."

"That's fair," Zooey said.

As we headed south, the skyscrapers and advertisements gave way to row houses and graffiti. We rolled past a huge banner of three cartoonish, yellow, squiggly stick figures surrounded by lines of motion, with red X's over their hearts. It read: IGNORANCE = FEAR, SILENCE = DEATH

Zooey saw me staring.

"That's by Keith Haring," he said. "Heard of him?"

I shook my head.

"Oh, he's the best. He used to do these chalk drawings in the subway; you'd see them all over the city. My mom and I had a game to spot them."

"His Majesty takes the subway?" I said. Zooey scoffed.

"Everyone takes the subway, sometimes. And Mom never liked the car."

"She did NOT," the driver, Max, chuckled from up front.

"But yeah, he did those stick figures everywhere, for free, then he got famous. Hung out with Warhol and designed outfits for Madonna and showed in all the big galleries and stuff. He's gone now . . ."

I noticed the men.

Men everywhere, chatting, strolling, holding hands. Something familiar about their mannerisms. It was like the Vicious Circle, but there was something different, something wrong. The men were thin, haggard-looking. Against the general grayness of the blocks, they looked like ghosts, haunting a graveyard of mausoleums.

"This is Chelsea, by the way," Zooey said. "One of the . . . the gay neighborhoods."

Then I knew what I was seeing.

Of course.

This year had been so full of death, I should have expected the arrival of ghosts.

"We're almost there," Zooey said.

Soon, Max pulled to a stop at the corner of Seventh Avenue and West Eleventh Street.

"Saint Vincent's Hospital," he announced.

It was an ugly collision of two brown buildings of different heights overlooking a banal little park.

"Thanks, Max," Zooey said. "Don't wait. I'm not sure how long we'll be. We'll take a cab."

We walked through its carved stone entrance, and I was hit with that sinister medical smell, like something horrific covered up by chemicals dressed as flowers. We approached the woman at the front desk.

"We're here to see a patient," Zooey said. "Maybe in the ICU?"

"Name please?"

"Breyer," I said. "Lucas Breyer." Saying the name in reference to a living person and not a mythical character from a story made my throat tighten.

She click-clacked her manicure across her keyboard for a few moments and raised her eyebrows.

"Seventh floor," she said.

What is that look in her eye? I wondered.

We got off the elevator at seven and, through a waiting area filled with haunted-looking people from seemingly all walks of life, found our way to another reception desk.

"Name?" the receptionist asked curtly. I'd never seen a man look more exhausted, so I didn't judge him.

"Lucas Breyer."

"Relationship?"

"Um . . ." The moment was upon me. It occurred to me that he might turn me away if I said "son."

"Just a friend."

"Wait."

We returned to the waiting area and took two seats by the door.

A stretcher went by. A skeletal man was strapped down to it, screaming for his mother as he bucked and writhed violently.

I took Zooey's hand. He let me.

Soon, they called for me.

"I'll wait here," Zooey said.

I was met at the doors to the ward by a young Black man in pink floral scrubs with big blue plastic glasses. He smiled, though his eyes were sad.

"Hello, I'm Terrence," he said. "I've been looking after Lucas. He's awake, but he's pretty weak. It's good you're here."

We walked back into the ward, passing room after room. I heard moans and swearing. I smelled shit and vomit. I tried to focus my eyes on the balloons, flowers, and decorations and not on the living dead who lay in the beds.

"He's on a full mask for oxygen now, not just the nasal cannulas, so it may be a little hard for him to talk to you, but please don't let him take it off. He's been doing that."

"Oxygen?"

"It's the pneumonia that's getting him. His lungs are like tissue paper. He'll have to go on a ventilator soon, and well . . . like I said, it's good you're here. We'll get you in a mask, gloves, and gown up here and then he's all yours."

"Sorry," I said, trying my best to focus on the information I was getting while ignoring the horror scene around me. "Does everyone need to wear that stuff in the ICU?"

He turned to me, concerned.

"Kid, this isn't the ICU. This is the AIDS ward."

A shudder coursed through my entire being, like Death itself passing through me on his way to another bed.

The grains of the picture around me all clicked into focus at once: the men, the screaming, the smell, the flowers.

Of course.

I felt that all of this must be some cosmic mistake. This had to be *another* Lucas Breyer who happened to know *another* Rona Scalfani. My Lucas Breyer was dead, just like my Rona Scalfani had always told me, and I was about to make a terrible fool of myself in front of some dying stranger. Still, I put one foot in front of the other, put on the mask, gloves, and gown, and entered the room. And then I saw his face, grotesquely thin and mostly covered by a plastic mask and tubes but still an echo of my own, framed by limp-but-still-fiery-red hair. That's when I knew this Lucas Breyer was, in fact, mine.

"I'll leave you two alone," Terrence said.

The machines around him whirred and hummed, punctuated by the steady beat of a heart monitor.

Lucas looked into my eyes and I looked back, some silent, primal recognition.

Beep . . . beep . . . beep . . .

"My god," he finally said in a guttural, wheezy whisper. "Is this how death comes for you? Sends your younger self? How cruel."

"I . . . no, don't worry," I said. "I'm really here. My name is Leo."

He looked perplexed.

"Sorry, they said a friend was here . . . I didn't think I was losing . . . my mind yet . . . but I'm afraid I don't remember you."

It seemed to take a great deal of effort for him to speak, drawing breath deliberately with each pause and reattacking his sentence with the utmost determination.

"That's just what I told them at the desk," I said. "I didn't want you to turn me away."

"Why . . . would I?"

"Well . . ."

There was nothing wrong with my lungs, so why couldn't I speak? I owed it to him to speak. Owed it to myself. This thing had to be done. I sat in the chair beside the bed. I took a deep breath.

"The hospital called asking for Rona Scalfani. Apparently, she was listed on old medical records of yours as an emergency contact."

"Rona . . ." he whispered.

Beep . . . beep . . . Beep. Beep. Beep.

"She was out, so I took the message. They said her . . . husband . . . was in the hospital and that she should come right away. I said that was impossible, because she'd told me her husband had been dead for fifteen years."

Beep. Beepbeep. Beepbeep. Beepbeep.

"So they checked the name, and sure enough. Lucas Breyer. That's the name she'd always told me."

Beepbeepbeepbeepbeepbeepbeepbeep.

I took down my mask so he could see my full face.

"Sir, my name is Leonard Breyer. Leo. I believe that I'm your son."

BEEPBEEPBEEPBEEPBEEPBEEPBEEPBEEPBEEP.

Terrence came running in, panicked, checking machines.

"Lucas, what's wrong?!"

Lucas started to speak but began coughing violently.

Shit, I thought. *I've killed him.*

"I should go," I said, and stood, heading for the door.

"NO!" Lucas croaked.

I stopped. Lucas held a hand up to Terrence and clutched his chest and closed his eyes. He drew deliberate, meditative breaths, willing his lungs to operate and his heart to slow.

I could finally notice the room around me, filled with cards and flowers, photos taped to the wall of a younger, healthier Lucas Breyer surrounded by friends, mostly men. He was drinking, laughing, posing in front of the Statue of Liberty. *Alive.* A whole life I never knew about.

Beepbeepbeepbeep.

Beep. Beep. Beep. Beep.

Beep . . . Beep . . . Beep.

Eventually, he opened his eyes.

"It's OK . . . Terrence . . . just a little excited," he said.

"Well," Terrence said, looking at me suspiciously, "Just don't get *too* excited."

He left, and we were alone again, my father and me.

"Sit," he said.

I did.

The sun was getting low in the sky over the dusty little park outside his window, turning the hospital room surreally golden. It would be fully down by the time he got through his story.

He told me that he'd met Rona in Cambridge while he was at Harvard, he a quiet student, she a beguiling bartender. They became best friends and maybe, he thought, could be something more. Maybe she could be his last chance at a normal life.

They married young. But then he started to lie and sneak off, seeking the things he desired in men's rooms and public parks. He knew it couldn't last. He left for New York without even a letter, used a different name for years, started a whole new life in Greenwich Village.

"Oh my god," I said, putting the pieces together. We shared a face and a hair color, sure, but what really made us kindred was far deeper.

He'd made himself invisible, too.

"But I swear . . . I didn't know," he said. "When I . . . left. I didn't know she was . . . If I'd known, I could have . . . Oh, Leo . . . I'm so sorry."

He began to cry. So did I.

I took his hand, and we just looked at each other, tears falling. I knew, and I think he knew too, that there was more to say than we could ever say. He'd have run out of breath, out of *time*. So, we said it all with our eyes.

And I understood.

When we'd stopped our crying, I wiped his face.

"You can't blame her . . ." he said. "I left without goodbye . . . never got in touch again . . . To protect her. To disappear."

His face darkened.

"Because it wasn't just . . . the lying, the men. I had to get away from . . . people. Bad people. A group I was born into . . ."

"The Oldfellows," I said.

He looked at me gravely, any misty medicated dreaminess in his eyes evaporating instantly to reveal utter, urgent clarity.

"*How* do you . . ."

"I'm a student at Blackfriars," I said. "I found Westcott's copy of . . . the book."

"The Book of Brothers," he whispered, the way you whisper the name of an enemy.

"Me and some friends . . . we ended up using it. Got ourselves into a lot of trouble. People are dead. My friend is dead."

"My god," he said. "But you're just . . . kids."

"We're going to find a way to stop them," I said. "Avenge our friend. Make it right."

He pulled his oxygen mask down off of his face, reached over to me, grabbed my sweater, and pulled me close.

Beep . . . Beep. Beep. Beep.

"You listen to me," he said. "The Oldfellows . . . are some of the most powerful men . . . in the world. They'll kill you if they find out . . . that you know what they know."

I thought of Steven. *Of course.*

Beepbeepbeepbeepbeepbeepbeep.

"Do you still have . . . the book? Do they know you took it?"

"No."

"Good. Then . . . let it rest. Your friend is dead . . . but you're alive."

He started coughing again, worse than before.

Terrence came running back. He saw the dangling mask and shot me daggers.

"What the *HELL*?!" he shouted as he rushed over to the bed.

"Don't . . . fight them," Lucas choked through coughing. "You will . . . lose!"

"He's desaturating," Terrence said as he wrestled with Lucas to get his mask back on. "Lucas, you're gonna go hypoxic. What did I say about the mask?!" He turned to me and shouted, "Kid, I'm sorry, but you gotta go. He can't take much more of this."

"Yes, sir," I said, and turned to leave.

"Tomorrow," Lucas wheezed. "Come back. I'll tell you . . . what I know . . ."

"Go!" Terrence shouted as he adjusted the machines.

I fled.

Back in the waiting room, Zooey stood when he saw me coming.

"Well?" he asked.

"I have to get out of here," I said, stripping off the protective gear and blowing past him.

He practically chased me to the elevator. My head was starting to pound. I realized I was totally exhausted, yet my heart was racing and I was panting like I'd run a marathon.

"Let's get some air," Zooey said when we arrived at the lobby. He took my shoulders and pulled me out into the arctic night. Once safely drowned out by the sounds of blaring horns, shouting NYU kids, and the roar of the subway steaming up from the grate beneath us, I let out a mournful wail.

All of it. *All of it.*

It came out of me like vomit, but the vomit was a scream.

I thought I'd cried myself dry up in the room, but fresh, hot, dripping sobs came forth. Zooey led me to a bench just beside the door and rubbed my back while I heaved.

A few strangers passed and paid me no mind. This kind of scene must have been common, outside this hospital.

And then, after what felt like ages. I could speak again.

"He's dying of AIDS," I said. "He didn't know about me. He left my mom high and dry when he knew . . . what he was."

"Jesus," Zooey whispered.

"And to protect her from the Oldfellows," I said. "He said to come back tomorrow and he'll give me more information. It sounds like they're . . . big. He said we can't stop them."

Zooey let out a sigh of white clouds, looked up into the buzzing yellow streetlight, and said, "Let's go somewhere and get warm. There's something I need to tell you."

❖

We walked a few blocks south to where a neon sign announced the Waverly Diner.

We sat and ordered coffee and pie.

I felt my bones begin to defrost and my head begin to clear.

"So . . ." Zooey began. "I didn't tell you everything about the note Steven left behind."

"Oh? Why?"

"I dunno, I guess I just wanted to be done with it. But I couldn't stop thinking about it. I actually grabbed it when you called, took it with me. So I could show you."

He pulled his bag around and reached inside to find a file folder.

"Are you . . . prepared to see this?" he asked.

"Why not?" I said. "Ready as I'll ever be."

He opened the file folder to reveal Steven's handwritten note. Seeing his scribbles seemed to summon him into my mind's eye. I was struck instantly with a clear image of his height, his glasses, his gait.

I missed him.

I read the note and turned it over to look at the thing Zooey had kept hidden from me: a torn page from the Book of Brothers.

"Christ," I said. "This thing still gives me the creeps."

"Tell me about it," Zooey said. "Sometimes it's like it's whispering to me. I catch myself having the darkest thoughts sometimes, the most aggressive outbursts. I feel like it marked me, somehow. Changed me."

"Made you straight?" I joked.

"Come on," Zooey said. "Be serious."

"How is she, by the way? Your beard."

"*Mallory* is terrific," he said. "You know, I actually really like her."

"I'm happy for you," I said. He gave me a skeptical look. "I know that sounds phony, but I mean it. You got out."

"What do you mean?" he asked.

"Oh, *you* come on, you know what I mean. Look at you, Zooey. You're just like Keanu in that movie. You're just like *them*, now. You dress like them, you even sound like them. You're gonna have everything you want in life. And me? Well, I'm probably destined to inherit the family curse."

"Don't say that," he said. "You're gonna be careful. You're not gonna get sick. You're gonna get everything you want, too. You just have to be very—"

"Clever," I said.

"Hiss hiss, bitch."

I had to laugh. I was also buoyed to hear his faggy S sneak back in, but I didn't say anything.

Then a man entered the diner and caught my eye. It was Terrence, in street clothes now, a puffy coat, baggy sweatpants, and sneakers. He saw me and gave a friendly nod. He came over to the table.

"Hey," he said. "OK if I join you for a second?"

"Sure," I said. "This is Zooey. Zooey, this is Terrence, he's been taking care of my dad."

"Your . . . ?" Terrence looked stunned.

"Yeah, long story," I said.

He sat down across from me.

"Fuck," he said. "I'm sorry about how I kicked you out of there, if I'd have known—"

"It's OK," I said. "You were doing your job."

"You OK?" he asked.

"I'm . . . full up," I said.

"I hear you," he said. "I leave most days like that. If you need somewhere to put all that energy, I know a place. I'm going as soon as I get a bite."

"But you just worked a full shift in that place," I said. "Don't you need to rest?"

"This is our war, and I'm a frontline soldier," he said. "I'll rest when the war's over."

CHAPTER THIRTEEN

ZACH

We took our seats in the crowded, smoky, deafeningly cacophonous meeting space.

After finishing up at the diner, we'd followed Terrence north, back toward the hospital and a couple of blocks further to a stone building indistinct from others that surrounded it. There, we'd waited in a long line to enter, took the handouts and brochures that were offered to us, and stood by as Terrence greeted friends and comrades with cheery air-kisses, somber hugs, and news about others in their community. I learned we were at the Lesbian and Gay Community Services Center.

(I tried to play it cool, because even though I kept telling myself I didn't belong here, not anymore, I knew inherently that I was surrounded by my own.)

Then it was time to gather, so we took our seats in that humid, cramped room.

For all the energy, the wit, the flirting I felt around me (kinda like the atmosphere of my first Vicious Circle meeting), the space was pretty brutal: some folding chairs facing in toward a place for the speakers, our view blocked by the pillars that interrupted the room here and there, the smell of cigarettes, body odor, and an aging heating system filling the air.

(Kinda like the Blackfriars locker room, actually; all this humidity, all this aggression, all these *men*. They came in kissing and gossiping with the fierce look of athletes about to hit the field and use their bodies to claim victory.)

It wasn't all young men gathered there. In fact, it wasn't all men, but lots of women, too: butch lesbians and transsexual activists and older mothers and nurses. It wasn't even all queer people, I later learned. But we all shared something that brought us to this room, and I felt that camaraderie from each of them, regardless of our differences.

Soon, a studious but furious-looking young man stepped into the center of the space and spoke.

"ACT UP is a diverse, nonpartisan group of individuals united in anger and committed to direct action against the AIDS crisis," he announced.

"ACT UP! FIGHT BACK! FIGHT AIDS!" the crowd chanted.

What followed was nearly three hours of speaking, arguing, and occasional uproarious chaos as various committees shared updates and plans of action. A treatment and data committee updated everyone on various drug trials as scientists looked for something better than "AZT," the current, only treatment for AIDS, which prolonged life but didn't save it and came with horrific side effects. A housing committee discussed options for those who could no longer work to pay rent due to their illness. A media committee instructed members on how to use succinct, clear talking points to shout their message into news cameras as they were being beaten and arrested.

It sounds boring, putting it down here, but I promise it wasn't, because every so often, someone would stand in the back and shout something like, "Why are we talking about the fucking media, people are fucking dying!" which would lead to someone else shouting them down, some sparring over procedures, and then ultimately unified chants like "HEALTHCARE IS A RIGHT!" and "AZT IS NOT ENOUGH, GIVE US ALL THE OTHER STUFF!"

The main event of the meeting was when a Black transsexual woman from the action committee stepped up to discuss a planned demonstration tomorrow night, New Year's Eve.

"Tomorrow night, we enter a new year," she said. "And so, like we do at the New Year, I'm looking back. *Ten years* of AIDS. In Nineteen Eighty-One, there were forty-one documented cases of what we called 'gay cancer.' Now, ten years later, we have over forty MILLION cases of AIDS worldwide."

The crowd made a noise like a wounded animal. I joined them.

I had no idea.

"Tomorrow night, we also enter an *election* year, and so far, no candidate has announced any action plan to fight the virus, support our community, and direct funding toward a cure. They won't even say AIDS on the campaign trail. So we're not gonna ring in this new year without raising awareness and demanding that our leaders address this plague. We're going to Times Square for the ball drop. HAPPY NEW YEAR, AULD LANG SYNE, FORTY MILLION WITH AIDS WORLDWIDE!"

"HAPPY NEW YEAR, AULD LANG SYNE, FORTY MILLION WITH AIDS WORLDWIDE!" the crowd chanted back.

I noticed I was chanting, too. As was Leo.

When it had died down and the woman began going over details of the demonstration, an older man with black glasses and short gray hair stood in the back.

"Speaking of candidates, what are we going to do if Eldridge takes the nomination?"

My ears pricked up.

"What?" the woman asked.

The man scoffed. "Are you kidding? Charles Eldridge! The representative from Massachusetts. He's challenging Bush in the primary."

The woman turned to her associates quizzically.

"I'm aware of the man. But we don't consider him a threat. No fringe candidate is going to beat Bush in the primary," she said. "If anything, he'll chip away some Republican support."

"Have you seen the polling?!" the man shouted. "He's doing well in New England. Too well. And if you think Bush is bad, you should check out Eldridge's record on gays. Bush just ignores us; Eldridge publicly compares our love to pedophilia and bestiality. He started a letter writing campaign to lobby Congress to ban people with HIV from entering the country. He makes Jesse Helms look like Mister Rogers. AND he's handsome! Which is to say, he's dangerous."

❖

After the meeting, I flagged us a taxi home, and somewhere along the FDR, Leo fell asleep on my shoulder. I realized the day he'd had, waking up warm in his bed, enjoying his freedom, his father still long dead, the affair with the Book of Brothers and the Oldfellows behind him. And now we were here.

When we arrived back at my house on the Upper East Side, it was almost midnight.

Thankfully, my dad had long since retired for the evening. Introducing Leo to the uninitiated could be a challenge in the best of times, but in the wake of the expulsions, I really didn't have it in me to explain our friendship. I was too exhausted from the day, my head full of noisy questions about the communities I had stumbled upon and where I fit into them.

(*If* I fit into them.)

I led Leo to one of the guest rooms and fetched him a set of pajamas and towels from the linen closet. He washed up fast and flopped into bed, totally spent.

"Good night, sweet prince," I said, shutting the door.

"Wait," he said, groggily.

"Yeah?"

"You were chanting tonight, at the meeting."

". . . I was, yeah."

"You seemed really into it."

"It was . . . really moving."

"But you're straight now."

I had to laugh a quiet little laugh. Leo was never one to beat around the bush, even in this state.

"I never said that," I said. "I said I was figuring it out."

"You also said you wanted something different. Different from us. And it seems like you actually have a choice. Like you've *made* your choice. But then . . . you were chanting," he said. "So, I'm just curious, after everything you saw tonight . . . do you still want something different?"

He looked so small in that big bed, surrounded by all the extra pillows my mother had insisted we buy. I felt like I was tucking in a child, but not like a son.

More like a brother.

"It doesn't matter if I want it or not," I said. "It's mine."

The next morning, we tiptoed past my father's office, where he was already making calls, and slipped away into the bright, slushy morning. Leo suggested a long, lavish breakfast at the Plaza Hotel, but I assured him that the best Manhattan breakfast was an egg and cheese on a roll with a coffee in a little blue cup from one of the silver carts that lined Fifth Avenue.

"But first," I said. "There's something we have to do."

I led him to a bank of pay phones near the park and handed him a quarter.

"Call her," I said. Leo began to protest, but I said, "She's probably called the cops by now. And I imagine he'd like to see her one more time. To clear the air before . . . Look, you don't owe it to her . . . but you also know it's the right thing to do."

Leo nodded, picked up a receiver, and plunked the quarter in.

"I'll fetch us that coffee and breakfast," I said. "Give you some privacy."

"None for me, actually," he said. "And maybe reconsider for yourself. You're gonna need a strong stomach for that place."

❖

I ignored the warning and got enough for both of us, which he devoured on a park bench upon my return.

"You let her know?"

"I did," he said, his face still fraught from what I'm sure had been a terrible conversation. "It was . . . a lot. She's on her way."

"Then we don't have much time. Come on."

We hailed a cab down to Greenwich Village, announced ourselves at the St. Vincent's front desk, made our way up to the seventh floor, and, after a wait, were led back to glove and mask up for our visit with Lucas Breyer.

I knew about AIDS, growing up in Manhattan. I'd watched the news reports with my mom and dad at night, saw the *60 Minutes* special from inside a ward, but still, I wasn't prepared to meet someone as late-stage as Leo's dad, face-to-face.

He was as thin as I'd expected but gray in a way I hadn't. His arms were covered in dark purple blotches, his face constricted by a plastic oxygen mask. I wondered who would be bound to these machines next, when the fleshy, temporary part of him gave way. Still, when he smiled and extended his hand, I smiled back and shook, as if we were meeting at a holiday party and not in a graveyard.

"Who . . . is this?" Lucas asked.

"I'm Zach- er, *Zooey* Orson, sir. I'm one of Leo's classmates."

"Zooey? I . . . love that. So . . . chic."

Leo shot me a grin.

"Thank you, sir. It's wonderful to meet you."

"Zooey is one of the guys who got mixed up with the book," Leo said.

Lucas nodded ominously.

"If only Sister Patricia knew . . . she had a coven of gay witches . . . in her Catholic hospital," he chuckled. "Have . . . a seat, boys."

"What can you tell us about the Oldfellows," Leo asked.

"Everything," he replied. "I was the son . . . of the Cardinal Brother. The . . . heir. I have more to say . . . than I have the breath to tell you . . ."

Leo's face was defeated, then intrigued as Lucas pointed toward the drawer of the bedside table. Leo pulled it open to find a mess of scribbles on a substantial stack of loose-leaf paper.

"So . . . I wrote it down . . . Took me all night . . ."

We attached the pages here, so you can read them for yourself.

(Thanks for letting us, Leo.)

LUCAS

Dear Son,

I can say more in a letter these days than I can in even a whisper, and I know there isn't enough paper in Manhattan or time left on my clock to tell you everything I'd like to. So I'll just tell you what you need to know.

You need to know that about a thousand years ago, I was once a student at Blackfriars School like you. My hair was real red back then, not this faded mess I've got now. Like you, I was also a legacy. My father, your grandfather, was Francis Breyer, the reigning leader of something called the Fraternal Order of the Oldfellows. Blackfriars School was but one of the many properties and businesses in the Order's portfolio, so naturally, I got in regardless of my bad grades. Oh, I hope you're a better student than I was. And I hope you've been having even more fun.

Growing up, I got occasional glimpses into what I thought was just my dad's social boys club: ceremonial robes in a closet, closed door meetings with other Brothers in the dead of the night, a large black leather book in the office that I was forbidden to touch. Men like my father had always been like aliens to me—were these quirks so much stranger than his love of classic cars or major league baseball? I never paid The Oldfellows much mind.

Besides, I was distracted by a Fraternal Order of my own I'd found at Blackfriars. I'm sure you've found your way into the Vicious Circle? Did you ever check for my name in the guest book? You'll find it there, alongside some slanderous gossip about me that is all absolutely true. Do me a favor and burn it when you get back there. No, on second thought, give it a big kiss.

Anyway.

You need to know that spring of my senior year, Nineteen None-of-Your-Business, my dad burst into my room to announce, like Moses with his tablets, that the time had come: I was going to become initiated.

He explained to me that since its founding, Blackfriars had been host to an annual Oldfellows event called the Invocation. It was a very special day for the Order, the day when new members could be admitted. However, once you were a member, you were a member for life, so the initiation ritual should not be taken lightly.

I asked what kind of society it was.

My dad said that only members could know.

This is the first of many turns in my life that I would need reams and reams of paper to explain to most men, but I'm afraid you'll understand acutely. It was my dad, reaching out to me with an offer to know what he knows. It was an acknowledgment that he saw something in me that I never saw: a reflection of himself. To be a Brother of the Oldfellows was to finally be not just in his orbit but in his world.

I accepted.

I wish I hadn't, but I think you understand why I did.

That spring, my classmates (and lovers) went home for break, but I stayed behind to greet the rich and powerful men from around the world that converged at the school by limousine or helicopter or seemingly from thin air.

"This is my boy, Lucas," my dad said proudly as I met their handshakes. "This is my son."

I was given robes like his, signed the vow he'd signed. My father took me to the auditorium to teach me how to perform the pageant-like ceremony that would symbolize my rebirth into the Order. I thought it felt like bad theater, but it was the only time I'd ever seen my father cry.

I performed the initiation ceremony with full-chested enthusiasm.

I wish I hadn't, but I think you understand why I did.

The crowd cheered. I was a Brother, like my father. One of them at last.

But I quickly learned that the Invocation wasn't only for initiating new members.

We gathered in the Blackfriars Chapel, all in our robes.

Incenses were burned, incantations chanted.

They called out to summon something called Frateroth, their god.

I followed along in the black book I was given as best I could.

I wish I hadn't, but I think you understand why I did.

We beseeched Him to bring us power, treasure, and fame.

A teenage girl was brought forward, bound. One of the Brothers had a knife.

But I said I'd only tell you what you need to know.

You need to know that the Oldfellows are the "They" you think of when people say things like "They planned his assassination," or "They control the banks," or "They will never let Us get too far ahead." Men who look like them and think like them are selected to become part of that great They, and They control the systems of the world.

And They do it with the power of the beast.

And the beast needs to be fed.

You need to know that I tried to play along. I tried to be like them.

I wish I hadn't, but I think you understand why I did.

I found a wife, even.

That part I don't regret. I regret what I did to her and, even though I didn't know it, to you. But I don't regret our union because I don't regret you, Leo. I regret who I've been to you, and who I haven't. But I don't regret you.

You need to know that.

CHAPTER FOURTEEN

LEO

I know I've been a garrulous narrator up until now, but you can understand that this part is difficult to write about.

So I'll be like my dad. I'll tell you what you need to know.

❖

"I'd seen too much," he said after I lowered his pages, my mind so full up that my pain and recognition and terror overflowed out through my eyes and down my cheeks. "I cast every protection in the book . . . Against curses, against being discovered. Then I ran . . . lived under a different name for so many years . . . But now, at the end of my life, I figured . . . what's the worst they can do? I checked in here as myself. Let them find me . . . I'm already cursed."

"Maybe there's still something you can do to stop them," Zooey said.

"I told Leo . . . there's no . . . way . . ."

Zooey looked to me for approval to proceed and I nodded. We'd already come so far. There was nowhere left to go but to the end of it. He unzipped his bag, pulled out the folder, and laid the torn page it contained on the hospital bed.

Lucas had the look of a soldier lost in a flashback of wartime carnage.

"My . . . god . . ."

"Before our friend died, he left this to me," Zooey said. "He said it was a solution. He'd planned to help me translate it but then . . ."

"They got him," I managed to say.

"I held on to it, not knowing what to do, how to translate it . . . and now we've met you," Zooey said. "Sir, could you help us?"

I could see in my father's eyes that even sharing a room with this thing was overwhelming. Still, his heart rate monitor kept a steady pace as he sighed and said, "Of course I can. Luckily, I still have . . . my mind and my eyes. Luckier than a lot of the others."

He picked up the page and began to look it over.

"Extraordinary," he said. "You have one of the . . . *original* copies . . . the handwritten ones . . . Every brother in the Order has a copy of the book . . . but not every copy has this page . . . Only the original founders' copies have this. They fear it getting into the wrong hands."

"What is it?" I asked.

"The final working . . . The spell to unleash Frateroth."

"Unleash as in . . . we'd sick the monster back on the Oldfellows?" Zooey asked.

"No, no," my father said. "Not unleash to attack . . . to *release* . . . to free . . ."

I looked to Zooey, who looked just as concerned as I did.

"Why would we want to *free* that thing?" I asked.

"Because . . . it's the source of all of their power," he said. "The Oldfellows . . . summoned and bound Frateroth in antiquity . . . he is chained in the space between . . . this world and the next. They feed it . . . lives . . . and command it to do their bidding . . ."

A shiver ran down my spine. Had we fed the beast when we sent it to take Ryan Godfrey?

"So, let's do it," I said. "Let's get what we need and do it right now!"

"The timing . . . has to be right," Lucas said, poring over the page, translating in his mind. "The Invocation . . . the last dark moon . . .

before the Vernal Equinox . . . a holy day for the Oldfellows . . . also, it is very dangerous."

"Why?" I asked.

"You must meet the beast . . . at the crossroads," Lucas said. "I don't mean streets intersecting . . . the space where he lives . . . between life and death. Kind of like this place," he chuckled, gesturing around the hospital room. "This page is a recipe . . . for the poison that will take you there . . . right to the brink . . . but not further. Its measurements must be . . . exact. Or you will cross over."

"Can you write down the translation?" I asked.

"Leo . . ." Zooey protested.

"We have time to think about this. Until spring," I said. "But . . . we don't have all the time in the world to get the translation. Let's at least do that."

He relented.

"There's paper and a pen . . . in the drawer," Lucas said.

For the next ten minutes, he scribbled a translation onto a small scrap of paper, which I slipped into the folder with the torn-out page and Steven's note.

Then, we just chatted—about New York, about where he'd been, about *who* he'd been in the sixteen years that we'd been apart. He'd worked as a barback at a leather bar in the East Village, a dresser for a Broadway musical, and a hustler for a closeted Wall Street millionaire. He'd attended a "die-in" protest at St. Patrick's Cathedral in Eighty-Eight, laying down in the aisle right in the middle of Sunday mass to protest the church's stance on safe sex education and condom distribution. He'd danced on piers, had sex in parks, taken care of other sick friends, and sang show tunes in Greenwich piano bars until dawn. He'd had a longtime lover whose name I don't want to repeat because the bastard left him when he got sick.

And then, in the middle of a howling story about the time his friends hired a witch in the Bronx to hex the bigoted singer Anita Bryant, Terrence arrived at the door with a trembling, disheveled blond woman half drenched in sleet.

"Mom . . ." I said, standing.

"Hello . . . Rona," Lucas whispered.

Tears welling in her lined eyes, my mom drew in several breaths but couldn't seem to form words.

"I'll leave you all alone," Zooey said, as he grabbed his backpack and slipped away.

❖

I think I'd like to keep what happened next private, if that's OK.

❖

You need to know that after we finally emerged from the room, Lucas asleep, my mother at peace, me in a daze, Zooey became an utter hero.

He took us uptown to the theater district, where he bought us dinner at Joe Allen with his dad's credit card. The posters of Broadway flop musicals that hung on the walls brought me some comfort after that day. I think he knew they would.

You need to know that we walked over toward Times Square, where thousands were gathering for the New Year's Eve ball drop. We stopped short of the scrum, though, because we found the crowd we were actually looking for, gathered just a block away at Forty-Second and Eighth, holding signs.

GEORGE, WHERE ARE YOU?!

$10,000 LAST YEAR FOR AZT,

HAPPY NEW YEAR TO ME

WHAT WILL YOU DO IN '92 TO FIGHT AIDS?

We found Terrence in the crowd, and he hugged us like family, even my mom. He complimented her manicure. She kissed him on the mouth at midnight.

We left when the arrests started.

Zooey got us a room at the Plaza, also on credit. They said they were fully booked until he dropped his dad's name. I smiled with satisfaction that I'd been right; they *were* the hotel Orsons.

We didn't get the news until the next morning, when we called to check in.

"Lucas Breyer passed over peacefully, just minutes into the New Year."

I'm not usually at a loss for words, but here we are.

You know what you need to know.

CHAPTER FIFTEEN

ZACH

My winter at Blackfriars, absent of my friends, the Vicious Circle, the mystery and terror of the Book of Brothers, and any joy or pain beyond pure academia, was as lonely and methodical as long-distance running. I know this, because part of my deal with Westcott to avoid expulsion despite my involvement in the VC scandal was to join the track team. Carpinelli had been talking about this transfer student who was a mess with a racket or ball but a machine on the track, and word had gotten all the way up to the headmaster.

So I ran.

The track guys were like the rugby guys, but different; they were quiet, tall, thin, like me. I introduced myself as Zach. They'd heard about my past, like everyone, but soon, the suspicious looks, the cold greetings, and the way they hid from me in the locker room when it was time to change and shower gave way to congratulations when I bested a run time, slaps on the back as I passed in the halls.

I became Zach Orson, track star.

The key to long-distance running is to find your rhythm and detach your mind, and that's exactly how I survived both marathon runs and my solitary time at Blackfriars.

Wake. Class. Track. Study. Call Mal. Sleep.

I was great at the rhythm. I was less successful at the detachment.

For instance, every time I walked by the senior dorm, I heard Madonna, tasted cheap gin, smelled incense, saw all the boys. Saw Daniel.

I wondered about him most.

Wake. Class. Track. Study. Call Mal. Sleep.

Now and again, on weekends, I'd check in on Leo and Rona, who had repaired their relationship. Leo had started in at the local public school and was grateful to still be invisible. He was going to try out for their production of *The Music Man*.

Still, neither he nor I, nor any of the old VC boys who still kept in touch had heard from Daniel in what was now months since his expulsion.

Of course, we considered that he might have met the same fate as Steven. That is to say, that he might be dead.

But Leo figured that if Westcott had hexed Daniel, the rest of us would have gotten it, too. Also, Daniel's dad didn't say he was dead or even missing; he said, "He doesn't live here anymore." I was glad to hold on to hope that he was alive, but still, those ominous words were very cold comfort.

Wake. Class. Track. Study. Call Mal. Sleep.

When I wasn't reminiscing about parties past or worrying about Daniel, my mind would linger on my experience with ACT UP, with the AIDS ward, with Lucas and Leo and what I felt in their company.

I'd wonder who I was.

I knew who Zach Orson, track star, was.

I also knew that wasn't the whole story.

I knew that I still needed to avert my eyes when my teammates would disrobe and roughhouse in the locker room. I knew how much I'd wanted Daniel when I thought he wanted me.

All the same, I knew how I felt about Mallory.

The last night of Christmas break, after a skate around the Bryant Park rink and a sneaky drag of a joint in a phone booth on Fifth Avenue, she led me back to her house, left vacant by her vacationing parents.

We kissed. She put my hand on her breast. She asked if she could open my fly.

I'd told her it was my first time and she said, "That's OK." I asked if it was hers, too, and she just smiled at me through strands of dark hair as she unhooked her bra.

(And as it happened, I swear to you, it didn't feel like a lie. When my hands and mouth searched her body for the places that felt right, I realized that unlike all the other ways I performed Zach Orson, track star, this moment had no audience. My hands, my mouth, the rest of me just wanted what they wanted.)

We went all the way that night. Just a few days into Nineteen Ninety-Two, and I was no longer a virgin. Boyhood was behind me. The biggest milestone of adolescence had been met and passed.

And for some reason, I'd kept this from Leo, even though he was my best friend.

I lacked the self-awareness at the time to call it what it was: shame. The way I felt hiding myself from the regular boys at Blackfriars—changing my voice, minding my lingo, managing my friendships—I would feel it all over again every time Leo asked me, jokingly or earnestly, about Mallory.

Everyone understands the concept of being in the closet. But imagine your closet has two doors instead of one, directly across from each other. One door leads to the normal, everyday straight world. It's the door you have to keep shut to be safe, accepted, and successful. The other door leads to a party where all of your friends are hanging out. This door must stay shut if you want to keep those friendships, stay invited to that party. Imagine the distance between the doors is just a few inches farther than your arm span, and each door is opening, little by little, all the time, unless you can actively pull it shut. So the more time you spend holding one door closed, the wider the other swings open. And between the doors? It's the real you. Completely alone.

That's what it's like to be a closeted bisexual.

(Yeah, remember at the beginning of this thing, when I told you I like boys? That was true, but it wasn't the whole truth. It still takes me time to open all the way up.)

Living in that double closet was isolating and exhausting.

Like long-distance running.

So I ran.

Wake. Class. Track. Study. Call Mal. Sleep.

And then one day in the frosty first week of February, on my nightly call to Mal, I tripped.

She was telling me about how bored she was with an English class assignment to read *A Midsummer Night's Dream*, and I let it slip that, "My friend, Leo, did that play here at Blackfriars."

I say slip, because I could tell from her abrupt silence on the other end of the line that this was not something I should have said.

". . . Leo *Breyer*?" she asked, after an eternity.

"Yeah," I replied. "Do you know him?"

"Only by reputation," she said. "I mean everyone at Hansard has heard about the expulsions. The *sex club*."

"The what?"

"Darling, how could you not have heard?! There was an underground *sex club* at Blackfriars! A *gay* sex club. They got found out and a bunch of kids got expelled, *your friend*, Leo Breyer, included!"

"No, I know that," I said, "but . . . it wasn't a *sex club*. It was just a club. Like any other secret student club."

"How would you know?" she asked. "You didn't *go*, did you?"

(I could have lied. I could have said that I'd just heard. That I'd met Leo in class and he'd told me about the parties and what was she having for dinner? Maybe I should have. But even Olympic marathon runners sometimes get tired of running.)

"I did."

I could hear the tiniest gasp escape her lips back in New York City.

". . . Are you . . . *gay*, then?"

"*No*," I said, "Jesus. I mean . . . you and I had *sex*, Mal. Or do you think that was some kind of act?"

Quiet.

"Well, I'm sorry, but given your *past* . . . Do you like boys?"

". . . I have, yeah."

More quiet.

"My god . . ." she whispered. "Zooey, did you have sex with any boys at that party?"

"I told you, you were my first time."

"What about Mister B?"

"JESUS, Mal!"

"Well, you've been lying to me about . . . what you are. Stands to reason you could have been lying about—"

"I *never* lied to you!"

"You weren't exactly honest, either," she spat. "So, tell me."

"I told you," I said. "Why are you doing this?"

"Well, Zooey, because I heard about the Blackfriars boy who died of AIDS and I'm just wondering if I should be scared for myself!"

Now I was quiet.

"*Excuse* me?"

". . . Hillman. I think. I know what happened to him. Everyone is talking about it."

"Mal . . . you *really* don't know what you're talking about. He died of a brain aneurysm. Not fucking AIDS. I mean, he was sixteen."

"Well, of course the family is going to *say* that," she scoffed in a really ugly tone.

"It's the truth!"

"How do you know?!"

"BECAUSE HE WAS MY FUCKING FRIEND!" I roared. "HE WAS MY FRIEND AND NOW HE'S DEAD AND I NEVER GOT TO SAY GOODBYE!"

I could feel the curious glances fall upon me from just outside the phone booth in the Bass common room. I didn't care.

Then there was the longest quiet yet. I let her take it. I'd rather her really consider what she wanted to say than do that Upper East Sider thing, spinning and sputtering just to keep the ball in the air.

"So . . ." she whispered, at last. "What *are* you?"

Human, I thought.

Lonely.

Tired.

Sad.

Confused.

But also Gentle and Loyal and Stalwart and Funny.

And fucking Yours.

(But I didn't say any of that. I knew those weren't the answers she was looking for.)

"Does it matter? If I'm with *you,* with *only* you?" I asked.

"It does . . . to me," she said.

I sighed.

I knew it was over. I only wished that things had ended in that bittersweet way you see in a movie: two different colleges, or she's moving to France, or a tender goodbye and a vow to remain friends.

I wish it had at least happened in person.

That night, though, all I could say was, "I'll have to get back to you on that."

At least she'd replied with, "I understand," in a tone that was sincere, not cruel.

We didn't speak for a few days.

When I finally did get her on the line, she told me she'd gotten an AIDS test and would let me know the results.

I informed her that we'd used a condom, but furthermore, it was impossible for me to have AIDS, because I'd never had sex before.

She said she was freaked out. That she couldn't do this. That she was sorry.

I didn't apologize back. I'm still proud of that.

❖

Wake. Class. Track. Study . . . Sleep.

The missing step was a hitch in my pace.

Without Mal, I had more time to work, to rest.

I also felt more alone than ever.

One day, February eleventh, just after lunch, I was summoned to Westcott's office.

Of course, my heart pounded, and I began to sweat like I'd just finished a long run.

My mind swirled with possibilities: a missed clue about the book that had pointed him in my direction? New testimony from a VC member about my conduct? News of Daniel?

When I arrived at his office, clammy and terrified, I was further alarmed to see him smiling, pouring brown liquid from a crystal decanter on his desk into one of two chunky rocks glasses.

"Orson! Don't worry," he said. "I phoned your father and got permission. This is sixteen-year-old Lagavulin, practically older than you! I know it's a little early in the day, but a celebration is a celebration."

He handed me a glass and poured the second for himself.

He looked years younger and healthier than when I saw him last, the gauntness in his cheeks refilled, his color restored.

"Sir?" I asked.

"Now don't tell me you haven't been following! I ought to take that right back from you. But I suppose with school and track, you might be distracted from the news."

He slid the day's newspaper across the desk to where I stood, flummoxed.

ELDRIDGE BESTS BUSH IN STUNNNG IOWA CAUCUS UPSET

Harkin leads Dems in first Primary Challenge

"Our man won! He actually won!" Westcott said as he clinked his glass against mine and raised it to his lips. He savored the drink while I tried to make sense of all of it.

"Of course, it was a close margin, and this is just the first primary caucus. A long way to go to the actual nomination, but it's WORKING! He's taking the full news cycle, which can only help, moving forward."

He was practically dancing. I managed a smile and raised the drink to my lips. It smelled terrible. Or I thought it was the drink that smelled, but after I took a sip (caustic in my throat, tasting of Band-Aids and bacon) and lowered the glass, I smelled it even worse. Like body odor and decay and garbage.

A smell I recognized.

"Still, when he takes the whole thing, I look forward to the day when you and I can say that we were on the train early," Westcott said, taking another pull on the glass.

I realized it was the smell that had clung to all of us for days after we'd used the Book of Brothers to hex Godfrey: the acrid, rotten smell of the beast.

The stink of Frateroth.

It was all over Westcott.

I strained to endure it as I finished the drink and made small talk about track, my studies, my unfortunate breakup.

"Long distance is tough," he said. "You don't want to be tied down, anyway, young man like yourself. Plenty of fish in the sea."

I raised my glass to that, though I was very close to vomiting from the odor.

"Thanks for this, sir," I said, placing my drained glass on the desk. "I'd better get to English. Congratulations!"

"And to you, Mister Orson. The Grand Old Party will be Grand again."

I didn't make the connection at first. I knew he was using the book again, communing with Frateroth, picking up his stink, but I didn't yet know for what purpose.

Meanwhile, the biggest story in America was the rise of a fringe Republican candidate, growing in popularity, seemingly poised to do what no one had ever done before: usurp a sitting president to become the party's formal nominee.

The anchors on the nightly news had never seen anything like it, but Republican voters were energized and rallying behind Eldridge in record numbers. After all, Bush had betrayed them with his tax hike. They found him soft on social issues like crime, abortion, and rights for homosexuals. Shouldn't they be able to use their votes to affirm what the party actually stood for instead of throwing their support on the incumbent president just because he won the last time?

New Hampshire and South Dakota tipped toward the charismatic newcomer. Bush picked up enough delegates to stay competitive, but it was undeniable that Eldridge had the power of momentum. If he could continue this performance through March tenth, Super Tuesday, when eight key states, including his native Massachusetts, cast their votes, there would be no stopping him.

❖

I was summoned to visit Westcott once more, the morning of February twenty-eighth.

Somehow, he smelled even worse than I'd expected.

"Happy Leap Year, Orson," he said when I entered the office. It was true, the next day would be a rare February twenty-ninth, and a Saturday at that. I longed for the Vicious Circle party that should have happened on this Friday evening.

"Thank you, sir," I said, struggling to breathe through my mouth to halt the smell from entering my nose. "Is there something to discuss?"

"I wanted you to be the first to know," he said. "This Monday, we will be hosting some special guests at the school, including one *very* special guest. I'm sure you can guess who!"

Judy Garland's ghost?

"Eldridge?!" I gasped, feigning delight.

"Keep it close to the chest until we announce at the assembly," he said, grinning paternally. "He's stopping on his way down to Maryland for the race on the third. The polling puts Colorado and Georgia in the bag for him, so he's not going to try to squeeze in another rally. He's got a day to breathe and he wanted to spend it visiting his alma mater, really get that home court advantage cooking ahead of Super Tuesday. Orson, he's going to take this thing."

"That's incredible, sir."

"And Mister Orson . . . Zach . . ." He beamed at me, proudly. "I'm going to arrange a personal audience for you. I've really come to think of you as an ideal Blackfriars man, the perfect ambassador to represent our student body."

"No, really?!"

"We'll get a great photo to hang in Bass Hall for the ages. A Blackfriars student standing shoulder to shoulder with our very first alumnus president!"

When I was finally released, I staggered out of the office, dizzy—not from excitement but from lack of oxygen.

❖

After a sleepy, snowy weekend, February became March.

Town cars and limousines pulled up the drive one after the other, delivering rich-looking old men who had come to see Eldridge. Oldfellows, I suspected. I remembered what Lucas told us about their holy Invocation. It was just a few days away.

The chapel was finally repaired fully from the damage of last October, so we assembled there, students festively brushing snow off of their coats and buzzing with excitement to get a glimpse of Blackfriars' most famous son. When he entered, gleaming white teeth, sharp slicked hair, broad red power tie, the place erupted into a frenzy of cheers and whoops that I hadn't seen at the school outside of a rugby match.

"Good morning, my *fellow* Blackfriars brothers!" he said, to another roaring wave of applause. Westcott was lit up like a Christmas tree.

He gave roughly the same speech he gave at Mallory's place, detailing the ways that Bush had let the Republican identity slip away but with a tone of optimism about what was possible for a new "Morning in America."

However, having stood shoulder to shoulder with the protesters in New York, having seen the AIDS ward at St. Vincent's, having felt the cloud of mourning hanging over the entire city, I couldn't feel optimistic. I knew his stance on homosexuals, on AIDS. What I once found inspiring about him I now found repellent. Looking around at the way my schoolmates beamed and cheered for him, though, I knew I was alone in that. He had the crowd totally bewitched.

I shouldn't have been surprised, then, when I was shuffled back to the vestry of the chapel where he waited, among that crowd of anonymous wealthy men, that my nostrils stung with a familiar, nearly unbearable odor.

"Bewitched" was the right word.

Him too, I thought.

We all thought we were celebrating a Blackfriars president. We were really celebrating an Oldfellow president.

"Mister Orson!" he said warmly as he clapped his bear paw of a hand around mine. "So wonderful to see you again!"

"You . . . you remember me?" I choked.

As badly as Westcott stunk of the beast, Eldridge and his entourage were a hundred times worse. I could hardly think, the place reeked so intensely of rot and pestilence.

"Of course I do! I'm usually good with faces—you have to be, in politics—but meeting another Blackfriars man? I asked Westcott if I could see you specifically!"

An upperclassman from the yearbook staff came in with a camera, signaling it was time for our big photo op.

"Whoa, ripe in here," the kid said. "I woulda thought they'd cleaned this moldy old place during the renovation."

"Erm, thanks for this," Eldridge told the kid. "Where should we stand? I know plenty about policy but precious little about photography!"

"There's good light there by the brick wall," the kid replied.

We stood side by side, locked in a handshake, surrounded by his accomplices, and I mustered everything inside me to force a smile for the flash of the camera. The smell was unbearable, but the revelation of what was really going on here was worse.

"Well," I said when we pulled apart, "I wish you great luck with the remaining primaries, sir."

"Thank you, Mister Orson, but luck has nothing to do with it. Rest assured, I *will* be the next president of the United States, and when I am, I won't forget you. I hope we'll speak again."

"Me too, sir."

I staggered from the space disgusted, not just from the foul stench but also from the sad reality I was faced with: The game was rigged, the election decided before it had even begun.

Leo's dad had been right.

The Oldfellows were everywhere and controlled everything, and it would always be so. These men were invincible. The rest of us would always live under their thumbs, punching our cards at their factories, consuming what they told us to consume, living with exactly as much prosperity as they allowed us to have and learning to be *grateful* for it.

But then, as I thought about Leo's dad, I remembered that there was a way to break the cycle.

He and Steven had left it behind for us.

I made a plan. I made a phone call.

❖

The next day, I called out of class sick and walked to the edge of campus, past the shed where we'd stolen the bikes those many months ago and down to the main road.

There, I was met by a junky green Volkswagen driven by a newly licensed chauffeur with bright red hair.

"Your chariot awaits, bitch," Leo said. "You ready?"

"The fact that you can now operate a motor vehicle unsupervised is far more terrifying than what we're about to do," I said, buckling my seatbelt for what was sure to be a bumpy ride.

Leo drove as chaotically as he spoke, danced, decorated, what have you—but we did make it in one piece to our destination: Ouroboros.

"Prepster!" Oona said, behind the desk as we entered. "Annyeong!"

"Hey, girl," I said, as I pulled a folder out of my backpack and slapped a handwritten spell down on the counter in front of her.

"What's this?" she asked.

"We're here to buy some poison and rig an election."

That's when I slapped down another piece of paper I'd been keeping. A crisp one-hundred-dollar bill my dad had slipped me on my first day at Blackfriars.

She looked down at the counter and then back up at us.

Her dark eyes darkened further.

"Punk rock."

CHAPTER SIXTEEN

DANIEL

"Magic isn't real," the man in the khakis and white polo announced to us.

I have news for you, I thought.

"But when hard work meets a strong will and the help of a loving God, the miraculous *changes* can seem like magic."

He pressed Play on the VCR connected to the television that one of his (also white, male, khaki-ed) teammates had wheeled into the beige room we all sat in.

After a few seconds of grainy distortion from so many plays of the tape, a video came into focus of a young child, sitting with a doctor and her parents (white, khakis) in a medical room.

I looked around at the handful of kids near me, all dressed, as I was, in that same white polo, with either khaki pants or a long black skirt, depending on whether they'd decided you were a boy or a girl.

Where's this going? I tried to mentally ask them.

All of them just looked straight ahead at the screen, though, so I turned back to watch the movie.

"Today we are testing out a new piece of technology that little Bethany here has received," the doctor on the screen said. "It's called a cochlear implant. You see, little Bethany was born deaf, unable to hear because she lacks the cochlea: the part of the inner ear that lets us transmit sounds from the outside world to our brains. This little implant will replace that function, and we are about to turn it on.

Bethany is about to hear her mother's and father's voices for the first time. We ready?"

The teary-eyed parents nodded.

"OK."

The doctor connected something on the side of Bethany's head. Instantly she stopped her childish squirming and sat up, startled. I thought she'd been electrocuted or something. But then, her mother said, "Hello, Bethany," and she raised her hands up to her head, confused.

"Hello, angel," her dad said.

Bethany turned to them as a smile spread across her face. Then she started to laugh. The parents began to weep as they said, "Hello. Hello! *Hello,*" over and over.

"Amen," the Filipino kid with the buzz cut in the folding chair next to mine whispered.

The man at the front of the room stopped the tape.

"Praise be to God," he said.

"Praise be to God," the others repeated, me included.

I'd learned over the past couple months that it was best to just play along.

After Westcott made my expulsion official, he had Mrs. Wesley call my parents to break the news while I sat helplessly by.

Luckily, it wasn't so late on the West Coast as to wake him up, but still, when the school called after business hours, my dad assumed the worst.

"No, no, he's fine—" Mrs. Wesley said into the phone before raising a hand over her mouth. "That is to say . . . he's *alive*. But I'm afraid Daniel has gotten himself into some trouble."

I was better off dead, I remember thinking.

As she explained the situation, certain highlights made me wince as I thought about his face on the other end of the line, back in the Hills:

". . . lewd conduct . . .

". . . drinking and drugs . . .

". . . *homosexuals* . . .

". . . expelled."

She pulled the phone a few inches from her face as I heard shouting from the other end. She looked at me, concerned, like she was about to say something, but only held there, frozen.

"I want to talk to him," I said.

She nodded.

"Uh . . . Mister Preston," she interrupted. "Daniel is here with me . . . and he wants to talk to you."

She was still as she listened, like one of the paintings of the school founders that hung around her in the office. Then she held the receiver to her chest and turned to me.

"He . . . he says no, dear. Not right now."

I grabbed the phone from her, as she gasped.

"But Dad," I said.

At that very moment, Leo passed me, led by Theo Breckenridge, on his way into Westcott's office.

Fuck, I thought, but I couldn't think about Leo and his safety long, because I had my father in my ear.

"I SAID I DO NOT WISH TO SPEAK TO YOU," my dad roared. "PUT HER BACK ON THE PHONE."

I knew enough to know that whatever I had to say, he wouldn't hear a word of it in that mood. I handed the phone back to Wesley, who looked at me like I was a terminal cancer patient.

Things happened pretty fast after that.

I was immediately sent back to our room to pack. I kept waiting for Leo to come join me until I realized they were keeping us separated.

I was terrified for him, not because I didn't think Leo couldn't handle himself with Westcott, but because Leo was the type of guy to just say fuck it and own up to the whole thing—the book, the murder, all of it—just to let Westcott know who was boss.

I just hoped that in this moment, he could be smarter than that.

When I was packed up, Theo was waiting for me downstairs in the common room.

It was late now, past eleven, so it was quiet; just a couple kids studying on couches and one in the phone booth. Their eyes all said that they knew exactly what was happening, though. They'd seen me get called in to the office—seen the van pull up outside, ready to take me to whatever was next.

We trudged out into the cold driveway, and Theo helped me load my stuff in the back of the van.

"Where am I going?" I asked him.

"The airport," he said. "Out of Boston. They got you an early flight."

"Nice of them," I said.

He looked down at the gravel.

"I don't know what we're gonna do," he said. "The team, I mean. First Godfrey . . . and now you."

"Maybe you'll finally get off the bench," I said.

He laughed, steam escaping his mouth into the night.

Then he looked down again.

"Were you . . ." he mumbled. "I mean, *are* you . . . really one of them?"

"They were my friends, yeah, if that's what you mean," I said. "Like how I'm your friend."

He looked at me, though he seemed miles away.

"Goodbye, Preston," he said. "I'll . . . Goodbye."

And he turned and walked back to the warmth of Bass Hall.

I took a last look. I always loved the look of the buildings here, like castles covered in ivy, so different from the new builds in Beverly Hills.

Goodbye, I thought.

Then we were gone.

It was about an hour's drive in the dark of the night down to Logan International Airport in Boston.

I arrived after one in the morning, groggily checked in, and finally lay down my head to get some semblance of a night's sleep on a row of chairs at my gate.

Thankfully, I didn't sleep through boarding for my flight at six. I even got a McDonald's breakfast of pancakes and hash browns. If I was flying to my doom, I might as well enjoy the final moments with greasy deliciousness.

It wasn't until I was in my seat (coach this time, my punishment already beginning) that I began to get scared. I wondered who would be waiting for me at the arrivals gate: my mom, muttering prayers and crying, or my dad, ready to berate me with all the ways I'd squandered the gifts he'd worked hard to give me.

Turns out, it was worse.

Five hours later, I staggered off the plane, grabbed my bags from the carousel, and walked to the arrivals, bracing for impact. I was totally confused, then, when instead of finding one or both of my furious parents waiting for me, I found a white guy in khakis holding a sign with my name on it.

Growing up the way my dad did, even with the fortune he'd made for himself, he wasn't one to waste money on things he didn't need. He'd never once booked a car service to take me to and from LAX when he was perfectly capable of driving me himself for just a couple bucks of gas. I knew something was up immediately.

"Daniel?" the guy asked me.

". . . Yes?"

"I thought so! How was the flight?"

"Early," I said. "Who are you?"

"Sorry, I'm Pastor Michael Davis, but everybody calls me Pastor Mike. I run a program called Right Path."

He was probably forty-five, an ex-football-looking type, like he used to be the star of the team in his glory days and now he drives a sedan and keeps his jock haircut tight just in case he gets that call from the big leagues he's been waiting for his whole life. I usually try to be polite, even when I'm suspicious of someone—I learned that's a good way to not come off as intimidating and stay out of trouble—but I was way too tired for his caffeinated grin. Still, I shook his hand when he offered it.

"Pastor?"

"You probably have a lot of questions," he said. "And that's OK, because we have a bit of a drive ahead of us."

"But my house is only, like, thirty minutes from here."

He cocked his head, quizzically.

"Ah, Dan—can I call you Dan? We're not going to your house."

Now I was awake.

I wondered if Westcott had intercepted my travel and sent some Oldfellows agent to take me to be interrogated under torture or something.

Turns out, it was worse.

"Then where are we going?"

"Your parents gave you a gift. A really special gift," Pastor Mike said. "The gift of a second chance through the love of Christ. We're gonna help you seize that chance at Right Path."

It's amazing what you can get used to.

For the last . . . what was it, three months now? I'd had the same daily routine.

Up at five.

Breakfast at five thirty.

Morning prayer at six.

Morning exercise at six thirty.

Shower and into uniform for "Secular Education" at seven thirty.

Lunch at noon.

Reorientation Therapy, or "RT," from one onward.

Every day, except for Sunday, where we'd have extended prayer and then extra time for "quiet reflection."

And it was quiet, all right.

We were somewhere a couple hours out in the desert, maybe Indio or something, but I had no idea where exactly. We never left the Right Path compound.

The people in charge were called "teammates," while those of us sent for RT were called "refugees," a term that rubbed me the wrong way considering how many Black and brown kids they had in the program. There were fifteen refugees in total while I was there, mostly teenage boys like me, but also two grown men in their thirties and a couple of girls, too. Any group gatherings took place in the large, beige Fellowship Hall, from meals to worship, RT, and our secular classes (which meant real stuff like math and science and history, but all taught through the Right Path lens). If we weren't there, we were in our cabins, separated by sex, carefully, constantly supervised by one of Pastor Mike's teammates. Everything we did was watched; I couldn't even take a piss or a shower alone. Apparently, any alone time with my own penis, even for purely functional reasons, was too dangerous.

I had no way to leave, contact anyone, or refuse any part of it. If it sounds like prison, yeah, that's exactly what it was.

And what was "Reorientation Therapy"?

That could mean any number of things, depending on the day.

Some days, RT was lessons on how to free our minds from the programming of the biased media. For example, we shouldn't call ourselves "gay" when we talked about why we were at Right Path. Instead, we should talk about the "same-sex attractions" that we struggle with, because giving those attractions a label like "gay" means that they're something we're born with, like my dark skin or my right-handedness, and not just a bad habit that we can unlearn.

Some days, it was guest speakers who would tell us how broken their lives became due to the homosexual lifestyle: the drugs and promiscuity and lies and, of course, the friends dying all around them. From suicide. From overdoses. From AIDS.

During my whole time at Right Path, I spoke to my mom exactly twice.

The first time was upon my arrival at the compound. After handing over my luggage to them to search for contraband and other "at risk" material, they'd had me sign a pledge of commitment to the process and then finally let me use the phone.

"Mom, what the hell?" I said when she answered. Pastor Mike shot a look to a teammate, but I didn't care. I'd be the "angry Black man" in their eyes. I *was* angry.

"My love, now listen—"

"Where am I, even? They won't tell me."

"You're somewhere they can help. Trust me, your dad called Reverend Waters, and he said they're the best."

"Oh good, I was worried you'd skimped on my kidnapping."

"Now *hold on*, young man," she said in a voice I'd come to learn was her "last straw" voice. Like a trained puppy, I sat at attention and shut my mouth without even thinking about it. "If I'm not mistaken, you were *expelled* from your school, the school we paid a fortune for you to attend, because you couldn't behave yourself, am I wrong?"

She'd be right if she was talking about the parties or the drinking, but I knew she meant the gay part, and thinking of my relationship with Leo as not "behaving myself" seemed wrong, to say the least.

". . . Daniel Darius Preston, am I wrong?"

". . . No, ma'am."

"So, your dad and I could have had them put you on a bus to wherever the heck we wanted, let you figure it out from there since you're so smart, but try as you might to push us away, we *love you too dang much.*"

I could hear something crackling through her last-straw voice. Something pained and raw.

My mom cleaned houses when she was young, just like her mother, and her mother before that. When my dad hit it big, she could have sat back and enjoyed her money with shopping sprees and hundred-dollar lunches like so many of the other ladies in the Hills. She wouldn't even have to clean her own house ever again. That's not what she did, though. Instead, she went into social work, driving an hour or more, six days a week, down to Compton and back to work with kids who have about as many options as she'd had back when she was scrubbing other people's toilets. And on the one day a week she didn't make that drive, she still scrubbed ours. She was a complicated, Christian woman, so sometimes her love took forms that didn't make sense to me, but no one could say she didn't love.

"Yes, ma'am."

She sighed on the other end of the phone.

"Just *try*, Daniel. We're giving you this chance. I just ask that you take it and try. For me."

". . . Yes, ma'am."

"Thank you, my love."

"Can I talk to Dad?" I asked.

She paused. I imagined her looking to where he surely stood, feet away, listening to every word and getting waved off. My dad could do amazing things with fabric and thread but was never good stringing words together into anything special.

"He needs some time, Daniel. You understand."

"Yeah, OK," I said.

❖

Some days, RT was drills and exercises meant to train our bodies and voices to perform more like men, or more like ladies, depending on which direction Pastor Mike thought each of us needed to go. These were the easy days for me, since I already seemed to have the posture, the voice, the comfort with a football or a power tool that Pastor Mike was looking for.

In fact, one day, after I'd aced a lesson in how to chop wood, he pulled me aside.

"Dan, I just wanted to let you know how great I think you're doing," he said in a low whisper. "Between us, some of these guys can only expect to learn *control* from RT, rather than expect real change. That is to say, God may be calling them to a life of . . . service. *Celibate* service, I mean. It will be a lifelong struggle, but that's their calling. I hope you can see that you're different, though. I really believe you are a normal, straight guy who was just in the wrong place at the wrong time. Boys' schools can be like that. You just got off the path."

That was the main message of Right Path, no matter what the day's Reorientation Therapy was: that we were all born straight and that something had interfered with our healthy development. That some moment of trauma in our past was responsible for our same-sex attractions.

The hardest days for me were the days where we tried to pinpoint that moment.

Who touched me inappropriately? I'd wonder, as instructed.

Pastor Mike insisted that there had to be *some* reason for my perversion, and that until I found it, I'd never be free. So even when my mind drew a blank, I'd still keep searching, not because I thought something was actually there, but because I knew Pastor Mike wouldn't rest until I delivered, like the others, some weepy admission about an uncle or a teacher, regardless of whether or not it was true.

There seemed to be two kinds of people that Right Path attracted. There were the ones so earnestly into the cause that you couldn't just have a conversation with them about music or the weather. They only wanted to talk about where they were in their recovery and what it would be like to feel God's love once again. Then there were the ones who were so shocked and ashamed by whatever circumstances brought them there that they didn't say anything, drifting from class to meal to RT like zombies. As you can imagine, I didn't make many friends.

There was one friend, though.

I won't call him what Pastor Mike called him, because that wasn't really his name, not anymore. Mike made him go by his old name and made him wear the black skirt instead of the khaki pants and called him "she" instead of "he" because this one friend I made was given that other name at birth and Mike thought his "recovery" demanded he return to that identity. I just knew him as Jackson, and Jackson was fucking *funny.*

We first noticed each other one day during RT when some *Sound of Music*–looking kid was speaking.

"I get scared that after I go through all of this, even when I'm restored, people will judge me for having gone through it," the kid said. "But then I think of Christ. He hung on a cross for us, so I can do this for him. And I don't love Jesus in *spite* of him having to go through hanging on that cross. I love Jesus *because* he was hung."

I heard a snort erupt from the seat over my shoulder, giving voice to the laugh I was working to stifle myself. I turned. That was Jackson, shaggy straw-colored hair in his face. I raised an eyebrow at him and he put a hand over the smirk he couldn't control.

"Very GOOD, Pete," Pastor Mike said to the kid, though he was looking right at Jackson. "That's a *beautiful analogy.*"

I sidled over to Jackson at dinner that night and introduced myself.

"Don't let this *stunning* piece from the Nancy Reagan Collection fool you," he said, gesturing to the frumpy skirt and dowdy one-inch heel they'd made him wear. "It's Jackson, and it's 'he.' "

"Nice to meet you, Jackson," I said. "Next question—you don't buy any of this shit, do you?"

"What do you mean?" he said, incredulous. "I think Pastor Mike is absolutely *full* of Christ's love! Totally and completely. *Full. Of. It.*"

We howled.

Pastor Mike saw us laughing and strolled over.

"Dan! ■■■■■■■■■■!" he said, calling Jackson by the name I won't say. "Is this a love connection I'm seeing? God works in mysterious ways!"

"He really thinks I'm a straight girl," Jackson said, rolling his eyes as Mike walked away. "Little does he know I'm a gay boy. And you are cute, Preston, but I got someone waiting for me back home."

No matter how the day was going, I could count on Jackson to shoot me some secret little wink or eye roll and remind me that there was still sanity inside this place.

Then one day I came down to breakfast to find a scene of total chaos: kids being interrogated by teammates, Pastor Mike running around red-faced, the food not ready.

I thought about the Perfect Storm.

"What's going on?" I asked Pete, the *Sound of Music* kid.

"It's ■■■■■■■■■■," he said.

"*Jackson*," I corrected.

Then I got scared. It really says something about gay life that you assume the worst when hearing something like that. ". . . What happened to him?"

"*She* made a run for it," the kid said, making a point to use the wrong pronoun. I didn't have the energy to school him a second time. Some people are just like that.

"What?"

"Flown the coop, a runaway," he said. "It happens sometimes. It's sad. Not as sad as the ones who off themselves, but still. Why would you refuse grace for a life like that?"

"That happen a lot here?" I asked, horrified. "When you say, 'the ones who off themselves'?"

The kid's eyes went dark.

"More than it should," he said quietly.

❖

Some days, RT was holding big chunks of ice, strapped to a chair, while a teammate made me watch gay porn videos. If I dropped the ice, I got time added to the end of my session. I was only free to go when I could make it through the five-minute video, my hands simultaneously frozen and on fire as I screamed.

❖

The second time I spoke to my mom was on Christmas. I thought for sure I'd have gotten a clean bill of health and a ticket home by then, for *Christmas* for god's sake, but all I got was a box in the mail with some gift-wrapped Air Jordans and that phone call.

"Merry Christmas, my love! Did you get the present?"

"Yeah, I *got the present*," I said, bitterly. "Really thought I'd be home by now, though. I mean, it's *Christmas*."

"I know," she said. "Trust me, I don't like it, either."

"So why can't I come home, then?"

I could hear her forcing a smile and an upbeat tone.

". . . Pastor Mike tells me you're doing great! That he thinks you're on the verge of a breakthrough, and—"

"Yeah, when he says 'breakthrough,' he means that he wants me to make up some event from my past that made me gay," I said. The teammate who was supervising my phone call sat up at attention with that, but I didn't care.

"What?"

"Yeah, if I lied and said that Reverend Waters diddled me behind the church a few years back, I'd be out of here. Maybe I should."

"Daniel!" she cried.

I saw out of the corner of my eye that the teammate had fetched Pastor Mike.

"Mom, it's all a load of shit, this whole thing. They're not scientists, they're not psychologists, they're just trying to get your money!"

"OK," Pastor Mike said, as he tried to wrestle the phone from my hands. "That's enough, son."

"Does Dad actually believe God can change me, or does he just think this is another way he can buy a perfect son? How much are you paying them?" I shouted. "They're robbing you!"

"Daniel has to go, Mrs. Preston!" Mike yelled, still weirdly peppy.

"WHERE IS DAD?!" I screamed before Mike finally got the phone out of my hand.

He slammed it down onto the receiver and slapped me across the face, hard.

If I wasn't so stunned, I would have given him one back, but the way he just dropped his whole "Up with People" act like that took me a minute to process.

"Give us a minute," he said to the wide-eyed teammate, who cleared out like a hit dog.

"*Now you listen here*," he said. "I'm going to level with you, because I can tell that's what it's gonna take. God's love, sin, fear of Hell—all of that is a way into what we offer here that works for most people. I can tell that isn't the case with you. So let me put it to you a different way."

He walked over to a filing cabinet, flipped through some folders, and found the one he was looking for. He pulled a newspaper clipping out and handed it to me.

THE FACE OF EVIL: BODIES LITTER MILWAUKEE MAN'S APARTMENT

Jeffrey Dahmer Says He Killed and Ate Seventeen Men

There was a picture of a man who, by gay standards, was a textbook stud: muscular build, wavy blond hair, mustache, tight T-shirt. He wore aviator-style glasses, but he didn't look nerdy. He looked like Harrison Ford.

I'd heard about Jeffrey Dahmer when he was arrested last summer, Ninety-One, but the newspaper in my hands brought the details flooding back. He lured young men, mostly young gay *Black* men, back to his apartment, where he killed them, cut up their bodies, ate their flesh, and kept their skeletons. He was able to lure them from a Milwaukee gay bar, because Jeffrey Dahmer was himself a homosexual.

"Is this really something you want to be a part of?" Pastor Mike asked. "Because you let a sickness fester long enough and this is where it leads, I promise you. Here, or to the end of a heroin needle, or to a bed in an AIDS ward. I'm just being honest with you, son."

I wasn't impressed.

"So there are gay monsters," I said. "There are Christian monsters, too. Am I asking you to answer for all of them? You might as well preach to me about Black-on-Black crime."

He flashed a sinister smile as he snatched the clipping back from me.

"Well, since you brought it up," he said, his voice changing from angry to gravely concerned. "Your dad and I talked about that when he called, late in the evening, to get you booked into this place. Because, as I'm sure you know well, being Black in this country, you're already fighting with one hand tied behind your back. You tie the other hand with your label of 'gay' and you know what happens? You're a damn punching bag."

He said it like he was letting me in on a secret I didn't already know.

I had to hand it to him. This gloves-off Pastor Mike knew exactly where to hit.

"Now think about everything your daddy told you about how it's been for him, being Black in America. Think about everything you've got ahead of you, everything holding you back *without* this gay thing, and answer me this: If you could do something to change it, to remove all those obstacles, wouldn't you?"

I stared at him, amazed.

". . . Would I like to stop being Black?"

"That's the question, yes."

"Well, it's a ridiculous question, because it's impossible."

"It's a hypothetical, Dan. Say you could take a pill and change your skin overnight, hypothetically. Because, in essence, that's what we're offering for your same-sex attract—"

"Would *you* like to take a pill and stop being white?"

He rolled his eyes.

"Now why would I wanna do that?"

"So you could tolerate seasoned food, I dunno," I said.

He didn't like that.

"You can be as smart as you like with me, Daniel, but you know what I mean. Now I can't make your life easier than it will be on account of your skin, but I know I can help you with that other hand tied behind you."

"You *know*," I laughed. "How do you know?"

"What if I told you that *I* was a refugee myself?" he said. "Married ten years now to a wonderful woman."

"I'd say I had a few questions for Missus Pastor Mike."

"KEEP TALKING, BOY!" he roared. "See where it gets you. You just see what happens."

There it is.

"To answer your question," I said, standing to get right up in his face, "no, I wouldn't take your magic pill. My race isn't the problem, *racism* is the problem. Just like my gayness isn't the problem, *bigotry* is the problem. You should make a pill for those, because those actually can be changed."

He sneered and turned away, but I laid in.

"But you know what? Even having to live in this country, the way it is, no, I wouldn't take the pill. *Either* pill. I mentioned Black food, but there's also Black music, Black art, Black history, Black language. Black *culture*. Black *joy*. There's gay joy, too, if you can believe it. I don't know if I believe in God . . . but those gifts give me a hell of a lot more reason to believe than whatever you're offering here."

❖

And so, months later, as February became March, as I watched the videotape of the Deaf baby hearing her parents with her new implant, all I could think was, *They gave her the pill. And she couldn't say yes or no.*

I'm sure there is Deaf culture and Deaf joy, too. I prayed that the little girl in the video would still find them.

Just then, I heard a commotion coming from outside the doors of the Fellowship Hall: a woman shouting and a teammate trying to shush her.

I was certain I heard my name.

Then the doors burst open and we all turned to see a middle-aged Black woman with short gray hair, formidable despite her short stature, storming toward us as a helpless young teammate chased after her.

"Aunt Deb?!" I gasped, standing.

"Oh, Daniel!" she said as she wrapped her arms around my waist and squeezed tight. "I'm here to get you out of this loony bin!"

Aunt Deb would turn out to be the gift from God I didn't know I had.

She explained everything in the car as we headed back west toward LAX and our flight to Chicago.

After all this time, I was going back to the neighborhood.

She was in the driver's seat, pushed all the way forward, straining to see up over the wheel as we rumbled along.

Growing up, Deb was like a second mother to me, but ever since we moved away, she had become weirdly distant; just a voice on the occasional phone call, a name in a card next to a twenty-dollar bill every birthday, Christmas, and Easter, and a face in some very old photos. I knew my Aunt Deb as a great cook, a big gossip, and a surprisingly good ball player despite her height, but I never knew much about who my Aunt Deb was as a person, and I'd soon find out that was for a reason.

"When I called on Christmas morning and you weren't there, I knew something was up," she said. "Darius said you had stayed behind at school, but I heard something strange in your mom's voice when I asked her why you would do that. So I decided to call the school myself. Well, did they ever have a story to tell!"

She gave me a sly little grin and slapped my leg a couple of times and I thought, *Wait a minute, Aunt Deb is cool.*

"I called your folks back and I said, 'Darius, I've been your sister for forty-five years. I knew right away that you were lying about Daniel, but now that I know the whole truth, I know *why* you lied. The only thing I don't know is where you're keeping him, so out with it.' "

"Damn, what did he say?" I asked.

"He hung up, of course. He was always scared of me."

"So how did you . . . ?"

"I tried back a few times, but I think they started screening my calls. Luckily, last month your mom called me herself, while Darius was working. She gave me the name of the place. Sorry it's taken me so long to stage my rescue operation. It took me a few weeks working overtime to save up enough for the plane tickets and rental car. In my mind, I'd scoop you up in a black Rolls and we'd soar away in a private jet, like James Bond, but you'll have to use your imagination."

"Why are you doing this for me?" I asked. "I mean, thank you, but . . . wow."

She began to speak but then stopped herself and, instead, reached into her back pocket to fish out a wallet. She tossed it into my lap.

I opened it and a strip of photographs accordioned open; photographs of my Aunt Deb posing at various tourist attractions around the country, posing in front of a Christmas tree, posing at a protest. In each of them, she was accompanied by another Black woman, a few years younger and about a full foot taller, beaming affectionately. I noticed the way her arm hung around Deb's tiny shoulders. I thought about how little Leo fit in the crook of my own arm.

"She's . . ."

"My wife," Deb said. "Keisha."

"Oh wow," I said.

In an instant, I understood a lifetime of mysteries about Aunt Deb. Why we never visited her or let her visit us. Why my dad scowled when she came up in conversation. Why I knew almost nothing about her.

"She's beautiful," I said.

"She can't wait to meet you," Deb said. "You're gonna come live with us for a little while . . . if that's OK with you."

Turns out, my dad was still not ready to even have the conversation about what happened at Blackfriars. About who I was.

Deb told me that after my altercation with Pastor Mike on Christmas, Mike had called the house to tell my parents that I was a tough case. They needed to either come get me immediately or commit to a full year of the program.

You'll be shocked to learn which my dad picked.

Luckily for me, Deb works as a paralegal and arrived with some very serious questions about the legality of the operation Right Path was running, since they weren't properly permitted as caretakers or psychologists. Even though she wasn't authorized to sign me out, they decided to look the other way and mark me as a runaway if she didn't pull those threads.

Once we were safely on the road, she told me she was absolutely going to pull those threads anyway, for the sake of the other kids.

We got to the airport and began to check my mountain of bags through to Chicago. They were each little time capsules, still unopened since I hastily packed them the night I got expelled from Blackfriars. I watched each of them climb the conveyor belt and wished that I had thought to grab a change of clothes so that I could leave my Right Path uniform in the trash. Then, just before the bag full of my school supplies and desk stuff disappeared from view, I remembered the thing I'd needed so much more desperately than a new look, all these months.

"Wait! Grab that one," I shouted to the attendant. "I need something."

She passed me the bag. I zipped it open and rummaged through the papers and books until I found it: my address book.

We were at the gate early, so I had time to hit the payphone, which I ran to like a man runs to an oasis in the desert. It was just after six o'clock—Leo ought to be home.

I flipped through the book, nearly tearing the pages, my hands were so shaky. Plunking in the quarter and dialing the number were just as challenging.

The wait as the phone rang on the other end was excruciating.

And then, he picked up.

"Hello?"

I don't know how I expected to react to hearing his voice, after so much time, after everything I went through at Right Path. I should have expected tears, I guess.

I didn't expect so many.

"Hello?" he asked again. "I can hear you breathing, creep! If you think you can shock me with some panting, you don't know the things I've seen—"

"Leo," I managed to say.

Then he was quiet.

". . . Daniel?"

"Yeah. Hi. Hi!"

I could hear his own breath quicken. I think he was crying, too.

"Oh my god, Daniel. Hi," he said. "Where have you been? We've been calling and calling. Your dad—"

"That's a long story that I'll tell you soon. But I'm OK. I'm OK now."

Saying the words out loud unlocked something in me. I really was going to be OK.

"I just wanted to check in as soon as I could before I got on this flight," I said. "Did you get expelled, too? What about Zooey and Steven?"

"Oh . . . Oh, Daniel, you don't know," Leo said.

There was that thing again, always assuming the worst.

This time, though, I was right.

"Steven's gone," Leo said.

". . . Where'd he go?"

"No, I mean . . . Daniel, he's dead."

I pressed the phone to my chest and clenched my eyes shut, trying to keep from crying out right there in the phone booth.

I drew in as deep a breath as I could and brought the phone back to my ear.

"What . . . what happened?" I asked.

"He took the fall for us, returned the book himself and said it was all him. He got expelled, too, but that night he dropped dead in his bedroom. Some freak aneurysm, they said."

"Westcott," I whispered.

"Had to be," Leo said. "But Steven got him off our trail. Westcott's left us alone since."

"Jesus," I said.

I pictured Steven at his post at the door of the VC parties, book in hand, thick glasses down on the bridge of his nose. He was always protecting us, even to the end.

"God, your timing is downright spooky," Leo said. "The dark moon is tomorrow, Oona's been working on the poison all day, and now here you are, back in our lives at the eleventh hour."

"Leo, what the hell are you talking about?"

"Right. Gosh, there is so much to catch you up on," he said. "How many quarters do you have?"

Ten minutes later, I was sprinting to the gate where my Aunt Deb was waiting, flustered, up on her tiptoes to look for me over the crowds.

"Daniel!" she cried as I approached. "There you are! Lord, you're gonna give me a heart attack. We're boarding soon!"

"Aunt Deb, I'm really sorry, but I need to speak to someone about changing my ticket," I said.

She looked up at me, stunned.

"Baby, what on earth are you talking about?"

I took her shoulders in my hands and looked urgently into her eyes. "I need to get to Adders Lair, Massachusetts, right away."

CHAPTER SEVENTEEN

ZOOEY

"One . . . two . . ."

I took a deep breath and looked to Leo, then Daniel, who sat on the opposite side of the table, their faces grim with the gravity of the task at hand.

They each nodded their readiness.

We'd all made our decision.

"THREE!"

We each pointed our fingers toward the golden slivers arrayed before us.

Then we shifted our gaze down to the platter.

"We picked the same again, Zo!" Leo cried.

It was true, we'd both pointed at the same French fry; a long, medium golden one with a gentle, even curve. (A textbook fry, by my estimation.)

"I mean I knew we had the same taste . . ." he said coolly, as he tilted his head toward Daniel.

"Shut UP!" I cried, tossing my balled-up napkin right at his red little face. I missed completely despite the close range and hit his plastic cup of water, very nearly toppling it and drenching the whole plate of fries. Daniel's Spider-Man reflexes saved the game and the evening.

"Smooth move, Z," he laughed as he waved away the stern-looking waitress who'd approached our table like a cop making a traffic stop. She'd been eyeing us up ever since it became clear that we had no intention of eating the fries we'd ordered, instead using them as props in this stupid little game to take our minds off of the task that lay ahead of us that night. She gave us another dirty look. I imagined just what kind of look we'd get if we told her that we couldn't eat the fries because we had to fast before ingesting the ritual poison that would nearly kill us. I shook the thought from my mind.

"And look at the one you chose, Dan," I said. "Another 'short and salty.' A man's fry choice really does say a lot about him."

"You can say that again." Dan beamed and tousled Leo's hair.

Apparently, when Leo picked Daniel up from the airport early this morning, they barely made it out of the parking lot, the reunion was so passionate. They did somehow keep their hands off of each other long enough to reach Leo's bedroom. Luckily, his mom had already left for work. Somehow, I wasn't jealous anymore. Seeing them back together was like easing into a bath. The more they flirted, the more my shoulders dropped. In fact, I was so relaxed, sitting in the booth of the sun-drenched diner on that (uncharacteristically, for Adders Lair) warm and sunny afternoon, I felt more at peace than I had all year, despite what I knew was coming in just a few hours' time.

"God, I wish we could eat these," Leo said, examining the textbook perfect fry before sadly dropping it onto his own plate. "If I die tonight, I hate to think that I went out without tasting the Sea Salt Diner's fries one last time."

"Hey," Daniel said. "No one is dying . . . and we agreed: Today is about us. Fries and catching up and each other. Save tonight for tonight."

A wave of something melancholy washed over the table, like that feeling you get on a Sunday night or on the last day of summer vacation, but immeasurably worse.

"So, next round," I said, trying my damnedest to steer us back into the carefree feeling of just moments ago. "Gentlemen, select your fries. What *exact* fry would you eat next, if you could eat it? One . . . two . . . THREE!"

We played the stupid game well past the time the fries got cold and the waitress got fed up and abandoned us and any hope of making a decent tip from our table. Each round, we selected our perfect fry from the remaining plate of available options and then discussed our choices in-depth, which inevitably led to stories and tangents: A particularly pale and limp fry brought out Daniel's stories of Pastor Mike and all that he'd endured at Right Path. We sat with jaws dropped as he recounted the horrors of the place and wrapped him in a group hug when he'd finished.

The longest fry in the bunch became a toast and tribute to Steven.

"This one's for you, Hillman," Leo said, holding the fry aloft. "We wouldn't be able to do this thing tonight without you."

"Save tonight for tonight," Daniel reminded him gently.

Leo nodded and wiped a fresh tear. We returned to the game and the present moment.

A skinny burnt fry reminded us all of Leo's very tanned mother, who, according to Leo, was doing OK after the shock of Lucas's final days. She was even dating again. Two stuck-together fries inspired jokes about Mallory and our breakup.

"No, I haven't returned her calls and no, I'm *definitely* not giving the CD back," I said to high fives from the boys.

I thought about my mother, who always said when planning dinner parties that the food was secondary to the company. She was right. Despite not eating a morsel, it was one of the greatest meals of my life. But, as ever, the party has to end at some point.

We looked down to see that the plate of fries was empty.

"I guess it's time," Daniel said as he looked out the window to see the diner's neon sign buzz on. There was something foreboding about the way its electric redness pushed back against the quiet navy evening, the dark moon of March fourth, Nineteen Ninety-Two, hanging ominously overhead. I felt sick and sad.

"Is it bad that I just wanna run away from this?" I asked. "Like, haven't we been through enough?"

"This is the last chapter," Daniel said. He laid his hand on mine, and this time, I didn't feel the kind of romantic flush I used to feel when we touched. I felt a kind of comfort I hadn't felt in a long time. I thought about my mother again. "And then we can finally put it behind us and, I *hope*, feel OK about it. I mean, I don't know if this will make it right, what we did . . . But *I hope*."

I nodded.

"You do realize," I said to Leo, "that if we succeed in this, if we can actually release their demon and remove their source of power . . . you won't be invisible anymore. You really ready to go public at public school?"

"Being invisible isn't all it's cracked up to be." Leo shrugged. "I've always been more suited to the spotlight anyway, for better or worse."

Just then, the waitress slapped our sad little check on the table before stomping up to the front counter to seat the growing crowd who'd showed up for dinner, shooting us the very iciest look on her way.

"I *think* she may be trying to tell us something," Leo said. "Well, boys, shall we go meet the devil?"

The easy flow of our conversations at the diner dried up entirely on the short drive to Oona's place. We sat in complete silence as Leo guided the car through the winding, trash strewn back streets of Adders Lair. I tried to keep my mind focused on the plan ahead so that it didn't race in all directions and make me chicken out.

The spell would be simple, by Book of Brothers standards: On the night of the last dark moon before the vernal equinox, mix and consume a poison to slow the heart to the brink of stopping without actually killing. Once at the "crossroads," as Lucas had called it, the magician would meet the demon Frateroth face-to-face. Then, they just had to recite a command: "Frateroth, your work is complete in this realm. I give you license to depart."

Easy, right?

The trouble was, according to Oona and her knowledge of herbalism, the concoction was so volatile, the slightest error in the mixture would be deadly. If the mandrake and datura and opium weren't perfectly balanced with the fly agaric and ghost pipe and henbane, then the drink could kill you with seizures, paralysis, heart failure, madness, or any combination thereof. She spent a whole day gathering the required ingredients and worked through the night checking and rechecking their measurements before infusing them into red wine as instructed.

And sure enough, when we arrived at Oona's door and she led us somberly inside, three little glasses of death-spiked red wine sat waiting on her coffee table.

"If your translation is good, then it shouldn't kill you," she said. "I mean, I *know* I mixed it right. I'm a chemistry major, believe it or not. Not at all my passion, but . . . immigrant parents."

"And what's all this?" Leo asked, gesturing around the apartment. The spell didn't call for any special lights or circles, but I supposed Oona couldn't help herself; she'd decked the place out in lit white candles, statues of saints and angels, and several dishes of burning incense.

She looked almost embarrassed, turning her heavily shadowed eyes to the carpet.

"For protection," she said. "Just in case."

"Thanks, Oona," Daniel said. "We'll take all the help we can get."

"Yeah, I'll tell the devil you say hey when I get over there," Leo said.

"You're not going," I told them.

I'd been trying to find a way to tell them all day, but I didn't want to ruin our time together with what I knew would be an argument.

". . . What?" Leo asked.

I stepped forward and looked my friends in the eye.

"You're staying behind. I'm going on my own."

"Zooey, we all agreed," Daniel said.

"Yeah, are you crazy?" Leo said.

"Are you?" I asked. "There's no reason for all of us to take the risk. It's a one-man job: Reach the crossroads, say the words, release the demon. It will only take one of us, and it needs to be me."

"Why would you say that?" Leo asked. "If anyone should take the risk, it's me."

"I can't tell you how I know, but you have to trust me. I know."

❖

(What I didn't tell them then is something I'd kept from them since. Until now.

I knew, because the previous night, when I'd finally been able to clear my mind enough to sleep, I'd been visited in the place where we dream.

I'd been visited by Steven.

I don't know if you've ever lost someone, but when you do, there's a certain kind of dream you have for years after that you just *know* is different from the normal kind. Sometimes the person you've lost shows up, and it's as clear as being awake that they're not a random face generated by your subconscious to pass the time until dawn. You just know that they're really there.

And in some blank, gauzy space, deep in my mind's eye, Steven appeared to me, his height seemingly doubled as he towered over me, his glasses glowing like twin moons, a trickle of blood coming from his ear.

"Hello, Zooey," he said.

"Steven! I've missed you! Where are you?"

"Between," he said. "Like you will be soon."

I could hear the crashing of waves. I could feel water lapping at the indistinct edges of my body. I realized I was floating on my back and Steven seemed so tall because he was standing above me, looking down.

"I'm scared to go," I said.

"You have to, though," Steven replied. "And you have to go alone. If anyone can survive the journey, survive the *monster*, it's you."

He had something in his hand. A sea sponge. He lifted one of my arms and began to drag the sponge across it gently.

"What?"

"You have spent the most time with the beast," he said. "It knows you best. It may not devour you instantly."

"That feels nice," I said, enjoying his scrubbing. "But why would it . . . devour me? We're trying to free it from its prison, aren't we?"

"Like a dog, it doesn't know what freedom is anymore," said a voice.

I turned to see Ryan Godfrey, holding his own head under the crook of his arm, wading toward me across the water's mirror edge. He didn't look angry, though. He looked peaceful.

"It just knows how it gets fed," he said, bending to grab a sponge off of the ocean floor. "And it's very, very hungry. It can't help itself. I know the feeling."

He began to wash my legs with the sponge.

"Ryan, I'm so sorry about what happened," I said. "If I'd have known . . ."

"If *I'd* have known, I wouldn't have done what I did to you, either," he said.

"And not to be rude, but . . . why are you here, *washing* me?" I asked. "I mean, it's kind of gay."

He laughed.

"I'd have thought so too, before. Here, the way things look don't matter at all. I wanted to be here."

"To prepare you for what is coming," Steven said.

Ryan nodded.

"And to let you know that you're forgiven."

Then the water rose above all of us, and I woke up.)

❖

Leo grabbed my arm.

"Zooey," he said. "I can't let you do this. If it wasn't for me, none of us would know a thing about that book. None of this would have happened. Steven . . . Ryan . . ."

"They're OK," I told him. He looked confused.

". . . What?"

"Look," I said. "I have to be the one to do this. OK?"

He looked to Daniel, who took his hand and nodded.

"OK," he sighed as he released his grip.

❖

There were embraces and deep breaths and a whispered prayer from Oona.

Then we were all sitting in a circle on the living room floor with a sole glass of murky scarlet poison reflecting the candlelight around us like an unholy grail.

"Drink every drop; it's an exact measurement," Oona said. "And I would lay back, if I were you."

"And then what?" I asked.

"And then . . . you wait," she said. "And after that, I have no idea."

"You off-book?" Leo asked. "I mean, you know the incantation?"

"Frateroth . . . your work is complete in this realm. I give you license to depart," I recited.

"Aces," Leo said. He smiled, but his eyes glistened, like he was near tears.

"We'll be right here," Daniel said. "Go get 'em."

I nodded, lifted the glass, and raised it to each of them.

"Cheers, queers."

Then I drank.

It tasted so foul, I began to cough violently when I'd gotten it all down. The others rubbed my back and helped me lie down.

"Zooey! You OK?"

"Did you guys fast before, like I asked?"

"Breathe, buddy . . ."

Their voices distorted and slowed, like a cassette tape winding down.

Then, everything became very still.

Finally, my coughing ceased, and I could get my breath, though my eyes were still flush with tears.

"Ugh, that shit's awful!" I said.

I expected some kind of response, but the room was deadly quiet.

"Guys?"

I blinked my eyes open.

I was completely alone on the floor of Oona's living room.

I sat abruptly upright.

"Guys?!"

I managed to stand, shakily. The edges of my vision blurred and smeared as I looked around for some sign of them.

Though night had fallen when we gathered, an ominous red-orange light now poured in through the windows of the house like it was the height of sunset.

There was no sound, no movement of air, and no sign of the others.

The only thing I could sense, other than the strange, fiery glow of the light, was a faint but undeniable stench in the air.

He was close.

I walked cautiously toward the front door as the stench grew stronger.

As my vision became clearer, I could now see that everything in her house, its candles, crystals, and furniture, fizzled and vibrated around their edges, tiny particles of them rising into the air like bubbles in champagne.

I'm there, I thought. *The crossroads.*

This is what it's like.

I reached the front door. The light coming in around its hinges was nearly blinding, the smell overwhelming.

Still, I braced myself, thought of my friends, and pushed the door open.

When I stepped out into the street of downtown Adders Lair, I was nearly swept off my feet by a raging wind like I hadn't felt since the night of the Perfect Storm. The stink of the demon wasn't just thick in the air, it *was* the air itself. The silence of the house was replaced with a roaring like a commercial airplane going down. I could now see that the strange color of the light was because the sky was a raging inferno, fed by the particles of the street, buildings, and cars, which rose all around me, like snow falling in reverse.

And towering above it all, an inky black abomination pinned against the burning red sky, was the beast, its thousand tentacles rising and falling all across Adders Lair, its gaping mouth drooling, its obsidian eyes searching for its next meal.

Its eyes found mine, staring right back.

"FRATEROTH!" I cried, stepping out into an open intersection, in full view of the demon. It unhinged its jaw and roared furiously, ropes of slime carried down by its putrid breath like acid rain.

"YOUR WORK IS COMPLETE IN THIS REALM! I GIVE YOU LICENSE TO—"

And then I couldn't speak, couldn't *breathe*, because a slithering black tentacle had struck down fast as lighting and coiled tight around my throat.

I tried to pull it loose from my neck as it tightened.

Two more tentacles came raining down from the sky to ensnare my hands.

". . . Frat . . . er . . . oth," I choked.

I was now being lifted off my feet.

". . . Your work . . . your work is . . ."

My vision began to brown out as I gasped for breath. The beast was lifting me toward its hungry maw of razor-sharp teeth, but suddenly I felt like I was falling instead, plummeting into myself as my consciousness gave way and the wind, fire, stench, and monster all faded into blank whiteness.

I awoke wrapped in soft cotton sheets and a heavy feathered duvet, warm and languorous in the morning sun.

I drew in a sleepy breath as I stretched my limbs back to life.

Somewhere, I could smell coffee brewing.

I sat up, blinking.

I was in a luxurious bedroom: navy blue walls with crisp white wainscoting, a four-poster bed, a big-screen TV, wide windows looking out onto Central Park.

It was my room, of course.

I didn't understand why that would be a strange revelation. I was in my own bedroom, where I'd lain down to sleep last night after I'd finished my homework.

But that dream.

It was taking me several minutes to return from wherever I'd gone between hitting the pillow and rising again. It had been so immersive, so detailed, as I dreamed it, but now, as I tried to recall the details, each was just beyond my grasp, like a missed trapeze swinging away from my groping hands as I fell back to earth.

I think there was a school?

I think it was a nightmare?

My neck was slightly sore.

Must have slept funny, I figured.

Anyway, the dream was gone now, replaced by my morning hunger and the feeling of peace that comes with greeting a weekend with no homework.

I padded downstairs in my bathrobe and slippers, into the kitchen and, I hoped, the source of the scent of the brewing coffee.

My mom turned to see me approaching and smiled.

"My darling, you're finally awake!"

"I didn't mean to sleep so late," I said, pulling a chair up to the kitchen island. "Is the coffee still warm?"

"I just made a fresh pot," she said, reaching for a mug. "You must have slept well."

"Yeah, I was really in outer space. I had this dream . . . It felt like another world while I was in it, but now I can't even remember it. Isn't that funny?"

"Happens to me all the time," she said. "Well, wherever you went, I'm glad you're back with me." She reached a hand to the side of my face, stroking my cheek lovingly.

"How are you feeling?" I asked.

Her brow furrowed.

"I'm feeling great, darling. Why do you ask?"

Why do *I ask?*

The question had come so naturally to me, as if there was a reason she would almost certainly *not* be feeling well, but what? The instinct was slipping away from me just like the dream. I shook my head clear of it.

"I . . . I don't know," I laughed.

"You'd better drink up," she said, sliding the full cup of coffee to me.

"Rip Van Winkle is with us!" my dad said as he strode in from the den with his paper. "I thought you might have pricked your finger on a cursed spindle!"

"You're mixing up your fairy tales, Dad."

"This is my house, I'll tell the story how I want to tell it." He grinned. "Anyway, fantasy is better than the reality this morning. Your very own school is in the news, Zooey. I hope you didn't know this boy."

He dropped a folded page in front of me.

SCANDAL AT HANSARD SCHOOL

Teacher Charged with Statutory Rape of Student

"Seems like one of your teachers, a Mister Barrett, groomed and . . . took advantage of a student," my dad said.

I stared at the headline.

Something in the back of my mind was calling out to me, like the dream, but I was too foggy to hear it.

"Terrible," I whispered.

"Yes," my dad said. "The teacher will rot in jail, but think of the poor boy. He's ruined, too, even though he's the victim."

"I don't know what I'd do if someone did that to my son," my mom said.

"Don't even let that thought into your mind," my dad said. "We're lucky. Zooey isn't so vulnerable."

I smiled, even as that strange half-remembrance swirled around the drain of my mind, lingering, if ever-so faintly, at its depths.

❖

Things like that would happen to me from time to time throughout high school and college.

I'd see a kid with red hair, or two boys sharing one bicycle, or a news report about an approaching tropical storm, and I'd stop dead in my tracks.

One time, when Mal and I were driving west from Cambridge to see a play in the Berkshires, we passed the exit for Adders Lair and I nearly crashed the car, the feeling had been so intense.

"Zach, what on earth?!" she cried as we swerved.

"Sorry," I said. "Déjà vu . . . or something."

"Just keep us alive until curtain," she said, rubbing my back with her hand. "This was the last thing I was looking forward to before finals. After the show, however, *please* run us directly into a ditch. It would be better than flunking Poli Sci."

❖

My English degree from Harvard and Mallory's political connections led to an internship with a GOP senator, which led to a coveted position as assistant press secretary for President Eldridge's second term, a meteoric rise for a twenty-one-year-old fresh out of school.

That was by design, though; the party needed young people.

While most of the country was beginning to panic about apocalyptic conspiracies surrounding the approaching year Two Thousand, Eldridge's office was more concerned about getting his chosen successor elected after eight years of his controversial policies. Across the country, young people on the other side of the aisle were becoming engaged in numbers that the party couldn't ignore. They were anxious about global warming, angry about racial injustice, and beginning to lobby at the state level to legalize civil unions for same-sex couples.

"There's a perception problem," my boss said. "We're seen as the old guard going into a new millennium."

The think tank had gathered in the Oval one night in early March to strategize about how to garner similar enthusiasm around Vice President Westcott, who would now run for the presidency. Westcott was in his seventies, looked like someone's diaper-soiling grandpa, and put his foot in his mouth basically anytime there was a mic and camera on him. Just last week he'd called a Black female reporter "uppity." I knew that our climb was uphill, to say the least.

When I stepped into the room, I was nearly knocked out of my loafers by a stench like sewage and BO that filled every corner of the room, but I dared not say anything. I'd mentioned it once, months ago, to my boss, and he swiftly, curtly explained that the White House had plumbing issues and that the Boss found it very embarrassing and not to utter a word about it if I knew what was good for me.

I breathed through my mouth and learned to endure it.

"So, you're bringing in a kid to tell us what to do?" some aide barked.

"He's been telling *me* what to do for six months now, and he's been right every time," the press secretary said.

"I want to hear this," President Eldridge said. "Mister Orson is impressive, and if we don't get fresh blood pumping, we die."

I looked to him, astonished. He hadn't so much as made eye contact with me since I'd joined the team. That's not to say he was unfriendly. He was generally well liked among the staffers and known to be jovial and polite to even the lowliest intern, an ideal boss. But the Boss he remained, unreachable and unknowable.

Then, suddenly, he knew my name. The president of the United States knew my name. Moreover, he wanted my *opinion*.

"Thank you, Mister President," I gasped.

"Now, I have every confidence we can win this race just like we won the last two," he said. "*Every* confidence." His eyes scanned the room of men nodding in understanding. "But this isn't just about the presidential race, this is about the party down the ticket, at the state and local level. I can't promise victory for every *single* race, and I certainly can't enact our agenda with a divided Congress. So, Mister Orson, the floor is yours. Bring us dinosaurs into the age of enlightenment."

I nodded, took a deep breath, and stood.

"So, I know from *all* the memos about the issues with our email server that everyone in this room is now an internet user."

"Don't remind me!" Westcott chuckled. "I'd trade the Pennsylvania electoral votes to go back to a stamp and an envelope!"

"It's evolving technology, yes, but it's evolving fast," I said. "We have data that says by next year, fifty-two percent of adult Americans will be online. The vast majority of those adults are young adults, and a lot of the organizing we're seeing on the left right now is through online forums and blogs."

"*Blogs . . .*" the president repeated, turning the word in his mouth like a strange exotic food.

"Yes, like . . . open journals, online. People can write whatever they want in their blogs and share them with millions of people, all over the world, instantaneously. We believe that someday, every single person is going to have their own blog, publishing their thoughts and sharing them constantly. We believe this limitless sharing of information . . . without journalistic *oversight* . . . is going to completely change the way news media operates inside of ten years."

"Go on," Eldridge said, leaning in.

My boss shot me a proud glance.

"Now, when people read something in print, or in digital text in this case, it feels different from just hearing something around the water cooler. It has a legitimacy to it, no matter what it says."

"You're saying . . ."

"I'm saying, Mister President, that we have an opportunity to . . . craft the narrative around the party and let that narrative spread organically, user to user, rather than continually trying to grease the networks. The internet is, of course, free, and I believe it's also the future. We should seize it, now."

Eldridge sat back in his chair, nodding, a satisfied little smile spreading across his face.

"You're right about this one, Bob," he said to my boss. "This kid might be sitting at my desk someday."

❖

Emerging from the White House into the cool spring evening on a victorious high, I decided to treat myself by taking the long way home, as I did from time to time.

(The long way home meant walking north through Dupont Circle, then west on P Street until I hit a certain little park along Rock Creek where I'd find a bench and take in the sights.

That is to say, I'd only ever watch.)

I'd never been disloyal to Mallory in all of our years together, and I had no intention to be. Still, there was an itch I'd left unscratched my entire life, and so yes, sometimes, when I had a victory at work like I had today or maybe a few too many drinks at the Hay-Adams afterward, I'd take the long way home, as a treat, just to watch.

Men drifted in and out of the trees and bushes like sirens emerging from a black sea, calling me into the depths, but I kept anchor, as I always had. The call itself was exciting enough for me.

But then I saw one man whose stare I couldn't wave away.

It wasn't because he was stunningly beautiful or anything. He was handsome enough, with striking red hair, but a few years older than I was interested in.

When my eyes caught his, my first thought wasn't "*I want him.*"

It was, "*I know him.*"

I didn't know how, but I knew that I knew this man.

That feeling.

He turned and slipped through the dark of the trees, and I rose instinctively.

"Wait," I whispered into the night, but he seemed not to hear.

It was that feeling I'd had my entire adult life, of another truth, just beyond my understanding, but this time, it wasn't fading like it usually did. I knew that I needed to follow him.

So I ran.

I brushed through the trees, past groups of men chasing their own sirens in the dark, squinting for the flash of red hair in the moonlight that led me deeper in.

It occurred to me as I pursued him that I should have reached the other end of the park by now. It was a small park, just a couple of blocks deep, and yet I'd been following the man for what felt like miles as the trees thickened around me and the manicured grass under my feet became raw forest floor.

Eventually, I emerged into a clearing I'd never encountered before, the moon hanging high overhead, the red-haired man waiting for me.

"Hello, Zooey," he said.

I gasped. No one had called me that since high school.

We stood in silence a moment, just long enough for me to notice how silent the park had become. I was used to the sounds of this park: the buzz of insects, the distant hum of traffic beyond its edges, the soft whispers and moans of the men within its darkness. All of that atmosphere had gone blank. The temperature of the air itself had gone blank. I dared to break the stillness and ask:

"I . . . do I know you?"

"Not yet," he said. "I was wondering when you'd come."

"I don't understand," I said.

"In another life, we knew each other briefly. You showed me kindness when I was at the gate to the crossroads. I'm here to repay that kindness."

"Another life . . ." I repeated. That feeling of recognition was returning to me, like a dream upon waking, but in reverse.

"Yes," he said. "Oh, Zooey, that thing inside of you that you've denied and hidden and hated? In that other life, you wore it proudly."

I opened my mouth to protest, but I couldn't speak.

"You didn't steal glances at it in the shadows of some lonely park, or a dirty men's room, or a crowded sauna. You danced with it, surrounded by friends, howling with laughter. You spoke it out loud to the people you loved, and they loved you all the more for it. Don't you see? All the nights you've come to this park looking for something . . . you weren't looking for the men, the sex. You were looking for me. To take you home."

"*Another . . . life . . .*"

"Remember, Zooey," he said, as he reached out and touched my arm.

My eyes snapped closed as my mind snapped open.

❖

I am ten years old, hearing my voice on a tape recorder for the first time, the voice betraying a secret I didn't yet know I was keeping.

I am twelve years old. I learn a new word. Someone says it to me in the hallway at school. I go home and ask my mom, "What's a 'faggot'?" I watch her face fall.

I am fifteen years old and I'm telling my secret to Mr. B, the only person I've ever told. He reaches over and touches my thigh. It's wrong, but it's the first time I feel loved for my secret. I am taken advantage of.

I am sixteen years old and I'm at a new school, at a new party. I meet new friends. They give my secret a name, and it isn't a cuss word. We dance. We drink. I feel loved again, but the love doesn't feel dirty this time.

I am with Leo.

I am with Daniel.

I am with Steven.

We ride bicycles through the night.

We wear Halloween costumes and drink terrible punch.

We are on the seventh floor of a hospital in New York City. Our brothers are dying. Still, we find reasons to laugh. We find joy.

We are in the street, surrounded by allies, holding signs, shouting for medicine, for support.

We don't want to be invisible anymore.

We are back in the hospital. We are talking to a man, a man who is fading. A man with red hair.

❖

My eyes snapped open.

"Who *are* you?" I asked the man again, though with each passing second, I became more sure that I already knew the answer.

"You remember," he said. "You tell me."

". . . Lucas," I whispered.

He looked different in this life. Healthy and vibrant, his eyes brighter, his face fuller, his hair redder. He looked the way he'd looked in the photos on the wall of his hospital room.

"Hi, Zooey. It's good to see you."

He smiled at me.

I smiled back.

". . . And . . . who are they?"

I was referring to the men who surrounded us.

I'd thought we were standing in a clearing of a forest, but now I could see that we were standing in the center of a crowd, thousands and thousands of men, standing shoulder to shoulder around us, silent as trees.

"The dead, Zooey. Those who went before me, and beside me, and after me."

I looked around at them. So many men, of every age and shape and race. To look at them, you wouldn't know the thing that made them all kindred unless you had it, too. It wasn't something you could see; it was something you could feel.

"I can take you back to that other life," Lucas said, "but only if you want it. I can't promise you'll be safe. I can't promise that road will lead you to a job at the White House, or to a happy marriage, or even to a comfortable life free of violence. But I can promise you that all of those memories you keep, the dancing and the weeping, the good touch and the bad touch, the life and the death, the joy and the agony . . . those are the truth. Your truth. And having lived mine, I can promise you that the joy outweighs the agony in the end. I only remember the dancing."

I remembered a night from my other life. I'd just lain Leo down to bed in one of our guest rooms after we'd first met Lucas, learned the truth about what happened to him, and wound up at the meeting with the activists. He'd asked me if, after all that I'd seen, I still wanted a different life.

I looked around at the crowd of men and then at Lucas. I repeated my answer from that other night with Leo.

"It doesn't matter if I want it or not," I said. "It's mine."

Lucas bowed his head, smiling to himself, like you do when you know you've drawn the winning hand.

"It's time to finish it, then," he said. "And then to begin whatever's next."

He raised a hand up to my eyes and swept it across my field of vision, tearing that reality away like a wet napkin.

❖

My eyes could finally see the world behind the illusion I'd been trapped in.

I was sixteen again, held aloft in the slimy clutches of a hellish monstrosity, halfway between the empty streets of Adders Lair and the churning red sky above.

I was about to be devoured.

But this time, I was *not* about to be devoured.

For Steven, I thought. *For Lucas. For all of them.*

I mustered the rage of the thousands I'd seen around me and wrenched one hand free of the beast's grasp. Then the other. I reached up to where it had its grip around my throat and pulled the arm just far enough down to allow myself a breath and a voice.

I looked the devil in the eye.

"FRATEROTH!" I cried.

The thing screamed desperately.

I screamed louder.

"YOUR WORK IS COMPLETE IN THIS REALM! I GIVE YOU LICENSE TO DEPART!"

And with a sound like a blast of thunder from the Perfect Storm charged by the roar of the crowd at the New Year's protest, the red sky ripped open, the beast was sucked backward into oblivion, and I was falling, and rising, and falling, like a feather in a hurricane.

I tumbled over and over myself, nearly torn apart by the forces that pulled me in every direction, until I landed, hard, on my back.

❖

I sat up, gasping for air, my eyes opened wide.

"He's awake!" cried a voice.

"Zooey! Breathe!"

"Christ, I thought he was . . ."

My eyes focused on the concerned faces around me.

Oona.

Daniel.

Leo.

We were in her candlelit living room, an empty wine glass in my lap.

I was home.

I threw my arms around all of them, drawing in hungry breaths and choking back sobs.

"Welcome back to Kansas, Dorothy," Leo said, hugging me tightly. "Did you melt the wicked witch?"

A few days later, on March seventh, Charles Eldridge narrowly lost the South Carolina presidential primary.

Then, on the tenth, Super Tuesday, George H. W. Bush won every contest in a blowout. There would be no path forward for an Eldridge nomination.

The next day, Eldridge formally announced the suspension of his campaign.

That night, Headmaster Westcott was shot dead in what the police deemed a botched robbery.

CHAPTER EIGHTEEN

US

Daniel here.

So, back in Chicago, even though the local public school that took me in was a far cry from Blackfriars, my Aunt Deb was determined I would get an education.

A few days after I got back from my detour to Adders Lair "to see the boy I love," as I'd told her, desperately, back in the airport, she came knocking on my bedroom door to say there was a call for me.

"Hello?" I asked, already nervous about whose voice I'd hear on the other end. Sure, it could have been Leo or Zooey, but it just as easily could have been my mother or father, and I definitely wasn't ready for that just yet.

To my surprise, it was Prof. Reyes on the other end who said, "Mister Preston! Quid agis?"

"Professor! Hi!"

"I asked you a question in Latin, Mister Preston," he said. "Thank goodness your aunt called the school to inquire about your old curriculum; otherwise, I wouldn't have known where to send your textbook. Does your new school have a decent Latin program?"

"We're lucky we have the lights on," I said.

"I thought as much," he said, sadly. "But! We'll just have to endeavor over the phone and through the mail. Your first correspondence course! I started you on this journey to the classics, and I intend to finish it. If you're game to come along with me."

I never thought I'd be so glad to get more homework, especially work I wouldn't get credit for.

"Yes, sir."

"Good man," Reyes said. "I'll make sure that your Latin is just as good as any Blackfriars student. Any student who didn't get the bum deal you all got. I *promise.*"

Aunt Deb was on me like a drill sergeant about my lessons; the ones from school, the ones from Reyes, and the ones she and Aunt Keisha taught me themselves.

See, before Aunt Deb took me under her wing, I always thought of my Blackness and my queerness as things I held in each hand separately, because at Blackfriars, the queer world was white. We worshiped white women like Judy and Madonna. We lusted after white boys like River Phoenix and Brad Pitt. We mourned white icons like Rock Hudson and Harvey Milk.

Turns out, there was a whole Black queer world too, hidden from most people behind double locks. Lucky for me, Deb and Keisha had the keys.

They taught me about Bayard Rustin, the gay pacifist who advised Dr. Martin Luther King Jr. on nonviolent protest and was a lead organizer for the March on Washington.

They taught me about Gladys Bentley, a butch lesbian musician of the Harlem Renaissance who became one of the most famous Black entertainers in the country.

They gave me a copy of *Giovanni's Room* by James Baldwin. The characters were white, but they were written by a Black man who dared to write about their homosexuality and bisexuality openly, with empathy and grace.

They told me about the Black women who led the Stonewall Riots that led to our liberation and the concept of "Gay Pride" today. Stormé

DeLarverie and Marsha P. Johnson were both drag performers who were regulars at the bar; Stormé, a drag king, and Marsha, a Queen. The story varies apparently, depending on who you talked to, but as Deb understood it, the Stonewall Riots started after Stormé threw a punch at one of the cops who'd raided the bar and tried to arrest her. Marsha arrived a short time later, like the calvary, to lead the resistance and channel the fury of that night into activism, founding the Street Transvestite Action Revolutionaries with her friend Sylvia Rivera. On the one-year anniversary of the Stonewall Riots, Marsha marched in the very first Gay Pride Parade.

Sadly, all but Stormé were now dead.

Marsha was the last to go, her body found in the river just this past July.

Deb told me there were more icons out there, waiting for history to find them. I told her she was my icon.

I'll forever be grateful to her and Keisha for all they taught me, but like I said, public school was . . . not great. Luckily, my tenure there lasted only until the end of the semester.

❖

Leo speaking!

That was due to *my* Mommie Dearest, working in concert with Daniel's Aunt Deb and her legal office. Ms. Rona Scalfani was nothing if not a relentless bitch (in the absolute *best* way) who got shit done (and still made sure her nails and hair were sickening).

Once the dust had settled after Westcott's suspicious death, my mom called Blackfriars to request a full report on the details of her son's expulsion, why he was made to leave immediately, in the middle of the night, and who was present at his questioning. She'd gotten accounts of other Blackfriars students who'd also actually been *caught* consuming alcohol and having unauthorized gatherings on campus and had received lenient punishment if they had otherwise good records. Her son, Leo, and the fourteen other expelled students had only been *accused* of these acts based on hearsay and rumors. Her *lawyers* were very interested in checking to see if there were any grounds for a discrimination case.

In the wake of Westcott's death, the third Blackfriars death that year, the dean of students who served as interim headmaster decided that another scandal would be the final nail in the coffin, pardon the expression, for the school's reputation. Thus, by the end of the term, all of us received letters stating that we would be welcomed back for the fall term on academic probation, should we wish to return.

In short, Miss Rona slayed them.

I wish I could report that all fourteen students returned, but we lost some for good. We VC boys pooled our address books and tried to get in touch to find out why. Barton told us that he would be homeschooled from here on out. We were always hung up on when we tried Reinhart's house. No one had an address or number for The Kid, and we never heard from him again. Humphrey Meier was sent to repeat his senior year at a military academy. In a twisted way, I imagined him happy there, at least, all that grunting and muscle.

Then there was Daniel.

❖

Yeah, like Leo said, I was almost one of the lost ones.

When we got the news about my readmission at my aunt's house, we celebrated until we realized that without my dad's money, I'd never be able to afford tuition.

We did finally talk, my dad and me, about a week after I'd arrived at my new home.

He told me he felt betrayed after all he'd done for me, which was pretty rich, considering he'd sent me to an actual prison and refused to even hear my side of things over the *phone*, let alone face-to-face. I told him as much, which just led to screaming, and I decided it was better for us both to go our separate ways and hung up.

My mom was, thankfully, doing better with it all. She started to call Deb's house about once a week, when my dad was off on an errand or something, to check in, hear about school, and tell me how much she missed and loved me. She said she was working on Dad and hoped I could come home soon. That still hasn't happened, and I'm not even sure if I want it to.

Luckily for me, Reyes and I had kept up with our Latin work by mail, leading up to a national exam he helped me apply for. My high score on the test and his personal recommendation letter got me back to Blackfriars on a full academic scholarship.

I still don't know if I believe in God, but damn if I don't believe that I'm blessed. And I'm starting to think that's enough.

We opened the champagne Deb and Keisha had been saving.

❖

(I swear I didn't cast any spells for that. —L)

❖

It's Zooey. With a Z. (Yes, that's a Liza Minnelli reference, and I'm not ashamed of it.)

And speaking of musicals, Daniel and I planned a secret final curtain to the school year when I booked Dan a flight east in late May so we could go see Leo in his school's production of *The Music Man*. He'd gotten the lead part, Harold Hill, and we were under no circumstances going to miss it.

For all the horror stories he'd told us about his new school, when the car pulled up to the very sixties-looking, ranch-style rectangle of a building, I have to admit I wasn't impressed. Based on Leo's description,

I'd expected roaming wild dogs, armed soldiers, and a hail of bullets as we raced for the front doors, but all I saw were white people in business casual gossiping about their own children.

❖

(Not *not* a horror story, but I also thought Leo was being a little dramatic. —D)

❖

As we collected our folded paper programs from the mom working the door, I heard a telltale jingle of jewelry approaching me at a breakneck pace.

"Zooey! Daniel! Oh my GOD, you actually made it, you angel babies!"

"Hi, Rona!" Daniel gasped as Leo's mother crashed into a tight hug.

"You look . . . amazing!" I managed to croak when it was my turn to be squeezed, her rings and necklaces stabbing my midsection here and there.

Rona was never one to turn a conservative look, but that night she'd really outdone herself in a sprayed-on leopard print minidress, the armory of metallic jewelry, and a red lip and smokey eye. I suddenly longed to see Leo in drag again.

"Oh, Zooey, careful flirting with a single woman like that, you'll break hearts. Some bitch selling Rice Krispies Treats over there told me this was a family event and I just said to her, 'YEAH, meet the FAMILY of the goddamn STAR OF THE SHOW,' stuck my dainty little hand right in her face and— Oh! They're flashing the lights! It's time!"

She took one of us on each arm, and as we walked to our seats, I felt the kinds of looks I used to get at Blackfriars and had an unexpected pang of nostalgia. In a weird way, I'd missed feeling like a freak. Being a freak alone is tough, but being arm in arm with your fellow freaks can feel pretty punk.

We took our seats. The show began with a number featuring salesmen all talking about their business on a train. Leo's character was actually onstage for the entire number, unbeknownst to the businessmen who'd been talking about him, until he reveals himself and exits the train, leavening them flabbergasted.

I smiled at the perfect casting.

Even though he's reading this, I can tell you earnestly that he was electric: funny, charming, tuneful, and, most surprisingly, very butch.

I admit I'd chuckled to myself on the drive down imagining lispy Leo romancing Marian the Librarian, but as soon as he delivered his first line, I was stunned at how easily he could click into the vocal transformation I'd worked so hard to achieve. And I wondered why he didn't employ it constantly to get people off his scent. He could easily sound and act like any of the other guys and would never have had to endure the bullying that led him to the book.

I asked him as much later that night, after Rona had showered him with flowers, kisses, and praise, and she'd left the three of us on our own at a diner nearby.

"Darling, I explained this ages ago," Leo said, mouth full of chicken fingers and honey mustard, which he swore was the most satisfying meal to have after any performance. "I like performing, but not *all the time.* There aren't enough chicken fingers in the world."

His answer unlocked something in me so immediately and profoundly that I just blurted it out: "I think I may be bisexual."

Leo feigned a theatrical gasp and acted like he was choking on his chicken. Daniel scolded him with a playful smack. "Oh darling, what next? Will you tell me that pro wrestling is fake?!"

"Leo . . ." Daniel chuckled.

"That the moon is not, in fact, made of cheese?!"

"Shut up!" I groaned, though I was smiling.

"I'm joking, my dear boy, we'd figured as much. I think I *asked* as much, once, but to hear you say it out loud is utter music. Congratulations."

"Hear hear!" Daniel cheered, raising his milkshake aloft in a toast. "We love you, Z."

"Thanks, guys," I said.

And I loved them, too. I'd never loved them so much as I did in that moment.

"Tough luck about your breakup with the Poor Little Rich Girl, though," Leo said. "I know you two were like Daisy and Gatsby."

"Well, look how they turned out," I said. "Anyway, I still have the Nirvana CD, so it wasn't a total loss."

❖

And now we're here. Believe it or not, "here" is VC headquarters: the student pub.

Leo, Daniel, and I have been coming here to write these pages since our first day back on campus as fresh juniors.

The Vicious Circle as we knew it is no more.

The returning members all decided we were too squeamish about getting in trouble to throw the kinds of parties we used to throw. Instead, the three of us went to Reyes, asking him to be the faculty sponsor of the Circle, a new student club for out queer students and their allies. He was very happy to say yes. We lobbied the deans to grant us legitimate access to use the pub for meetings and they agreed, provided we stick to the school rules.

So far, we are the only members.

That's fine by us. We know the others are out there and will come when they're ready. After all, we'd learned that coming out can turn out like Leo's amazing relationship with his mom, or Daniel's troubled relationship with his dad, or something in between. Like mine.

My dad picked me up himself after the last day of my sophomore spring semester. We asked Max to crack the windows in the car so that those first warm breezes of the coming summer could creep in. Everything was blooming.

"You going to miss your friends from track this summer?" my dad asked me.

"Those aren't my real friends," I said.

"Oh?"

It was a slip I didn't mean to make. But I'd made it.

And I knew it was time.

"My real friends got expelled last term," I said. "You heard about the fourteen?"

". . . Yes?"

"Well, I should have been the fifteenth, but I got lucky."

He turned to me in his seat for just a moment, then turned to look out the window again.

"Zooey, what are you telling me?"

"I'm telling you I'm one of them, Dad."

Max rolled up the privacy screen that separated his seat from ours.

"But . . . Mallory . . ."

"She broke up with me for it . . ."

I took a deep breath.

"For being bisexual, I mean."

He let out a little snort, like I'd told a joke. I'm sure such a reaction could damage a person for life. Luckily, I'd stared a demon in the eye, so I was tough.

"Zooey, I don't want to talk about—"

"That's fine," I said. "We don't have to talk about it if you're not ready. But I think we should. I think we should talk more, about a lot of things. About me, about *you* . . . about Mom."

"Please—"

He was looking desperately out the window for something to draw our attention from this moment, but I wouldn't let him.

"I know it's scary," I said, taking his hand, feeling it tense instantly. "But it doesn't have to be. It's important to share yourself. I learned that this year, from my brothers. This is what it's like, to be family. *This is what it's like.*"

He still won't talk about it, but he hasn't kicked me out, either.

I wish I could have given you a happy ending to that story by the end of this one. But know that I'm happy with this beginning.

❖

So, what are these pages? Why have we spent so much time putting all of this down; all the grisly, sad, sordid details of the entire affair?

Well for one, the VC guest book is lost. Mrs. Wesley looked and looked for us, but to no avail; Westcott either threw it away when he had no more use of it, or maybe used Steven's signature therein to throw the curse that killed him when he got the Book of Brothers back. We'll never know. All that history is gone forever. Our own Book of Brothers disappeared when he did.

So, we wanted to start a new record of who we were and what we lived through in Nineteen Ninety-One and Ninety-Two.

Also, the Oldfellows are still out there.

They may not have their demon anymore, but they still have all the money and power they need to stay in control for a long time and to do to us what they did to Westcott if they ever found out about us.

We don't know exactly what happened after Eldridge's campaign loss, but our theory goes something like this: After election night, it was clear that their spells had suddenly lost their power. Westcott had to come clean about his copy of the book going missing. They examined it and found the last page torn out. Westcott said that he was sure he took care of the student who'd stolen it, but he must have missed something. He got punished. He turned up dead, not by magic, but at the end of a gun.

If that's actually true, then they know that there's a sleeper cell of teenage witches out there who know their secrets and deliberately stole their power to cost them the election. They'd know that those students are likely a part of the fourteen who were expelled along with Steven. We can only hope that Westcott didn't know that we three were Steven's closest friends. We suspect they're already in the school somewhere, watching. Leo thinks the new headmaster looks at him funny, but that might just be because Leo's gayer than pro wrestling.

◆

(I take that as a profound compliment. —L)

◆

All this to say, we might not make it.

Just in case something happens to us and we meet quiet, mysterious ends like Steven or Westcott, we wanted there to be a record of everything we knew. If we've learned anything this past year, it's that history lets us carry the work of those who came before us forward, so that we might finish it.

So if you've read all this, you know, too. Welcome to the resistance.

But we're cautious, not scared.

Because we still have that torn-out page.

If things start to get weird and we think they're on to us, we can still get back to the crossroads to summon the power we need to take them on.

And we're not talking about another demon.

We're talking about Freddie.

Marsha.

Bayard.

Harvey.

Lucas.

Steven.

Our own saints and angels.

❖

Which brings us to today, October ninth, Nineteen Ninety-Two.

Upon completion of this document, we're going to stash it in Leo's trailer for safekeeping and then Rona is driving us all down to Washington, DC, to see a quilt.

Long way to see a quilt, right? Let us explain.

Back in the Eighties, a gay activist from San Francisco named Cleve Jones started the NAMES Project AIDS Memorial Quilt: a square for every soul lost to AIDS, sewn into a patchwork quilt, to show the scale of the losses to people who might not understand. By the time the quilt was first displayed on the National Mall in Nineteen Eighty-Seven, it was larger than a football field. The one thousand, nine hundred and twenty names that the quilt represented were read aloud. Half a million people came to see it. Then the quilt went on tour. Every city added squares of its own. There were six thousand by the end of its journey. Over eight thousand by Eighty-Eight.

Today, the quilt is returning to the National Mall.

It now has twenty-one-thousand squares from every state in America and twenty-eight countries.

We're bringing a square for Lucas.

It's an offering to just one of our many saints, but we know they'll all feel it, because we are connected like a quilt ourselves.

A fraternity that stretches from the very dawn of man through us today, on into the future, forever and ever.

Patchwork, but tightly sewn, and never again invisible.

ACKNOWLEDGMENTS

A profound thank-you to Maggie Lehrman for reading the skeletal pages of this idea many years ago, keeping on me about turning them into a book, teaching me how to write a book in the years leading up to its first draft, and then crafting that draft into the book I always wanted to write. You've actually changed my life.

Special thanks to Kyle Beltran and Daniel Isaac for lending your minds, hearts, and experiences to the creation of Daniel and Zooey. I owe you any and all favors, forever.

Thank you to Geoff Soffer for being such a champion of and valuable set of eyes on this project from its most nascent stages through to now, and hopefully, beyond.

Thank you to Arvin Ahmadi for innumerable pearls of writer wisdom and invaluable pep talks. Also for talking me out of a truly terrible plot twist on an otherwise lovely drive upstate.

Thank you to Jackson Teeley, Nicole Tingir MacMillan, and Conor Norton for being some of my earliest readers and providing such smart and useful feedback while also protecting my fragile little ego. Thank you to Michael Mahan for continually altering your job description as I explore new job descriptions myself. Thank you to Dr. Barry Kohn and Jean Mientus, BSN, for providing crucial medical details.

Thank you to Michael Arden for creating an actual temple of creativity in which to write, and for providing the love, support, space, and gin required to get any writing done.

Thank you to my bullies for giving me so much to say.

Thank you to my queer ancestors for giving me a reason to say it.

CHRISTMAS IN THE *SOUTHWEST*

Holt, Rinehart and Winston / New York / Chicago / San Francisco

CHRISTMAS IN THE SOUTHWEST

Photographs by Taylor Lewis, Jr.
Text by Joanne Young

ACKNOWLEDGMENTS

The authors are grateful to the Southwesterners who shared their knowledge of the area and their Christmas customs with us. In Texas, our special thanks to Miss Marylee Battiato, Mrs. Sharon Eason, San Antonio; the J. M. McDonalds, Mission; Miss Lena Sturges, Bill Brandon, and A. G. O'Brien, Kerrville; Mrs. Letycia Palacio and the Robert O'Connors, Laredo; in New Mexico, to the Bud Lewises, Albuquerque; Mrs. Barbara Egan, the Walter L. Goodwins, Jr., and Miss Audean Davis, Santa Fe; in Arizona, to the Ed Worsleys and Mrs. Betty Krause, Phoenix; the Hermosa Inn, Scottsdale; in California, to Ruth and Harrison Brent and Mrs. Parley Johnson, Downey.

Library of Congress Cataloging in Publication Data

Lewis, Taylor Biggs.
Christmas in the Southwest.
1. Christmas—Southwest, New.
I. Young, Joanne B. II. Title.
GT4986.S64L48
394.2'68282'0979 73-3701
ISBN 0-03-010741-5

Published simultaneously in Canada by Holt, Rinehart and Winston of Canada, Limited.
First Edition
Designer: Winston Potter
Printed in the United States of America

BRIGHT with December sun, the great Southwest basks in a holiday mood from the lush Rio Grande Valley in Texas, across New Mexico's rugged mountains and the vast cactus garden of Arizona desert, to the flowering southern California coast. South of the sleepy Rio Grande, Mexico tunes her guitars and fashions her paper flowers for fiesta.

Christmas approaches in a twinkle of lights, a blaze of poinsettias, and the captivating rhythm of dancing feet. It is a festival blending the rich mix of cultures woven into the colorful fabric of the Southwest itself—Indian, Spanish, Mexican, and that of the nineteenth-century pioneers who rolled westward with the best-loved customs of many European nations to adapt to this new land.

The brilliant bloom of poinsettias in Mission, Texas, sets the stage for Christmas.

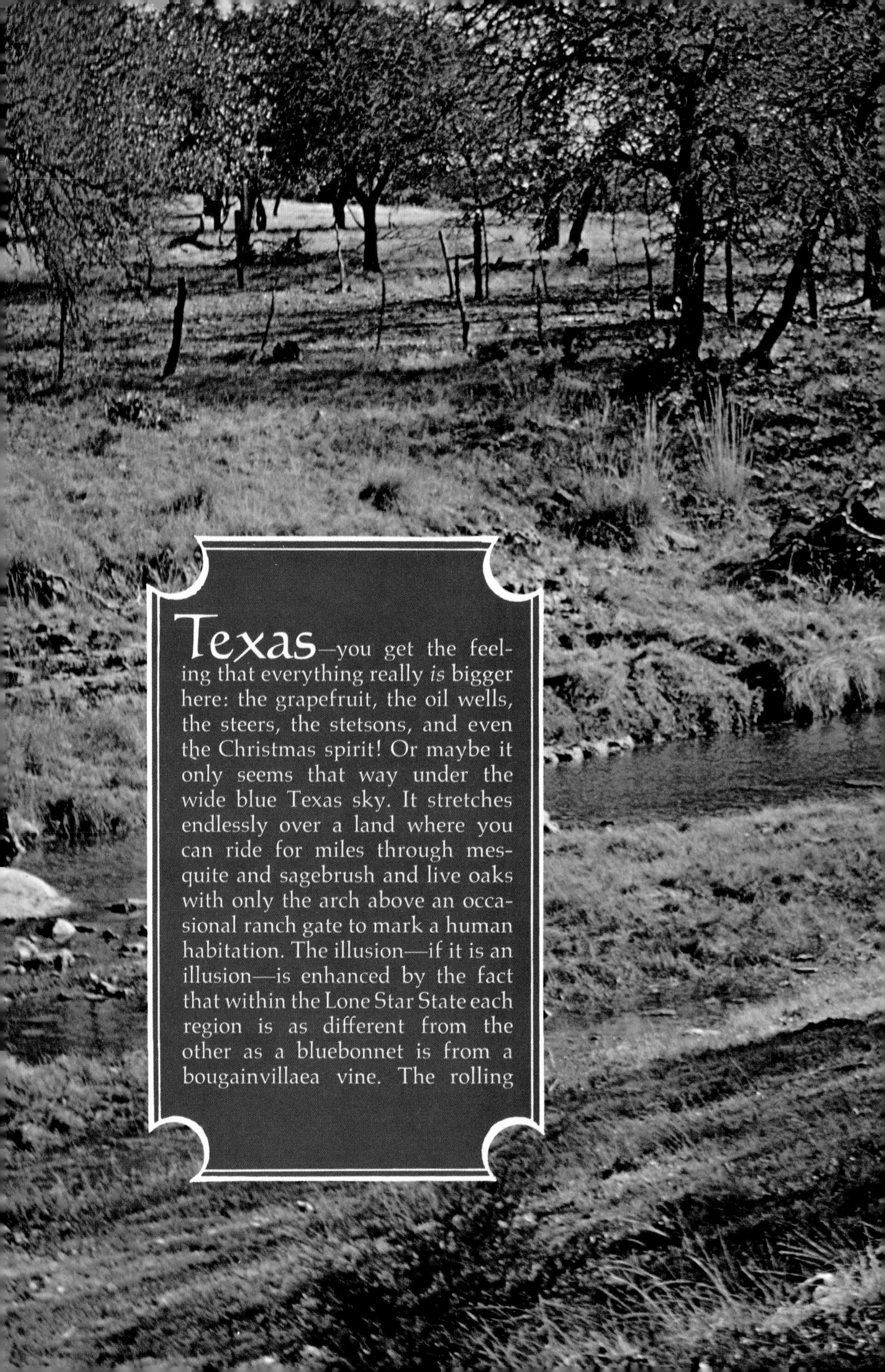

Texas—you get the feeling that everything really *is* bigger here: the grapefruit, the oil wells, the steers, the stetsons, and even the Christmas spirit! Or maybe it only seems that way under the wide blue Texas sky. It stretches endlessly over a land where you can ride for miles through mesquite and sagebrush and live oaks with only the arch above an occasional ranch gate to mark a human habitation. The illusion—if it is an illusion—is enhanced by the fact that within the Lone Star State each region is as different from the other as a bluebonnet is from a bougainvillaea vine. The rolling

The Steves Homestead in San Antonio reflects the German Yule customs that enrich Texas traditions.

plains and prairies of the north, the mountainous west, the sophisticated metropolitan areas around Dallas and Fort Worth, the historic Brazos Valley just south of them, and the Gulf coast are each different countries.

In central Texas, the wind can whip across the hill country on a December day, and a light sprinkling of snow may dust fenceposts and tumbleweed. Glossy mistletoe clusters in green balls high in oak trees, ripe for cutting to decorate a Christmas party. The whitetail deer take cover until twilight, and then cautiously slip from the brush to graze on the sweet range grass.

On one of these chilly mornings, you'll see a cowboy, cradling his youngest child behind the saddlehorn, ride out to chop down a cedar for the family Christmas tree. He may have spotted it first on a hot August day when he was riding fences, checking for broken wire that would mean straying cattle. By now its branches have filled out; and it will look pretty Christmas morning with lights and tinsel and lots of red and green and gold balls. The six-year-old will find his first pair of leather boots under its branches—he was fitted for them last week, but a wink to the clerk let him think his folks weren't buying them after all. A boy's first boots are mighty big—Texas-big, you might say, even if they are only a little boy's size twelve.

The Pedernales River is lined with windmill-dotted ranches. Among them is the LBJ Ranch, which has shared the warmth of its holidays, its barbecued beef, pinto beans, and chile con queso with visitors from all over the world. From New Braunfels to Fredericksburg nestle the stone houses of Texas's early German settlers. They landed on the Gulf coast in 1845 and came up by two-wheeled oxcarts and on foot, plagued by cholera and one of the worst rainy seasons in history, while war raged between Mexico and the United States.

The following year, John Meusebach led a group of them from New Braunfels to found Fredericksburg. He made a peace treaty, which was never broken, with the Comanche Indians, on whose land they settled.

Signifying their friendliness to all who traveled the territory, the settlers named their streets from the center of town southeast, so that the combined initials spell "all welcome," and to the northwest, "come back."

A Victorian tree at the Steves Homestead holds German ornaments and tiny candles in gay profusion.

By December, they were more than ready to bring a touch of Christmas at home to the new frontier. A Texas cedar or a holly tree became their Tannenbaum—bright with candles, paper chains, candy, and gilded nuts. Around the tree, with its candles lighted on Christmas Eve, the tender notes of *"Stille Nacht, Heilige Nacht"* rang out as the eyes of children glowed.

In 1848, Ed Steves, who had been a cabinetmaker in Germany, moved to San Antonio and opened a lumber and mill-working yard. In less than thirty years, his own American dream had come true. He was prosperous enough to build a splendid Victorian mansion for his family on King William Street. (The area of fine German homes near the San Antonio River was humorously referred to as Sauerkraut Bend.) A formal garden in front, a fountain on the side which he purchased at the Philadelphia Centennial Exposition, and the city's first indoor swimming pool—it was a Texas showplace.

Now the property of the San Antonio Conservation Society, which has done so much to preserve the customs and landmarks of the past, the Steves Homestead is open to the public. At Christmas, every room reflects the charm of a Victorian holiday.

Of the twenty-six national, racial, or cultural groups who have contributed to the development of Texas, the Spanish have left one of the strongest, brightest imprints on its Christmas celebration. This is radiantly visible at the lovely old Spanish Governor's Palace.

The long, low, white-plastered building was erected in 1722 as part of the old Spanish fort, or *presidio.* After the city became the capital of the Spanish province of Texas, its governors resided here, as did Mexican officials after that country's successful revolution against Spanish rule. Here Jim Bowie courted his bride-to-be, and Moses Austin contracted with Governor Martinez to bring the first Anglo-American colonists to Texas.

A century plant bright with pears and partridges in Laredo is truly Texan!

A Mexican "tree of life" adds the touch of one more land's traditions at Christmas time.

Three wise men from Mexico at the Steves Homestead.

Facing page: *Pan dulce and candies in the dining room of the Spanish Governor's Palace in San Antonio are ready for the Fiesta Navideña.*

Candles glow in the Palace chapel where Christmas mass was heard in 1722 when the commandancia *was a Spanish fort in the Texas wilderness.*

A fire blazes on the hearth of the high, open-throated fireplace in the dining room which was the scene of gala Spanish Colonial banquets. Was it *cabrito* or roasted wild turkey that was prepared for His Excellency's Christmas dinner in the adjoining kitchen, its charcoal fire glowing in the open stone brazier?

The Palace's family chapel, the heart of all Mexican haciendas, is mentioned in the will of Mexican Governor Ignacio Perez, dated January 25, 1849: "The small room called 'of the Blessed Virgin,' will be for my daughter, Trinidad." Rare primitive wood carvings of saints (santos) look out from niches, and religious scenes painted on tin (retablos) hang from the chapel walls. Even today no Mexican home is too small to devote at least a special corner, if not a room, to family worship.

One of the most beautiful Christmas traditions of the Southwest and Mexico, from which it comes, is Las Posadas (The Inns). In symbolic pageantry, a procession reenacts the journey of Joseph and Mary to Bethlehem and their search for a room where the Baby Jesus would be born. Then, in the happy combination of reverence and gaiety typical of the Mexican people, their welcome to the inn is followed by a festive piñata party. The custom, introduced in Mexico in the 1500s by Father Diego de Soria, was adopted as readily by Southwesterners as the German Christmas tree and Santa Claus.

Along the beautiful Paseo del Rio in San Antonio, Las Posadas is combined with another delightful tradition—the Fiesta de las Luminarias. Four hundred years ago, in Spain and later Mexico, crossed piñon boughs were set ablaze on Christmas Eve to light the way for the Christ child. The custom continued until Yankee peddlers introduced brown paper wrappings and

Above left: *The spire of San Augustine Church in Laredo.*

Hundreds of luminarias line the Paseo del Rio in San Antonio as eyes and candles glow in the Las Posadas procession, ending at La Villita.

The piñata party climaxes festivities at La Villita.

long-burning candles. Today the Southwest's luminarias are candles in sand-weighted paper bags.

At dusk they reflect in the shimmering, palm-lined river with Christmas lights on shops, hotels, and sidewalk cafes. The crowd gathers in the Spanish-style courtyard of La Mansión Motor Hotel, where it takes its place behind a brown-eyed, brown-haired "angel" with tinseled wings carrying the *Ojo de Dios* (Eye of God)—crossed sticks wound in a kite shape with colored yarns. Two young girls in long white dresses carry the *misterio*, a platform bearing clay figures of the Holy Family. They start down the steps to the river walk, each person holding a lighted candle, singing a litany as they go.

A few blocks away, a boy and girl in their early teens start across an arched bridge over the river. In the blue of not-quite-dark, they glimpse the winking luminarias and the approaching line of candles. The girl's breath catches in her throat.

"Oh—Las Posadas!" she whispers. Its lights are twinkling pinpoints in her eyes. She reaches for the boy's hand, and they run lightly down the stone steps to join the age-old ceremony. In a moment of wonder it is Christmas!

"In the name of Heaven I ask for lodging," sings the crowd in Spanish at the procession's first stop. A choir inside the building replies, "No room here; go on your way." Tens of hundreds of candles shine as the pageant moves on until they reach La Villita, the restored Mexican village in the heart of the city.

Silver trumpets blow as the wrought iron gates swing open, and the choir within the plaza sings: "You are Joseph? and your wife is Mary? Enter, pilgrims; I did not recognize you."

The rejoicing marchers fill the walled plaza; and when the misterio has been placed on an evergreens covered table, the crowd of some three thousand people sinks to its knees and sings The Lord's Prayer: "Padre nuestro, que estas in los cielos . . ."

No need to tell the children what comes next! There is a sudden cry of "Now the piñata!"

Bright blue and red and yellow Star of Bethlehem Christmas piñatas are lowered on ropes in four corners of the courtyard. (The soft clay beanpots, filled with candies and tiny presents, are traditionally decorated with bright crepe paper in the forms of stars or birds or bulls or even Mickey Mouse!)

Like dozens of jumping jacks, the children wait for their turn to be blindfolded and swing the stick at the piñata. It dances tantalizingly just out of reach. One blonde six-year-old just misses, and they squeal their disappointment. At last, with a mighty swat, a small boy connects with the target; and candy showers down like a shattered rainbow. What a shout! What a scramble! The excitement is ear-splitting as every child dives for his share.

When the last bit of crepe paper has fluttered to the ground, the last piece of candy has been claimed, there is hot chocolate and buñuelos—the crisp, lacy Mexican Christmas cookies—for everyone in the crowd. A flamenco guitarist plays, and a lovely Spanish dancer twirls and flirts through her black lace mantilla. Exuberant shouts of *"Feliz Navidad!"* mingle with "Merry Christmas!" in one joyous international carol.

For three days of the pre-Christmas holiday, "SALT's Off Stage" riverboat of the San Antonio Little Theater is "on stage" at points up and down the Paseo del Rio.

Rowdy and religious by turn, like the Elizabethans they emulate, the cast presents a modern verse adaptation of *The Second Shepherd's Play*, a medieval miracle drama. The barge drawn up to the river's edge substitutes for the

A riverboat is the stage for Los Pastores, a modern version of a miracle play.

Piñatas for sale are a sure sign of Christmas in Nuevo Laredo, Mexico.

horse-drawn wagon platform on which it was originally performed on holidays in merry old England. Their audience is equally informal, made up of Christmas shoppers, tourists, Air Force men on leave, or school children on vacation. They join in when the players sing familiar carols, wave as another riverboat goes by, and clap as enthusiastically as any first-night audience on Broadway.

On the other side of town, near *El Mercado* (the Public Market), there is a great air of excitement as streets are roped off, and merchants prepare for the Fiesta Navideña. Pizzinni's Spice Shop is a fragrant hub of activity where children buying chocolate, pralines, pumpkin or cactus candy vie with señoras shopping for the ingredients for tacos, buñuelos, and all the mouth-watering specialties that fiesta-goers will buy. The aroma of *pan dulce,* sweet, light holiday pastries in infinite variety, wafts through the open door of Mi Tierra Cafe and Bakery where the Cortez brothers act as a clearing house for news of the evening's events.

Strolling mariachis will play and sing until dawn, and there will be a blessing of the pets, piñatas, and arts and crafts for sale.

At Pizzinni's, Mrs. Henry Guerra, Sr., whose father founded the store in 1893, observes the preparations thoughtfully. "This is what we must bring back to America," she says in warm approval, "these traditions—this heritage. This is what made America great, and we need them to keep it great."

Mrs. Guerra, Jr., agrees, for she has watched a successful exchange of cultures firsthand. "Here is this Italian in the nineteenth century who comes over to America and marries a pretty girl from Durango, Mexico. And what happens? I'll tell you what happens! Today, two generations later, we're eating spaghetti *con mole!*" Her thoroughly American twins, rushing by to take two piñatas to a customer, grin their approval. Doesn't everyone flavor their spaghetti sauce with chocolate?

Candy made of pumpkin, cactus, or chocolate is a specialty at Pizzinni's Spice Shop in San Antonio.

In the tropical Texas valley, where tourists and Canada geese are winter visitors and the Mission Garden Club holds an annual Christmas Poinsettia Show, citrus groves are like no others. Their boundaries are marked by rows of royal palms, a custom dating back to a time when palm trees were more plentiful than wood for fence posts in the valley.

Dawn breaks over the Rio Grande River at Laredo, with

South of the border, in Mexico itself, festivities which started on Guadalupe Day in mid-December are now in full swing. The market places in Reynosa, Nuevo Progreso, Laredo, and Juarez—always a mecca for tourists, are even more frantically busy with Christmas shoppers. The traffic on International bridges across the Rio Grande rushes in both directions. (You can walk across for a penny.) Mexicans shop for bargains in Texas stores, while Texans find them in Mexico!

Shoeshine boys and paper flower vendors are everywhere, and sidewalk salesmen offer their wares, from serapes to steer horns. Steam puffs up from tubs of roasted corn on two-wheeled carts, and charcoal braziers in the open

Mexico lying beyond and Texas bordering it on this side.

fronts of butcher shops send out a fragrant advertisement. The raucous sound of horns blown by fearless cab drivers are syncopated by the clip-clop of burros' hoofs.

Strings of garlic and red and green peppers decorate vegetable stalls, while bins hold red, white, and speckled beans in a colorful mosaic. On one corner of a tiled sidewalk, a vendor sells fresh fruit—tangerines, slices of papaya and pineapple—to grinning children who rush up to hand him their pesos like American youngsters greeting a Good Humor man.

Through the wrought iron gates of private homes, you catch a glimpse of courtyards where bougainvillaeas bloom and Christmas tree lights shine through the windows. Wreaths hang on gates and

Christmas cards in a Nuevo Laredo store window, and a nacimiento (below) in the yard of a Mexican home in the town of Roma, Texas.

doors and windows, and elaborate *nacimientos* (nativity scenes), some of them life-size, decorate yards or patios.

In dozens of shops, bright tree ornaments are for sale. There are gaily painted tin angels, stars or flowers, handmade figures of straw, and white birds with paper wings and candlewax bodies.

Corn husks are a very large sales item, much in demand at this season. In many Mexican homes on both sides of the border, tamale making is at its height on Christmas Eve. Dozens and dozens are made for families and friends, most of them filled with the traditional mixture of pork, spices, and chile, but some made with chicken; or raisins and chopped fruit for a special dessert. And how could you possibly make tamales without corn husks to wrap them in for steaming?

The town square in Nuevo Laredo is a great spot for flower vendors, shoe shine boys, tired shoppers.

In Mexican homes, hundreds of hot tamales are made on Christmas Eve, just as they were for Spanish Governors.

The old Longhorn Saloon is a San Antonio museum now, but the Lone Star Brewery keeps beer on tap.

Surrounded by so many Yuletide customs older than the United States itself, it is hard to remember that the days of the Old West are comparatively recent. Many Southwesterners learned about cattle drives along the Chisholm Trail, range wars, and covered wagons rolling westward not from school books but from the reminiscences of older members of their families. At the turn of the century, Christmas meant family reunions, as it does today, and tales told and retold of round-up time, sourdough bread and chuck wagon meals, Indian raids, and outlaws.

Landmarks keep the Wild West alive, such as the Buckhorn Saloon, which originally stood on Houston Street in San Antonio, bright with poinsettias and gold tinsel. Once a favorite gathering place for ranchers and oil men (it had a cabinet in which cowboys were asked to hang their guns while they drank), it is now a museum. Teddy Roosevelt propped his foot on the old brass rail when he stopped in during a trip to recruit his Rough Riders; and Sam Rayburn's famous ten gallon hat hangs on the wall.

Chile con carne and tamales are the spicy favorites on the menu at the gala Christmas celebration at Mission San José. All the color and laughter, reverence and drama of the season are combined at the "Queen of Missions" which had its first celebration of Christ's birth in 1720.

It is chilly on this December evening as a full moon rises over the adobe walls. Colored lights are strung between the live oak trees, and bonfires are ringed with spectators warming cold hands and toes. On the outdoor stage, young lariat twirlers display their skill; boys and girls of the parish perform the delightful Mexican folk dances of their ancestors; while young Indians keep alive their own rich heritage with matachines dances that are at once an expression of worship and dazzling pageantry.

The history of Texas beef cattle, from the Longhorn at the top to the Hereford, is dramatically displayed at The Stockman restaurant in downtown San Antonio.

A Las Posadas begins at Mission San José y San Miguel de Aguayo (known as the Queen of Missions).

A mariachi mass blends the voices of the mission choir with guitars and trombones and the age-old sacred words.

Within the chapel, a mariachi mass is celebrated. A choir wearing magnificent serapes sings of the recurring Christmas miracle while the mariachis' guitars and trombones add a rich accompaniment. The congregation leaves the church carrying candles in a Posadas procession to the creche on the stage.

Then the centuries blend as an old and primitive pageant begins. *Los Pastores* is a mystery play which was first presented in Texas missionary settlements in the early 1700s. The drama was handed down by word of mouth from generation to generation. Indian imagery and Mexican folklore were added to the original Spanish script, but it still depicts the eternal conflict between good and evil. An interpreter translates for the audience as the players speak their lines in Spanish. But as the Devil tries to keep the shepherds from reaching Bethlehem, and they defeat him, the meaning is clear.

The shepherds tap their crooks, and their small bells ring in unforgettable rhythm. They sing as the pageant ends:

Good-by, beloved Child,
    Your little shepherds are leaving;
Now close those beautiful eyes
    And go back to sleep.

Matachines Indian dancers and Mexican folk dancers bring color and rhythm to the Mission's Christmas celebration.

New Mexico

—they call it The Land of Enchantment, and at the Christmas season, it could be named The Land of Enchanted Lights. Nowhere in the Southwest, where the Yuletide season has a glow like no other part of the country, does it shine more brightly than in New Mexico. It twinkles with starlight and candle flame, gleams with golden luminarias and farolitas, shines with colored lights that outline trees and houses. In the Santa Fe area, a luminaria refers to a Christmas bonfire, while the paper bags with candles inside, which the rest of the Southwest calls luminarias, are known as farolitas—"little lamps."

At Raton, the hills are aglow in Climax Canyon, where rocks, cedars, and piñon trees surround the lighted nativity scenes which are known as the "City of Bethlehem." Farther south, at the little town of Jemez Springs, a forty-foot living Christmas tree sparkles; luminarias flicker on rooftops; and on the hillsides, Christmas scenes handmade by the families in the area are brilliantly illuminated.

In New Mexico where mountains, caverns, mesas, and deserts all speak of antiquity, it is fitting that Christmas customs date back four hundred and fifty years to the

arrival of the first Christians. (Alvar Nuñez Cabeza de Vaca of Spain; Estévanico, a black Moor; and two other Spaniards were shipwrecked on the Texas coast in 1528 and were the first to traverse the Southwest. In an unbelievably arduous eight-year walk, they finally reached the Gulf of California and Sonora.)

To the Indian performing his Christmas deer dance at Tesuque Pueblo or the matachines dancer at Taos, even the span of time since the Europeans' coming is no more than a trickle of desert sand. For centuries before that, his ancestors held their ceremonial dances at this season, to pray for the return of the winter sun after

Under the wide starry sky of New Mexico, an adobe ranch house is lighted with golden luminarias.

At Rancho Encantado near Santa Fe, enchilladas, roast beef, Indian bread are on the Southwestern Yuletide menu.

its annual withdrawal. Now at many pueblos the Indian dances for the Christ child after midnight mass in the mission church. He does so without conflict; for he recognizes the natural clock of the universe, and this has always been a time for dancing.

Nowhere, perhaps, have the Anglo, Spanish, and Indian cultures blended so easily as in the happy customs of Christmas. With them are mixed the influence of the Southwest itself—the gay strings of red peppers, called *ristras,* on the door; the Zuñi basket filled with pine and holly; a cedar wreath hanging over a Navajo blanket in the den; English carols played on a Spanish guitar.

On Christmas dinner tables, the juicy prime ribs of beef or roast turkey are surrounded by platters of enchilladas, guacamole salad, and a hearty casserole of pinto beans. The loaves of homemade Indian bread baked in a pueblo's beehive oven are as often part of the menu as feather-light *sopaipillas*—little popovers dripping with wild honey. Dessert may be a German chocolate cake, English apple pie, or sugary *biscochitos*—the crisp Spanish Christmas cookies.

Christmas means candles—in all shapes and sizes.

Even a rare three-hundred-year-old Penitenté cross at Rancho Encantado is decked in greens and ribbon.

At La Mesita ranch outside Santa Fe, primitive santos hang above an old Spanish shepherd's bench.

The snow-covered terrain along the road to Taos has changed very little

The trader who drove his mule train from Missouri down the Santa Fe Trail in the 1800s may have shocked the housewives of Independence when he went back and demanded his eggs scrambled with green chile peppers! At any rate, much more was traded than furs and silver, tea and trinkets on the Santa Fe Trail; and in New Mexico today it's apparent that it was a valuable exchange.

The city of Santa Fe seems to have grown out of the earth itself. Its brown adobe buildings (none more than three stories high by city ordinance) seem carved out of the mountainous plateau from which the city rises. Cottonwoods line the streets and shade the secluded patios. They have probably done so since the old Palace of the Governors was built by Don Pedro Peralta in 1610, a decade before the Pilgrims set foot on Plymouth Rock. The oldest government building in the United States, the adobe wall around it enclosed not only the governor's rooms, a powder storeroom, and chapel, but quarters for soldiers and a corral for their horses. This fascinating old structure on the Plaza now houses exhibits of two millennia of New Mexican events, as part of the Museum of New Mexico.

since Alvarado searched here for the Seven Cities of Cibola in 1540.

At this time of year, its halls echo the footsteps of the ghosts of countless Christmases Past. Men and women who served there under five flags—Spanish, Mexican, American, and briefly, the Pueblo Indians (1680–1692) and the Confederacy (1862)—have each in their own way paused in late December to celebrate this holiday. Among them was Lew Wallace, who wrote his classic *Ben Hur* in the Palace while he was New Mexico's territorial governor.

At the Rancho Encantado, north of Santa Fe, thirty youngsters are bubbling with excitement as they wait for Santa Claus. The guest ranch, on a quarter section of chaparral country bordering Pojoaque Indian land, holds an annual Christmas party for youngsters eight-to-ten years old from nearby Guadalupe School.

Tantalizing spicy smells of dinner drift through the kitchen door, and dancing eyes reflect the fire on the hearth and the twinkling lights of the Christmas tree.

"I think I hear sleigh bells!" exclaims Mrs. Barbara Egan, their hostess.

"Hey, I think I do, too!" cries an excited nine-year-old, and his classmates echo him. "I think they're on the roof!"

Snow adds its own brush to a Taos artist's window.

Thirty pairs of eyes turn to the ceiling above the fireplace, and there through the skylight—one of them spies a jovial white-whiskered face.

"It's Santa Claus!" they shout. "El Santo Closs!"

The skylight slides open, and a pair of boots (suspiciously resembling cowboy boots) dangles through. Someone brings a ladder, and Santa descends with his bulging pack. The sleigh bells jingle merrily outside, and laughter rings within.

(A few days later, a group of profusely illustrated thank-you notes arrive from Guadalupe School. "Dear Mrs. Egan," writes one little boy. "Thank you for telling us you heard Santa Claus. We might have missed him otherwise.")

A few miles south of Santa Fe, two ghost towns swing silent doors to the December winds, mute testimony that man leaves only a transient mark on the landscape. Madrid, once a prosperous mining community known for its Christmas decorations, lies deserted, a billboard proclaiming that the entire town is for sale. The rows of hillside houses, the Mineshaft Tavern, the school, the church, an off-Broadway theater (a long *long* way off Broadway!) that once wore Christmas lights in gay profusion, are now as barren as a well that has run dry. A roadrunner, grown unaccustomed to the sight of human beings, strolls instead of running down the main road.

Cerillos (the Little Hills) a few miles down the road is slightly better off. The Schmidts, one family holding out against time in a neat little adobe house, have put

The chapel at the old Taos Pueblo wears a green wreath.

luminarias along the wall and a sign proclaims to all who pass, "Feliz Navidad!"

The town was founded in 1879 when the railroad first came through, opening up the turquoise, copper, silver, and gold mines to a rich eastern trade. But the mines must have given out, for L'Église de San José looks almost deserted, and the Tiffany Saloon has a message scrawled across its windows: "Sorry—closed till Easter." There appear to be more stray dogs along the dusty streets than human inhabitants. Still, the Metropolitan Hotel has a tinsel-decked tree in its lobby, and the sign as you leave town says *Hasta la Vista,* so there are at least a few hopeful residents.

Twentieth-century travelers speed along the route of the Camino Real (the Royal Road) through the Rio Grande Valley at Christmas time. Their destination differs, however, from the traders, missionaries, or soldiers who journeyed this way to and from Mexico City in the Spanish Colonial era.

Today they head for the powdery ski slopes of the Sandia or Sangré de Cristos ranges, or take off cross-country into the Pecos Wilderness. Just riding up a ski lift is a breathtaking experience. (If the altitude doesn't take your breath away, the scenery will!)

Handcrafted gifts from the nearby Indian pueblos are eagerly sought by Christmas shoppers in Albuquerque.

Indian boys sweep snow off the roof at Taos Pueblo.

Facing page: *An outdoor mural in Albuquerque's Old Town depicts the colorful early history of New Mexico.*

Seemingly endless miles of snow-covered, pine-dotted ridges and valleys spread out below, where deer and bighorn mountain sheep are in their element.

To skiers or travelers homebound for the holidays, the road to Taos unfolds its panoramic beauty as it did to Captain Hernando de Alvarado in 1540. This officer in Coronado's expedition found several thousand Indians living in the eight hundred terraced rooms at Taos Pueblo. Instead of the legendary Seven Cities of Cibola with walls of gold, the Spaniards glimpsed adobe pueblo walls reflecting the morning sun. These well-established Indian civilizations had existed for more than fifteen centuries. The Taos people were already masters of the art of irrigation, and their fields produced abundant crops of corn, beans, and squash. Other nearby Indian tribes had skilled craftsmen —basket weavers, pottery makers, workers in silver and turquoise.

In spite of the stormy years between, the ancient arts are not only still alive but flourishing. At the Christmas season, handcrafted gifts of exquisite jewelry, intricately designed, and woven rugs, famous Nambé silver, and black-on-black potteryware from San Ildefonso are in particular demand. Christmas shoppers crowd the trading posts. Sidewalk displays do a thriving business in Albuquerque's Old Town and the ancient Plaza in Santa Fe.

Taos is a mecca for artists. Like Santa Fe, its narrow streets and softly rounded adobe buildings seem like a painting themselves.

Snow has added its magic brush to the ropes of evergreens, the nacimientos, the spruce and holly wreaths. In the town square, a group of little Indian children, bundled up from boots to parkas, are putting finishing touches on a rotund snowman. The window of an artist's studio frames an abstract painting, and the pungent scent of burning piñon logs drifts on the wind. The warmth of Christmas is in the air, and it helps to dispel the temperature's chill.

The weather is milder in Albuquerque on Christmas Eve. Early in the day, trucks begin to deliver thousands of luminarias which will line the streets, sidewalks, balconies, and roofs of Old Town. As they are put in place, workers move along the rows placing a vigil candle in each one, nestling it carefully in the sand.

The sun sets in a sky gaudy with color, fading from purple to rose to palest pink. The gaslights around the Plaza flicker. One by one, candles are lighted in the luminarias on the quaint Victorian bandstand, the shops, and San Felipe de Neri Church. In the window of La Placita Restaurant, red lights wink on a white Christmas tree, decorated entirely with red chile peppers.

Now in the last rays of the sun, the Plaza has a golden aura, jeweled with the deeper gold of the luminarias. As though on signal, a crowd begins to gather, walking along the sidewalks in the glow of a Southwestern Christmas.

When it is fully dark, a caravan of cars begins to move through the residential areas, interspersed with buses provided by the Chamber of Commerce for visitors at local inns and hotels. Headlights are dimmed; horns silent. For the most part, it is a quiet crowd, hushed by the beauty of the little lanterns; but children in lighted homes along the way merrily call out Christmas greetings to the passersby.

If Christmas is a visual thing, then in New Mexico it is a golden luminaria saying "Welcome—come in!" to the Christ child and all those who celebrate His birth.

Since 1706 Christmas Eve mass has been held at San Felipe de Neri Church in Old Town, Albuquerque. Nearby homes and streets glow with luminarias.

Arizona—on an early December morning, the air is soft as the down of a cottonwood tree. Breathe deeply, and it is heady like a fine clear wine, not too dry nor too sweet. The hills may be veiled in blue mist until the sun reaches golden fingers into the valleys. Then the desert comes richly alive, teeming with bird and animal life. It is fragrant with its special scents of creosote and flowers and sand that hold remembered heat from yesterday's sun, even the delicate aroma that water has, carried on a desert breeze.

Jackrabbits romp like gazelles. A horned toad blinks gently at the landscape like some tiny Socrates; and roadrunners begin their comical track races for the day. Cactus wrens dart from hidden nests; and

Sabino Canyon, northeast of Tucson in the Santa Catalina Mountains, holds all the delights of a desert garden.

mockingbirds, tired from their elaborate midnight serenades, hunt out the shade of a paloverde tree to rest.

To the north, the Grand Canyon is stilled in majestic snowy splendor; the Painted Desert is quiet as a frozen rainbow; and in the Navajo's Monument Valley, the buttes sculpted by time stand sentinel.

Arizonans have a great fraternity. It cuts across all lines and makes them brothers. Its members are all those who think Arizona is the greatest—in fact, the *only*—place in the world to live! They do not recruit members. It is becoming too sadly apparent that the more the clan grows, the more Arizona takes on the formerly unfamiliar evils of urban civilization with its smog and traffic. But for those who succumb to the siren call of peacocks roosting in trees at dusk, orange blossoms sending out perfume by moonlight, purple hills, and most of all, a life style deliberately unsophisticated and free from pretense, the fraternity opens its arms.

Near Tucson, at San Xavier del Bac, the beautiful Spanish mission known as the White Dove of the Desert, the Christmas season really begins on December 3, the feast day of San Xavier.

The chapel bells at San Xavier are framed by the graceful wrought-iron gate, the ocotillo and cholla. The mission was named by Father Eusebio Kino in 1692.

Near Tucson, on the Papago Indian reservation, stands San Xavier del Bac, the White Dove of the Desert.

Inside, the mission has been lovingly decorated for Christmas, its angels dressed in starched white lace robes.

From Squaw Peak, sunrise is golden over Phoenix.

As the day approaches, the Papago Indian women of the parish carefully launder the colorful, elegant vestments in which they dress the statues of the saints. They starch and press the exquisite lace robes for two angels suspended on the arch at either side of the altar, and tie red velvet capes around the lions that were modeled after the Spanish Lions of Navarre. In the angels' hands they place green satin banners emblazoned in gold with the words first sung over Bethlehem's hills—"Gloria in Excelsis Deo."

When all is in readiness, special services are held in the chapel, and three days of music, dancing, and all the traditional processions and pageantry of fiesta time begin.

Father Eusebio Francisco Kino named the mission for Saint Francis Xavier when he first visited the Sobaipuris Indian village of Bac (meaning springs) in 1692. Five years later he reported that the foundations were laid for "a very capacious church and house of San Xavier del Bac." The great missionary-explorer was a totally new type in an era when Spanish soldiers, who accompanied a priest on expeditions purportedly to convert the Indians, usually pursued gold more arduously than souls, often with murderous effect. Father Kino mapped the entire southwestern Arizona region, explored an overland route to California, and discovered the ruins at Casa Grande of a Hohokam civilization which were then already seven hundred years old. He established ranches in several areas and taught the Papago and Pima Indians to raise cattle and grow the grain to feed them.

After the death of the resident priest in 1702, the little mission was largely unattended until the arrival of another Jesuit, Father Alonso Espinosa, in 1756. He built a convent which is still in use, but the present mission was not begun until about 1781 under the direction of the Franciscan father, Juan Bautista Verderrain.

With Indian workers, he fashioned the walls of fired adobe.

On the outskirts of Mesa, sheep and new lambs graze.

They were then sheathed in plaster which was whitewashed with a combination of limestone, from nearby pits, and cactus juice. This mixture is still applied every three years to keep the graceful old building a dazzling white under the desert sun.

There are many stories as to why only one tower was completed. Some say it was to avoid the Spanish tax on finished churches; some blame it on workmen, superstitious after one of their number fell to his death while working on it; and others say the money simply ran out.

The fortunes of the White Dove waxed and waned a number of times in the next two centuries. In one period it was almost abandoned, and weather and neglect began to take their toll. Indian parishioners had to take the mission's furnishings into their homes to preserve them from vandals. In the past three decades, however, scrupulously careful restoration has preserved and enhanced its ancient beauty.

Moonlight spills mystically over its domes, its balustraded walls and arched gates on a December night. Within, its frescoed ceiling is gray with the smoke of countless votive candles, and its niches and vaulted ceiling are filled with the breath of a million prayers.

In the Holy Land, the first Christmas morning may have dawned much as it does in the Valley of the Sun in which Phoenix is located. Light rims the hills first and then the tops of palm trees, and gradually drifts down to pastures where sheep are grazing.

Sun sparkles on the gold and crimson decorations that line Phoenix streets—Santa Claus wearing a sombrero, and a sunburst that has become the Valley's symbol. In Scottsdale it smiles on three saguaro cactus wearing the robes and crowns of the Three Kings. Homes, guest ranches, and shopping centers twinkle with lights on olive trees, century plants, and all manner of cactus. Obviously, you don't need a spruce or a pine tree to get the Christmas spirit!

In downtown Phoenix Santa wears a gay sombrero.
Left: *A desert home in Lincoln Hills has a red tree.*

A tumbleweed tree is built on Chandler's town square.

Only in the Southwest will you find Three Kings who are really saguaro cactus. These are in Scottsdale.

In the town square of Chandler stands a "tree," as high as the roofs of surrounding shops, made entirely of tumbleweed! At night it shines with brightly colored lights and a golden star on top. Santa Claus has a stopping-off place at the base of the tree. Between his other chores before December 25, he takes note here of the gifts Chandler children hope to find in their stockings Christmas morning.

He also checks in at a number of homes in Phoenix where parents or grandparents have gotten word to the North Pole that a particular small girl or boy is listening for reindeer hoofs and hoping Saint Nick will make a personal visit.

A Christmas cookie dance is in full swing at the Phoenix Saddle Club.

In this project, he seems to be assisted by gentlemen whose usual occupations are not toy-making at all, but run instead to such vocations as selling insurance, teaching school, or growing cotton or grapefruit. But that's Christmas!

It's holiday party time, and the Phoenix Saddle Club is holding their "cookie dance" in the clubhouse that members built themselves. The moose head above the mantel is even wearing Christmas lights on his antlers for the occasion! Members arrive in their newest and brightest square dancing clothes—full-skirted dresses that swirl out like paper parasols, and rodeo shirts often colorfully embroidered and worn with a *bola* (a western tie of silver-tipped braided leather).

The ladies arrange the choicest cookies from their Christmas baking (the recipes were brought with them from Ohio or Iowa or Pennsylvania or Georgia) on a table close to the coffee pot. Then Johnny Schultz, the caller, starts the toe-tapping music and announces: "Choose your partners." The dancers move quickly into sets around the floor—teen-agers, gray-haired grandparents, the college professor, the lady gas-station attendant. It's "Allemande right" and "Left square through" or "Rollaway with a half sashay." It sounds like another language, but it's clear to the smiling dancers.

> Do sa do your corner, girl,
> Come back home and swing and whirl!

It's a good old Southwestern custom; and as they say that "Square dancing is friendship set to music," it's a natural part of this happy season!

On Wilder road in Phoenix, even the mailboxes are decorated. Santa Claus doesn't need snow to make his rounds.

California — the Golden State—stretches out along the blue Pacific for 840 miles. In the south, the cliffs that overlook the beaches, the parks, the yards of modest homes or huge estates all seem, in December, to be part of a lush tropical garden. It is hard, if not impossible, for a wreath on a door or a tree hung with tinsel icicles to compare in beauty to the profusion of roses, the exotic Bird of Paradise flowers, the date palms and banana trees on every hand. Crimson poinsettias bloom, and pyracantha and holly trees put out their brightest berries in celebration of the season. Nature herself has decorated the state for Christmas, and Californians have taken her hint as they look to New Year's for the holiday's climax with the Tournament of Roses.

Whimsical Mexican ornaments, all made of straw, trim this tree in Downey.

Just in time for Christmas the exotic Bird of Paradise bursts into bloom and seems ready to take flight.

Sun sparkles on a crimson Christmas tree among the palms at Shelter Island.

"Red hot pokers" frame a view of Laguna Beach where waves break gently on the white sandy cove below.

While most ocean-front roads along the southeastern coast of the United States are on a low flat coastal plain, in southern California, the highway hugs a cliff-top. Rolling waves break whitely on half-moon beaches, and fishing and pleasure boats, from the traveler's vantage point, look like toy ships floating on a lily-pond.

As the sun sets, the water turns to an unbelievable turquoise, almost luminescent in the pearly light. Keeping your eyes seaward, it is almost possible to forget the miles of urban sprawl, the oil wells, and the traffic, which mark the twentieth-century coast.

How different it must have looked to Juan Rodríguez Cabrillo —who had put out from Navidad (Christmas), Mexico—when he sailed into San Diego Bay in 1542 and claimed the land for the king of Spain. Or to Sir Francis Drake in 1579 when he cruised the Cali-

fornia coast and marveled at its beauty, its climate, and its natural harbors.

Today there is a special enchantment to those waters at Christmas time when marinas are a fairyland of lights that outline the mast and rigging of even the smallest boat. The great gray Navy ships are gaily decorated, and they ride at anchor off Coronado like Christmas islands floating in the Bay.

In spite of the treasures of the past which California holds in profusion—the lovely eighteenth-century Spanish missions, San Diego's Old Town with its historic homes and buildings, the old Customs House and Presidio at Monterey among them, its mushrooming growth gives the state a "new"

Ice flowers are in bloom for the holidays on a hill overlooking San Diego Bay.

A holiday brunch in Downey has California's fabulous fruit in the place of honor.

look. It is still the mecca of a westward-moving population no less than when the gold at Sutter's Mill lured the forty-niners.

Among the national groups who have left their unique imprint on California's holiday customs are the Japanese-Americans for whom New Year's—*Osho Gatsu*—is the most festive day of the year. To start out with "a clean slate," thousands of Japanese families clean their houses from ceiling to garret on New Year's Eve, and every person takes a bath shortly after the clock strikes midnight. At the Buddhist Temple in Gardena, 850 members gather outside the church as a one-ton bell is tolled 108 times to cast out the 108 evil passions of the human being. New Year's Day is spent in visiting old friends, feasting on traditional foods (rice balls, black

It is the season of roses at Ranchos las Gertrudes in Downey, where a pink crepe myrtle grows from a tree brought across the plains by covered wagon all the way from Alabama in 1860.

beans, dried herring eggs, a tangerine) and exchanging toasts in sake: *"Shin Nen Omedeto"*—"Happy New Year!"

You will hear the American translation shouted back and forth along Pasadena streets on New Year's Eve, also; but here the resemblance in the two celebrations seems to end. The crowds camping out on every street along which the Tournament of Roses Parade will move the following morning, have been gathering there since noon on the day before New Year's Eve. Whole families have moved in with sleeping bags and picnic baskets, a charcoal burner in case the temperature drops, and odds and ends of paraphernalia, which transform Colorado Boulevard and surrounding sidestreets into a holiday gypsy camp.

If you are decorating a float with crepe paper, there is nothing to stop you (except possibly the lack of a building to keep it dry) from putting on the finishing touches days in advance. But if you are working with millions of fresh flower petals, the possible time lapse changes into hours! Work goes on around the clock on New Year's Eve, and the last petal may be put in place only moments before the Grand Marshal leads off

Early on New Year's Day, the Tournament of Roses Parade in Pasadena caps the Southwestern holidays.

the parade. The finished floats are works of art, unbelievable in their shading of colors and the intricacy of the figures and the illusions that can be created.

Bands play, horses are wheeled in precision formations, flags fly, pretty girls smile and smile and smile in spite of the shivering wind that may turn a bathing beauty blue by the end of the march. Celebrities wave to cheering crowds; and vendors sell color film to amateur photographers who are as numerous as the roses.

Most of all, the new year is welcomed in with a medley of fun and noise and laughter and beauty, a golden sun, and the absolute certainty that it's bound to be the happiest new year ever!

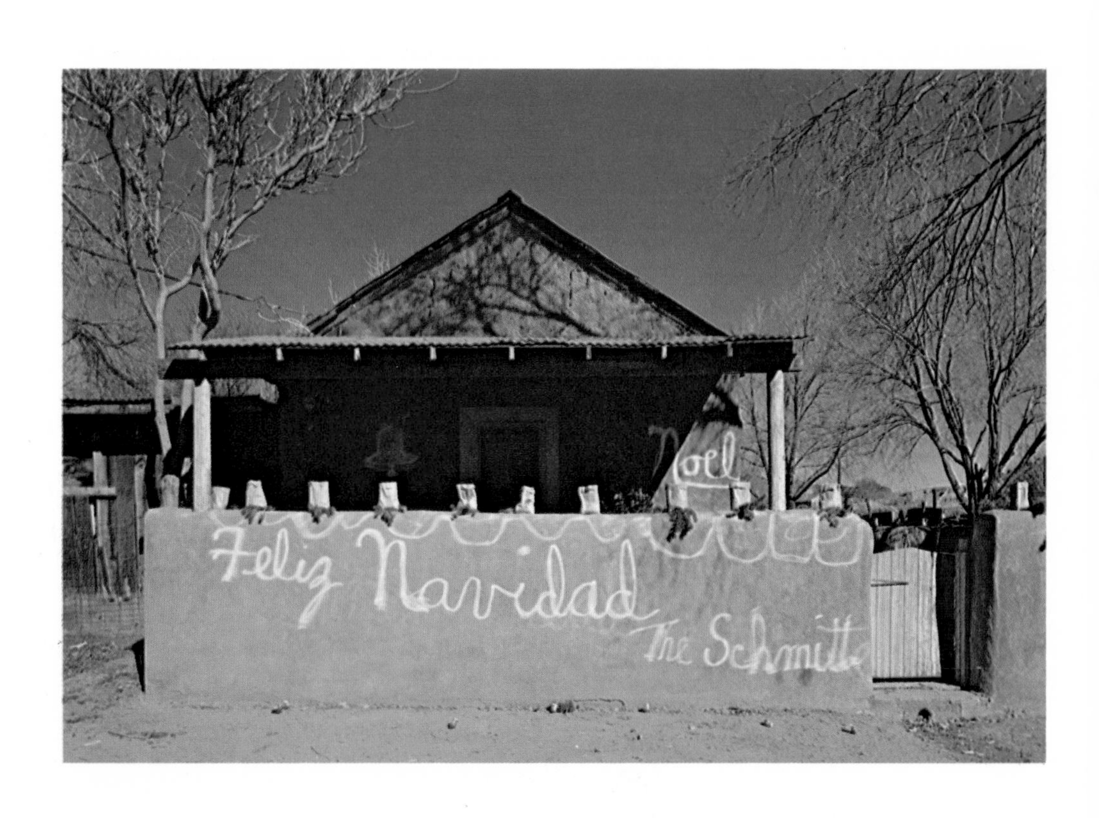
Noel
Feliz Navidad
The Schmitt